BARREN FIELDS

THE LAST BLADE OF GRASS BOOK II

ROBERT BROWN

SEVERED PRESS
HOBART TASMANIA

BARREN FIELDS
THE LAST BLADE OF GRASS II

www.severedpress.com

ISBN: 978-1-925342-40-6

CHAPTER 1

Shell Beach, Louisiana.
Eight Months Before the Plague.

"Hello. You got JeeJee's Airboat rental."

"George, this is Maggie. Maggie Roach."

"Hello Maggie, what can I do for you?"

George is an educated man. He was born and raised in Louisiana in a family that was considered old money. His education growing up was of a dual nature, as it was with most of the very wealthy. He was sent to the best private schools, and along with other educational requirements, he was taught to speak impeccable English in the proper manner according to those with money. Having power and influence in this state required those who want to fit in to have an unblemished Louisiana Southern drawl, with the usual French words or catch phrases thrown in at the right times. George had his accented speech for business and his proper speech for his closest friends.

Maggie's husband, Keith, had become one of George's friends ten years earlier, when they were working together at one of the shipping docks along the Mississippi River. Keith was in charge of safety and maintenance at a loading facility, and George was a new manager coming in to inspect the facility and do hands-on learning of the whole operation.

George was working as a manager but was actually the owner's son. There was no part of the family's holdings that a son or daughter could run or manage later in life without direct experience in those business operations. The children learned early in life they had to earn their place in running the business or accept a smaller cash inheritance and have no controlling interest in the companies when the parents died.

George took that to heart and spent his evenings during college and the years after getting his degrees working on family fishing boats, at small oil refining plants, and at the shipping docks where he met Keith. George had plenty of scars from the difficulties in working at the various family businesses, and each scar gave him a profound sense of respect for the employees that he would one day call his own. He received his biggest scar on the third day working with Keith. That day Keith should have been home during his day off but went in to work because a storm was wreaking havoc on the docks and loading equipment.

Keith's arrival to work that day put him in the unique position of having saved George when a secure line broke causing it to snap in George's direction. The line embedded itself a foot into the concrete wall of the warehouse they stood next to. If George wasn't pulled out of the way, the line would have cut right through him.

The scar he received was from taking a step back after being saved and falling on a large bolt at the base of a support beam. George knew he was lucky to be alive. Since that time he and Keith had become friends, and they made it a habit to go fishing or watch a New Orleans Saints football game.

"George, I need a safe place to go with Keith. We're getting out of town."

"Can't stand the rioting anymore?"

"I wouldn't call it rioting, George. It sounds like a warzone out here. Keith's son, Eddie, called to tell him it is some kind of plague."

"And you want to move, Maggie?" he asks, ignoring what must be embellishments of their situation.

"I have to get out of here, George. Keith won't leave without me, and if he stays here we'll both die. I can hear the shooting from the city at my window, and it's non-stop. Please, George!"

Maggie is sick. She needs oxygen, and any stress of travel could end her life, which increases the seriousness of what she is asking. Maggie has only one lung remaining and doesn't qualify for a transplant because she has cancer. She is at home for *end of life* care, and while she has made peace with the fact she is dying, she can't bare the idea of Keith's love for her getting him killed as well.

George knows Eddie from a few previous fishing trips with Keith. Eddie was always relaxed and mellow like his father, but had strong ideas that he wasn't afraid to express about politics, guns, or survival if you got him going. He knows Eddie is a *Prepper* and owns a gun shop in Oregon somewhere. On one particular visit, Eddie said some things about survival that particularly bothered George and caused him to make some extra preparations of his own.

Prepping isn't such a big deal in Louisiana where people have to deal with hurricanes and potential floods, so that aspect didn't bother him. What bugged George was the reason Eddie gave for not moving to Louisiana when he had the chance. *There's no way I will move to an area with so many nuclear power plants. The entire Eastern U.S.is a dead zone if any national disaster hits.* That statement by Eddie bothered George enough to buy a retreat property in Mexico after he did some of his own research.

"Do you know what Eddie said, exactly?" George asks with concern.

"He said the CDC is warning about a plague starting at military bases that's making people attack each other. The Navy base is only twenty miles from here, across the river. That's probably why I can hear the shooting."

"Maggie, if you can hear the gunfire, it is a lot closer than New Orleans. Is Keith there? Can I speak to him?"

"If I let him speak to you, do you promise to come and get us no matter what he says?"

"I promise, Maggie. It will take a while though. I'm out on my boat now, so I have to—"

"Don't go home, George. If you go home you'll never make it here by car. I told you it is a warzone out there right now. I called you because I knew you would be on your boat. There is no place on land Keith and I will be safe. I need you to get us out of here."

"I'll do it Maggie. I'm on my way."

George spoke with Keith, and as much as Keith insisted that he not come to get them, George respectfully declined the refusal of help.

"I'm doing this for Maggie, not for you, Keith. She made me promise."

George owed Keith his life and wasn't about to let him die when there was something he could do about it. There was also a chance, if whatever is happening ends quickly, they could ride out this mayhem in some level of comfort on one of the oil platforms the family manages. They aren't luxurious, but the one he is thinking of does have a medical bay that can keep Maggie stable.

Turning his boat around to face the shore, George's heart sinks as he finally notices two important things: the number of boats heading in his direction toward open water and the amount of smoke rising from New Orleans. For the last two years fires and shootings had increased as the economy sank, so seeing smoke every day from a fire was common. Now it seems like the whole coast is on fire. The truth is there are fires spread throughout the city at various spots giving the whole coast a dark billowing look from this distance. He doesn't remember ever seeing this many vessels on the water—especially with them all heading out to the Gulf at the same time.

The ride to Shell Beach will take nearly half an hour, so George starts using that time to try reaching his family and friends to give them a warning. He also decides to call the oil rig to get it ready for Maggie's arrival. He curses at himself for turning his phone and radio equipment off when he left yesterday to go fishing. It was supposed to be a relaxing escape away from everything to deal with his girlfriend breaking up with him.

Now all the text messages that showed up this morning from his family when he turned on his phone have a more ominous meaning than he had first imagined. He was curious why they kept writing urgent and thought they were worried about his break up and that he wasn't responding. Now he wonders if his family is dealing with problems from the rioting, or a plague, if Maggie is right.

*

When George maneuvers his boat up to the dock outside Keith's house he is worried about many things, but his greatest fear is that he can't reach any of his family. They all live in the city, and his father is in the hospital, with a respiratory virus. He tried calling them all continuously on the boat ride to shore, and the lines kept going to voicemail. He couldn't get anyone working at his parents' house and knows Evelyn and others should be there today. He wasn't even able to reach anyone at the main office or on their private lines. Every number went to a message, and there were no responses to e-mails. Yesterday he wished the whole world would leave him alone. Today it seems his wish came true.

He is also worried about transporting Maggie to an oil rig in his boat and what the trip will do to her in her condition. Her decision to leave with Keith is tremendous, in consideration of her recent return from the hospital to live her final days in the comfort of her own home. The magnitude of what she was doing and *why* compounded his feelings of anxiety with each unanswered call.

The fear building in him is of the *empty bottomless pit* variety that comes from being helpless in a situation. It builds into desperation as he ties up the boat and listens to the sound of shooting that isn't coming from distant New Orleans, but a mile or two up the road, in the adjacent town of Yscloskey. There is also another sound in the air. Something that makes the hair stand up on his neck, but he's not sure why. It's like the deep groaning sound a large ships hull will make when it is being hammered by waves, but this sound is constant and overlapping.

Keith comes out of the house with a bag in his hand, a shotgun slung on his shoulder, several portable oxygen tanks in a rolling carrier, and a face full of tears. George knows the pleading Keith would have done to try and get her to stay, but he also knows Maggie wasn't one to have her mind changed once it was set. Keith would do anything for her, and she would do anything to keep him from harm.

"Do you know what's going on out there?" George asks. "Have you gone up the road to check?"

Keith shakes his head and steps into the boat to load what he brought.

"I haven't left Maggie alone since we started hearing the shooting this morning," he calls from inside the cabin. "But I have a pretty good idea of what is happening. Is it anything like this at your place?"

"I have no idea. Heather and I broke up, so I took a few days off and took the boat out by some of the rigs yesterday morning to do some fishing. I left everything electronic off through the day and last night, so I haven't heard a thing. I had a bunch of messages my family sent last night on my phone, but I couldn't reach them. I mean, I couldn't reach anyone, not at home, or at the office."

George is surprised to see Keith step off the boat with the shotgun still slung over his shoulder. He assumed Keith was just bringing it out to load with the other items, but with the shooting in the town just up the road, it makes some sense.

Keith puts his hand on George's shoulder, and says, "I'm sorry to hear about Heather. Have you tried contacting her at all?"

"I tried, but it's just like my family. I didn't reach her. She left to visit her sister in Colorado, so there isn't anything I could do for her from here anyway."

"You know I don't like the idea of moving Maggie, but I'm glad you came. I'll need your help bringing her out, but first you should come in and listen to what we know. It isn't good, George."

*

"Hello, Maggie," George says as he leans over to give her a hug.

"You better sit down before Keith tells you what's happening," Maggie says with less strength than she had on the phone earlier.

"Last night we saw a report of rioting at both of the military bases, the Joint Reserve Base and the Naval Support Activity base. I didn't listen closely and thought it was some protesters attacking the bases. This morning I got a call from Eddie, and he tells me the CDC is warning hospitals that a plague is spreading across the U.S. and the origin is military facilities. Hospital staff are supposed to be on the lookout for people acting aggressively and trying to bite each other."

George finally takes Maggie's advice and sits down.

"This disease is everywhere, and it's manmade," Keith says angrily and hands George a letter. "Eddie e-mailed that to me and told me to print it out because he thought the internet would get shut down soon."

George laughs. Even with all of the smoke he saw over New Orleans and the gunfire close by that seemed like a ridiculously funny thing to say.

"They can't shut down the internet!" he says expecting some smiling faces to stare back at him, but he only receives two faces with dead serious expressions as a response.

"Our internet service is out, George. Are you getting anything on your phone?"

"I thought I couldn't get anything because I was on the boat," he says while looking at his phone's screen.

"Read the letter, George."

Turning it over in his hand he reads:

"I verified that the Zeus drug was administered to The Tiger Squadron and to General Taggart as well without incidence. It is assumed that the current batch was contaminated somehow as most of the men who were inoculated started showing tremors and violent behavior from ten to twenty-five minutes after injection. By the time we realized the reactions of the men weren't fitting the guidelines, we had already managed to inoculate over 300 men. Those men with immediate symptoms were able to attack and infect the remaining base personnel and the infection spread exponentially. Those personnel that received the infection from attack, usually in the form of a bite started showing tremors or violent action from one to five minutes time. I am currently trapped in my office with a small group of surviving soldiers under my command and this is the only way left for me to get the information on this drug out.

I am sending this letter to the non-classified accounts at the CDC due to my inability to contact Washington and Homeland Security through my secure-line. I fear that all major branches of government may be in the same state of infection that my base is and need to get this information out in the hopes that someone may be able to stop this infection from spreading. The following letter I received from my colleague, General Taggart. Something must have changed with this drug to be causing the violence we are experiencing."

"General Francis,

In response to your query regarding the safety and efficacy of the Zeus drug.

Due to the deteriorating condition of law and order within the Continental United States and abroad, nationwide martial law has been planned for and it is expected that the President will give the declaration for enacting it next week. The continuing societal unrest is expected to be compounded on Wednesday when the World Bank is set to announce an end to the dollar as the world's reserve currency. This will cause massive inflation and dollar devaluation to our already crumbling economy.

The troops under your command will be required to ensure the safety of the citizenry as well as the prevention of violence and property destruction. As such, you and all of your troops are ordered to take inoculations of the Zeus drug. This injection has been shown to minimize blood loss, reduce fear and anxiety and remove pain detection. The combination of which will ensure a minimal amount of casualties with our soldiers in violent interactions with a rioting populace.

This drug has been tested safely on the Tiger Squadron of German soldiers working in Moldova for the last six months. There is a side effect of a high fever which takes place on the sixth hour after inoculation and lasts one to five hours after initial administration. As such, only one third of all troops are to be inoculated at any given time to ensure all soldiers are not inoperative due to the fever at the same time. The time frame for the drugs' effectiveness is two to three weeks depending on the individual. All troops will be re-inoculated with the drug at such time as it becomes ineffective and as long as the order for martial law due to societal unrest is necessary.

I appreciate your concern for the welfare of your men and I have the same concern for mine. This is why I have written more than the required "follow your orders or be relieved" reply. I have observed the Zeus drug being administered to the German soldiers and have had it administered to myself while in Moldova with the Tiger Battalion and can personally certify its effectiveness. I will also mention that the reduction in fatalities to your troops resulting from armed conflict will help to prevent your troops from building grudges and animosity against the populace they must keep under control. Anything we can do to reduce casualties in the expected upheaval must be done.

Inoculations are expected to begin with the arrival of Zeus on Monday. In coordination with the military the CDC will be distributing inoculations nationwide to select first responders in high value areas.

Sincerely,

General Arthur C. Taggart"

George looks at the paper a moment longer attempting to make sense of the information his brain doesn't want to accept.

"This is happening at every base in the U.S.?"

"*Every base* was yesterday. Today they were injecting that Zeus drug into first responders. That means police and hospital personnel as well."

"My father is at the hospital!" George yells as he stands up and turns for the door.

"George, you can't go into the city," Keith tells him and grabs his arm.

"I have to try, Keith. Maggie, I'm sorry, but I need to at least check if I can make it to the hospital."

"You can take our truck," Keith says with a small amount of relief.

With George leaving, he can stay here with Maggie and won't have to put her through the stress of travelling.

"Keith, please go with him."

"I'm not leaving you alone when the shooting is so close."

"Then make sure George has a gun before he leaves."

*

Driving up the Yscloskey Highway, not even a mile from Keith's and Maggie's house, George sees the origin of the shooting. A crowd of some young hoodlums are shooting across the canal at people on the other side. George slams on the brakes to keep from hitting people that are standing in the road. He squints his eyes and tenses up expecting the murdering gang of armed people to turn their guns on him at any moment, but they ignore him and the screeching of his tires as he comes to a stop.

What he witnesses over the next few seconds is something he can't comprehend. The shooters on this side of the bank aren't a bunch of young punks or criminal looking people at all, but an assortment of men and women who are shooting at the people on the other side. The crowd of people over the waterway is no less strange. They are also men, women, and even some children. It appears to be hundreds of them crowding along the edge—just like they do along the streets during the Mardi Gras parades.

George's stomach lurches, but he is able to keep himself from vomiting at the horrendous sight of bodies falling to the ground or into the canal as they are killed. More than the nausea, there is a cold and fearful feeling George gets while watching the scene. The people shooting look terrified and the people being shot look, how can he describe it, they look vacant. They are just standing there with their mouths hanging open watching everyone on this side of the canal. They aren't running away, flinching, or noticing when the person standing next to them falls dead from being shot. They are doing nothing but standing there as one after another is killed by the bullets these shooters are sending their way.

As repulsive as what he is witnessing is, he has to get some answers. If any of the shooters wanted to harm him, they would have by now. Other than some glances his way, they seem to have more important things to do than speak to him.

The true horror of the situation hits him when he opens the door of the cab. The groaning sound of waves hitting a metal hull he heard earlier is actually a wet, guttural moan coming from the people being shot at. It is the sound of the infected when they cannot reach their prey. George climbs into the truck bed to get a better look at the crowd on the other side. That awful sound is not coming from hundreds, but rather what appear to be thousands of bodies pressed up against each other along the other bank of the waterway, and more are approaching from behind them.

He climbs back down from the truck and walks over to the shooters—almost in a trance-like state of disbelief at the whole situation.

"What the hell is going on?" George finally gains the presence of mind enough to ask the closest shooter.

"We have to shoot them. We have to keep shooting them, or they will make it over here and kill us."

"But they are stuck on the other side of the water."

"For now they are. These things are attracted to sound, and a police officer is down the street trying to get the drawbridge raised so we can try keeping this area free from the sickness. We don't want to keep shooting them, but we have to keep them from moving south to the bridge."

"Can't the police do anything about them?" he asks before he can stop the words from escaping his lips.

The man stops shooting and looks at George.

Normalcy bias took over George's thinking for a moment before he remembered the numbers he saw while standing in his truck bed. What could police do to stop a situation when so many people are infected at once? How many police officers are left to help if that letter from Eddie is right?

"Do you live out here?" the man asks.

"No, I was out fishing and came in to help a friend. I'm heading into the city to find my father."

"You have no idea what's going on, do you?" he asks but doesn't wait for George to respond. "Those people we are shooting at are the good residents of the city. We got pushed back to this spot early this morning from St. Bernard Parish. New Orleans is a wasteland of disease. Everyone left there is either infected like the ones we are shooting or hiding from them."

"They can't all be infected," George says in a desperate tone. "The hospitals must still be taking care of people."

Shaking his head in a slow depressed manner, the man replies, "No, I'm sorry, the hospitals fell last night. I tried making it to one of them with my wife but..." He trails off in his description after mentioning his wife. "As far as I know, anyone that could make it out did. If you want to make it into New Orleans you'll have to go through all of those sick people to do it, and trust me when I say this group in front of us stretches all the way back to the city."

"My father..." is the only thing George can say.

The man he was speaking to puts his hand on George's shoulder in a show of support and returns to shooting at the moaning host before them.

George walks back to the truck, gets in, and shuts the door muting the calling sound of the sick people and gunfire. Even though he can't accept that New Orleans is already lost, his brain is working through the logic of it all and it does make sense. The city is flanked by two military bases, and if they were exposed to this drug yesterday, then infected soldiers would be able to converge on the city from two sides overnight spreading the infection as they went. The inoculations of Zeus would have been rushed to the hospitals and police yesterday as well to deal with the infected people coming out of the bases and surrounding areas.

It's a perfect storm of medical horror. A drug designed to protect people from violence is actually the cause of it. If people react as quickly as the letter had said, then hardly anyone would be alive to give a warning. They would all be infected from the injection or bites.

George makes one final attempt at seeing if he can reach his father or remaining family. Even with the numbers he would be facing, he has to try. He drives down the road to the bridge but it is up. The control shack for the bridge is on the other side of the bank, where a police car is sitting and the body of the police officer is laying on the ground. There are a few infected people near the body looking over at George. He must have been bitten in the process of raising the bridge and took his own life.

*

"We have to go now!" George says surprising Keith and Maggie when he walks back in.

"Did you hear from your family?"

"The city is gone. There are people just up the road shooting at hundreds, if not thousands, of infected people across the waterway. Those people got pushed back here from St. Bernard Parish and are making their last stand. We have to leave now."

Keith grabs George's arm, and asks him, "Are you sure?"

"If I had any doubt, I wouldn't be back. The hospitals got overrun last night, and my father was in one of them. If I knew where my sister or brothers are I wouldn't be able to make it to them if I tried. St. Bernard is overrun and that's the only way back into the city. Please, let's just go."

They begin the delicate process of getting Maggie transferred into his boat.

CHAPTER 2

THE THREAT AT WAL-MART?

Grants Pass, Oregon.
Present day.

No good deed goes unpunished. I wish I knew who came up with that phrase because it seems so fitting to our situation right now. My group and I managed to outwit Stockton and his criminal gang at this store and free all of their prisoners without having to fire a shot. It looks doubtful that our departure from this place will go as smoothly.

With only an hour of preparation left to transport most of the store's remaining vital supplies and the freed prisoners back to my ranch, we now have to deal with the armed group of men that have pulled into the parking lot and most likely have surrounded the place.

Standing next to me, Timothy Weyland asks, "Who are they?"

"They are a survival group that did some training at the ranch," I reply with a concerned look on my face. "When they trained, those two men in the front there were in charge. They are brothers," I say while pointing them out. "The younger brother seemed like a decent guy. The other one was all right, but at times, kind of an ass. They stopped training at the ranch after they found out I was an atheist."

"Are you sure that's why they stopped?"

"Yes, unfortunately. The older brother was pretty upset with me when he found out. That's also the reason they gave you, isn't it, Arthur?"

"Yep," he says and nods while looking over the shelving and out the glass doors at the group.

"That doesn't mean they're bad guys," I add. "They just didn't like giving money to someone that doesn't share their beliefs."

"And are they a threat or potential allies?" Timothy's girlfriend, Dianne, asks.

"Both at this point," I reply and pause for a second to think. "Get some shooters on the roof and have everyone ready to fight. There are a lot of unknowns in this situation, like what they've done since the collapse and why they are here. It's also doubtful that they know who we are and why we are here, so we need to work that out first."

The well-armed men in the parking lot interrupt our impromptu discussion session with an announcement, "Criminals in Wal-Mart, you are surrounded! Lay down your arms and release the people you are holding hostage or we will flush you from the building you are cowering in and bring vengeance upon you for your sins."

I chuckle a bit and turn to Arthur with a questioning look on my face at the sins statement. "At least we know they aren't here to reinforce Stockton's group. Now we just have to convince them we aren't the bad guys they came here to fight."

Arthur grabs my arm as I reach out to move one of the shelves to gain access to the door.

"Eddie, we don't know they aren't here to free Stockton from us."

"We know those men, Arthur. Not all of them, and not well, but I think they are decent people and doubt they are the type to hook up with the scum that was in this place. At least they were decent before the collapse. Besides, if they were here to free Stockton then they would have said as much and said Stockton's name. You dealt with them more than I did. What did you think of them when they were at the ranch?"

Arthur squints a little while bringing up a memory. "Well, you remember the older brother, Jeremiah? He was a bit of a hothead."

I nod in remembrance.

"Well, I had an issue with him when they said they wouldn't be training at the ranch."

"Go on."

"Nothing major happened. At least, not at the time. He accused me of turning my back on Christ by working for you. I told him you were decent people and trying to do your part to help people get prepared, but you could tell by the way he spit out his words talking about you that he hated the idea that people like you even exist. Atheists, I mean. The younger brother, Isaac, was embarrassed by the scene Jeremiah was making. The reason they left wasn't a big deal for us then, but it might be an issue now with the world changed."

"I guess we'll find out if it's an issue shortly then. Help me move the shelf so I can talk to them before an unneeded gun battle starts."

We slide the shelves away a bit, and I pull the sliding door open enough to yell out. I am completely exposed to being shot through the glass if they choose to shoot before we come to an understanding. Hopefully the older brother has learned a bit of self-restraint since the world fell apart, because he certainly didn't have enough of it before.

"Isaac and Jeremiah, this is Eddie Keeper of the survival training ranch. You and your group have arrived a day late I'm afraid. Yesterday my group arrived here and we freed the people that were held captive.

The criminals that were controlling this place are dead, and we are preparing to take the people we freed to my ranch for recovery."

The two brothers look at each other, and Isaac responds, "Mr. Keeper, if that is you and your story is true, then come out where we can see you better."

I look back to Arthur, and ask, "Is everyone ready?"

He nods back at me.

I wave through the glass door and call back to him and his men, "Isaac, I know you were a good man before this disease hit, but we all have to be cautious of others these days. You can already see me from where you are, and I am exposed enough to your gunfire as well. Allow me a few moments to prepare my people into defensive positions. Once they are in place, I will exit the building with a group of the prisoners we freed so they can verify my story for you."

"I'll give you a few minutes," Isaac replies. "But don't try anything, we have the building surrounded."

His older brother starts to argue with him. No doubt over his giving us time to prepare a defense rather than just moving against us.

I don't bother waiting for time to go by. I slide the door all the way open and walk out toward the group with my rifle slung over my shoulder. I hear footsteps behind me and look back to see Simone stepping up to be beside me while Arthur is catching up as well.

"What happened to a few minutes?" Arthur asks.

"If they wanted to attack us, they would have when they thought we weren't ready. He gave us time which was a show of goodwill and decency."

Reaching Isaac and Jeremiah I smile and shake Isaac's hand. His brother shifts back just slightly letting me know he doesn't want me to try shaking his, so I don't try.

"It's good to see decent people again," I say while gripping Isaac's hand tightly.

"It's good to see you too, Mr. Keeper, I'm surprised to see you alive," Isaac replies and looks at his brother.

Jeremiah just gives a blank poker face stare.

"Just call me Eddie, Isaac. Did you say you have the place surrounded?" I ask with concerned urgency.

"Yes, we have men all around the place. But don't worry. We have radios so they know not to attack unless we give word."

"Do you know about the running infected? Have you seen them yet?"

Just when the questioning looks appear on the brothers' faces, gunfire erupts from the back side of the building followed by a faint yell when the shooting stops. Lucky for us, Arthur has been coordinating the preparations to leave, so he has one of our radios on him and calls back to our people, "Protect the armed men from any infected. Shoot any runners you see."

Four shots ring out from the roof of the store, and Isaac's men all chamber rounds in their guns and aim them at Simone, Arthur, and me thinking this is some type of trap or setup. Fortunately Isaac's men follow a strict hierarchy and will only fire when given the order. It is actually Jeremiah that steps in and shields the three of us from the gun barrels and tells his men to stand down. There are many questions that they want to ask, but another call on the radio interrupts the brothers before they can get a word out.

"Arthur, there are two men down. Two men are bitten, what are our orders?"

I grab the radio from Arthur, and I start to run to the side of the building leaving the two brothers at their vehicles and allowing them to decide if they will follow. Keying the radio, I call, "What are the locations of the bitten men?"

"Back side due west. Head out from each corner of the building about forty yards from southwest corner and fifty yards from the northwest corner."

"We're approaching on foot. Don't shoot them unless they have turned and start to run," I say heavily while running alongside the building. "Keep two shooters on the northeast bite victim. He's the farthest from us."

We reach the first man just as he starts to shake from the fever. A twisted body of a dead infected is lying beside the man's shivering body and another one of Isaac's men is just standing there looking at his fallen compatriot. Isaac and Jeremiah step up closer to the man along with three others from their group. They don't wait for the change to finish. Isaac puts a bullet through the man's head and says a quick prayer before we head to the next location.

"You could have let him change first," I say. "What if he didn't turn?"

"We don't wait for people to turn," Jeremiah says in a flat angry tone next to Isaac.

I know it was unlikely that the man was immune. No one has been immune yet that started having symptoms so quickly, but we haven't had enough experiences with immunity to be certain what does and doesn't happen in each circumstance. That being said, I wouldn't shoot someone I know before they turned, especially in our current situation of having multiple armed people available for protection. It wasn't necessary.

Isaac's group must have had things pretty rough so far to be reacting like that.

I want to mention immunity to them but am interrupted by another call from the radio that lets us know that the second man is luckier than the first.

"It looks like we have another lottery winner, Eddie."

While quickly walking toward the next group of people off of the north corner of the store, I tell Isaac and Jeremiah to get on their radios and make sure none of their people are on their own.

"Everyone has to be doubled up now with one person always watching the rear approach. I take it none of your group has encountered the running infected yet?"

"This is only our second trip away from camp since the winter began," replies Jeremiah in a frustrated tone and looks at Isaac.

"I didn't want to risk losing anybody," Isaac shrugs as he replies. "Not that we could have made it far if we wanted to go anywhere. Our camp is away from main roads, so when we were ready to make an excursion, the abnormal snows that we had this winter locked us in. We also started out reasonably well for supplies and didn't have to travel, so our first trip out wasn't until four days ago."

"We made it to the outskirts of Grants Pass and found a wounded boy. At first we thought he was bitten and dead because of the blood on his shirt. When we tried moving him out of a doorway we wanted to go through, we realized he was just unconscious, and that he had been shot."

Jeremiah cuts in to add, "We only saw three of the possessed people on that trip, and since the boy survived without being attacked by any of them, we figured it was a sign that most of them were dead."

"These people aren't possessed. It's just a disease," I say to them while rolling my eyes.

"It isn't a disease," Jeremiah says and stops in front of me. "If you were a believer, you would see what this actually is. This is the End Times that is spoken of in Zechariah 14:12: *And this shall be the plague wherewith the Lord will smite all the people that have fought against Jerusalem; Their flesh shall consume away while they stand upon their feet, and their eyes shall consume away in their holes, and their tongues shall consume away in their mouth.* I don't expect someone like you to understand," he says in a brusque tone.

I chuckle and give a smile before telling him, "But I do understand, Jeremiah. I understand very well." And I continue the with the next bible verse where he left off. "Zechariah 14:13: *And it shall come to pass in that day, that a great tumult from the Lord shall be among them; and they shall lay hold everyone on the hand of his neighbor, and his hand shall rise up against the hand of his neighbor.*" His surprised look is all the satisfaction I need. No one runs a survival supply store without being well versed in apocalypse theories or prophesies.

"Don't assume because I don't believe in a God that I don't know the Bible or your religion."

"So you think this is a disease? People are eating each other!" Jeremiah yells attempting to get his point across. "Have you ever heard of a regular disease like this ever happening?"

"Yes, have you heard of rabies?" I say with a calm shrug.

You can tell a light just went on with Jeremiah, but there is an awkward silence of seconds with his face turning from embarrassed to angry.

I move around him and continue on to the next attack victim.

Isaac goes on with their story: "We thought for this wounded boy to survive out in the open without being attacked, that most of the people we thought were possessed must have died during the winter."

"Isaac you do understand this is a disease and not possessions or a curse, right?" I ask out of concern that his entire group has become some religious end time's cult. Of course the world as we know it did come to an end from all the information we've been able to gather, but even so, falling to a superstitious answer when dealing with a disease will only create more trouble than we already have.

"Honestly, until you just brought up rabies with Jeremiah, I can't say any of us seriously considered this was anything but Biblical prophecy. I would like to see it as a disease, Eddie, but this fits the descriptions of Armageddon fairly accurately, don't you think? It looks like demonic possession, the work of the Lord."

"Is that why you shot your man back there so quickly, because you thought he was possessed? I take it you don't know some people are immune?"

They both look at me like I've sprouted a new head, and I continue talking, "We haven't had much experience with immune people either, but if your group has been secluded this whole time and haven't thought of it as a disease per se, you might not know about it at all. I'm actually shocked you shot your man before he completely turned, even if you don't know about immunity."

"There are no immune people," Jeremiah says strongly with a slight hint of desperation in his voice. "A bite allows a demon to enter and gain control of that body. We kill our bitten people while they are still human so they can die without their souls being tainted."

I shake my head wondering what spending time with these people must have been like while surviving these past eight months, and am about to respond, but the conversation stops when we reach the second group of people. The lucky lottery winner isn't a man, but a woman. She has a bloody bite on the back of her right shoulder and a cut on her forehead from an impact with the ground, but isn't showing any negative signs or symptoms from her bite.

Before the collapse, many of the people in Isaac's group were related. The woman sitting on the ground is Isaac and Jeremiah's sister, Mariah, and if they haven't added anyone new, then their group is still comprised of three or four large family units.

Isaac grabs her and gives her a hug, apologizing for not running to her first.

"Why were you back here? What were you thinking?" he says in a tender moment of concern amongst the horror.

Jeremiah is not so happy to see her, and yells loudly at her, "What do you think you're doing here? You were supposed to stay back at the camp, and now look what happened to you."

He raises his gun and points it at her.

Isaac jumps up and he, myself, and a few others step between Jeremiah's gun and his sister.

"Jeremiah, she's probably immune," I say in a stern but pleading tone. "You need to put the gun down."

"Isaac, you know I have to do it. We shoot before the possession takes hold." He has a look that says he will shoot through all of us to kill her, until Isaac tells him to put his gun down.

"Jeremiah please, put the gun down. We might have been wrong," he says. "Even if we're right, she isn't showing any of the signs."

Jeremiah slowly lowers and then holsters his gun, and takes a few steps back but has a look of complete anguish on his face. Something else is going on here that I don't know about, but it will have to wait.

I turn to Isaac, "Is she going to be safe with him here?"

"She's safe," he says while turning back and helping her to stand.

With the stress of this little encounter ebbing down, I laugh a bit too exuberantly when I see a cat pin on the front of her shirt making Isaac and the others stare at me.

"I'm sorry for laughing, but it's the end of the world and your sister is accessorizing her clothes with cat pins?"

Isaac smiles at her, and says, "Her and her stupid cats. Jeremiah and I have had to endure them ever since she was a little girl."

"Well Isaac, if she is truly immune, then her stupid cats saved her life today."

Before more is said, another two groups of Isaac's men approach from around both sides of the building and those that arrive from the north side of the store raise their weapons at Arthur, Simone, and I.

"Don't make any sudden moves and hand over your weapons!" one of them tells us without any wavering of seriousness.

Another says with urgency, "Isaac, Jeremiah, you need to see something!"

"Eddie, Arthur, what should we do?" calls one of our rooftop shooters while watching us being held up.

"Hold your fire, but be ready to shoot if these men do anything to us," I reply on the radio, and then the three of us slowly raise our hands to show we are complying.

"Lower your weapons," Isaac says to his own men.

"Not until you see what's by the building," the man says with finality.

The men take our weapons from us and lead us toward the grocery loading dock on the north side of the building. That loading dock happens to be filled with the discarded dead bodies of Stockton and his group.

"What do I have to see so badly?" Isaac asks.

Trying to head off an already bad situation, I tell him what is coming, "The bodies of the people you came here to stop are piled up ahead."

In his typical confrontational manner, Jeremiah stops the group then steps right in front of me less than a foot away and looks me in the eyes. Out of the corner of my eye I see Isaac drop his head.

"You have a pile of bodies up there?" Jeremiah asks in a more than agitated way.

"Yes," I reply dryly. "The people we freed and my people took two votes to decide what to do with the criminals that were running this place. Once you speak with the former captives and find out what was done to them, you will understand why we chose not to let those criminals go free."

"Oh will I?" Jeremiah says unconvinced.

"Yes, Jeremiah, I think you will understand. I know what you think of me. Remember what you said to me on my ranch two years ago? You said *I can't possibly be a decent person because I don't share your belief in God.* I know you think there is no morality without God, and you think I must be some devil or evil person or whatever must go through your brain.

"Despite what you think I am, it is possible to make moral decisions without religion. I have a pile of fifty bodies over there, and once you hear the accounts or read what the victims wrote in journals, you will agree with what was done here. I promise you."

*

Standing in front of the bodies isn't pleasant. It reminds me of the mountains of bodies we had cleared from the ranch after it was attacked. The smell is disgusting.

Isaac turns to me and with a fierce sincerity, says, "Eddie, you better be right about what you did here. We don't allow murderers to go free."

"If you include rapists and abusers with murderers then I have nothing to fear from what you will find," I reply then point at the bodies. "We don't let their kind go either."

*

After two hours of talking with the former prisoners and reviewing the notebooks filled with accounts of what was done to them during their capture, Isaac, Jeremiah and three other men from their group walk up to Simone and me.

"You are right, Eddie," Isaac says, speaking for his group and shaking his head in disgust at what he's heard. "The pile of bodies is a horror, but we have all decided we would have taken the same actions based on what those men were."

"It took you two hours to figure that out?" I say pissed off while grabbing my guns back from his men.

"Actually, that was agreed on in the first thirty minutes. The last hour and a half were used discussing in detail your use of infecting Stockton's group with the disease and also putting to death the family members of his group."

Isaac's group believes that the people that get bitten are possessed or their souls are tainted somehow. This poses a particularly awkward situation for me and my people, in that we were assisting in the spreading of demonic possessions in their eyes.

"I pray that the good Lord accepts the choices we have made so far to survive and blesses us with the wisdom to choose wisely in the future," Jeremiah adds.

Several people nearby us that overheard Jeremiah's proclamation issue *Amen* in response to his words.

Jeremiah finishes by saying, "I am thankful we didn't have to fight those men or with your group today."

There was no malice or false pleasantry in his words. He seems genuinely relieved that he and his men not only didn't have to fight Stockton's group, but didn't have to fight us either. Even with the honesty of his feelings, the word that echo's in my head is his last, *today*. They didn't have to fight us *today*. Hopefully there won't be a tomorrow when they feel they do.

"So you would have taken the same actions?" I ask Isaac. "Even the experiments?"

"No. We would not have done experiments on them. Most of my men are against the reason you had them bitten, but considering what their group had done to others, what you did to their souls before they died seems a fitting punishment. If we had more experience with what is going on when people are attacked, maybe we would see things differently, but we aren't convinced that this is a disease let alone that any people can be immune to it."

"Well, if you don't accept your sister's current condition, take a look at my arm then," I say while removing my bandage.

After another round of telling the *where, when, and how* of my bite and subsequent immunity to the disease, at least some of Isaac's group seem swayed that this is a disease that people contract and not some supernatural possession. Not all of them seem inclined to accept the evidence of my survival. After listening to most of my account, Jeremiah seemed even more repulsed by me. He backed away and left with some of his men after apparently hearing enough.

We haven't told them about Erde Fleischer's roll in all of this, and I'm glad of our discretion on that for now. Jeremiah would probably consider him to be the devil incarnate and kill him on the spot for creating the Zeus drug. Maybe they'd try to kill us as well for doing the experiments at his direction.

CHAPTER 3
WATERFORD STEAM ELECTRIC STATION

Louisiana.
Eight Months Earlier.

When they arrived at the rig called The Mallory it was largely deserted. The warning call George gave to the platform was spread to many in the area, and the crews from this and many other drilling rigs opted to go aboard any passing crew change ships so they could head home to help their own families. Leaving was the only choice most of the men could make at the time with little information and no understanding about what was truly happening. It is also a decision that condemned most of them to death as none have returned in the three days' time Keith, George, and Maggie have been on the rig.

Only Jack and Frank remained on the platform. Jack was the driller, like the name sounds, he was in charge of drilling on the rig. Frank is the rig foreman. They don't have any family nearby to go help, so staying at the distant tower seemed the most sane with a disease spreading on land.

Each day since their arrival has been touch and go for Maggie. She is holding on but is in a great deal of pain, and even with the oxygen mix set on high, she is struggling to get enough air into her system through her compromised lung.

George stands in the doorway and waits for Keith to turn his way, waving his hand to motion him over.

"Keith we need to talk about our next step. We have to make plans to move on from here."

"She won't be able to move again, George. She is barely recovering from the trip out here." He looks back at Maggie sleeping.

"Keith, she's sleeping now. Let's go talk."

Keith follows George as he walks to the upper platform deck on the outside. They both know the situation is serious because of the complete absence of communication since the day they arrived. The internet was down before George made it to Keith's house. All phone service was off by the afternoon, not that any calls would go through earlier than that, but at least they would still ring. All radio and television service was preempted by a looping emergency alert broadcast that was never updated. It keeps repeating the message: *Stay indoors and avoid people behaving strangely.* Nothing else is heard and the sudden vacancy that the departure of instant communication leaves is filled with the worst doubts and fears the trio can come up with.

"I've been speaking with Jack and Frank about where we should go when we have to leave."

"I told you Maggie can't move again."

"Don't get angry with me, Keith. We won't have a choice."

Keith shakes his head and begins to counter the argument he thinks George is going to make. "When we run low on supplies we can scavenge from on shore. Also most of these rigs are built to take hurricane winds and waves, and we aren't that far from the end of the season."

"I'm not worried about hurricanes or supplies. I'm worried about radiation."

Radiation isn't something Keith or most other people around the world gave much thought to. Nothing could be done about a dropping bomb and the fears of that diminished significantly since the end of the Cold War. Dirty bombs were a concern, but there wouldn't be a point for a terrorist to set off a dirty bomb now when there isn't a population to terrorize. Nuclear power plants are the only source radiation that anyone has to concern themselves over. It is the cleaner energy that actually worked for the masses unlike wind or solar. With a radiation leak being so dangerous, multiple layers of protection were put in place at power plants to ensure accidents couldn't occur.

"You are too paranoid about things, George. You're starting to sound like my son."

"That's who I got the idea from and being too paranoid is exactly what I thought when he said it. Unfortunately, your son was right," George says dejectedly while moving to sit at a table. "He moved to Oregon because they only have one nuclear power plant in the Northwestern U.S. We have one just outside of New Orleans, and if goes into meltdown and breaches containment, the normal wind patterns will take the fallout right across the city and out into the ocean. Directly at us!"

"They have safety measures to keep that from happening."

"Yes, yes they do. And each one of those measures requires a team of plant workers to keep those safety checks in place."

Keith looks at him skeptically, not wanting to believe their situation could get any worse.

"Trust me, Keith. I've checked into it. My family does have a stake in the energy sector, after all. I mean, *we did*. I bought a property in Mexico three years ago after your son mentioned why he wouldn't move to Louisiana. He said the entire eastern U.S. would be a dead zone of radiation if only a few of the power plants melted down. It took over four years for the Japanese to get control over the Fukushima nuclear plant after the tsunami knocked out the diesel generators. Four years with every resource being thrown at containing the problem and no diseased maniacs trying to attack the workers at the same time.

"How many workers do you think stayed on the job at Waterford Steam when New Orleans was collapsing? And how long can the ones that stayed survive against the numbers of infected leaving the city? The Waterford Station is literally a ticking time bomb, and to make matters worse, you have to multiply that effect by every nuclear power plant east of the Mississippi. We have two plants just in our state alone. It is just a matter of time before we have to leave, and I want to include you and Maggie in on our plans."

"I keep telling you Maggie won't survive another move, and I won't go anywhere without her. For all we know the plant could have melted down already and we are soaking in fallout right now."

"Ten years ago, *yes*, but not today," George replies. "You can thank the Department of Homeland Security for this save. With all of the terror attacks and the collapse of Middle Eastern countries, DHS put radiation monitors on most of the rigs out here. That way no one could sail a dirty bomb or worse up to one of our cities and set it off. We will know if radiation is detected, the sensors are wired into the alarms."

"I still can't move Maggie. She won't survive the trip."

"She won't let you stay when I tell her what we have to look forward to, Keith, and trust me, I will let her know. You know I care about her and how much you two love each other, but she is already dying. She has come to terms with her situation. You're the only one that doesn't seem to accept that fact."

Keith wants to hit him; he wants to knock those words back into George's mouth. It is a truth he hasn't been able to run from these last few years, but he has managed to comfortably ignore the progression of her cancer. She is the woman he loves, and he wants to be with her until the end.

"I know what she means to you, Keith. I feel the same way about my family, but there's nothing I can do for mine. At least you have a chance to keep protecting Maggie if we have to leave, and you have other family out there that might still be alive. I'm not going to let the two of you stay on this platform when we leave just so you can slowly die of radiation poisoning."

*

Standing in the medical bay, George is going over the situation with everyone, including Maggie.

"The Waterford Steam Electric Station is our main concern. I'm sure we will know if it has gone into meltdown within another five days with the direction the wind has been blowing."

"Why five days?" Maggie asks with a tone full of increasing strength.

"From what I've read, it only takes a few hours to a day for a plant to go into meltdown. That is if there is a failure that can't be corrected in one of the safety measures. We can expect the same amount or more of the diseased people leaving New Orleans and heading west toward the power plant as those that came across the bridge and through St. Bernard Parrish. The station is only twenty-five miles from the center of the city, so it takes less than a day to walk there. Anyone that was alive and stayed at Waterford to keep it running is most likely gone or dead by now. Another five days and we should find out if they had the time to shut it down properly."

"That doesn't sound as grim as what you told us earlier," Frank mentions.

George gives Frank a look trying to make him shut-up, but Frank doesn't stop talking, he just points out the obvious.

"Maggie is a tough lady, George—probably tougher than all of us with what she's dealing with right now. Tell her everything you told me."

"George, tell me. I need to know the truth," she says.

"We need to leave within five days but preferably earlier, before the radiation alarms start ringing. We don't know how much fallout we'll be dealing with when it starts, and even a short term exposure could be fatal."

"I thought you said we would have some time?" Keith says in frustration.

"I didn't create this situation, but I understand it. Please, let me explain what I researched and we all need to decide what to do together, okay?"

Everyone nods or mumbles their acceptance so George continues.

"If the workers at the Waterford plant were able to shut it down properly, a power plant takes continuous upkeep and maintenance to ensure those shutdown protocols keep functioning the way they should. Just like at this platform, complex machinery needs regular maintenance. If there were workers still there, unless they were underground, they would have been killed or run off by now. No army can stop the whole population of New Orleans from overrunning the power plant, and the military was the first to be infected. The entire area had one and a half million people, so at best, only two hundred thousand people will walk by or through the power plant property. That's a lot of bodies to break something as they move by."

Then, let's say best case scenario, the workers are alive, stay alive, and no equipment or generators are damaged. Power stations usually keep one week of fuel on hand for emergency generators. Even if they kept a month supply of diesel on hand, eventually the generators will shut down."

This dramatic information in George's mind is met with blank stares by everyone in the group but Frank.

"The generators run the coolant circulation for the reactor. No generators means no coolant, and no coolant means meltdown. No matter how carefully maintained they kept Waterford, even if it was one hundred percent automated, the generators will eventually stop, the fuel rods will heat up and make the plant meltdown. Even the security measures won't hold it if a reaction starts, the whole containment building will be blown up just like in Fukushima and Chernobyl, and that isn't the worst part."

"Now I'm beginning to get concerned," Maggie says dryly making everyone, even Keith laugh.

"I'm sorry for the interruption, George. Please continue telling me how a disease destroying civilization isn't our biggest threat," she says in a serious tone but follows with a smile.

"The worst part is other power plants and cooling ponds," he explains. "Each nuclear power plant has cooling ponds where spent fuel rods are kept, and they aren't enclosed in containment buildings but they rely on the same generators to keep the coolant circulating. So even if a reactor doesn't explode, the ponds will heat up, burn off the coolant, and the rods will catch fire and explode. That has to be multiplied by the sixty nuclear power plant locations in the U.S., many of which have multiple reactors and cooling ponds at each site."

"Keith's son, Eddie, told me he would never move east of the Rocky Mountain states because of the nuclear power plants. I bought my retreat property in Mexico after I looked into what I thought was his overblown paranoia. Fifty-seven of the sixty power plants are east of the Rockies. The other three are located in Washington, California, and Arizona. That is why he moved to Oregon, even if this disease burns itself out in a month, it will be too late. The Eastern half of the country will be a maze of radioactive wastelands, and there is nothing we can do about it but run."

A few quiet seconds go by allowing the group to absorb what George just told them, when an alarm starts ringing and makes them all jump with terror.

"I am so sorry," Maggie says laughing as she turns off her alarm clock that she surreptitiously grabbed while George had everyone in rapt attention to his speech. She has tears in her eyes and is struggling to breathe and speak through her laughter. "You should see your faces!" she is finally able to say with considerable effort.

Jack seems more upset than all the others at Maggie's joke at their expense. He turns and starts walking out the door.

"Jack, I'm sorry," Maggie says calling after him. "Don't be mad."

"It was a good joke, Maggie. I'm not mad," he calls back. "But you made me wet my pants, and I need to change."

This brings another round of tension releasing laughter that they all need. The laughter is short lived as the reality of what George told them sinks in, and Maggie especially has a very serious expression take over from the joyous one.

"Frank, if we move again soon it will kill me," she says. "Keith and George know this, and you need to tell Jack as well. I have made my peace with God, and I am ready to die. Do not let my illness slow down your preparation to leave, no matter what my wonderful Keith may try to plead you to do otherwise. My time is up, and I am ready to go to a better place but I am not going to be the cause of any of you fine men going with me. It is not your time."

She gives Keith's hand as much of a squeeze as she is able, but the whole episode has taken too much out of her. She takes some pain medication and lies down to sleep.

Once Maggie is sleeping, Keith finds the others in the dining hall. He sits at the table in resignation of what they are discussing, and Frank puts a plate of food in front of him.

"It's not half as good as what the chef used to make us, but it's decent and you need to eat."

"I was just telling them about my place, Keith. Should I continue or do you need a minute?"

Keith nods his head and says to *go on*.

"My place in Mexico is on the western edge of a city called Coatzacoalcos, in the Vera Cruz region, and like our current situation, there is good and bad about that location as well. Mexico has a lot of empty land in between cities and no capabilities to do a one day national inoculation of Zeus like the U.S. Most likely this disease hasn't made it there yet, and if we get really lucky, it won't reach there at all. I have a retreat full of supplies with its own water well, and we can cruise the boat right up to the dock on the western edge of the river.

"The bad news is Mexico is corrupt, so there is a chance the local police or military could give us grief or even try to take my supplies. There are also local gangs that might do the same, especially as word about the disease spreads and it approaches the city. The final problem will be where we should go from there if and when the disease arrives. We will have to consider leaving before it makes it there because Coatzacoalcos has a population of three hundred thousand people to run from if they get sick."

"Do you have any idea where to go if we have to leave Mexico?" Frank asks.

"I have one idea, but it's a long shot. I was hoping I could hear your ideas first."

"My only family is my grandfather, and he lives in New York. My house and all of my friends are in... *were* in Louisiana, so I've got nothing," Jack says.

"I have an ex-wife in Indiana and a forty year old son in Chicago that won't speak to me," Frank offers. "I'd give anything to speak with them again, but there's no way we would make it anywhere near Chicago with the disease or possible radiation. My own house is just outside of Denver so even my property in Colorado is an impossible trip."

Everyone looks at Keith.

"I've lived in Louisiana most of my life. I have a huge extended family in Champaign, Illinois. A brother, sisters, cousins, the whole nine yards, but I doubt we would find anyone alive if we made it. Champaign's a city of eighty thousand people and it isn't situated any better than New Orleans. Clinton Nuclear Power plant is thirty-five miles west of Champaign, and I would see it when we went fishing in Clinton Lake.

"The only person I know that isn't by radiation is my son Eddie, in Oregon. We would have to travel across most of the country and the Rocky Mountains to get there. I wouldn't be able to make that trip even if I was still eighteen years old. I hope your idea is a good one, George, because I'm all out."

"My plan is to try and reach your son, Keith," George offers.

"I appreciate you trying to cheer me up and give me some type of hope, but I just said it's impossible. That's a two thousand mile trip over mountains, through deserts, and a world filled with disease. Any survivors will shoot at us to keep what is theirs or try to kill us to take what we have. Give us something real to hope for," Keith says angrily.

"It's a two hundred mile trip," George replies. "I bought a house in Coatzacoalcos because it is a two hundred mile trip across that part of Mexico to the Pacific Ocean. I never had a place in mind to go before, but I liked the idea of being able to make it to the Pacific and have access to the West Coast if the East Coast went radioactive.

"Don't look at me like that, Keith. Talking with your son is what started me down that road of thought."

"Is your son a *tin foil hat* type of guy?" Frank asks with concern.

"No, he's not a conspiracy kind of man. I asked him about it once, and he said he loves his family so it's his job to know how to keep them safe. I'm surprised he was so dramatic with George that it scared him so much."

"He wasn't dramatic at all, and I bet he doesn't even remember that conversation. I asked him if he had any plans to move to New Orleans to live by you and Maggie, because I knew you would love to have the grandkids here. He gave me this quick look like I asked if he wanted to cut off his arm. I thought he might have an issue with living near you, Keith, but then he told me about the nuclear problem with this area. It wasn't more than a two minute conversation, but he was serious and direct with his reply. It gave me the chills, but I dismissed as him being crazy and paranoid until I looked it up myself. Doing my own research is what really freaked me out."

"Do you think we could make it?" Frank asks.

"It took me four hours to drive to the Pacific Ocean by car. It would take a day or two on horses and maybe a week on foot if we don't have any other options for transportation. There are cities and towns in between the coasts so there are all sorts of dangers besides the disease we could face along the way."

"It's still a long way to Oregon," Keith adds. "Even if we go by boat, which is what I guess you're thinking."

"Exactly, I was thinking we could buy a boat when we reached the coast. If the disease is already there then we might have to fight for one. It won't be easy, but I have no other idea where to go. We could head to Alaska or South America, but I hate the cold and I don't speak Spanish."

With a somber look on his face, Keith says, "I appreciate the thought of heading to see my son, but even if we make it to Oregon, you realize he might not be alive."

They all nod their understanding.

"I do have one request," Keith adds. "I want us to wait until the alarm sounds. We can load the boat with everything now and wait to make a quick escape as soon as the radiation reaches us. I want to give Maggie as much time as possible, and I want to have that time with her as well."

They all look at each other and Keith. Their looks are a mixture of remorse, understanding, fear, and shame.

"Please."

Frank and Jack both look at George with expressions of unease and shrug.

"Is there a way we can protect ourselves against the effects of radiation? What good is surviving a plague if we die from fallout?" Frank asks.

"We can check the medical supplies to see if they have Potassium tablets, I don't have any. Potassium Iodide or Iodate will block radioactive iodine from building up in the Thyroid. We will need to start taking them now to make sure our bodies are saturated before any fallout reaches us."

"You bought a property in Mexico to prepare for a nuclear escape location and didn't bother getting any of those Potassium pills?" Jack asks.

"I have a supply of them at my house in New Orleans and in Mexico, but I didn't think the end of the world would happen when I was fishing. If we can't find any Potassium pills we can try red wine if the kitchen has any, or even broccoli. If we're going to stay and wait for the alarm, we should have all three of those things in our system by the time it sounds. Keith and I can check the medical room for the pills, and you two can gather the wine and broccoli out of the kitchen if there is any. All five of us will have to start consuming those items today."

"Can't we just wait until we need them?" Keith asks. "I don't want to go in and disturb Maggie by searching through the room."

"You mean you don't want to disturb Maggie by telling her what we're looking for? You can't keep the truth about this away from her. If we stay here, she is going to need this stuff in her system just as much as we are before the radiation hits. She may be struggling to live but that doesn't mean she's dead, or doesn't get a say in what we do."

Keith quickly stands up to face George against his accusation. Instead of arguing his point, he turns and walks out, knowing that George is right about his intentions to hide the dangers from Maggie.

*

No potassium pills were found on the rig or in George's boat. He double checked the first aid kit he had on board just in case he threw some of the pills in there, but he didn't. He meant to, but didn't.

They spent the evening loading as much water, food, and medical supplies into the boat as they could and refueling it. There is no guarantee that George's house will be accessible or intact anymore, and if not, they need everything they can carry and more.

After everything is secured the men return to the medical room to speak with Maggie.

"We have everything set to leave, but we've decided we are going to stay until the alarms sound," George says for the group. "With the broccoli and red wine in our systems, we should be fine with the short exposure we will receive before we can leave."

"And if you're not fine with the exposure?" she asks.

"We are all adults and are doing what we think is right."

Maggie looks at each of the men's faces. She sees strength and pride, but also fear. Jack is only able to keep eye contact for a second before his eyes look to Frank, and then scan to the floor. The men are staying longer for her benefit, and as much as she would like to usher them all off the rig right now, she knows her urgings would fall on deaf ears.

"When the alarms sound, how do you four propose getting me down to the boat both quickly and safely?" she asks them.

"We'll use the same empty cargo box that we used to lower supplies to the boat. We can use the crane to lower you and Keith the same way.

"You will all continue to get exposed to radiation while this process of loading me takes place."

"We've made our choice." George says, and they all nod with expressions showing varying degrees of commitment.

"I assume you will be staying on board to run the crane, because you are in charge of the rig?" Maggie asks Frank directly.

"Yes ma'am."

"In that case I want all of you to leave so I can get some rest, but would like Frank to stay to explain the whole process of getting me loaded so I don't screw something up and slow you down even more. Keith, that means you too. Go get some sleep. How are you going to carry me to the crane if you don't have enough rest?"

Keith leans in for a kiss and stands up from beside her bed. The men say goodnight and trudge out the door to get some sleep. The days have been far easier on Frank and Jack without the physically demanding job of running the rig, but the stresses of the known and unknown versions of death that are knocking on their doors is causing serious fatigue to affect them all.

"Could you make sure no one is in the hall, Frank?"

He checks and shakes his head when he turns around.

"No one is out there."

"Frank, I want you to make the alarm ring tomorrow afternoon."

Frank just looks at Maggie and waits for an explanation.

"I know you think you're staying here for me, but you are really staying here for Keith. It is his feelings you are all concerned about, and his feelings are secondary to all of your physical well-being. You set the alarm to go off tomorrow afternoon and don't tell Keith. He will think we are leaving because of the radiation and won't feel guilty about moving me, and I won't feel guilty that my condition put all of you in danger."

"I think we'll be able to get you off the rig fast enough that we won't be affected."

"You think but you don't know. Tell me, Frank, have you ever gone through chemotherapy?" she asks but doesn't wait for a response. "It isn't fun. There is nausea, vomiting, hair loss, and you boys could get what I have now, *cancer*. Now I love Keith with all my heart, and I appreciate what you men are trying to do for me, but your pain and suffering won't help me live any longer. I won't die in peace if I know I was the cause of your deaths. You set the alarm, or trigger it, or do whatever you have to, but you get us off this rig no later than tomorrow evening or I will jump from the edge and start swimming to Mexico on my own."

"I'll make sure we leave tomorrow evening."

She gives him a stern look.

"And I'll make sure Keith doesn't know there is no radiation."

"Thank you, now go get some sleep. You look terrible."

*

The night's rest did everybody some good. The comfort of knowing they are ready to leave at a moment's notice also helps. Today is an especially good day for Maggie. Not only has she recovered from the stress of being moved to the oil rig, but she is feeling better than she has in weeks. At her insistence she had Keith bring her to the dining room, on a rolling office chair, since there aren't any wheelchairs on the rig.

"I'm surprised to see you join us," Frank says cheerfully to Maggie.

"I am glad to be out of bed. I felt so good this morning I was standing up on my own. Nearly gave Keith a heart attack when he walked in the room."

"It's good to have you doing so well," Keith says while standing behind her chair squeezing her shoulder.

"I should warn you, Frank, when we get off of this rig, I'm going to complain to the owners that this place is not a bit handicapped accessible. Keith is having to wheel me around on an office chair."

"I look forward to hearing my reprimand from the boss," he says back and follows with a smile.

George walks in after everyone else is sitting around a table with their food.

"Looks like sleeping beauty finally joined us," Maggie teases.

"Ha ha. I've been awake for a while. The wind has picked up, so I went up top to check that the boat is still moored to the buoy. We've been lucky that the water has been so flat."

There are some plates on a second table with a bunch of eggs, bacon, and pancakes. The jovial mood shifts a bit for George when he sees there is also a bowl of broccoli and everyone is drinking red wine.

He makes himself a plate and sits down, exclaiming, "Red wine for breakfast. What a bunch of alcoholics we're becoming."

The group laughs.

The morning chatter goes on with ease. They even talk in a relaxed manner about their predicament and eventual escape. They speak about the property in Mexico and hope that there will be papayas and pineapples for breakfast while they are there. It is a morning that they all needed after the stress and turmoil of the last few days. After a few more laughs and a general relaxed sigh, the group falls silent and into their own thoughts.

"I love you," Maggie says in a softer tone than she managed earlier while grasping Keith's hand. "Thank you for always being there for me and trying to protect me."

"I love you too," he says in return.

"You don't have to feel guilty when I'm gone, Keith, and not just because you feel you have done everything you can. It isn't our choice when we die. It is the Lord's choice when He wants to call us home."

"Do you want me to take you back to your room?" Keith asks concerned as her grip on his hand is getting weaker.

"Now I know why I felt so good this morning, Keith. It's time for us to say goodbye."

The rapid change in Maggie's condition is shocking to the other men. Keith has seen this several times before. The color drains from her face, and she starts to sink in her chair as she becomes too weak to hold herself up. Keith gently picks her up and begins to carry her out of the dining room.

"I'll take her to bed."

"Is she going to be all right?" George asks before he can stop the words.

"This happens from time to time," Keith says back to him. "She just needs to rest again. She pushed herself too hard."

He says the words but isn't convinced she'll come back this time.

The men sit back at the table and stare off in various directions. They don't have jobs to do and each has a million things to consider about their pasts and possible futures. Jack breathes in and is about to say something when the lights start flashing and an alarm starts blaring. The three men look at each other with faces full of terror at getting caught in radioactive fallout, and then start to move.

"I'll get the boat and get it ready," George says and runs off.

"You get the crane started. I have to get Maggie and Keith," Frank yells at Jack, and they each run in different directions.

Arriving at the medical room, Frank yells, "Keith, bring Maggie, we have to leave now. That's the radiation alarm!"

"She's too weak to move!" Keith yells back. "I know you set the alarm to ring. I heard her talking to you last night!"

"I set it for this afternoon like she asked. This alarm is real. We have to leave now."

Keith looks hard at Frank and see's the truth of what he is saying in the expression of fear in the return gaze. He looks at Maggie, and she says weakly, *"Let's go."*

Keith scoops her back up in his arms and follows Frank. They weave their way to the crane amidst the blaring siren and blinking lights on the interior hallways. Stepping outside there is a slight smell of smoke in the wind that is blowing. Burning particles from all the fires in New Orleans have finally reach the oil rig with the increased wind.

When they arrive at the crane, George is still standing on the deck, and Jack is sitting at the controls and hitting them.

"It won't start!" Jack yells and everyone looks at Frank for a solution.

"Let's get in the emergency lifeboat."

Lifeboats for oil rigs are large and orange. They are usually big enough to hold up to thirty people. This one has a capacity of twenty-eight. It looks like part boat and part submarine which it technically is in a way. It isn't designed to operate underwater, but because of how lifeboats are launched from oil rigs, they need to be watertight.

The lifeboat is sitting on a ramp angled down to the water at forty-five degrees. There is a ninety foot drop for it once it is released, and it will become completely submerged before its buoyancy pops it back out of the water to float on the surface. It is quite like an amusement park ride designed to drop you and give you that instant stomach churning sensation of uncontrolled falling.

They climb aboard and all help to get Maggie secured before strapping into their own seats. Frank pulls the lever and the lifeboat begins its freefall into the water. Keith is across from Maggie and can see she is barely there. The feeling during the impact and the subsequent bouncing is as disturbing as the drop. Frank starts the engine and drives the lifeboat over to George's moored fishing boat.

"George, get out and get your boat going. We have to head east and try to get ahead of this wind," Frank calls out to him.

"Head south instead," George says while climbing out of the lifeboat hatch to get onto his boat. We'll leave the radioactive winds quicker and can turn east when we need to. As soon as we don't smell smoke we should be out of it."

Frank doesn't wait for George to get his boat started. He guns the engine and heads south trying to get clear of the invisible death in the air. Keith has unstrapped Maggie from her seat and is sitting on the floor and cradling her in his arms.

Jack climbs out of the cabin and sits outside with a rag wrapped around his head, covering his mouth and nose. He is smelling the air to tell when they clear the smoke coming from the city. He also wants to stay out of the smoky air remaining in the cabin out of a justified fear that it is radioactive and he doesn't want to filter it with his lungs.

The smell of smoke disappears ten minutes south of the rig, and Frank keeps going another ten minutes just to be sure. George's boat is much faster. He caught up with the others before they cleared the affected area and bounced alongside them as they sped along the small waves.

Jack lashes the two boats together once the engines are cut, and George climbs back onto the bobbing orange escape craft.

"I don't think she made it," Frank says quietly to the others as he steps down to the bow.

"I'll go check on Keith," George says. "You two need to start cleaning up. Take off your clothes and dump them overboard. Grab a bucket and the deck scrubber, and scrub each other down with lots of water, keep dumping the water over yourselves and scrub hard. If it doesn't hurt you are leaving something on you. Keith and I will do the same when I bring him out."

"I need to get a drink first."

"No! Don't drink or eat anything until you get yourselves cleaned off. You don't want to ingest any more particles than you already have. We have to scrub the boat as well, both of them if we're taking this orange beast with us."

Frank and Jack begin to strip down while George climbs back into the cabin with Keith and Maggie.

"She's gone," Keith says as George kneels next to him.

"Keith, we have to go outside and scrub the radioactive dust off of us."

"Help me carry Maggie out of here. Before we went to breakfast, she asked me to bury her at sea if she didn't make it to your house."

George nods and lifts her body up to Keith, who raises her out of the hatch hole, and places her gently onto the deck.

"Keith, I know this isn't what you want to hear, but we need to hurry. We need to get out of these clothes and scrub each other down to remove any radioactive particles. There isn't time for a long goodbye, and we shouldn't handle her body after we have scrubbed down."

Keith nods at George and kneels at Maggie's side. "I love you, Maggie. You were my best friend, and I will miss you until the day we meet again."

He kisses her forehead, and then he and George lower her into the water, where she sinks into its depths.

With every second counting, George climbs over to his boat and begins stripping out of his clothes to begin the decontamination process. Keith lingers for a second, staring blankly into the deep blue before he finally turns and joins the others.

CHAPTER 4

FINDING OUR WAY

Grants Pass, Oregon.
Wal-Mart—Present Day.

"What do we do now?" one of Isaac's men asks him.

I turn to Arthur, and say, "Tell everyone to stand down."

My group had instructions to casually shadow the members of Isaac's and Jeremiah's group while our story was checked out. Isaac did his interviews, and my people followed him and his men or *hung out* with them. Our youngest members and women stayed closest to those who looked like the most competent and alert members of the opposing team, and were accepted as non-threats until Arthur's stand down order rings out over the radios.

Surprised looks appear on the faces of Isaac and his men when my people, whom they were having casual conversations with of some sort or other, put their guns back on safety and holster or sling them in less accessible positions.

Jeremiah looks from my twelve-year-old daughter Hannah, who is standing next to him, back to me, after she re-holsters her handgun. She had been so relaxed in her behavior and handling of the weapon that he didn't realize she wasn't actually wiping it down for the last thirty minutes. She looked directly at him when she put it away to let him know she was ready to use it if she needed to.

Both Jeremiah and Isaac look at each other, and then at me and those of my group gathering near me. We have already lost three hours of the day to this encounter with them, and by the looks on all of their faces, I can see they want something more than explanations of what just happened.

"Can we join your group?" Isaac asks.

That question catches me by surprise and apparently his brother as well. Jeremiah walks over to Isaac and gives him a fierce look that has only one meaning.

Giving back a look just as intense as he received, Isaac says, "We need this!" appearing to settle the matter for now. At least this lets me know which one of them is really in charge. I'm glad it is the more *level headed* Isaac, but regardless of who is running their group, they have been holding us up, literally, for three hours.

"My first inclination is to say *no*," I reply to him. "I'm not really in the mood to add even more people than the ones we saved to our ranch roster. There is only so much space, you understand. We've already been delayed by your showing up here, and now you say you want to join us after threatening us several times. I could go on about your brother's attitude and what to me is your group's excessive religious fervor, but right now all I want to do is get this group of survivors on their way."

"Look, Eddie, I know we have been holding your group up and threatening you, but with everything that we've seen here, we had to know you weren't really the bad guys. You've got to admit your group looked guilty. Imagine if you were the new arrivals to find us with a pile of recently killed people."

"I would have trusted your word after a quick check with those people on who you were," I say and point to the group of starved former captives off to the side. "Why should I take you in, and why do you want to join us? It looks like you already have a strong group to me."

With what I consider an unnecessarily pleading look, Isaac asks, "Let me lay out our position so you can decide."

I hesitate a second, nod to Isaac, and then turn to Arthur, "Get everyone on top of the trucks now." Turning back to Isaac, I say, "Walk with us to the trucks, and we can discuss it while everyone else prepares to leave. We should have at least thirty minutes to speak while my people get everyone safely situated."

A make-shift railing barrier of posts and chains was secured around the top of the truck trailers. With the trailers full of food and other supplies we had to figure out a way to get all of our people and the thirty people we rescued back to the ranch without finding other working vehicles. Most of the survivors are too ill or weak to make the journey on foot or bicycle. The railing allows the people to ride up top away from any infected and prevents us from having to leave any of them behind for a second trip.

Taking a few steps, I start the brief inquiry, "So why do you want to join us?"

"Our group isn't doing that well," Isaac replies. "We made it through the winter all right, but we aren't set up for this situation. We were somewhat organized and had supplies, but lost a lot of our stuff in a fire after we were attacked by a large group of the infected people."

Our own overwhelming attack jumps into my head at that comment, and my skin crawls uncomfortably. I get a small comfort from hearing him say *infected* and not *possessed people.*

"We had our own run in with a large group of the infected," I reply "How many did your group get attacked by?"

Jeremiah, who is following, answers me, "We lost seventeen people during the attack and ended up killing two hundred and eighty-seven of the possessed."

Ignoring his continued belief in possessions, Simone and I all look at each other when he says 297 infected people killed seventeen of his group.

"Did they overrun your fences all at the same spot?" Simone asks.

He shakes his head. "We don't have our property fenced off. They came at us in the middle of the night on Christmas. Our place is out in the woods like yours, and we got lazy. We hadn't seen any of the possessed come our way until that night. I think the singing brought them to us."

"Singing? Did someone send the infected after you too?"

"Send them after us?" Isaac asks with a curious expression on his face. "No. We were singing Christmas carols throughout the day, and were just trying to celebrate, especially for the children. Off and on throughout the day someone would start a new carol, and it made us all feel...more than happy, we felt blessed to be alive. The infected showed up about an hour after dark. They just appeared there among us, all around us, they were everywhere."

A sadness creeps across Jeremiah's features as Isaac is telling us about their attack.

"We had seventeen souls taken that night," Isaac continues. "Jeremiah lost his wife and daughter. We lost friends and family, both to these creatures and unfortunately to our own stray bullets in the darkness. We aren't set up the way your people are on your ranch, Eddie. Like I said, we weren't expecting the end of the world. Half of the food we had burnt with our house the night we were attacked after a fire started. We barely have anything left now and were hoping to gather the remaining supplies here at the store after we freed Darren's mother."

"Is Darren one of your men?" I ask.

"The wounded boy we found four days ago when we made our first trip from our property. That's right. I didn't get to finish telling you about him."

I nod wanting him to get on with his story.

"We found Darren, and he had been shot. He told us that three men grabbed his mother and shot him when he tried to stop them. They laughed and said they were leaving him as a snack for the possess... for the infected, and he could visit his mom later at Wal-Mart."

"So you decided to gather up twenty-five of your men and announce to the group of fifty armed criminals here that you are what, *the Army of God*, and they should lay down their arms?" I say with enough incredulous sarcasm that several of Isaac's men hang their heads slightly with embarrassment.

"We didn't know how many people were here," Isaac replies in his defense. "We knew there were the three that grabbed Darren's mother and expected maybe five to seven more people."

"We didn't think Satan would build his army so quickly," Jeremiah adds trying to defend his brother.

"Look, Jeremiah, you're really not winning me over with all of your religious crap. You need to tone it down a bit, okay?" I say trying to fathom how they could make such a stupid mistake by driving up to the doors and announcing themselves without scouting the place first.

"We don't need them, Isaac," Jeremiah says to his brother, clearly angry and not just at my rude remarks. Turning and pointing to me, he loudly says, "These men you killed were doing the work of Satan. And even if you don't believe it, you were doing the work of God."

Isaac turns to his brother, and forcefully says, "We will all die without help, Jeremiah. If they can take in all the people they saved from this torture pit after such a brutal winter, then they are the ones that can teach us how to survive!"

Jeremiah looks at me with angry and fearful eyes, shaking his head, and says, "We can't trust him, Isaac. He has no morals without God!"

Angrily I get in his face, and say, "My supposed lack of morality brought me here to risk almost certain death to try and free these people, Jeremiah. Unlike you, we knew the numbers of people we would be facing and we still came. I didn't do it to get my name in the paper or drum up customers for my business. I did it because it's the right thing to do. I doubt you would have even bothered to show up if you knew how many men Stockton had, so who's morally superior now?"

Turning back to Isaac, I say, "This isn't going to work. There is no way he and I will get along at our ranch. And if more of your people are like him it will be even worse."

"Eddie, I know Jeremiah can be abrasive at times," he says while pushing his brother back and giving him another stern look, "but I don't understand why talking about God bothers you."

"It's not just talking about *God*. It's how he does it. Try to look at this conversation from my point of view. I've heard what Jeremiah is spouting my whole life from different religious people. *Atheists don't believe in anything. Morals only come from God.* Blah blah blah. I've heard it ad nauseam all while I lived a law-abiding life and been a decent person like any regular family man does. I know exactly what he thinks of me, but let me tell you what I think when I'm told I'm doing *God's* work. To me anyone who preaches about God with every breath sounds like they are literally crazy. I know you believe you are honoring the higher power you believe in, but it makes you sound unstable to me, and I don't want unstable people at the ranch."

"So no one at your ranch believes in God?" Isaac asks with clear concern in his voice.

"Actually, me and my family are the only Atheists at the ranch—at least I think we are. The others at the ranch do some sort of church services on Sundays, but God and religion never really gets brought up to us or thrown in every sentence like it does with your brother." Looking at Arthur, I say, "I don't even know what sect of Christianity all of you are?" But not having my gaze linger for an answer, I turn back to Isaac. "I know I am a jerk about religion at times, but it usually comes out when it is being thrown around constantly the way Jeremiah is doing. No one at the ranch shouts out to the world about *the glories of God* with every breath like your brother does, and I like it that way. Even before the collapse he would seem extreme. You see that, don't you?"

"I am just giving the Lord credit where He deserves it," Jeremiah cuts in trying to defend himself.

"Fine, Jeremiah, but just so you know, when you say *God*, that's not what I hear. I hear Santa Clause. When you say *Satan*, I hear *Tooth Fairy*. To me you are thanking one of the many make believe creatures that humans invented, and you sound like you're fucking nuts spouting off like that. How would I sound if I told you, *you are doing Allah's work* or *Zenu*, the Scientology God? You'd think I was crazy and rightfully so."

"Eddie, please!" Isaac says. "My people aren't set up to handle life without society. We were barely prepared for this situation before the winter came. And after the attack wiped out so much of what we had, we won't make it long without some serious help and training."

"We are a better group of people for you to take to your ranch than the scarecrows you rescued from this place," one of Isaac's men says from behind him.

I nod a bit while looking side to side to my wife and the other de facto leaders of our group. "You aren't starving and are probably better trained than those people you're calling scarecrows, but they are at least grateful to us for saving their lives. We saved your lives, and for gratitude, we've had to endure the threat of your gun barrels since you first arrived."

"When did you save our lives?" Jeremiah demands.

"You came in here with a chip on your shoulders thinking you are doing *The Lord's* work and He would protect you from all harm," I say accusingly. "If Stockton was still in charge when you made your announcement about atoning for sins this morning, his men would have opened fire on your group and killed most of you before you could scratch your ass and wonder what went wrong. Then he would have had his people head out to gather up the women and children you left behind. Your arrogance nearly got you all killed and only the actions of my people saved your lives today."

"That is one of the reasons why we need your help," Isaac replies and turns to his brother. "You know we need help. Even if we had the supplies that were here, we don't have the skills to make it."

Jeremiah nods knowing it's true.

"Go back to the front of the store with the men and let me speak with Eddie alone."

Isaac's men and Jeremiah leave, and the rest of us step through the doors into the back of the store. Simone stays by me and the others head off to finish with the trucks.

"Eddie, you need to take us in. We won't survive without some help and training."

"Do you speak for *all* of your people?"

"Yes."

"So there is nobody back at your camp that will override what agreements you make if we agree to help you?"

"No one. I'm in charge of the group, for now," Isaac replies. "I run the camp and keep things in order and under control, but if I don't bring back some type of hope for how we can continue to survive, I won't be running things for long."

"That probably means Jeremiah would be in charge, right?"

"Yes, if I'm out, he would be running things. You need to know we already planned on going to your ranch before we arrived here. I thought you would be there and we could ask you for help, but Jeremiah was certain you would be dead and any supplies that were there we could take. Maybe even move everyone there and stay at the ranch if its condition wasn't too bad."

"I can understand why he would assume we were dead. Most of the world is gone."

"It's more than that, Eddie. My group, *my family*, we are all God fearing people and without anyone to communicate with after the fall, all of our time was focused on finding repentance for our sins. I thought you might still be alive, but he was convinced you would be dead or possessed because of your lack of faith."

"And what does that mean?"

"He and several of the men that are closest to him said they would take your ranch even if you were still alive. To him it would be better if you were a Muslim than a non-believer."

"And you expect me to welcome your group in when some of you are willing to kick me off my ranch or kill me and my family because I'm an Atheist?"

"I want you to know that if you bring us in, I will be in charge and those people won't be able to do anything. If you don't help us in some way, I don't know if I'll even be able to keep Mariah safe, and won't be able to do anything if they decide to try for the ranch."

"He would kill his own sister?"

"He believes he is trying to protect her soul. Hell, you saw me out there today. Even I shot our man before he could change because we all believed it. Sure, a part of me thought it was a disease we were dealing with and not demons, but I wasn't sure. Now I know for certain it's a disease, but it will take some time for the others. With Jeremiah, I'm not sure any amount of time or evidence will help."

I nod trying to take in everything he's telling me, and then look at Simone, who just shakes her head and shrugs her shoulder at my gaze.

"How many people did you leave back at your camp?" I ask while exhaling a sigh.

After looking at a small notebook, he says, "We left eight men to guard the camp, seventeen women and seventeen children. Seventeen women, including my sister, who shouldn't be here."

"Give me a few minutes to get the trucks on their way and talk this over with my people," I say to Isaac, and he nods back at me.

"Are the trucks loaded?" I ask as I reach the loading dock.

"Most of our people and all of the Stick People that are going are loaded up. We were just waiting for your say-so to get everyone else on board to leave," Donald replies.

Donald, Arthur, Samantha, and Simone gather close so we can figure out what to do. I motion for Hannah to come over so she can be a part of the discussion as well.

"They have over sixty people, including seventeen kids, who we would have to add to the ranch. Any idea's or comments?" I ask.

"It will already be a stretch dealing with the thirty people we saved from this place. We'll have to start some serious scavenging for more resources to take care of everyone through the winter," Arthur says. "On that note though, Isaac's people could be a big help in guard duty and caring for the Stick People we are bringing with us. However, they might be a danger if many are like his brother and consider anyone not adhering to their brand of Christianity as the Devil's helpers."

Simone and I look at each other knowing how true that is after what Isaac just told us.

"They seem like good Christian people to me," Samantha adds. "Maybe some are a bit overzealous to my liking, but I don't see what harm they would pose to us. Especially if they already know you and your family are Atheists and they still want to join our group."

"Just being a Christian doesn't make them trustworthy or your friends, Samantha. I know exactly the type of danger Arthur is talking about, and it is more real than you understand. Isaac thinks his brother and more of his men will be a danger to us if we don't help them out."

"Did he threaten you to get onto the ranch?"

"Isaac warned us that he wouldn't be in charge anymore if this trip of theirs ended without major supplies and a better idea that they can survive another winter. Jeremiah doesn't look kindly to people like Simone and me existing, and he won't think taking what we have is wrong because he doesn't think we are worthy of having it, at least not in the Lord's eyes."

Samantha gives an expression showing she's unconvinced that they could be a real threat. "I think you might be inflating the danger a bit, Eddie."

"Just think about how well the Catholics and Protestants got along in Ireland, and you'll understand how dangerous even a small difference in religious belief can be, let alone something as serious as my family not believing at all. I'm not exaggerating. Isaac thinks his brother is a threat. I haven't heard much from you, Donald. What do you think?"

"I think we have to let them join us and don't think we have much of a choice at this point, do you?" he asks.

"No. We really don't, I guess."

"Why don't we have a choice?" Hannah asks. "We can't let them bully us into taking them in. We are better trained than they are, and the ranch is secure."

I frown at the thought and think how to answer. "They are an armed group that trained at the ranch so they know the inside layout. They have a large group of women and children that they need to protect and are low on supplies. They know our group will be stretched to the breaking point trying to care for the Stick People, and they know the people we are taking in have less to offer us than Isaac's group does. If we turn Isaac away, as decent a person as he is, he won't be able to stop his people from trying to take the ranch from us. In fact, they would have every reason to turn against us and try to take what we have. I just hope the more zealous members of their group don't disregard Isaac's control of his group because they'll be giving up too much."

"And what would they be giving up?" Donald asks.

"Control," I reply. "They didn't let their women come here to fight, and I don't remember any women training with them before when they were at the ranch. They also said they left some men to guard the women and children."

"I did catch that. Why can't their women defend themselves?" Simone asks.

"Exactly!" I say while nodding. "If they want to join our group, then they will be joining our group, not working as a secondary group on our ranch. That means even the women and able children are armed and trained to fight. That might be a deal breaker for them if they are segregating jobs by gender. It is also still my ranch, and I have you leaders and advisors picked out, whatever you want to call yourselves. Whatever hierarchy Isaac's group has, they will have to earn their place and our trust on the ranch like everyone else we encounter. On a separate note, have we had any problems from the six survivors we told we weren't taking with us?"

"No. They have stayed out of our way so far and are all by the rear bathroom last time I checked," Arthur says, obviously disturbed by the subject. "Eddie, I don't want you killing them. It isn't something any of us want to see happen."

Everyone nods with Arthur's objection.

"Letting them live will end up costing us something eventually, you understand that, right? We know they are trouble makers and those types of people thrive from the misfortune of others."

"We know some of them may cause problems eventually, but it doesn't feel right killing all six when they haven't done anything wrong yet."

I look at each one of them, wishing they could step beyond the veneer of civilization they are holding on to so desperately. Letting these six people live is no different to me than letting a rattlesnake live in your garden. It's ridiculous to choose what people think is the moral route if the moral choice could get you killed.

"I'll let them live, but you all have to accept responsibility for what they do to us in the future. What they do will be on your shoulders like Chad Hansen's actions are on mine."

"They may not do anything," Arthur offers.

"And they may not let you live to regret this decision," I counter.

"You know they can't survive on their own and what that means, right?" Simone asks.

"Yes... I know. We'll have to take them with us. I hate the idea of trouble makers like them at the ranch, but with the threat from Isaac's people, those other six skeletons don't seem like much of a problem now. Maybe they'll insist on not joining us and make all of our concerns a moot point."

"What about not having Isaac's group on the ranch at all?" Hannah asks.

"Do you mean killing them?"

"No, that's not what I meant, but it is an option isn't it? If they are threatening to kill us and take our supplies, they wouldn't just kill us Atheists, they would kill everyone that worked with us. They would kill everyone at the ranch."

"I can't kill them because they are decent people. At least some of them are."

"More decent than the six from here you were going to kill? None of them said anything about killing us or stealing our supplies."

"Jeremiah is delusional because of his beliefs but at least he has a reason to think ill of me, even if I don't agree religion is a good reason to do so. Those six others are just bad people and seem like the type that cause problems just for the sake of causing them. I'll take a crazy religious person over a genuinely bad one any day."

"I still don't think we need to let them live at the ranch," Hannah says reiterating her point.

"Besides the trouble we could face if we don't let them in, they have seventeen children that will die if we don't help them learn to survive. I don't know their ages yet, but I can't let that many young people go without help."

"No, Dad, that's not what I mean. If we are going to help them, why not have them move to the farm instead of the Ranch?"

"That is an excellent idea," Simone tells Hannah and gives her a motherly hug that makes Hannah blush and look like the little girl I remember.

"That could help with all sorts of issues with them not feeling stifled and your lives not being threatened," Arthur offers.

"That sounds good. If we can make the farm secure it would be a great place for them to stay. If you all think that will work, I'll make that offer to them."

A round of agreement is heard, and the group splits up to leave.

"Hannah, good idea. I should listen to you more often."

CHAPTER 5
GULF OF MEXICO

Eight Months Earlier.

The four men are a ridiculous looking group travelling across the Gulf of Mexico. George didn't have much clothes below deck on his boat. His girlfriend, Heather, got seasick so he didn't spend much time on it. He bought it right before he purchased the property in Mexico so he would have a large enough boat to make the journey across the Gulf. He was able to find one pair of shorts, two t-shirts, and a bunch of towels. Due to Keith's grieving state, they opted to give him the shorts and a shirt, which fit him as well as George. The rest of them wrapped the towels around their waists and looked like they were headed to the showers.

The boat is stopped now and even under the canopy, the sun is oppressively baking them. The relieving wind of a breeze occurs with such little frequency and duration that they are certain the air is only torturing them when it decides to appear. They would take turns running the air conditioning in the cabin, but they don't want to use the extra fuel for those generators. There is no guarantee that their destination in Mexico will be safe, and they need to save every drop of diesel in case they need to travel several hundred more miles after Coatzacoalcos.

They took turns piloting the boat through the night, foolishly not fearful of running into anything. By morning there were three close calls where they almost ended the journey with a spectacular crash. Twice with different oil rigs whose lights were off and once with a large oil tanker that was heading somewhere unknown.

Keith was at the wheel when the silhouette of the large ship came into view, creeping through the water at about five knots. Like the oil rigs, the tanker had no lights working but the engines were taking it to some unknown port or crash point. When he told the others about it in the morning they all speculated that the crew might have become infected during the day while escaping some port. When that tanker finally runs aground it will undoubtedly add to the unplanned ecological disasters that have occurred due to the absence of man.

Of their seven hundred and forty mile trip to the port of Coatzacoalcos, they estimate about six hours remaining or just under three hundred miles. They are stopped and waiting to leave so they can arrive shielded by the night. Besides their unusual appearance, none of the men speak Spanish and none of them brought their passports. The local government officials in that city are heavily corrupt as they are in most of Mexico, but bribing a port entry officer only works if you have something with which to bribe them. This group has nothing of value besides the food onboard.

The hope is that they can enter the mouth of the river and pilot the craft to George's house without detection. The port police will either have to be asleep or busy to ignore them, and it is too much to hope that any of the port officer's he dealt with in the past would be working when they arrive. George's *fishing* boat is a 70' open bridge convertible Viking yacht, so sneaking in is an impossibly long shot, but it is the best chance they have.

"We have some company coming," Frank says while looking to the west.

What looks like another fishing boat is headed toward them. George looks at it with his binoculars.

"Looks like only one guy on board. He's got some balls taking that boat out this far. It looks like a thirty-five footer."

After he says the words, he realizes that the man may not be so brave as much as he might be running from something. That isn't good news because west of their current position is Mexico. George grabs his shotgun and checks that it's loaded, while they all wait for the boat to get closer.

"He isn't slowing down," Keith says as the approaching vessel continues on its course.

They can clearly see the man as his boat gets closer, and all except for George wave to him. The man sees them as well, but makes no effort to slow or turn his boat. There isn't a concern of collision, although the man could destroy both of their boats if he decided to turn the wheel sharply into them as he passes. Keith, Frank, and Jack all see for the first time what George saw at the banks of the waterway in Shell Beach.

As the boat passes them by, it is obvious the man in it sees the group of four staring at him. He stares back at them with wide eyes and turns his body to keep facing them as his engines keep the boat he is in moving past and away. He looks odd as he is walking in place on his boat and running into the chair that is blocking his way from walking toward them. With a small bump from a wave knocking him to the side, he is free of the chair and walks to the end of his boat, climbs over the back, and steps into the water while never taking his eyes off of his potential meal.

George sits down, but the other three continue to watch the strange vision of a boat cruising off into the distance while its owner bobs a few times in the water before sinking out of sight.

"He didn't even try to swim. He just walked off the boat and let himself sink," Jack says with amazement.

"You don't look too surprised," Frank mentions to George.

"I saw them outside of New Orleans when I was picking up Keith and Maggie. I thought I could go into the city and find my family, but there were already hundreds of them lined up on the opposite bank, with what looked like thousands more still approaching. They had the same strange wide eyed expression on their faces and no other emotion. They make a horrible moan however, that is something I don't look forward to hearing again."

"Where did that guy come from?"

George takes out his Gulf map and traces the trajectory.

"If he didn't change the direction of his boat, he must have come from Tampico, that's about five hundred miles north of Coatzacoalcos, and three hundred miles south of the Texas border. I doubt he could have made it out here from Texas unless he refilled his gas tank somewhere along the way. That means the disease is already in Mexico as well."

"How could it get down here so fast?" Frank asks.

"The letter my son sent me said they were giving the drug to first responders nationwide, and with the rioting and terror attacks around the globe, it's a good bet that many other nations tried to use Zeus to solve their problems as well."

"It could also be random boats with infected people like that last guy," George offers. "When I came in from fishing to pick up Keith, there were hundreds of boats spread out leaving Lake Borgne. Many of those boats could have had infected people that were bitten but not yet turned. If that happened at every port, which is likely, then the boats will cruise until they run out of gas or run aground and take the infection with them."

"So what should we do?" two of them ask at the same time.

"We should head in now," George says. "It will still be light out and we won't be able to sneak in, but if they are having issues with boats of infected crashing into the docks, they will probably be blowing up any vessels that attempt to sneak ashore. We also need to be able see what is happening on land before we tie up to my dock. It won't do us any good to get off the boat if the banks are lined with infected people like in Shell Beach."

CHAPTER 6
THE JOURNEY HOME

Oregon.
Present Day.

Once again I find myself yearning to get home without the certainty that I will arrive safely. Simone and I are riding in an SUV with Isaac, Jeremiah, and two of their men on the way to our ranch. The semi-trucks loaded with supplies were sent ahead of us an hour ago so we could stay back and work out the details of Isaac's group joining us by the ranch. I also wanted our group to arrive ahead of time so they could prepare a credible defense against this group in case the discussions didn't continue in a reasonable manner.

I have to admit that, even without the threat Jeremiah poses, my own concerns and prejudices against people of religion are the main problem I had with immediately accepting Isaac's group into our fold. More than my typical distrust of people in general, I am afraid of what religious people are capable of, because in my mind, *anything* can be justified if you claim to be working for the benefit of a higher power.

Jeremiah's demeanor is much the same as it had been before the collapse, but his religious fervor has increased and he is still a reactionary hot head. It doesn't help that I keep being the asshole that pushes his buttons, but in this short interview period, I have to push him to the extreme to see if he will continue to be as dangerous to my family as Isaac said he was. So far, he is begrudgingly accepting the fact that he and his people need us. My biggest concern with him at this point is the loss of his wife and daughter; it makes him a man with nothing left to lose. All he seems to cling to are his beliefs about religion, his ideas about God causing this outbreak, and loyalty to his family. Though I'm not sure how strong his family loyalties are with his attempting to kill his sister earlier.

On our way to the ranch we will be stopping at the house of Ruben and Maria Castellanos, the couple that Simone and I encountered on our bike ride into Grants Pass. Maria had been bitten by Rubens infected parents, and they were both trapped in their fifth wheel trailer waiting for her change and his eventual attack. I told Arthur to stop on the way by to check that they were still alive and to ask them to back their fifth wheel trailer into the road blocking the way once the semi-trucks pass. This was to be the first obstacle to Isaac's group rushing to the ranch and taking it by force.

As it is though, all of this paranoia of mine and the plans and preparedness were unnecessary. Isaac is the decent fellow I believed, and for all of the trouble Jeremiah is and the grief I gave him about his beliefs, they both agreed to my requirements about moving onto the ranch. Their women and any child capable of properly using a firearm would be trained to use them and required to carry a weapon of their choice for personal and ranch defense. Even having them agree to include their women into all forms of defense planning and possible leadership roles wasn't the hang-up that I thought it might be from my original impressions.

Apparently the roles of their men and women weren't religiously ordered or controlled, but their group sort of fell into a general segregation of roles due to people's personal interests. Most of the women that married into Isaac's group wanted to be homemakers and care for their children, while having little to no interest in fighting or guns. The few women that did have the aptitude to fight happened to perish during Christmas when their group was attacked by the infected. Only Isaac and Jeremiah's sister Mariah, the last fighting female of their group, survived that Christmas attack.

Only the six of us will arrive at the hasty road-block, and then travel on to the ranch with whoever decided to stay behind. The rest of Isaac's group split into two teams when we left the store. One group went back to Isaac's property to let them know what will be happening and have them start packing things to move. The other group is remaining at the store to keep it secure so the semi-trucks can return and gather more supplies that will help our combined groups survive.

Isaac's group is sixty-five people, and of those, seventeen are children with eleven below age ten. That is the best news of their joining us. After our ranch was overrun by the infected and eight children died, our group almost collapsed, which would have been the death of all of us. It feels good to know that there will be more children running around among everyone again. The hope that brings makes this trip worth every risk we took in freeing the Stick People from Stockton's group.

There is an old joke that success is the feeling a man has between the time he accomplishes something and when he tells a woman about it. Looking ahead I'm having the same reaction to my feeling of hope. The happy thoughts of playing children fades as I look through the SUV's windshield and see three infected in the road ahead of us. They turn quickly at the sound of our approaching vehicle, but they stand their ground and just watch us as the driver pulls to a stop. Them, turning quickly, is the unfortunate act, because this means the three infected are runners.

We are in the town of Rogue River, and there are quite a few infected left here but there were no survivors that we ever found. At least none that showed themselves when we called out offering help while driving through.

"I don't understand where these things are coming from," I say to the other occupants of the vehicle. "How are new runners being made if there were no survivors here to infect?"

"Maybe these are people that heard the trucks, followed them, and got infected," Simone offers.

"You don't think your trucks had trouble coming through here and lost a few people, do you?" Isaac asks. "Those infected look pretty skinny and could be some of the people you rescued."

The thought has its merits and is a terrifying proposition to consider, but it doesn't seem likely. They are skinny, but something about them doesn't seem right. "Their clothes," I say and everyone turns to me.

Simone and I are sitting in the second row. One of Isaac's men is in the back row with him, and another is driving, while Jeremiah is in the front passenger seat. When Jeremiah and the driver turn back to hear what I'm about to say, the three infected up ahead seem to take notice of their inattention and start to advance on us.

One of them starts to run outright at the SUV, and the other two seem content to walk briskly toward us without making the effort to go quickly. With only fifty feet to travel, I think I understand why the other two didn't run. They think we are trapped and there is no big hurry, especially with one that will stop our escape by running.

Isaac behind me and Simone are the first to point and yell a warning about the advancing infected. By the time we all look out the window, the runner is two strides from the SUV and where I thought it would jump on the hood or bang against the front of the car. It sharply turns to head around the driver's side. I'm on that side of the vehicle, right behind the driver, and I literally jump back into Simone when I hear the driver's door handle get pulled up. Thankfully we only hear a clink sound that the handle makes when the door is locked, but the thing outside is angry now and keeps pulling on the handle, *clink, clink, clink, BANG!*

Simone screams and Jeremiah yells as the other two runners made it up to the passenger side of the vehicle, while all of our attention was given to the door grabber.

I love automatic car locks on doors. One of the passenger side runners apparently did try a door handle as well, but that sound was drowned out by the other runner who just hit its hands against the glass trying to break its way in. That window hitter is what gave us the shock of the day, and if I didn't get out to relieve myself a few miles before we made it to this town, I would be sitting in wet pants right now.

The driver finally puts two and two together and hits the gas pedal to drive us farther down the road. I'm glad those runners decided to attack the sides and not climb on top. If we had a climber it could have made it into the open sunroof window.

"Stop the car," I say when we are far enough down the road that we have time to get out before the runners catch up.

Simone and I step out of our respective doors when the SUV stops and draw our pistols on the approaching infected. Simone drops the closest one with two shots when it is twenty feet from the back of the vehicle. The next two runners are ten feet behind the first. One starts to turn away from us after the first one starts to fall, and it takes me five shots to hit it in the head. The last one just keeps coming, and Simone gets that one right before I hit mine.

I have the feeling that we're being watched, so I look out into the buildings near us and see a body disappear around a corner when my eyes come up. I yell *Hello!* in the direction I saw someone and start walking that way when Simone grabs my arm.

"What do you think you're doing?" she asks me as if I'm a child reaching for the cookie jar.

"I saw someone by the corner of that building. Everyone get out here and stand guard." I say to the others that haven't bothered getting out of the vehicle. "I think there is a survivor over there."

"Eddie, no. There were three runners here. There could be more," she says still holding onto my arm.

"I know, but if there are any survivors here, they'll become runners when they get bitten. We have to at least check."

She looks at me not convinced.

"I know I saw someone, and they ducked behind that building when I looked up. Does that sound like an infected to you, Simone?"

"It sounds like a runner that is capable of setting traps," she says causing chills to shoot down my spine. "Call a few more times to be sure, but we aren't going over there. The buildings are too close together, and the infected are too fast for just six of us to survive an attack up close."

I call out several more times as does Simone. Even Jeremiah calls out a few times with what he thinks are comforting messages of Christian friendship, none of us get a response. Simone is right that moving into that area is too dangerous with all the buildings so close together.

"We're leaving now, so if you want or need help, now is the time to get it," I yell one last time with still no response. We all climb back into the SUV and continue on our way to the ranch.

After driving for a short while, Jeremiah turns to Isaac, and says, "I don't know how safe it's going to be by their ranch." And then points out the windshield to another *not so welcoming* view ahead.

Maybe a quarter mile up the road there is a charred and smoking hulk of what was once Ruben Castellanos' parents' house. The truck and trailer are backed into the road where they should be, but the house they once stood in front of is gone.

The driver, who I found out at our last stop is named *Luke*, pulls over to the shoulder farthest away from the house, and we all get out with guns at the ready.

"Check the ground for signs of a fight," I say. "Bullets, bodies, or anything that could point to what happened to the house."

"Are your people okay?" Isaac asks with a serious tone of concern while eyeing the road-block. "Is this the same way the trucks would have come?"

"Yes, I'm sure they're fine," I say and watch Jeremiah walk around the collapsed wreckage of the smoldering house. "The road-block was my idea," I reply looking at him quickly before scanning the area a bit more and finding no evidence of any problems. When I finally look up, I see he is just staring at me waiting for some type of explanation.

"I'm not a trusting sort of fellow, Isaac," I say while looking at him. "Just as you weren't sure who we were when you arrived at the store, I wasn't sure you could all be trusted when we sent the trucks ahead to the ranch. This road-block was set up to slow you and your group down if you decided to try and take the ranch by force. I always try to plan for the worst."

"Do you ever hope for the best?" asks Matthew, the other of Isaac's men with us.

"My wife and I stayed alone with your entire group, and we have five children under age twelve that depend on us. I think you can call that hoping for the best. We bet our lives on you being decent people and accepting our conditions for joining the ranch."

"But you didn't risk the people at your ranch or their supplies. You sent them ahead to prepare a defense, didn't you?" Isaac says while nodding and starting to appreciate a little more who I am.

I give a small smile and shrug to answer his question, and say while looking around, "What I don't understand is the house being burned down. It looks like it burned down yesterday, or last night, with the amount of things still smoldering."

"Marco!" Simone yells out but receives no reply, so she key's her radio, and again says, "Marco."

"Polo," is the squelched reply. "What's your status, Simone?" says a female voice which sounds like Samantha.

"We're all good here," Simone replies. "Isaac's group will be moving to the farm next to us."

"We'll be down shortly," she says, and after minute, a truck drives down the road.

"Hi Samantha, I thought that was you," Simone says as Samantha steps out of her truck.

Ruben Castellanos steps out of the passenger side, and I wave at him. Everyone either says hello or acknowledges each other with a wave or a head nod.

"What happened to the house, Ruben?"

"That was my fault," he says a little embarrassed. "I broke an oil lantern last night. I turned around with a box in my hand, and it went right over and burst into flames. I was in the garage and it lit up the wall with a few gas cans on it, so I had to run out and we had to just watch everything burn down."

"Is Maria okay?" Simone asks.

"Yes, thank you. She survived just like you said she would," he says smiling and grabbing Simone's hand into a vigorous handshake. "She went with your people to the ranch. I thought I should stay with Samantha to help if I could. I could drive, and she could shoot if it was necessary."

"It's a strange world we live in to have neighbors helping in such ways isn't it?" Simone says drawing a few chuckles from Ruben and Samantha.

"So how do we get around the trailer in the road?" Jeremiah asks.

"Oh, it'll move easy enough," I tell him. "Ruben moved it here when the trucks came by earlier. The truck is running, and we'll take the whole rig to the ranch when we go. It would be smart if we make trips to that RV and trailer sales yard across from the Grants Pass Wal-Mart to provide more shelters for people at the ranch. We won't be able to build proper rooms quickly enough to house all the new people we are taking in."

"So let's move it and get going then," Jeremiah urges showing he's a little agitated.

The hair stands up on the back of my neck and my paranoia kicks in again when he says that. *Why the urgency?* I wonder.

"Ruben?" I call out since he walked back around the trailer to the truck they drove here in. "Do you have the keys to the truck that's hooked to the fifth-wheel?"

"No, I put them under a rock over in the ditch there. I didn't think it would be smart for Samantha or me to have them on us in case…well just in case."

"Good thinking, would you mind getting the keys?" I say and turn to Simone. "I want you to take the other truck and go back to the ranch with Ruben."

"We're not all going?" she asks a little concerned.

"No, I want to stay here for a while to make sure no one else is coming up behind us," I say while looking at Jeremiah.

"You still don't trust us do you?" he says clearly frustrated with me.

"Trust is earned, not given, and you seem a bit too eager to get to the ranch considering your strong dislike in the idea of joining us. It makes me think that you might have told your men to hold back and follow you in an hour or two to make sure our defenses are down with distractions from all the new arrivals."

"If we were going to do something like that, we could have planned on doing it any time without bothering to try and join up with you," Jeremiah says while briefly glancing at Isaac, probably wondering what Isaac might have told me. "We do know the layout of the ranch after all."

"While I think the possibility is slight, you don't know the layout of the outer perimeter we put up since our large attack, and you might feel this is your only chance to take over the ranch and get rid of me and any people loyal to me since we were able to repel such a huge group of the infected."

"We had a huge group of infected attack us as well, if you remember us telling you. And we lost seventeen people during our attack. From what I heard you only lost thirteen people, so your attack must have been the same size as ours right? That makes us equal as fighters, I think," Jeremiah replies with bravado.

The memory of the ranch being overrun and facing our certain death is still painful and frightening to think about. I lower my head a little and frown. I know that only the extreme cold saved our lives during those two days of hell. Our firepower and level of preparedness helped, but without the cold, we would all have died with the numbers we faced. I am angry that I'm even having to deal with Isaac's group at all, let alone be questioned by them about something they know nothing about.

Isaac sees my reaction and speaks before I can build the will to answer calmly, "You mentioned you were attacked, and one of your people spoke about your losses. We're sorry for them, but we have lost people as well. No one alive today has made it here without having someone die, but none of your people would talk about your attack aside from mentioning those that were lost. I'll willingly wait with you here to show no one is following us, but I would like to know about your attack."

"Attacks," I say.

"What?"

"Attacks...We had three attacks, all in increasing numbers over a two month time frame. There was a man, someone I turned away from my survival store the first day of the outbreak that joined with a group of criminals. Together they figured out a way to drive groups of the infected at the ranch to attack us." I look at each of them as I tell our story.

"The first two attacks were simple enough. Forty-nine infected attacked the first time. They didn't make it onto the property, and we didn't lose any people. When the second attack arrived a few weeks later, we had our first clue that someone was sending the infected at us. Music...someone was putting radios in the forest to draw the infected to the ranch with music. That's why I thought your attack was set-up when you said singing brought your infected to you."

"Two hundred and seventy-six infected hit us the second time. They came grouped together and managed to breach the fence but didn't get far into the property. They weren't a threat to overrun the ranch, and we killed them all without losing anyone but they did kill our dogs. The third attack came a month later during the deep cold."

"So you lost your people after a third attack behind fences and you knew they were coming?" Jeremiah says with derision, completely unaware of the numbers we were facing. "At least we were caught off guard."

Simone moves to attack Jeremiah for his insult but Samantha is closer. She walks up to him and punches him in the face, busting his nose, and continuing to swing at him.

Isaac jumps in between the two to protect his brother from the attack but also trying to apologize for what his brother said.

"You have no idea what we went through, you bastards!" Simone yells at Jeremiah and the others.

"Please, Eddie," Isaac says. "What happened during your last attack?"

Samantha shakes her arms loose from Isaac and walks past me grabbing Simone as she moves by. They go ten feet away, to the front of the truck hooked up to the camper, and wait there. Once I see they aren't going any farther, I turn back, remove my hand from the pistol at my side, and continue the story:

"We were completely overrun," I say shaking my head and shrugging. "Every shooter was on the line, and we kept knocking them down. Headshot, headshot, headshot. We kept killing them and more kept coming. The only thing that saved us was the extreme cold that slowed them down to a slight shuffle, that and our ammo supply. Our group went through thirty-five thousand rounds of ammo during those two days, and we killed between twenty-five thousand and thirty thousand infected."

"Bullshit," Luke says, but he says it in a sympathetic way. "It would take an army to kill a group that size."

"I used to think so too, but that's what we killed. There were four thousand two hundred infected we killed beyond the fence before they were able to break through. We counted all those bodies during the weeks it took to clean up. We had thirty-four shooters on the line, so we only had to average a hundred and a quarter kills each. Once they breached the fence, most of our people went into mostly buried storage rooms for shelter, and only eight of us on the storage container towers were left to deal with the remaining infected. We didn't plan on such a large group ever attacking at once. Hell, I couldn't even imagine a group that size was heading our way. We would have left more people topside to deal with it if we knew, and it was stupid luck that we had enough ammo on the towers. We put enough up there to fend off ten attacks like the second one, not one attack with ten times the number."

Isaac and his men look between each other as I continue, and Jeremiah just holds a rag to his nose trying not to look at anyone.

"We have three of the buried shelters, but one never got their doors closed. That is where we lost twelve of our people, including eight of our children. I don't know what the exact number of the infected we killed is. With the cold, most of the bodies were frozen and fused together. They were scooped up by the tractor, and we did rough counts before we burned the bodies. Maybe one day someone will go through the ash piles and count skulls or jawbones, but for now, our best estimate is twenty-five to thirty thousand infected. None of us thought we would live through it, and for a while it felt like none of us did."

I turn my back on Isaac's group and look at my wife. "Simone, please take Ruben back to the ranch now. We will follow you in an hour if nothing comes up. Get everyone ready for an attack, and if I don't come back, I love you."

"How are we going to work together at your ranch of you distrust us so much?" Matthew asks.

"You'll earn your trust, and you'll prove your abilities just like everyone else that we bring in. This is the first stage of building that trust and possibly proving your abilities."

"We don't have any people following us," Jeremiah says with a muffled finality, trying to force the obviousness of his truth into my brain.

"No, you might not, but that doesn't mean *no one* is behind us," I say while looking around at faces finally registering the possibility. "Before a few days ago, I didn't know there were any runners and we didn't find any large groups of survivors even though we've been moving around for well over a month. Now we have runners everywhere, and I've encountered Stockton's group of fifty plus his prisoners and your group of sixty-five. Who knows how many more groups might be out there and are just starting to travel like yours? No one has been driving vehicles for a while, and all of a sudden trucks and cars are all driving down this road. Any group of survivors or infected in the area will have heard the traffic, and I want to stay here with you to see if anyone follows us." I then look at Jeremiah directly, and say, "That shouldn't be too difficult, should it?"

CHAPTER 7
COATZACOALCOS, MEXICO

Eight Months Earlier.

The situation on shore doesn't look promising, but the view in front of them on the water looks worse. The water along the shore is dotted with burning hulks of various sized boats. It looks like a fisherman's naval battle occurred and many of the fishermen died.

Two Mexican military boats come screaming through the water at them, and a loudspeaker from one yells *ALTO! ALTO!*

George brings his boat to a stop and cuts the engine. All of the men raise their hands in the air as the approaching boats pull up.

"*Estás Mordido? Estás infectado?*" is called out to them.

"We aren't infected. *No hables español,*" George calls out hoping the soldiers don't open fire.

"Move to back of boat," a new voice calls from the loudspeaker in broken but understandable English.

The patrol boats pull up to each side of George's Viking yacht, and as large as his boat is, both of the patrol boats are just as large. There are seven guns trained on the four men from the back decks of the two flanking boats, and all of the men holding the guns look ready to use them. More likely, they are ready to use them again as it seems they have had a busy day.

"Turn in circle," the voice orders and all four comply. "Clap hands."

Now the orders are getting strange, and the four men glance at each other but still do as they are told and start clapping their hands.

"Jump up and down," the voice now calls.

George is certain someone is screwing with them now, but the four men still comply and begin jumping up and down with their hands in the air.

Frank looks the most ridiculous, because the towel he is wearing falls off as he begins jumping. Each of them expect the soldiers to start laughing at the gringos that they made jump and act like fools, but the guns remain aimed at them and no smiles or laughter erupts from the performance.

"Is only you on boat?"

"Yes, only the four of us," George calls back.

"Throw dock rope. We will board your boat." That statement comes out quite clearly as it must have been issued many times over the years.

George grabs the stern line, tosses it over to the closest patrol vessel, and drops the fenders over the side used to protect the boat from damage when docked. Then he moves to the front to throw the bow line over. The other three remain in the back with their hands in the air. George returns to the others and raises his hands again while his boat is secured to the patrol boat.

Frank is allowed to climb up to the patrol boat while the soldiers motion to George, Keith, and Jack that they must remove their towels and shorts as well. They take them off and are ordered to spin around once again before being brought aboard the other vessel.

"They had to check you for bites," a man says in clear English as he walks up.

"We figured as much," George says in return.

"My name is Thomas," he says.

"You can put hands down now," the soldier that was talking over the speaker says as he walks up as well.

"There is no one else on your boat, correct?" Thomas asks. "If you lie they will kill you."

"No one else is on board," George says, and the others nod in agreement.

"*Buscar el barco*," the soldier commands, and the armed men board George's boat to check its interior.

"You have no more clothes on board?" the soldier asks looking curiously at George.

"We had to leave quickly and our clothes were ruined. We have nothing else to wear."

George intentionally leaves out any mention of radiation. These men are on edge as it is and are obviously ready to kill anyone that is a danger to the area.

"*Conseguir que la ropa*," he says to another soldier that walks off.

"They are getting you some clothes to wear. It's a good thing you stopped as quickly as you did," Thomas says. "As you can see by the burning boats in the water, not everyone is following orders today."

"Or not everyone is able to follow them," George replies.

"Who are you, and where are you going?" the soldier asks.

"My name is George Beauchamp, this is Keith Roach, Frank, and Jack," he says as he nods in each person's direction. "We are going to a house I have on the west bank of the Coatzacoalcos River."

Thomas and the soldier speak to each other for a while in Spanish. His men return from George's Viking, one of them says *Todo claro* and nods before walking away. Another soldier walks up carrying t-shirts and pants for the group. The man in charge speaks with Thomas again, while George and the rest start getting dressed. Before they are done, he says *Good luck* before shaking their hands and walking off. The second patrol boat cruises off after the *all clear* is relayed to them.

"Once you are dressed you can get back on your boat and continue toward shore and into the river," Thomas says before filling them in on what has been happening in the few moments they have left. "The infection first made it to shore here early yesterday by boat, and they started shooting at anyone that didn't respond quickly. Captain Alvarez says the uniforms you are wearing should help you get by any other patrols, although not speaking Spanish could get you killed anyway. The infected can't speak, so if someone doesn't understand you they might kill you rather than take the chance. The infected people also can't clap or jump, which is why you were put through that humiliating ritual and you were stripped down to search for bites.

"The city is probably lost because one of the patrols let someone in that had been bitten on the buttocks and wasn't stripped down. He made it to shore and attacked five people before he was killed. Four of the five people ran off after they were attacked, because they knew they would be killed by the soldiers. That is how the disease started spreading through the city. If your house is on the west bank as you say, you might have some time. They blew up the bridge that crosses it, but eventually someone will be infected and cross on a boat or the infection will reach that side over land."

"You don't have much faith that this thing can be stopped," Keith says.

"You are here instead of where you came from for a reason I think," he says in response. "The day after this began, Alejandro Molina, the Mexican President ordered all available military personnel to the U.S. border to prevent anyone from crossing. Their orders were to kill any living thing on sight, and they followed the orders. Even the drug cartels joined in the fight to keep the infection from spreading south. Now, none of the border cities or locations are responding anymore. Tijuana, Ciudad Juarez, Nuevo Laredo, and Reynosa are all gone, that's the entire northern border. Worse still, Mexico City has gone silent after the infection has been there for only three days."

"That's a long way from Coatzacoalcos, almost four hundred miles," George says.

"Yes, but even farther from the border with the U.S.A., that is over six hundred and fifty miles. The disease didn't spread that far over land in the last five or six days. The military men who were with me told me President Molina announced some infected bodies had been brought into Mexico City. They were taken to several Universities for research. The medical personnel there were being given the latest medicines to help prevent them from catching the disease. There was hope they might be able to do something to fight this thing, but then a report came out that a plane landed at Benito Juárez international airport in Mexico City. When the doors were opened the infected poured out. Someone got on the plane with the infection, and the disease spread to every passenger on board. Air travel is the only reason why Mexico City and the rest of the world are lost to this disease."

"The rest of the world?" Jack asks.

Thomas nods somberly.

Captain Alvarez yells something quickly to Thomas and motions with his hands that the group should get back on George's boat.

"He says they need to leave now. You should get back on your boat."

"Are you working with them, Thomas, or do you need somewhere to go as well?" George asks as the others walk over to the railing to climb over the side.

"I was working with them to help translate, but they don't need me any longer. They haven't stopped to check if people were clear of infection all day. If your boat wasn't so nice and you weren't already undressed, they would have shot you too. They could have used your boat for patrols."

"Do you want to come with us?"

Thomas turns and calls over to Captain Alvarez. They say a few things, and then wave and say *adiós*.

"I'll come with you. There isn't anything else I can do on this ship."

And they both climb over the side into George's boat.

*

George cruises his boat into the mouth of the river between the two walls built out into the Gulf to protect the land on shore from erosion. They have an hour left before sunset and should make it with time to spare.

"Do you really have a property here?" Timothy asks.

"Yes, I bought it a few years ago. If you weren't sure I had a house here, why did you want to come with us?"

"I wanted to get away from the soldiers and what they are doing. I understand the point of trying to keep the disease out, but I can't handle the way they are doing it."

"How did you get hooked up with them in the first place?"

"I was meeting with Captain Alvarez at a cafe to discuss shipping and customs issues. We were near the beach when the boat ran aground that spread the disease here. Captain Alvarez is in charge of the soldiers and patrol boats, so he took it personally that an issue like that occurred when he just finished telling me my shipments would be well protected in this region. He offered to take me aboard his vessels personally—to show me what they were capable of. At that point we still didn't realize things were as bad as everyone was saying. It seemed like just another disease that people worried over, like the swine flu. Four hours later I was on that same ship with him, and we saw three ships sailing through the waters along the coast that had only infected people on board. He fired on and sunk them all.

"After that he asked if I would remain on board to help with English translation if it was needed. He didn't want to kill a bunch of Americans and start a war. Even by that point he had *hope*, we all did, hoping that there was another explanation for what was happening around the world."

"You mentioned the rest of the world was lost when we were still on the patrol boat," George says. "It isn't the air travel that spread this disease, although I am sure it hasn't helped. It is the fault of a drug called *Zeus*."

"Zeus, yes, that's it. I couldn't remember the name earlier. That is the drug that was mentioned on the radio to protect the doctors in Mexico City."

"The Zeus drug doesn't protect anyone. It causes this disease," George says with a sad and frustrated tone. "Keith received a letter from his son about that drug. I wish we still had a copy of it. It spoke about how it was supposed to protect people from harm, but there was something wrong with it. It didn't mention worldwide distribution, but it was tested in Moldova and I would bet any overseas military would be given the inoculation as well. Even if no other nation used the drug, it could spread through our U.S. military installations alone."

Thomas is quietly absorbing what George is saying when a rumbling explosion echoes in the distance to the north.

"That is somewhere in the center of town," Thomas offers. "Do you have any plans beyond making it to your house?"

"Oregon," Keith says in a confident manner surprising both Thomas and George.

"I wasn't sure you spoke. You were being so quiet," Thomas says.

"I just lost my wife."

Thomas nods. "This disease is taking many good people, and I'm afraid it isn't done with us yet."

"She didn't get infected. She had advanced stage four cancer, and our escape was too difficult for her body to handle. She would have lived longer if we could have stayed at home, but unfortunately that couldn't happen. So in a way this disease *did* end her life."

Thomas nods.

"Do you have any family? You must be from stateside," George asks.

"My parents died a few years ago, and I haven't settled down yet. There are too many beautiful Latin women down here for me to make up my mind. I have been living and working in Mexico and Columbia for the last eight years, so I'm an expat."

"Columbia?" George asks.

"Coffee, not cocaine," he replies and gives a knowing smile. "I moved down originally working for Lukafe Gourmet...well, it *was* a specialty coffee company. I branched out and got contracts with multiple producers and buyers, and the rest is history. I've been down here ever since and was working on some issues with Captain Alvarez about the coffee supplies."

"We're almost here guys," George says to the men. "You can see my dock up there. We'll have to walk to my house. It's across a small field beyond those trees."

"I'm glad we're here. I'm starting to get sick," Jack says.

"You too?" George asks. "I haven't been feeling good for the last few hours. I was hoping it didn't show when I was speaking with Captain Alvarez."

Taking a step back from the men, Thomas asks, "You haven't been infected, have you?"

"No, it isn't the infection, but for us, it might be just as bad. I think we were exposed to too much fallout."

"Couldn't it just be seasickness?" Jack asks fearfully.

"I've been on boats most of my life and have never gotten sick, have you?"

"No. No I haven't. We waited too long to leave."

"It could be something else," Keith offers. "I'm not feeling bad. How about you, Frank?"

"I'm feeling good as well, so far, but we weren't outside as long as they were, Keith."

Keith and George jump off the boat together to tie it to the dock, while Jack leans over the back and vomits into the water. No one wants to speak about the possibility of radiation poisoning but they are all thinking it.

*

The western bank of the river is crowded with the bodies of the infected now. Coatzacoalcos proper is lost, and close to three hundred thousand infected are wandering around the city, looking for their next meal.

"How many do you think are there?" Keith asks George while acting as a crutch to keep him upright.

"It doesn't matter how many are there. The point is the city is lost, and we can't stay any longer."

"I don't think you and Jack should move yet."

"We can't stay any longer. We've been taking the potassium iodide, and whatever help it can offer at this point is what we have to deal with. There's nothing else we can do about the radiation, but we can avoid getting trapped by the infected."

Jack is lying down in George's house, his nausea, vomiting, and diarrhea have increased over the last two days. He is unable to take more than four steps—even with support—and has blisters on his skin. George is weak and needs to be supported when he walks, and all four of them are experiencing some degree of nausea.

The two men turn away from the river bank and begin walking across the field back toward the house.

"I'm sorry we didn't leave earlier."

"This isn't your fault, Keith."

"I read your medical books on radiation exposure. We're all dying now."

George stops and lurches forward grabbing his stomach in pain. He hasn't been able to eat anything for the last few days but has been forcing himself to drink water regularly. He isn't able to hold the water down long but having something able to come up is less painful then being wracked with dry heaves.

"You and Maggie didn't slow us down," he is able to rasp out after emptying his stomach. "You know that, Keith. We had everything loaded and wouldn't have left that night even if we weren't giving Maggie more time. It hit us before we would have left on our own, so you can't take the blame on yourself."

Thomas has stayed with the men and is taking the potassium iodide pills to protect himself from any residual radiation they may be putting off. He will continue to take them for two weeks, although eight days is enough to be beyond the radio-isotope's half-life danger zone. It will take six months for the isotope's to be broken down to zero. At least that is what the literature George has states. The concern is in not knowing which isotopes they were specifically exposed to at the oil rig and how much of a dose each of them was subjected to.

It took over twenty-four hours for Jack and George to start getting sick, and another day after that for Frank and Keith to have any symptoms occur. They agreed that there must have been a thicker cloud of radioactive pollutants that passed the oil rig when Jack and George first exited the oil rigs interior. *The smoke did seem heavier when I walked out the door* Jack told them trying to remember his chaotic exit, but George didn't remember it.

*

Thomas rushes in to the main room. "I found a truck we can take to Salina Cruz! I spoke with your neighbor, Senior Maldonado. He has the trucks that can take us there if we will share the supplies."

"Are there any other options?" George asks with concern about dealing with his neighbor.

Senior Maldonado's house is three stories tall and has an ornate design most likely representing the ancient Mayan or Aztec cultures, George doesn't know which. In front, there is a manicured garden which could easily be featured in any top horticulture magazine, and all of it is designed to be seen only by the occupants of the house or the rare few people that would travel down this private road to Senior Maldonado's house or George's. The expense and extravagance of the dwelling convinced George early on that his neighbor must be involved in some type of illicit trade, either drugs or guns. In his thinking, a hardworking man wouldn't spend his money so lavishly on decorations and architecture when no one else could enjoy it unless it was easy money.

"There might be other options, but we don't have the time to seek them out. Senior Maldonado will be here with his family in thirty minutes to begin loading everything. His family is coming with us to the coast. He is thinking of heading into South America by boat once we reach the Pacific."

"Do you think we can trust him?"

"Yes. You may have been right about what he did to make his money because his family is very well armed, but he seems to be an honest business man, even if his business isn't an honest one. We will need the armed escort his family will provide to make it through whatever we run into out there. So, our only other easy option would be trying to join with a group of deserting soldiers that might go to the coast. Senior Maldonado is the safest choice for us right now."

George has his own Range Rover at the house, but it isn't large enough to fit all five of the men and supplies for the trip. It also isn't the type of vehicle they should be driving across Mexico during a time of upheaval like the country is experiencing right now. What is left of the Mexican Army is scattered throughout the nation, and many soldiers are abandoning their posts to help care for their own families in any way they can. Thomas has found out the same has happened with the police. The absence of any organized peace keeping force will fill areas with chaos and criminal behavior anywhere they travel. If they don't leave now, it is likely that they will never be able to escape.

CHAPTER 8
NEW ACQUAINTANCES

Oregon.
Present Day.

"This is a waste of time. It's been over thirty minutes already. If someone was following us they would have made it here by now," Jeremiah says in his usual aggravated manner but with the added ridiculous smeared blood on his upper lip from his busted nose.

Getting your nose busted by a girl is still a funny thing to happen, even in this post-apocalyptic world. I know his men will mess with him about it. There's a good one hundred pound difference between him and Samantha. Jeremiah is a big guy.

I ignore him and continue to watch and listen. The six of us are spread out and hidden in the area of the burned down house. Luke and Samantha are watching the area behind the charred building, it is a large field that ends with a narrow tree belt and continues into another field. Someone would have to crawl through the tree line to make it past us unseen. Matthew and Isaac are by the trailer and are watching the road.

I stuck myself with Jeremiah in the wooded area to the south of the road. The trees are too thick to see very far, and once you are ten yards into the treeline from the road, the brush gets too thick to be able to move. We are here to listen for anyone or anything walking up through the open wooded corridor.

I needed to stay with Jeremiah to see how much of a danger he actually poses to my family and me. The only danger I felt pre-collapse from religious people was from Muslim extremists blowing themselves up or randomly shooting people. Their attacks became more frequent as the economic collapse dragged on, but the threat was still vague, not direct. It wasn't something I could deal with, because no one ever knew who the bad guy was or when they would attack.

Now I have to deal with unrestrained religious fervor of a different sort. I wish I had grown up in Ireland to know what it must feel like to be directly targeted either as a Catholic or Protestant. I feel totally unprepared to deal with this type of danger and have a harder time seeing it as real. I keep thinking I can ridicule the stupid out of Jeremiah but know I am most likely making things worse in how I am dealing with him.

A rock hits near us, and I look through the trees and see Isaac waving from behind the camper. He points to his own eyes and then back down the road, so Jeremiah and I creep to the edge of the woods where we can look that way without being seen.

One man is slowly making his way up the road. He is carrying what looks like an M4 or other AR-15 variant, and keeping closer to the wooded side of the road where Jeremiah and I are.

I hit Jeremiah on the shoulder and give him an *I told you so* look.

I whisper to him, "I can't tell if he's scouting for a group or just being extra careful because of the infected."

"Do you think he's the person you saw in Rogue River?"

"No clue. I only saw quick movement—like a shadow disappearing around a corner. I could tell it was a person but didn't register any details."

The man is still far enough away to not be a threat, so I call to Isaac in a soft voice, "Do Luke and Samantha know?"

Isaac nods and lies down, getting into prone position to watch the approaching man, from under the trailer. Matthew is already in prone behind the truck's rear tire.

"Jeremiah, move deeper into the woods. If this guy is a scout his people could be on either side of the road."

He nods and moves off. I'm thankful I don't have to argue with him or explain further why he should go. I return to my original position and wait. I can just see the top of Isaac's head from where I am standing if I look his way so I can see if he needs to signal us.

As the man on the street gets closer, so do his hidden companions in the woods. There are three people walking through the woods behind him, one man and two women, so I signal their numbers to Isaac. They are casually walking toward us in opposition to the cautious way the man in the road is, but then they aren't walking out in the open alone in this dangerous new world of ours. After about eight minutes the man makes it roughly fifty feet away from the trailer. He stops and signals to the people following to stop as well and turns left and right to make the signal. So, I have to assume there are more people following him on the other side of the road as well.

He is just standing there in the road either trying to figure out what happened to the house or because he knows some of us are here. It's an awkward situation, and Isaac motions to me that he is going to speak. I relay the signal to Jeremiah, and we both wait to see how the three ahead of us react.

I sincerely hope this turns out to be a good encounter and we are looking at possible new friends. I'm nervous though with the increased potential for conflict at the ranch with so many new people arriving. There are already too many people who will all have their own agendas and ideas about the ideal way to survive. At least Isaac and his group will be staying at the Carpenter farm next to the ranch and not right with us, that is a big headache we won't have to worry about.

"You there in the road, hello," Isaac calls out. "Put your rifle on the ground in front of you."

"I'm not alone," the man calls out clearly not wanting to put down his gun. The three in the woods all set up behind trees aiming at the truck and trailer to defend their companion.

Putting the rifle on the ground isn't what I would have called out, and I'll have to speak with Isaac and his men about that.

"Put your rifle on your back if you don't feel safe without it—your friends also," I yell causing the three in the trees to see where I am with my rifle trained in their direction. "If we wanted to shoot you we could have. It's your turn to show some restraint."

"I think we'll just go back the way we came," the man in the road yells and takes a few steps back.

"That's not going to happen. A few more steps and we start shooting," I yell in response.

I hope Samantha and Luke have eyes on the other people, I think to myself just as the man in front of me in the trees starts turning his rifle in my direction. He is probably thinking I turned my gaze to the man on the road and could take a shot. He has a bolt-action hunting rifle and may have experience making quick shots in the woods, so I can't let him finish turning in my direction. I intentionally shoot the tree next to him. I know it might make everyone start shooting, but I am hoping it scares them into submission rather than fight. I have killed enough people lately and hope I can avoid doing so today.

The man I shoot near drops to his knee and peripherally I can see the man on the road drop down. I didn't hear another shot with mine and it looks like he dove, so I'm hoping he wasn't shot. Relationship dynamics start playing out in the next few seconds as well. One of the women in front of us screams and starts running to the man in the road, the other drops her rifle, turns and bolts back in the direction they came, and a familiar high pitched crying starts following her through the woods. She has a baby strapped to her back.

The man I shot at turns around to run after her, but this time Jeremiah shoots at a tree ahead of the man halting his progress.

Finally raising his hands with his gun over his head, the man yells to us, "If I don't stop her she'll be killed."

The woman continues to run.

I want to respond but am stopped by at least ten shots that ring out from across the road between our group and theirs. Someone has been shot according to the screams I hear. They are the anguished cries of severe pain.

"What the hell is wrong with you people?" I yell bringing the man's attention back to me but ensuring my aim is right at him this time. "We didn't want to fight you!"

"Let me get her," he says, and the pleading look on his face lets me know he has a genuine concern for her or the baby, probably both.

"Drop your rifle and you can go," I say not wanting our people to be on the receiving end of that gun from down the road. Perhaps he is just as good a shot with whatever handgun he is carrying, but at least this way I minimize some of our risk.

He takes off after her, and I start to run following him. Turning to face Jeremiah as I go by, I call out, "Isaac's in charge. Find out who's hurt."

I'm close behind the man, but I can't see where the woman is and the crying has stopped as well. Ten more running steps behind this guy and I see what will probably be my death out of the woods on the road ahead of us. These people must have been part of a larger group and were a scouting team, because there are another six people spread out and running up the road.

I just separated myself from the protection of my group by falling for what might be a trick this group uses. Strap a doll in a kid-carrying backpack, and if trouble starts, hit the *play* button on a radio to make the sound of a crying baby start.

The only problem with that scenario is the man ahead of me raises his revolver and starts shooting at the people in the road—the runners in the road. He should have stopped running to get aim at his targets. Not only did he miss with all of his shots and only succeeded in attracting the runners' attention to us, but he didn't see the branch that swung out from behind the tree ahead of him hitting him in the face.

The baby starts screaming again after the man shoots so closely to it. So, I'm happy to know I didn't fall for a *sick baby sound* trap. I am still caught though as the woman steps out holding the branch, apparently surprised she hit the man on the ground and not me. As much as I would like to protect myself from the swing of the branch she is preparing for me, the greater fear in me turns my head and rifle in the direction of the runners that will be on us in just a few seconds.

As slow as time has been moving with just about a minute passing since the first shot was fired, it slows down now even more as I work to steady my breath and focus my vision on the task ahead.

I love my rifle. It is a wonderful FAL in a real caliber; 7.62x51mm or .308 Winchester for when I took it hunting. I never really liked the AR-15 platform and its little twenty-two caliber sized bullets. I've always said that the .308 is the best two-legged varmint round out there. Two-legged varmints being people, of course. I would prefer to have my shotgun in the close quarters of these trees and the proximity of the runners, but as rifles go, I have exactly what I need.

What I see before me is just a vision of beauty that I have to appreciate before my inevitable end. I keep pressing the trigger, and each time I do, bullet followed by flame makes its way out of the barrel and into the oncoming group of runners that turned our way.

I miss a few times, but the runners are forced to crowd together to make it through the trees to get at the three of us and the baby. The bullets that do hit these things basically tear them apart. The gore and mist exploding from the backs of the first two infected is painting the four behind them red, and the carnage continues with the bullet trajectory. I'm not taking careful aim because they are so close and moving so fast, but my bullets stop them just the same.

I pull the trigger two more times on empty before I drop my rifle to hang by its sling and grab for my pistol. The last infected falls in *movie fashion* just a few feet away from us, and the three of us take aim at the bodies on the ground and place bullets into each of their six heads.

With the communal killing of the greater threat over, the man, woman, and myself turn our guns on each other in an attempt to regain superiority on the situation. When I aim my gun at the man, I am thinking I will have two barrels facing me, the woman's and the man's. She is pointing her gun at him though, which is a twist to what I thought, because I believed they were together.

Jeremiah walks around a large tree next to us, and I am thankful that his gun is also pointed at this strange new man instead of at me.

"I think you're outnumbered," I say motioning with my eyes for him to see the guns pointed at him from each side of his head. "Lay down your gun."

He doesn't speak and just places his gun on the ground. I reach in my pocket with my free hand for a zip tie to secure his arms. The woman turns her gun's aim to my head and starts backing up.

"You can't go out there alone. It's not safe," I say not taking my guns aim away from the man.

"I'll take my chances. I'm not getting free from Toby here just to be controlled and traded by you two and your group."

"Look lady, I'm not sure what you've been through with this guy, but I'm not letting you just walk off into the woods with that baby." Mentioning her baby at least stuns her or reminds her why she shouldn't leave. She stops backing up. "If you can't take the way things are any more, then you'll be free to go as soon as we determine you aren't a threat. You won't be taking that baby to its death with you, though."

"You're not taking my baby from me!" she yells, and I see Jeremiah edge around the man so he can more easily take aim at her if he needs to.

"We have other children at our camp and women that are more than capable of taking care of your baby. I don't want to take your baby from you, but I will not let you take it with you to die in some bid for freedom from this man or his group," I say trying to redirect her anger at her initial target. "If you care about your baby at all I need you to holster your gun. You may be able to shoot me, but you won't make it away from this spot alive. I don't want the baby hurt by one of our bullets or by your body when you fall."

I say to the man, *turn around* after I pull my left hand out of my pants pocket, holding a zip tie.

The woman lowers her gun's aim from my head but doesn't put it away.

She begins, "How do I know—"

"You don't," I say cutting her off while zipping Toby's hands together behind his back. "You don't know who we are or what we are like, but we could have shot you, this guy, and that other woman while you were trying to sneak up on us. We didn't and that is all the comfort I can give you right now. Your safety with my group depends on what you have done since the world became this mess. Your baby will be safe with us no matter what you have done. Now holster your gun so we can find out what is going on with everyone else."

"I'd rather her drop the gun than hold on to it," Jeremiah says with his rifle now aimed at the woman.

"And I would rather have one extra gun available if more runners come at us," I say back to him. "If we die during another attack, do you want her and that baby out here without a gun? Just keep her in front of us, and we should be fine."

We cautiously walk to the inside edge of the woods and peer down the road to make sure no other runners are visible. Then we look up the road to the trailer and see our people and several others standing by bodies lying in the front yard of the house.

I take the rear, walking backward, to make sure we don't get surprised by any more infected. Jeremiah is behind the woman and man. I finally turn around to see the new chaos as we arrive to the group by the road. There are two dead people, neither of which look like infected based on them having guns and backpacks; one woman and one man. The zip-tied man we captured in the woods walks over to the dead woman's body and drops down to his knees by her. There are also four other people I don't know; three women and a man.

"What happened?" I ask looking at Isaac and Samantha.

"They shot each other," Isaac says. "Right after you guys shot in the woods, these two turned their guns on each other. The man got a shot off first, but his rifle is a bolt-action and she has an M4. She got three shots in before he shot her again."

"I thought I heard at least ten shots."

"That was us," Samantha and Luke say together. Samantha points to two of the women I don't know while continuing, "They were coming up behind the houses. When the shots came from the street these two dropped to the ground taking cover, and two infected ran up behind them, so we both shot."

"I thought you were shooting at us until that body fell on my legs," one of the women says and is clearly shaken both by the shooting and the body hitting her.

"You're lucky we didn't shoot you since you were following us. Why is your group shooting at each other? One of you tell us what your story is," Jeremiah demands with his rifle waving around at all the newcomers.

He is still on an adrenaline high from the encounter in the woods and looks a bit spooked. Probably because there are so many armed strangers.

"Don't talk yet," I say to one of the women as she takes a breath to begin speaking. "Isaac, Samantha and I will get their stories one at a time inside the trailer. Jeremiah, you Luke and Matthew watch the guy we tied up, keep a look out for more runners, and make sure these people don't speak to each other until we've heard what they have to say."

*

"So, tell us who you people are," I say to the first woman.

"Are you a cop? I mean, were you a cop before everything happened?"

"No."

"Sorry, I just thought since you wanted us separated and you seem a bit...bossy."

Samantha smiles at me being called bossy, and Isaac gets a concerned look on his face. I have been called much worse than that and by people whose opinions I actually care about, so it doesn't bother me at all.

"I wasn't a police officer. Yes, I *am* bossy at times, but I'm not a bully unless someone gives me a reason not to like them. I try to be fair to everyone I meet, at least under normal circumstances. This isn't a normal situation though, and you should know that I have a certain skill when it comes to interrogating people."

It is Samantha's turn to show concern, which the woman notices. Samantha physically shifts away from me, almost recoils, and her face blanches white when I mention interrogation. She is obviously recalling how I tortured those men at the ranch. My wife was right when she explained why she wanted me to continue with the torture. Samantha's reaction to me, Isaac's look of concern, and the unfortunate smile that appears on my face probably make me seem like the worst possible person to be with, in a confined space like this. At least that is what I'm reading from the sudden look of fear that is on this woman's face.

"I want to get back home to my family," I tell her and ease my expression a bit, which doesn't seem to calm her down at all. "Tell us your story. Who you are, who the people you are with are, and why your group members are attacking each other. If what you tell us doesn't match what the others say, I'll know someone is lying and things will get painful until I find out the truth."

She is staring at me as if she's afraid to talk, so I just turn my palms up and give her an *I'm waiting* look.

She nods and mouths *okay*, and then begins, "You probably won't get a straight story out of Toby, the *prick* you tied up. The woman that Roger killed was Toby's wife, Paula. Roger, the man that shot her, has only been with us for two days. We met him in Rogue River. I'm sorry he's dead. I thought he was a good guy, and if he shot at Paula first, then it was to help us get away from Toby and her."

The tension on her face starts easing up a bit only to show an expression of embarrassed sadness as she sits stiffly and nervously talks fast.

"Rachel is the girl I was with. Donny and Amanda are the couple who was out there. Heather is the mom, and her baby girl is Victoria. There were four more of us when we arrived in Rogue River five days ago, they were killed by those damn runners."

"And you are?" I ask when she pauses.

"I'm sorry... I'm Abigail."

She doesn't seem like an Abigail to me, even though she is used to calling herself that. There was the slightest hint of something when she said her name, but I don't question it right now.

"Our group was heading out of Medford, hoping to make it to the coast..."

"Can you just give me the quick version first," I say interrupting her.

"Um, well. Toby and Paula were trading us for supplies and people with skills."

"Us?"

"The women. We were the incentive to keep guys with certain skills in the group."

"You mean *sex*, right?" I ask wanting to be sure.

"Yes."

"And you went along with it or were forced?"

"I went along with it, but I didn't have a choice, if that makes any sense."

"All right, now give me the details."

"They didn't threaten us personally, but trading sex for supplies were the rules if we wanted to stay in the group. If a man had skills or something that the group needed, we traded ourselves to him to get it, whether it was ammo, bolt cutters, or in Donny's case, welding skills. I'm not a G.I. Jane and never even looked at a gun before things fell apart. I have no survival skills and don't have anybody to take care of me, so I don't have any other option if I want to live more than a few days. It's the same for all of us girls—except for Amanda. Donny agreed to stay with the group and be the welder or builder when needed, but he made them agree no one could mess with Amanda."

"He wanted her for himself?" Samantha asks in a disgusted tone.

"No, I think he just wanted to protect her at first, but they spent so much time together they got close. He never tried anything with me or the others, before or after, he and Amanda got closer. He even mentioned a few times he would like to get us away from Toby and his wife, but it is too dangerous to split into smaller groups."

"And what did Toby and his wife have to offer?"

"Protection. They are both really good with guns. I mean, at least he still is. He's quick and deadly accurate. I've never seen him miss until we were being attacked by the runners, and I swear he was missing on purpose."

"What do you mean?"

"He didn't use his rifle. We left Medford because of the runners— there were just too many starting to show up. They would keep their distance and try to sneak up on us, and it was wearing us down always having to be on alert. Anyway, Toby could shoot them with his rifle no matter how fast or which direction they were running, and yesterday when we were attacked, he left his rifle on his back and just used his handgun. He can't hit anything with that thing. I think he wanted to get rid of the other men from our group before we found you people. '*Men are a liability when interacting with new groups, you women are the commodity,*' he used to say."

"You only lost men in yesterday's attack?"

"Just men," she says, nodding. "I'm not sad they are gone, though. They were exactly the type of men that enjoyed the arrangement Toby and Paula set up. None of them were very strong or could shoot well. They needed Toby and Paula almost as much as me and the other girls do. They just happened to have some skills that could come in handy: electrician, cook, and two computer geeks that were friends and happened to survive with others until they were on their own. They were good with electronics and radios."

"So you think Toby let the infected kill those four so he would have better leverage in dealing with our group?"

"Yes, and that's what Roger thought too. He told me this morning he thought Toby might let the zombies get him before we reach your group. The only reason Donny and Roger survived yesterday was because they stayed back by us ladies to make sure we were safe. Toby told all of the men to form a perimeter around the building we were in to make sure none of the runners could sneak up on us. They were set up too far away and too spread out, according to Roger."

"Besides Toby, is there anyone else in your group that is, for lack of a better term, a bad guy?"

"No."

"And is there anyone else from your group that might be straggling behind or waiting for you to return?"

"There isn't anybody waiting for us, and we have no place to return to but our bike trailers filled with supplies. The trailers are back in Rogue River. We were all hoping to make it to the coast and try to survive the next winter there. There aren't as many places we can scavenge from out there, but we can go fishing and there shouldn't be as many sick people as there are in the cities."

"I hope the others back up your story. You seem nice even though you lied to me about your name."

Her eyes go wide letting me know I was right on my feeling about her name before she sputters, "They only know me as Abigail."

"That's fine," I say and get up to bring in the next person. "Your real name isn't as important as the other details you gave, and if you didn't have a reason to tell your group who you were before you met them, I don't expect you to tell us right away either. Please sit in the trailer's bathroom and close the door. I'm going to bring Donny in next."

*

After Abigail, I ran through quick interviews with Donny and the other three women. I don't think I spent more than five minutes with any of them. My first concern was, *are there any more of this group out there somewhere?* They all told me *no*. Of course, I asked them, *when is the rest of your group that is waiting in Rogue River going to get here?* They all denied there was anyone else and didn't know why Abigail would tell me that.

My second concern was, *did Toby and his wife force the women to trade sex for protection?* To find that out I told them, *Toby seems like a decent fellow and his wife was probably the same. Why would Roger want to murder Paula?* I got some pretty direct comments about how I'm blind or an idiot if I thought Toby and his wife were decent people, and they then backed up what Abigail had said about the sex trading arrangement.

My final concern was, *did Toby set up the other men in his group to die?* For that I asked them, *If those other four men were your main security force and defenders, how did they all die while none of you were injured?* Roger only told Abigail that he was concerned that Toby was going to kill him and only Donny shared in that concern. Until I posed the question the way I did, the other women, Rachel, Amanda, and Heather didn't think anything was strange about the attack that killed the four men yesterday. After they each chuckled in their own way at the four men being capable protectors, they expressed surprise that the men were set up so far away as they were and that Toby always arranges the defense set-up of the group since he was the best at it.

Stepping out of the trailer to give my final interview to Toby, I see Jeremiah next to him and they are both kneeling by Paula's body.

"We need to speak with Toby now. What are you two doing?"

"We were praying," Jeremiah says as he stands up.

"I have no doubt you were praying, but I think what Toby was doing is a thing called playing and he's taking you for a fool."

As usual, Jeremiah doesn't like what I have to say, or how I say it, and believes it is intentional malice toward him on my part.

"He has a good soul, Eddie, even if he threatened us in the woods."

"I'm sure he led you to believe that, Jeremiah. I don't fault you for him misleading you but tell me what you think of him and his wife after you hear what he has to say about how his group functioned."

79

Jeremiah looks at Isaac, who nods back at him as if to say *It's the truth,* and Jeremiah steps away from Toby.

*

"As you can probably guess, Toby, your version of events up until now don't exactly mesh with what these other five are saying. It's pretty close, but not exact, so let me run over a few things with you just to be sure. You say it was the women's idea to trade sex for supplies, but they all say it was your and Paula's requirement for getting your protection and staying in your group. Why would all of them have the same lie when I spoke to them separately?"

"I didn't touch them. I thought everyone should contribute something to the survival of the group, and they had nothing else they could offer."

"Did he touch any of you?"

All of the women shake their heads *no.*

"Paula would have killed him," Heather replies.

"Last thing, Toby, about the attack yesterday. You said you lost four men when your group was surprised by the runners, but the others say you had given each of them specific areas to guard, and they were all far away and spread out. I know, and I'm sure you do as well, that the runners like to attack solo targets. What about that?"

"Those men were a liability," he says echoing Abigail's words from earlier. "Those men used these women for sex..."

"And how is what you did any different?" Rachel interrupts to accuse him.

"I never touched you or any of the other women. You all had a choice of what you wanted to do. I can't help it if you were all entitled princesses before the world fell apart and never bothered learning how to survive or defend yourselves."

"Get back to your point," I tell him.

"The day after we arrived in Rogue River we saw a large group of people move through on bicycles heading toward Grants Pass. I thought they were escaping to the coast like we were, but I heard someone mention bringing people back to a ranch so I knew they would come back this way. I thought when those people came back by we could barter or maybe join up if they had a safe place to stay. No decent group of people would have let those men in, and any other group wouldn't want them because they would be competition for getting access to the women."

"So you set the men up to get killed by the runners."

"Yes, I did. They would have been turned away or killed by your group anyway. If they were turned away they would end up getting

80

attacked and catching the sickness. I don't want to have to fight any more of them than necessary."

"And that's it?"

"Yes. That is it," he says looking at me and the others like an innocent man wrongly accused. "So what now?"

Samantha uses the opportunity to give Toby a little scare. In a completely serious tone she says, "Everyone will go back with us to the ranch. You women will be safe there, and probably Donny as well, but our ranch was a former gay commune before the disease hit and the men have been complaining about no new single men showing up for a while. You can stay with us for protection, Toby, but you're going to have to perform for our boys if you want to stay alive." She walks behind Toby, smacks his ass and loudly whispers in his ear, "You are going to be so popular."

I have to give credit where credit is due, and Isaac steps in to play supporting role to Samantha and gives Toby a flamboyant wink and a flying kiss. For a few seconds we are all able to silently hold on to the moment and I imagine I can hear Toby's sphincter muscles tighten up, but then the moment is lost and we all start cracking up.

"So what are we really going to do with him?" Jeremiah asks, chuckling along with the rest of us.

I pull out my gun and shoot Toby in the head. "That, I guess," I say to the suddenly silent and serious looking crowd. "I want to get home, let's go," and start walking away from Toby's body to the truck.

"We shouldn't leave them here."

"Well, we aren't taking them with us," I say more coldly than I intentioned. "If you want to bury Roger, we can take him with, but I don't care what happens to Toby or Paula."

"Sadly, burying them isn't what I meant," Heather replies. "I wish I still had that kind of concern for the dead, but I don't. Not anymore, not after everything I've seen. Still we should take them with us or we have to burn their bodies."

I start feeling sick with the urgency of her tone. I've read too many zombie stories to think there is any meaning behind her words other than a new evolution of this sickness is starting to make the dead rise.

"Can't we just shoot them in the head to prevent them from getting back up?" I ask, fearing maybe even that won't stop them. *Is that why there are so many runners out there now? Are the infected that are dying finally starting to rise again?*

"Get back up? What are you talking about?"

"Real zombies. The dead getting back up and walking."

She looks at me like I'm a lunatic in a completely normal world. "You know that's impossible, right?"

"Yes, well it has been an interesting eight months, and the last week has gotten even stranger with the runners showing up. I just thought the *worst-of-the-worst* case scenarios might be happening when you said we had to burn the bodies."

"The infected are starving to death. You must have seen their corpses everywhere. If you leave an uninfected body out, they will eat it. I watched it happen once. If we leave them here, they should be burned or you will just be feeding the infected."

"That's good to know. Let's take the bodies with us then. We'll have to bury them at the ranch."

"Those two don't deserve a burial," Rachel says.

"I agree, but I've had enough experience with the smell of burning bodies to fill ten lifetimes. I don't want to smell it again."

"It's too bad we don't have any poison," Donny says. "We could use it on the bodies to kill any more infected that come this way."

"Too bad Ruben's house burned down, they might have had some rat or ant poison. It'll take too long to search other houses in the area, so let's just get the bodies loaded up and keep the idea of poisoning the infected available for another time."

CHAPTER 9
THE CARAVAN

Mexico.

Senior Maldonado and his family have been told about the radiation exposure George and the others received. There was concern that the sickly way they look and move was related to the disease that is everywhere, but a quick inspection by Maldonado's personal physician confirmed what they were saying.

The supplies from George's house have been loaded into two dump trucks from a local construction yard. Smaller bags and backpacks have been spread throughout the ten vehicle convoy for individuals to use if they have to get out and run. The only thing delaying their departure is Senior Maldonado's mother. She is saying her final goodbyes at the graves of her husband and daughter in the back yard.

The whole scene, when taken in, comprises the entirety of the effects the Zeus drug has wrought in the world. Sadness, terror, and confusion are etched on the faces in the vehicles. Sickness and impending death are embodied by George, Keith, Frank, and Jack. Upheaval and destruction are represented by the vehicles loaded for exodus. Destruction is the smoke and flames rising over the city across the river. A bright spot in the turmoil is the hope that is represented in the scene as well. Hope has its place with Milagro, Maldonado's newest grandchild that was born two days ago.

"Senior Maldonado is getting his mother in their truck now. Are you all doing okay?" Thomas asks the four other men in the Range Rover.

Keith and Frank are doing better now, they still have a slight level of nausea remaining but their strength is returning. George is still weak but has started to hold down water and chicken broth, which is a hopeful sign. Jack is in the worst shape of them all. Along with the ailments the others have, he has popped blisters on his upper torso and legs which they are treating to try and prevent him getting an infection.

Senior Maldonado's physician, Dr. Morales, examined all of the men and gave them the same prognosis that they were able to glean from George's books themselves. They were probably all exposed in the 2-6 Gray (Gy) of radiation range. Jack was likely exposed to the higher range and could die in eighteen to twenty-eight days. George might have a little less exposure than Jack, and with proper medical care, he might survive up to six months. In their current situation he probably has two to three months to live.

Keith and Frank are the real unknowns. Their symptoms have come and gone relatively fast—in terms of radiation exposure. It's even possible that they are reacting to residual radiation from Jack and George, rather than something they encountered directly at the oil rig. The real sign will come over the next few weeks for them all. The level of hair loss they experience, from moderate to severe, will determine more than anything how much exposure they received.

"I'm doing fine," Keith says.

Frank nods, and says, "Let's hope we can make it through the country safely."

George is lost in his own world as he stares out the window—tears flowing down his face. Jack is sleeping in the backseat between George and Frank.

*

The first test of their possible escape to the coast is approaching. They have only driven eight miles and reached the city of Minatitlán.

"There is a roadblock ahead," Thomas tells the other men. "We will find out shortly if coming with Senior Maldonado was the right choice."

Frank and Keith grip their guns tightly, but keep them low and out of sight, not knowing what to expect from a military blockade in Mexico. The vehicle Thomas is driving is the fifth vehicle in line. Senior Maldonado and his mother are in an SUV behind them, and the two dump trucks are in the rear followed by two more trucks filled with many armed men. The four SUVs in the front speed up as they approach the checkpoint. Thomas stops their vehicle to watch what will happen.

When Maldonado's sons and guards reach the check point their vehicles spread out and stop, gushing armed men from their doors like water bursting through a dam. The soldiers, or men pretending to be soldiers at the roadblock, all take off running at the show of force. One or two of them appear to have real rifles, but the rest are holding sticks painted black.

A guard walks up to the Range Rover and hands Thomas a radio. They exchange a few words in Spanish, and Thomas drives forward to the men getting back into their vehicles at the roadblock.

"He told me I acted wisely by stopping when I did, and they thought I should have a radio so they can let us know what they are planning in the future."

"Why did they take the chance of driving up to the roadblock like that?" Keith asks. "Some of them could have been killed if those were soldiers and they reacted like the military along the coast."

"They knew those weren't real soldiers. There haven't been any military or police in this area for two days. Most of the people around here are also familiar with Senior Maldonado's family and know to run when his sons or their security get out of a car," he says back.

"What about the fires in the distance? Is that from rioting because the military and police are gone?"

"Unfortunately, no. The disease is here now, and we'll have to move through the city fairly quickly once we get moving."

Another call comes over the radio. Thomas replies once they start moving along with the convoy again.

"They told us to keep moving no matter what we see and to shoot anyone that approaches the vehicles, no matter who they are. We have to assume anyone moving toward us is infected."

Keith rolls down his window in the front seat, and Frank does the same behind the driver. Their guns are ready for action, even though neither of the men is sure they are ready to take another human's life.

Looking in the side mirror, Thomas watches the two dump trucks fall back slightly and the vehicles guarding the rear drive up to each side of Senior Maldonado's SUV to flank it for protection.

"I guess the supplies are secondary to getting their boss and themselves to the coast," he says to the others.

The sides of the highway are covered in trash. It isn't an apocalypse thing. The streets here are just generally dirty. There are no street sweepers that come through this area, and the only saving grace for the garbage littering the landscape is the paper material it is comprised of. Very little foil or plastic packaging is used on the products here so the litter will eventually degrade and disappear, along with the houses, the roads and the bodies of people that are also laying on the ground in various places.

"How did the disease cause so much damage in this area when we haven't encountered any infected yet?" George asks coming out of his depression for a moment.

"These bodies aren't from the disease," Thomas says back to them. "When the military pulled out of the area, many of the people wanted to escape with them. These people were killed because they got to close to the departing trucks."

"And we're supposed to do the same thing?" Keith asks with disgust.

"It probably won't make you feel any better to hear this, but when the military pulled out, the disease hadn't arrived yet. Or at least no one knew it was here. Now you can see the fires all over the city up ahead. We won't truly know if anyone approaching our cars is infected, but there is a good chance they will be. When the military drove through, they knew the people they shot were healthy."

"You're right," Keith says. "It doesn't help."

*

Five minutes later, flashes of light and reports of gunshots erupt from the lead vehicles. A few at a time at first, but with increasing tempo as they drive farther along highway 180D skirting the edge of the city. Men, women, and the occasional child walk toward the roadway they are on.

"They look like they're in shock don't they?" Thomas asks. "I mean, the way they just slowly wander around with those blank stares."

The area they are driving through is completely infected. The vehicles in the lead are shooting the people that are too close to the road, but so far as they are driving, none of the infected out to the sides are moving fast enough to reach the vehicles. It is more depressing than it is terrifying while in the security of this caravan.

The fear starts to creep in as they approach another curve. The vehicles were forced to slow down to drive around several cars that wrecked against a wall on the last curve, and there is a concern about the same thing or something worse being up ahead. Some quick words on the radio ring out, and Thomas slows down their SUV to prepare.

"There is a tight spot between some wrecked cars around the curve, and the trucks are driving through but scraping as they go. They want Senior Maldonado to go next, and we will go after him."

"What about the supplies?" George asks.

"That is the problem. We'll have to stop ahead and shoot any approaching people while the dump trucks smash their way through."

The curve is a classically designed horror movie death trap. During normal times it is a perfectly functional two lane underpass that stretches for a quarter of a mile. It is recessed into the ground under an overpass and has tall ninety degree concrete walls on each side. Today it is filled with wrecked vehicles and diseased people approaching at both ends.

Thomas drives the Range Rover through the gap, occasionally scraping the sides along the wreckage. They are followed by the two security trucks. He pulls the SUV up to the other vehicles at the end of the curve in the road and watches as the men from the lead vehicles shoot countless people walking toward them.

An echoing screech and scraping sound erupts behind them as the first dump truck starts muscling its way through the pile of twisted and intertwined cars. They chose to go slowly to prevent front end damage to either of the trucks rather than attempting to slam their way thru with force and speed.

The men of the four front vehicles jump back in their SUVs and drive off, followed by Senior Maldonado. The remaining guards yell at Thomas, presumably to get him to move as well as the first dump truck approaches. The driver doesn't appear to want to slow down.

Looking out the back window as they drive, the five men watch as the remaining guards open fire on the rear dump truck. They aren't shooting at its driver or passenger but at the infected people at various stages of climbing onto the truck. Two of the guards are attacked by infected people while their attention is on the last dump truck. The men's view of the situation behind them disappears as they take another turn.

"We're entering the final stretch of Minatitlán before we head into the open countryside," Thomas tells them. "We'll be staying west on highway 1450 until we turn south on 185. That will take us all the way to the coast."

"Are there many cities between here and there?" Keith asks.

Thomas swerves the SUV away from a man that walked in front of them. He bounces off the side of the vehicle and falls onto the pavement. Like everyone else out there, he must be infected. He doesn't yell or wave his arms in anger at having been knocked down. He just slowly starts getting back up only to be run down by the dump truck that is speeding to catch up with the convoy.

The radio squelches out more quick Spanish phrases, and Thomas fills the group in again.

"Three men died back there, but we still have all the vehicles and supplies. The second dump truck and final two guard trucks are catching up."

"What's up ahead for the rest of the trip?" Keith asks, reminding Thomas of his earlier question.

"Once we clear the city we should have forty-five minutes before we reach the next town. It only has eleven thousand people in it, so we shouldn't have a problem making it through."

"Unless the entire population is infected and standing in the road," Jack says with a weak sarcasm.

"Well, yes, there is that possibility," Thomas says while shifting in his seat. "More likely though is the distant towns won't have the infection yet."

"Sorry to be a downer, guys, but my luck hasn't been the best in this whole *escape from danger and death* episode. Let's hope this trip is based on someone else's destiny and not mine."

"Or mine," says George, ending with a sad smile beside him.

Thomas pauses a moment in thought, and then continues telling them what's ahead.

"We have a hundred forty miles to go over the mountains before we get to the next major city, Juchitán de Zaragoza. It is smaller than Coatzacoalcos, only seventy-five thousand people, but if the infection is there we'll have to figure some other way to the coast because Tehuantepec and Salina Cruz would be infected as well. We want to get to Salina Cruz to get to the Pacific. We might be able to get to the ocean through Laguna Superior, a large brackish water lake south of Salina Cruz."

The radio squelches again, but the men can see what the problem is this time. A large crowd of infected have surrounded a building near the road. Two people are trapped on the roof and are waving frantically to the moving convoy for help.

The screams for help are recognizable to the men even with the language barrier and over the moaning sound the infected make. No shots are fired to kill the infected because their numbers are too great. If anyone in the vehicles shoot, they could draw all of the infected at them and there is already a large group heading away from the building and toward the more accessible vehicles. The men all hang their heads in shame as they drive by the trapped people, without helping in some way.

"We're supposed to pull over up there and wait," Thomas tells the group. "They have an idea how to help those people."

The armed guards of the convoy get out of their vehicles and form a perimeter to prevent any of the infected from getting to them. The plan doesn't involve actively shooting at the infected though.

Senior Maldonado says something in Spanish while walking up to Keith and the others, Thomas translates:

"He said we may lose some supplies."

They stand and watch as the dump trucks turn around and drive in reverse through the crowd of diseased people. They each work their way over the crowd several times as they mow down the new infected that walk out from behind the building as well. With the number of infected dropped from over a hundred to no more than ten visible, one of the trucks backs up to the building and the two people on top jump aboard.

Senior Maldonado says something else, pats Thomas on the shoulder, and walks back to his car.

"What did he say?"

"It is better to live this way. To help instead of leave them to die."

*

The trucks stop several miles outside of Minatitlán where no buildings or people are around. It is time to check the vehicles and

88

especially the dump trucks for any surprise hitchhikers besides the two they picked up earlier.

One legless and two headless corpses were found attached to the trucks in different spots. They were either tangled in a chain or crushed against the back and got stuck.

Thomas listens in and translates while the two people they rescued tell their story.

"My family ran when they came, but I don't move well anymore. My son and his wife all left us and only my grandson, Joaquin, stayed to help. We couldn't run, so he boosted me up to the roof where we could get away and he was bitten before he could get up there with me."

The guns all rise at the pair as they learn the boy has a bite. The old man steps in front of the boy to plead for his life and continues speaking rapidly and pointing back at the boy.

Thomas steps out to join the old man in blocking Joaquin without translating, and asks George and Keith, "You said you had a letter about the drug and what it did to people, right?"

"Yes, but we lost the letter."

"Did it say anything about transmission times?"

Thomas translates their English dialog for the others.

"People that got the injection became violent in five to ten minutes, and with a bite, it takes one to five."

"What about a *fever*? Did it say anything about a fever?"

"Six hours. People are supposed to get a fever six hours after the injection."

Thomas speaks rapidly to the group, and while no one shoots, no one lowers their weapons either.

Dr. Morales is brought up and inspects the boy. He was bitten three times, once on the shoulder, once on the arm and once on the leg.

"The boy was bitten over a day ago," Thomas explains. "They were trapped on the roof since yesterday morning, and the boy had a bad fever and convulsions six hours after he was bitten. He almost fell off of the roof because his tremors were so bad."

Dr. Morales says a few more things to the group, and then directly to Senior Maldonado.

"The doctor thinks the boy is immune," Thomas translates. "They haven't seen anyone that has stayed themselves for more than five minutes after being bitten. The two of them are going to drive in the car with the doctor so he can clean the boy's wounds and make sure he stays alive."

The boy and his grandfather are being guided to the main car, but the boy runs back to the dump truck and begins to call and blow kisses. His pet cat looks over the side and jumps onto the boys shoulders.

The old man says something about *el gato* loudly and puts his hands in the air before the boy walks back to them.

"He said that boy is always with the cat. He's not sure if the boy stayed to help him or his cat in the end."

*

The drive through the plains and the mountains were uneventful, even disturbingly calm. The disease hadn't made its way to the remote towns they passed but word of it had. Many of the citizens were setting up defenses and preparing road blocks, but what could they really do against a walking enemy? They would have to build walls around the entire town to keep out one infected person that wants to come through. Still, they were working together to prepare for the coming storm the best way they knew how.

CHAPTER 10
HELLOS AND GOODBYES

Oregon.
Present Day.

Isaac's entire group arrived an hour ago. I was surprised they were able to get here so quickly, but according to Mariah, Isaac's sister, the families didn't have much left in the way of supplies or belongings to slow their departure. They threw what they had left in their vehicles and came here immediately when they heard they had a safe place to come. It will take a few days to a week to make sure the farm is secure enough for people to live there permanently, so Isaac and his people will be staying on the ranch until then.

Stockton's former prisoners, the Stick People, have been at the ranch over four hours now and have been getting checked out by Simone and Michael Palmer, our resident EMT.

Arthur called an emergency meeting so most of the leaders of my group are here, as well as those from Isaac's group. Danielle Hartley is the only person from the Stick Peoples camp that is well enough to attend, so she is their designated representative.

"There are too many people for us to deal with effectively," Arthur tells everyone at the meeting in a frustrated tone. "Everything is going to fall apart with these numbers."

"Thank you for the boost of confidence, Arthur," I say. "I know it's going to be tough and confusing at first, but maybe we should leave the forecasts of doom out for a few days until we can get people more situated. Are supplies the main problem?"

"No, it isn't the supplies. We *will* have to collect a great deal more to prepare for the winter with these numbers. There are still all the grocery stores and houses out there waiting to be scavenged so we should be good on supplies for a couple more years. At least until we can start safely growing crops and perhaps find some cattle to raise.

"I've crunched the numbers these last few hours and we just don't have the facilities to take care of so many people. Sleep is one problem,

Eddie. A person can only stay so long on the ground in a sleeping bag before they will demand something better."

"We've already thought about bringing as many campers and RVs up here as possible, so we should be able to take care of that," I reply trying to calm him down. "If we can manage it, we'll start tomorrow or the next day and run scavenge teams to get supplies to build separation walls in the riding stable. That could be temporary living quarters for people as well or storage spaces for personal belongings and supplies we need to stockpile."

"Okay," Arthur replies. "Those trailers should help with where people can bathe, cook and use the toilet, but the trailers will hurt us with space. We were planning on taking down some of the buildings so we could turn more of your property into fields for crops next year. The goats need more room to move around right now."

I shake my head and smile. I never wanted to be a mayor but that is technically the position I'm in.

"What's the biggest priority right now? What should be taken care of first?" I ask of everyone.

"Bathing," Simone says and everyone looks her way. "The people we rescued from the store are all in bad shape, and several have severe colds and coughs that could turn into pneumonia if they haven't already. Some have diarrhea, possibly dysentery.

"Isaac, some of the people from your group aren't in the greatest shape regarding cleanliness and health either," she says while looking his way. "A few of them also have signs of spring colds. If we don't get these people cleaned up, bathed, teeth brushed and in fresh clothes, then more of them will die than should. The illnesses they have will probably spread to the rest of us."

"Our generator broke down a short while ago," he offers in an apologetic way. "We think our fuel went bad, and since then, we didn't have electricity for the pumps on our wells. The only treated fuel we had was in our vehicles, and we weren't about to use that and force ourselves to escape on foot if we had to. That's why we are a bit rank."

"I'm not trying to embarrass you. We just need everyone to get cleaned up now that they aren't on the run so we can once again avoid the preventable deaths."

"Since you mentioned fuel—" Arthur begins.

"Let's get back to the fuel later, Arthur. How many pools do we have? Didn't we have like three or four of those two foot deep pools that we bought for temporary duck ponds?" I ask.

"We have six of them," he says.

"Great. We have probably an hour of light left. Simone, grab whoever you need from outside, and set up a few of the pools in the riding stables. We can use those as giant group bath tubs. Maybe one for men and one for women or one for soaking and one for rinsing, however you think will work the best."

"I don't think any of our people will want to jump into a pool full of cold water to wash off at nightfall," Isaac says.

"Not to mention washing in public where everyone can see you," one of Isaac's people offers.

"The water won't be cold. We have extra tankless water heaters in one of the storage buildings that we can run off the generator in the stable. They should only take fifteen minutes to hook up, add to that the time it will take to fill the pools and then everyone can get a nice bath with hot water. People can even sit in them and soak while they are still filling up."

"We can set up tarps to separate the men's and women's pools for a bit of privacy. We have plenty of bubble bath, soap, and shampoo so getting everyone clean shouldn't be a problem," Simone says and starts heading out.

"If you have any problems getting the pumps hooked up just come and get me," Arthur calls after her.

"Sorry for cutting you off about the fuel Arthur. What did you have in mind for that?"

All I get in return is a blank stare, the same one I always have when trying to remember something Simone tells me not to forget.

"I have no idea," he says and shrugs to a few chuckles. "Next I guess is cooking and toilets."

"Toilets should be next. I don't know what your people's diets were like Isaac, but I know the Stick People are going to be getting far more calories and spices than they are used too. That means more possible cases of diarrhea and vomiting. We'll need easy access toilets for that.

"Again, I think for expediency we're going to have to forego the niceties of private toilets and do things military outpost style. Arthur, pick someone to get a bunch of our folding chairs and cut holes in the seats. We can put buckets under them that can be pulled out and dumped periodically. We'll have to make a burn hole we can dump the waste into for now. Use some of the sheets from the house for makeshift walls for the toilets and set them up close to where the Stick People will be sleeping tonight. I mean close enough not to cause issues with the smell but still be easy to reach by sick and weak people."

Arthur heads out with two of Isaac's people to show them where they can get the supplies they need, as well as grab some extra hands to help setting up latrines. I wait for him to get back because the next item is completely out of my area of expertise.

"I have no idea what to do about food for three people, let alone over a hundred. Someone give me some ideas."

"Our problem isn't food being available," Arthur says. "We still have plenty of canned goods and bulk storage like rice and beans, but we don't have enough kitchen space to cook it for so many people. Even if we use our bigger cooking pots I think people would only get a small portion or will have to wait for more to be cooked."

"I think that is my department," a woman from Isaac's group offers while standing up.

"This is Gayle," Isaac says. "She is an excellent cook and baker. If you have the supplies she can make anything taste delicious, even if it shouldn't."

Gayle smiles and nods. "He's not exaggerating either, I might add. But for tonight, I think it would be best to just make a warm staple of rice with some veggies for the sickest people. I've seen the kitchen in your house and the bunk house, between the two I can make enough food for all of the sick people. If you have something to hold the children over, I can make them a warm meal after I finish with the first group, and everyone else I can cook for after that."

"You can make that much food so quickly?" I ask.

"If your people didn't keep your food stocks so organized, no, but there are plenty of helpers to move pots around and fill up plates so it shouldn't be an issue. I have a good two hours before the first group will be out of those pools your wife is setting up, and I shouldn't need much more than an hour to make enough for them to eat."

"We have some canned mixed fruits that the children might like," I offer. "But anything that we have on the ranch that you think will hold them over until they can eat is up to you. Maybe the rest of us can skip out on the warm meal today and hit cans of beef stew to make your job a bit easier."

"I'm sure I can manage something," she says warmly in reply. "I'll just grab my usual helpers and maybe take your *Michael Palmer* with me too. I hear he's the man that's been taking care of most of your cooking at the ranch."

"You'll find Michael on the roof of the house, doing watch with his wife," Arthur tells her. "Just grab any two people from outside that look like they are too comfortable and have them take over the watch for Michael and Jennifer, and he can help you with things."

Things are going smoothly, and I get an idea that might help us out in another department.

"Erde, you're a chemist, right? Do you know how to distil alcohol?" I ask.

Erde looks at me oddly with that question, and a few others just smile.

"I think with the world having ended you will find more than enough alcohol of all varieties to satisfy your needs," he says and follows with a smile.

"I agree, but I need to know if you can distil?"

"Yes."

"Great! Isaac, you think your generator died because of bad fuel, right? What about distilling the gasoline? There is enough fuel sitting underground around this country to last us all of our lives, but it will go bad, drawing in water and other contaminants. Can you distil bad gasoline into a cleaner usable form?"

Erde nods. "I will need the right equipment and have to do it away from any buildings we wouldn't want to lose, as there is a danger to doing it, but it can be done. First however, I would insist upon getting a medical laboratory set up so I can do the more pressing work of attempting to culture basic toxoplasmosis to immunize people."

I nod, conceding the importance of what he wants to do. "So we've got the food, bathing and toilets settled for today, at least. Possibilities for gas are there but space and future crops are an issue."

"We can't eat canned goods forever," Jessica Dixon adds. "And with so many extra people we won't be able to raise enough chickens, rabbits, and goats to keep everyone regularly fed here. Like Arthur said, there won't be enough space to grow grass and plants for them to eat when the place is filled up with vehicles and trailers."

Jessica has assumed charge of the animal care on the ranch, along with her sister, Ashley.

"I thought they were going to be put on our farm?" Brain Carpenter asks.

The Carpenter farm next to my property is where we are already growing most of the crops we have set for this year.

"We were going to have plenty of potatoes, corn, peas, and onions for canning in the fall to make it through the winter, but with so many extra people, we won't. The rest of the farm will have to be planted now, if it isn't too late. With Isaac's group moving there, we won't have room to raise animals as well, and we can't let them run around eating the crops we try growing for ourselves."

"It's a bit late in the season but not too late," a man from Isaac's group offers. "With so many extra hands we could till up the property here at the ranch to grow some things and still leave some room for people to live. Especially if we move those shipping container towers."

"That's Steven," Isaac says introducing the man to everyone. "Steven was a farmer before the disease arrived."

"I appreciate the suggestion, but the land isn't ready yet."

Steven starts to protest about the condition of the land when I raise my hand up to stop him.

"It looks good on the surface, Steven, but too much blood was spilled here this past winter for us to want anything growing on it right now."

By now word has spread among Isaac's people about the numbers of infected we dealt with when the ranch was overrun. Steven nods his understanding and stops pressing his point. I know after they arrived several groups of people wandered to the back of the property to look at the piles of charred bones beyond the fence line. I overheard several comments by his people unable to imagine dealing with the numbers we faced during the attack. I lived through it and still have a hard time dealing with what it was like.

"Now that we are talking about space," says Danielle, the chosen spokesperson from the Stick People. "Isaac's group is moving to the farm next to the ranch and some of my people were wondering where we will end up?"

I shrug and shake my head because it's something I really haven't thought about.

"Everyone will get a choice, I imagine. Once your people are healthier, they're going to have to decide whether they want to stay at the ranch or move to the farm."

"Could I offer something about the space issue?" Mike Sawyer asks.

"Please go ahead, Mike. I'd be more upset if you had a good idea and didn't tell us."

Mike is sitting next to Hannah again. It seems that they like each other quite a bit. Probably just because there aren't as many people of the same age alive these days, but I will still have to keep an eye on them.

"Why not just clear out more of the forest for land? We are going to have to clear a bunch for firewood anyway, so we can clear acres of land and start using it for crops."

His point is clear and obvious. One that any of us should have seen, but didn't, probably because we're so used to things remaining as they are. Several people laugh at his point, and he sits down, embarrassed, thinking he said something wrong.

"Don't be embarrassed, Mike. They're laughing because your idea is clearly the obvious one that we all should have seen. Good job. Isaac, instead of keeping your and my groups technically split, we can clear out the woods between the farm and the ranch first so one day we can pull everyone together and unite the land."

Isaac nods, and Simone walks back in with a new problem. "The pools are filling and some of the Stick People are already bathing or being helped to bathe, but we don't have enough towels or clothes, not even for this first group."

"Jeremiah can help with that, Simone," I say. "When he and Isaac went back for the rest of their people I asked him to grab as many towels and sets of clothing from the store that they could fit in their trucks. Everything they brought is still loaded so we can grab it now, although I imagine it might be mixed up a bit."

She gives me a surprised look at my insight, and I offer, "I didn't think we would send the semi-trucks back to the store today for a second supply run, and I knew we would need it. We should probably break up this meeting and help out with getting everyone cleaned and fixed up."

"Great, let's go," she says, and everyone stands up to start the simple, yet tedious, task of helping the former captives start feeling human again.

"I don't remember you asking for towels and clothes?" Isaac asks in an odd questioning tone.

"It was a last minute thought before your group was leaving. I told Jeremiah..." I hesitate because I think he didn't get what I asked for. "Did you guys grab any towels or clothes?"

"No. My brother..." Isaac says accusingly, and points at Jeremiah, "said when we arrived at the store that you said we should grab whatever was left in the pharmacy area, so we loaded up what was there and came back."

"I thought the leftover vitamins and medications would be more helpful to have than towels and clothes."

"Eddie, I need to get back to the pools to help out. Figure this out," she says firmly, pointing between Isaac, Jeremiah, and me. "Everyone else that can help, follow me. I'll give you a job to do." Then she walks off, clearly upset.

"What exactly did Eddie tell you?" Isaac asks Jeremiah.

"He said they were all set for most supplies but needed any towels and clothes that we could grab." Jeremiah looks at me, and says, "I didn't see why we would need towels and clothes and thought you were trying to make a point of sending me out for something useless."

The three of us stand there awkwardly for a few seconds exchanging various expressions of frustration, embarrassment, and anger.

"Fine," I say. "Check with Randy at the house to make sure Simone grabbed all of the towels already, after that, you'll have to scavenge through your groups belongings to try and come up with enough. That means some of your people will have to wait until tomorrow to bathe."

"I can already tell you we didn't bring any towels," Isaac offers. "We told everyone to pack light and move out quick, not that we had a lot of supplies at our place anyway. Our property isn't a permanent living location for most of our group. It's our camping and hunting property, and we were not set up for long term survival. Our plan after getting here was to return to our homes over the next week and bring whatever personal items that we can. Most of us lived in or around Grants Pass," he says finishing his thoughts.

"I'll send a group of men back to the store now to get what we need," Jeremiah says, turning to walk off.

"It's too late for that, Jeremiah. It's already getting dark. You're not sending anybody out there now or you'll be sending them to their death. Just get some of your people together and go in my house to grab whatever clothes of ours that you can, so the survivors have something clean to put on when they're finished washing up."

I turn and walk toward the riding barn, and Isaac steps in beside me, while Jeremiah goes off with some of his men to gather clothes from the ranch house.

"Why didn't you tell me what you needed?" Isaac asks. "I'm sure you thought he might not listen to you. You weren't just setting him up, were you?"

I look at Isaac while we're walking. "I don't set people up for failure. I ask people to do things and expect them to do it or tell me why it shouldn't be done. I guess I expected too much from your brother."

"You should have told me directly, Eddie. You know you should have."

"Yeah, I know, but I've been an ass to him all day and thought I should give him a chance." I stop and turn to face him. "Look Isaac, I asked him where you were and he said you were in your truck ready to go. I was going to go ask you and he asked me if I needed anything. I told him towels and clothes, and he said that he would tell you. I kept walking to your truck wanting to tell you directly, but he grabbed my arm and said I needed to start trusting him. He said he would tell you what I needed, and I told him exactly what he said I did. I said '*We are good on everything but we need all the towels and clothes that you can fit in your trucks.*' I trusted him, but he obviously thought I was screwing with him by asking for towels. I'm beginning to doubt that you will be able to keep him under control if he will lie to you about something so basic as this.

"I don't trust him, and the rest of your group is also about a stone's throw behind him on the trust meter. So, you better get your brother and the rest of your people straightened out while they are here. I may be an asshole to you and him about religion, but everything else I say or do is to keep as many people alive as possible. If you or your brother don't accept that, you can forget about the farm or staying anywhere close to us."

"Calm down, Eddie. I get it. We all have to work on the communication but it hasn't even been a full day. It's going to take some time to get everyone used to each other."

"I'm sorry, Isaac. It's been a shitty couple of days, and I'm pretty wound up about it all. Especially being forced to take your group in. Just tell all your people that we don't usually do things around here just for shits and giggles, and we never send someone outside of the fence on a fool's errand. If someone asks for it then they need it."

"I know I didn't give you much of an option with my warning about Jeremiah, but I can keep him in check now that we are here. My people feel safe again. They won't back him if he wants to try anything, and he wouldn't act alone. I don't want you to feel like my people are holding you hostage by our staying here."

"Don't you? You have sixty-five armed people that knew the layout of our ranch. You say your brother would have knocked you out of power somehow and come here to take what we have, and you don't want me to feel like I am being held hostage?"

"You let us in because you knew the danger in turning us away, but we will earn our stay. My people are workers, and they will know if someone from our group isn't doing their fair share of work. You have a good setup here, and my people want to be a part of it. If someone gets kicked out later because they weren't contributing, then everyone will know what they did to get themselves kicked out and it shouldn't lead to repercussions against you or your group. My brother isn't a killer and neither are my people. However, I heard that you tortured some people to their unnecessary deaths."

Thrown off a bit, I stare at Isaac for a second. "The people I killed were a threat to our survival, and we could not let them go without risking another attack." I smile remembering their screams, and step closer to Isaac, invading his personal space and whisper the rest to him, "What I did to those men was an added bonus I got for our losses, but I didn't torture those men for my satisfaction alone. Everyone needed to see how far I will go to keep my family and friends safe, and what I will do to those that threaten us. Now, I would love to continue this chat, but I'm sure you would like to get your people situated and move your cars down to where you'll be setting up your tents."

Isaac nods uneasily, and while he is walking away, I call, "If your brother isn't a murderer, then how do you explain him trying to kill your sister earlier today?"

He stops and looks back at me, but then turns and continues on his way. It isn't easy to be confronted with a dangerous human, and Isaac has just been made aware of two. I am willing to torture and kill uninfected people to keep those I care about safe, and his brother is willing to kill to keep people from having imaginary souls tainted by demons. I think I have the sane and reasonable standing on this issue.

*

It's the first morning after everyone has returned to the ranch both old and new. We rotate all the jobs to keep anyone from feeling persecuted, or more important than others, like they would if they were always doing a particularly suck-ass job or a sweet one. I'm up early today because it is my day for laundry duty. I normally hate this job, but today I am actually despising it. Most of the clothes we will be washing will be particularly rank since it comes from the Stick People's and Isaac's groups. None of them had things as good as us and they weren't able to wash regularly, if at all.

So after yet another night of not enough sleep, I am trudging along with several other unlucky laundry detail people to begin the days toil. I hope rather than think that I might receive a temporary reprieve from my servitude when I see Isaac walking toward me in a determined and hasty manner.

"If he thinks he's going to pull you off laundry to help him pick out decorations for their new housing arrangements, you both have another thing coming," Arthur says to chuckles from the group.

Arthur pulls more than his share of work around the ranch and has earned mine and everyone else's respect for his fairness and diligence. If this was the military, he would be the sergeant that everyone respects and knows they can't live without.

"If you say I can't go, I won't," I say to him honestly and fully committed. "Good morning Isaac," I say as he reaches us.

"I'm missing some people, Eddie."

"It's a big place, Isaac. Have you checked—"

"They left the ranch last night. Jeremiah sent them to the store."

"You can go," Arthur says from beside me.

"I'll send some people to help you, Arthur," I say before starting to walk with Isaac to get the details.

We aren't able to make it ten feet before another person calls out my name for something. Greg Munoz walks up, and if he says what I think he will, it's going to be a sad day.

"Hey, Greg. Can you walk with us while we talk? Isaac's brother lost some people last night, so we need to send out a recovery party."

"I can talk to you later if it would be better," he says stepping alongside the two of us.

"There's never going to be a good time to hear what you want to say, Greg."

"So you know we want to leave?"

"Yes, Simone told me last night. You are a good man and a friend. I'll be sorry to see you go. I assume Jessica and Lilly are going with you."

"Yes, they are."

Greg, Jessica, and Lilly came to the ranch two days after we survived our largest attack. They also suffered at the hands of the men that tried to kill us with the horde of the infected. Having them here after we finally killed Chad and his group helped everyone heal. Greg's actions help to remind us that not every person outside of the ranch is evil, and Jessica's rescue gave us something beyond survival that we could hope for. As corny as it sounds, it gave us the opportunity to help. We needed something more than just our own group to believe in, and the idea that our survival could help others mended some of our emotional wounds from that attack.

I stop walking and look back at the ranch house in the distance, and then back to Greg. I think of how peaceful things were before a few days ago and see the chaos of human traffic that is already occurring at such an early hour of the morning.

"If this wasn't my ranch, I would probably go with you. I understand why you want to leave. I'm not a big fan of crowds either."

"But you will let us go?"

"Of course I will. This isn't a prison, and I never wanted you to feel that you had to stay here any longer than you wanted. I am truly sorry if you had that impression."

"Oh no. I didn't. I mean, not until last night when we finally decided to go. I was concerned that day in the sheriff's office when you found us, but I have never felt trapped since arriving until last night."

I look at him waiting for an explanation, but he doesn't get the hint, so I have to ask, "What happened last night?"

"Jessica and I could have stayed and adjusted to fit in with all of the new people, but Lilly isn't ready to be around so many yet. After the meeting I was going to tell you we were leaving when I heard you tell Jeremiah that he couldn't leave, and I panicked, thinking the worst."

"Well, if Jeremiah had listened to me, we wouldn't be missing any people. You did hear me explain to him why no one could go, right?"

"I did," he says while nodding. "I just panicked and thought the worst. Jessica reassured me and calmed me down."

"You've been through a lot, Greg. Far more than any of us have had to deal with, so I understand where your concern comes from. I'm glad you didn't ask me last night, though. I wouldn't have let you go after dark either."

"Eddie, this is a touching conversation and all," Isaac cuts in. "But I have four missing men out there I need to get back."

"Your men are dead, Isaac," I say plainly and without emotion. "This won't be a rescue mission. It will be a recovery, so if you want to go somewhere and pray for the dead, I want to spend some more time speaking with the living."

Turning back to Greg, I say, "There are too many people here now. I don't like it either, but this is the start of a new society and I have to do my part. Please take one of the HAM radios and whatever battery setup you need to run it. I don't expect you to tell us where you're going but would like you to check in now and then to let us know you are okay. Maybe we can even drop off extra supplies when you find a safe place to stay."

I grip his hand firmly and offer a tight lipped bittersweet smile with a nod before walking away with Isaac.

CHAPTER 11
BLOCKADE

Salina Cruz, Mexico.

Keith and the others are sitting nervously in the Range Rover waiting for Thomas to return. The caravan was forced to stop at a military check point heading into Juchitán de Zaragoza and is getting instructions. Thomas is with the others. He can explain to everyone what needs to be done, where they should go, and most importantly, how they should act.

"Let's hear the bad news first," Frank says when Thomas walks up.

"The disease has just been detected at Tehuantepec city, only fourteen miles away. That, of course, means the infected will eventually be heading here and to the west. We will have to take side roads to reach Salina Cruz, and that will add an hour to our travel time."

"That's it?"

"Yes. Everything else is good news for a change," he says smiling. "This city is clear of infection, and all of the roads are guarded like this one, but the soldiers know it is only a matter of time before the sickness gets through. We will all have to be checked for injury, and Dr. Morales is already speaking with one of the senior medical people about Joaquin and his immunity.

"They told us Salina Cruz is locked down even tighter than this place, because its ports are a means of escape if it comes to that. I think it might be difficult to find a boat, especially a sailboat, when we get there, but Senior Maldonado told me not to worry. I guess he made some arrangements."

"Hopefully his influence to have people stay is stronger than their drive to escape out of fear," George says.

*

The medical check looks fairly routine. Everyone must walk through a curtained off area and strip down for a complete visual inspection. The vehicles were taken to a different area, and the dump trucks are being held up outside until some special equipment can be brought over.

Standing on the other side of the inspection tents, a soldier approaches Keith and the others, and speaks rapidly to them all, to which Thomas answers:

"Now that we are finished getting dressed, he needs us to follow him back out to the dump trucks," Thomas tells them, leading the way.

The supplies are all being unloaded. In addition to the guns the soldiers are carrying, several of them have black and yellow scanners of some type in their hands. They are being waved over and around each box as it is taken out of the trucks.

"Those are Geiger counters," George says. "They're checking our supplies for radioactivity."

The soldier that brought them over says something and motions for Thomas to ask.

"They are surprised that they haven't detected any radiation yet and are questioning your story," Thomas tells them.

"Most of the stuff on that truck was at my house in Coatzacoalcos, so it wouldn't have been exposed. The items I would be concerned about were on my boat, but those were secured below deck in the cabin and shouldn't have had much exposure, if any."

After a few more quick exchanges, the soldier calls over one of the men with a Geiger counter to scan the five men. Thomas makes it through with no issue, of course, as he wasn't with them at the oil rig. He still feels a wave of relief knowing he is radiation free since he was with them when they were still *technically* radioactive.

Frank goes through next and is also beep free through the scan.

Jack isn't as fortunate, and the counter beeps loudly at his head prompting a quick retreat by the soldier.

The soldiers with the scanners put on protective suits and return to the men to scan them once again.

With a slower circular motion, the detector beeps on Jack—around his neck and wrist.

"I feel so fucking stupid," George says to the men while he takes his own necklace off.

"What's going on?" Jack asks.

"Take off your watch and necklace," George tells him. "Radioactive particles stick to metal, or interact with it somehow, keeping it radioactive much longer than other things. The Russian's had to abandon all of the equipment they used during the Chernobyl disaster clean-up because the metal was too radioactive. Keith, you'll probably have to take off your ring."

"What does that mean?" Jack asks in fear.

"We might have survived the radiation at the rig, but probably killed ourselves because our jewelry kept us exposed to it this whole time." George drops to his knees in the dirt and throws his necklace on the ground in front of him.

As the Geiger counter approaches Keith's left hand, it beeps like mad as well. He reluctantly takes off his wedding band and places it in a special box the soldiers bring over.

One more scan over Keith's hand lets him know he is finally radiation free. The scan on Jack and George isn't as comforting. While the radiation levels have dropped, they are still emitting some in the areas they had their jewelry. The group is advised to start taking potassium iodate again for the next eight days, although the benefit will only be for Thomas, Frank, and Keith.

"We've been poisoning ourselves this whole time," George says again angrily while they are led back to Senior Maldonado's group.

"At least we aren't on your boat anymore," Jack offers in sad comforting way. "Can you imagine how much radiation its metal railings and fittings are putting off? That's probably the reason we've been sicker than you two. We've had radioactive necklaces around our heads the whole time."

*

Keith, George, Thomas, and Senior Maldonado are sitting in the shade of a building waiting for the trucks to be reloaded with their supplies. They have been sharing stories about their backgrounds and retold the journeys of how they each met.

The back story of Maldonado wasn't specific and mostly covered topics simply referred to as *the business*. For him, the work or criminal activity he was involved in was a means to an end, and not a life encompassing pursuit. Once he made enough money to take care of his extended family, he turned over most business dealings to his sons.

They all can tell that there is a side to Maldonado that they haven't witnessed, and it is reflected in the eyes of everyone they meet that knows the man from the past. *It is comforting to be on the good side of a man that has so much power,* George thinks, knowing that many of the powerful people he has met in life would not be as gracious as this man has been with them.

The displayed character of Maldonado, which George is pondering about, represents itself in physical form as a helicopter flies over their heads. Landing near the roadblock staging area, several soldiers get out and are directed to come to where the men are sitting in the shade.

Thomas translates what is discussed for the pair:

"They are looking for Joaquin and his grandfather. Senior Maldonado is insisting that the boy gets taken to whatever secure location the government might have. They are assuring him the boy will be protected at all cost."

Senior Maldonado stands up and faces the soldiers. When he does, a group of his men run over and the soldiers step back. He points his finger at them and speaks in an angry tone that Keith and George knew was lurking in the man somewhere, and are waiting to hear what he is telling these men.

"He is telling them that they have the future of humanity in their hands. When they take Joaquin with them, they must make sure they fight to the last to protect him or they will be damning their souls to Hell. He made the local captain order this helicopter to come for the boy, and they should treat him like he is the baby Jesus. If they fail to protect Joaquin, the Devil himself will have to stand behind Senior Maldonado to take out his vengeance upon these soldiers."

Joaquin and his grandfather walk up and thank the Senior for his help and kindness, and are led by the soldiers to the helicopter. After it flies off to the south, Maldonado turns to the others and speaks to Thomas:

"I have taken many things, and many lives, when times were good. I know I won't be able to be this kind to people when things get worse, but it pleases me to do something that may one day help people more than the harm I have caused in the past."

*

Entry into the Salina Cruz area is following the same protocols as entry into Juchitán de Zaragoza. The only change is the absence of radiation monitors and the position of the checkpoint. They are still half a mile away from any standing buildings, and the area looks like it was recently destroyed. There are foundations of former houses alongside the road and small rubble and garbage everywhere.

As they move farther into the city past the checkpoint, a dust cloud ahead allows the men to start deciphering the mystery of the missing houses. There is a line of soldiers standing in the fields before them as far as the eye can see. They are all standing guard and facing away from the city, protecting the workers behind them.Dust clouds and dirt are billowing into the air as houses are being demolished. The debris is being scooped up into dump trucks like their own and driven farther into the city.

Squelching chatter over the radio fills them in on what is happening.

"They are building a defensive wall a mile up the road. This same construction is going on around the entire city. They are trying to get it finished before any infected make it here from Tehuantepec."

"That's only six miles away. They'll never get it done," George says.

Thomas rattles off some things into the radio and more is spoken back.

"They say the infected are drawn to sound, and they have dropped something to the north to attract them. There are soldiers in the fields outside of that city using suppressed weapons to kill infected that try to head in this direction. They are letting nothing escape from Tehuantepec."

The vehicles drive by the wall that is being built. It is more an immense pile of rubble than a wall and can be climbed in its current state, but more will be done to it before they finish.

"Thomas, ask Senior Maldonado to stop so I can speak with him," George says.

A moment passes and the convoy halts its progress.

"Senior, they are your dump trucks and our supplies, but I think we should unload them and let the people use the trucks for the wall."

Thomas sends the message over the radio. More talking ensues over the line as they wait and eventually, Thomas turns to face the others.

"The army is sending over several troop transport trucks that we can transfer our supplies to. Those vehicles are useless for this construction, but the dump trucks are in desperate need. Your suggestion has just earned Senior Maldonado a favor from the local General."

The entire city population is working in some way to fortify Salina Cruz. The houses on the outskirts were willingly abandoned in the hope that the rubble could be used to secure their safety. Salina Cruz has many resources worth protecting. Besides a naval base and air wing, there is an oil refinery which has a strategic resource significance to any long term survival scenario.

The land beyond the city is good arable land, and while it won't be easily accessible from behind the wall, they are hoping the walled in portions can be extended over time as they push back the infected that might arrive. Until that time they can rely on the abundant fishing that the Pacific Ocean already provides the city.

The gesture of turning over the trucks is viewed as nothing less than saving the lives of the city. Senior Maldonado gave his personal thanks to George and the others for the idea while they were stopped for the transfer of supplies.

*

The caravan stops once more on the way to the coast to let a large herd of cows cross in front of them. All of the cattle from the surrounding areas have been brought into the city. A flock of sheep was witnessed cruising along a side street a few minutes earlier.

They finally reach the dock after being ushered through the main gate by the soldiers standing guard.

"We're here," Thomas says waking Jack up.

"I hope Senior Maldonado was able to find a sailboat for us," George says in a skeptical tone.

Everyone looks at him.

"What? I trust the guy. He's been more than decent this whole trip and didn't have to take us along for the ride. He could have easily stolen our stuff if he wanted. I just don't know what he can arrange in terms of resources during a time of war."

The men step out and are greeted by many soldiers standing guard. Maldonado's mother is ushered along with some of the others into a nearby building.

After a short wait, a man walks up that is obviously in charge.

"Maybe he's the General," George says quietly to the others.

Thomas begins translating.

"Senior Maldonado, I am General Torres. I know of your plans to get on the boat that you arranged with the supplies you have brought." He is speaking loudly and in an almost embellished way to ensure everyone in attendance can hear him. "We are trying to prepare the city to survive a siege and have a great need for such supplies, as I'm sure you know."

The men all look uncomfortably at each other knowing where this conversation is headed.

"We have had many individuals such as you and your group attempt to go through Salina Cruz to reach the ocean to make their escape. They showed no concern for our great country or the people of this city. You should know I have confiscated all of their supplies and the large ships in which they were planning on making their escapes. I have currently enacted a blockade on the coast, and no vessels are allowed in or out.

"We would have seized your dump trucks and your supplies when you arrived here at the docks, but you have given the trucks to us freely while they were still at the wall, which saved us time and possibly our lives. Even with this act of generosity, I cannot allow you to leave this city with the supplies you brought. They will be desperately needed before our fight is over. I also cannot let you take the ship you were hoping to make your trip south in. In its place I have arranged to let you take a large sailing yacht that we have no military purpose for. It is only slightly smaller than the boat you wanted but with more comforts, I believe."

Senior Maldonado looks over at George and the others, and gives a big grin to them. They don't understand his reaction to losing all of the supplies.

"Thank you, General. You are sure you have no need for the yacht?"

"The yacht is a pleasure vessel, and I need ships for work and war. You can leave when you choose once you are boarded."

"I accept your generous offering and am grateful you are allowing us to leave. May I ask about the other sailing vessel that was requested?"

"Yes, it is available as well. That boat belongs to a couple. They are staying in the marina motel and are American, like your friends. They are anxious to make their way home and will appreciate receiving approval to leave."

The men shake hands, and the General walks to the building Maldonado's mother entered. The formation of soldiers disperse. Maldonado motions for Keith and his group to follow him after the General.

Walking through the door, Keith and the others see a most unusual spectacle. The stoic and boisterous General is tightly embracing Maldonado's mother, with tears in his eyes, and is talking to her. The only word that is understood and keeps getting repeated is *mama*.

After a brief inquiry, Thomas explains the situation to the others:

"That is *Señora Torres*. She is the General's mother. Maldonado was married to his sister and built the house in Coatzacoalcos, so his wife's mother, father, and sister could stay with them. That is why the house was so beautiful. He wanted every comfort for them and his wife, whom he had a tremendous love for."

"What happened to his wife?"

"She died of cancer a few years ago. Her father had a heart attack and passed away shortly after that."

General Torres walks around the room embracing his cousins, nephews, and nieces. He finally stops at a woman holding the baby, Milagro. He gives her a strong embrace, and then lifts Milagro into the air.

"Milagro's mother is his sister."

Senior Maldonado walks up to the men, who are strangers in this show of familial affection, and begins to speak to them.

"He says not to worry about the supplies. What was said outside was mainly to give the appearance that the General was still being firm. It is important to stick to protocols when dealing with emergencies such as these. Turning over the dump trucks did help provide the basis for allowing their two groups to leave. Without that act, General Torres would have had to lose face in front of his soldiers by allowing his own family to leave. The supplies are being loaded as we speak, and someone will come to get us when our boat is ready to leave."

*

The two groups are standing together on the dock. Senior Maldonado's family is already getting on board. The yacht that they are taking is magnificent and the crew is happy to be leaving, but the former owner of the ship was not thrilled at all when he was escorted away. He made too much of a show on entitlement and ruined his chance for escape or freedom with the General.

The owners of the smaller sailboat haven't said a word since arriving at their boat. They were told to go get on their vessel and wait for Keith and the others to board.

Senior Maldonado comes by and shakes each of their hands. Speaks a bit to Thomas, smiles, and walks off.

"He said it was good fortune for us to meet and help each other make it away from the disease. He wishes us all luck and hopes we find a safe place to live."

CHAPTER 12

LOST AND FOUND

Oregon.
Present Day.

"Eddie, are you in here?" Arthur calls from the door of the barn.

"Yeah, I'm up top."

I've been stacking supplies for the last two hours with Donald Chapman, his son Joshua, and Franklin Dougherty, one of the people we rescued from Stockton's men at the store three days ago. Many of the former captives want to do something useful, but besides Danielle, only Franklin has the physical strength to be able to help out at this point. Franklin was only captured a week before we rescued their group, and he was surviving fairly well before that time so he wasn't beaten down and starved to the point needing a long recovery.

"Eddie, I think we have a problem. You need to get to the house and speak with Gayle."

Gayle is a great cook and baker but is also a profound worrier and world class gossip, so I'm not looking forward to this particular encounter. Still, if it wasn't serious, Arthur wouldn't have come to get me.

"What's the problem this time?" I ask while heading down the ladder.

"Today's scavenger group hasn't come back yet," he says with clear concern in his voice.

I look at him knowing what this means, and he just nods in agreement at the silent conversation we just shared. We both start walking toward the house, and Gayle meets us halfway, obviously not wanting to wait for Arthur and me to get back.

"What are you going to do about this, Eddie?" she asks, stepping in line with us as we continue heading to the house.

"Has anyone heard anything on the radios?" I ask Arthur, ignoring her question for now.

"No. We haven't heard a thing. Tim and Dianne were there when Gayle came up to ask about the group not being back. They are getting a truck ready to head into Grants Pass to look for our people and are probably getting some volunteers together as well."

As we walk up to the house, one of our SUVs driven by Tim drives up from around the back of the house. Tim's wife Dianne, my wife Simone, and several others come out of the house, carrying guns and gear in preparation for a possible rescue mission.

"You can't go into Grants Pass," I tell everyone as I walk up. I don't think I've been met with more severe looks in my life, especially from my wife.

"You are not going to stop them, Mr. Keeper," Gayle yells at me. "My husband and son are out there. If your family had any understanding of what people have lost you would know why your people are ready to leave."

I spin and step right up to her, sticking my finger in her face. "If you were a man I would knock you in the teeth for that. Hannah is out with the missing group, and I'm telling you and everyone here that we aren't going into Grants Pass. It will be dark before we get there, and going into the city at night will be suicide. Every one of you knows there are too many runners out there for us to deal with in the dark."

"You pretend to be some kind of leader here, Eddie, but you're nothing but a coward."

Simone steps between Gayle and me, and pleadingly says, "Eddie, we have to do something!"

"*You*, what's your name?" I say pointing to one of the men from Isaac's group that is ready to head out.

"Jeremy."

"Jeremy, give your gun and pack to Gayle. She's going into Grants Pass."

Gayle steps back with a face full of fear at the prospect.

"You want to prove your love for your husband and son, Gayle? Grab that gun and let's head out to rescue them. I'm ready, aren't you? I mean, if you're so ready to send others out there on your behalf you must be desperate to do it yourself as well."

I cruelly let her back up a few more paces while her face is awash with new tears and terror before I go on.

"Fine Gayle, you've proven your undying love and loyalty to your family," I retort sarcastically. "Now, keep your comments about me being a coward to yourself, and let me think. I'm not going to let anyone go into an unwinnable situation like Jeremiah did."

Three days ago, Isaac's brother sent four of his men into Grants Pass after dark, even though I told him it would be sending them to their deaths. He was desperately clinging to the idea that things weren't as bad as I made them out to be, and that the runners were a fluke. The men went out fully armed and ready for the worst, and they didn't return.

We found their truck undamaged and some of the remains of one of his men still strapped into the back seat of the crew cab. The truck had the ignition turned on and the gas tank was empty, so it was running and the tank ran dry after they were attacked.

They apparently stopped it there with the intention of getting out to check something and were swarmed, or had to stop for some reason, and were swarmed. In any case, there were only thirteen empty shells on the ground near the truck and none beyond it, showing that the men made their brief failed stand right at the truck's doors.

The unlucky fellow that was eaten probably had an infected runner open the door on him before he could see that anything was outside the truck. The other three haven't turned up yet, but I have no doubt we will see them again as long as they weren't completely consumed as well.

Jeremiah accidentally sending his men to their deaths did help us in one aspect and possibly two. First, even I didn't know things had gotten so dangerous out there. With the runners able to hunt and coordinate, they use the night to their advantage, and while Erde says they probably don't have any enhanced night vision, they are more than capable of running up to a pair of shining vehicle headlights in the dark to see if anything tasty is attached or near.

The second thing we will learn, if any of those three infected men of his show up at the ranch and attempt to attack people here, that would show us that infected people still have some memory of their previous life. Right now I need to figure out what we can or can't do to get my daughter and the rest of our people back.

"They might just be broken down on the road between here and Grants Pass," I say. "Let me grab another truck from the back real quick, and we'll drive as far as I feel it is safe to do. If I turn back then we all turn back. Agreed?"

I get nods, but Gayle pleads as I start walking off, "Please just leave now. Why are you getting another truck?"

Without slowing or turning back, I simply call out, "And how would we bring them back if we should find them without a working vehicle?"

I drive up and pull to a stop next to the other truck, and Simone gets in with me. I see Timothy set to drive the other vehicle, and Dianne is next to him. Daniel Palmer and his sister are in the next row, and Isaac's man, Jeremy, and one other I don't know the name of, are in the back. Our two vehicles drive out the gate into a world that has become a nightmare of running infected within the nightmare we were already living.

A week ago all of our thoughts were that soon we would be free from this disease because the infected were finally starving to death. Then, we encountered the first runners. My wife and I were so confident that the infected of the world were dying off that we foolishly took all of our children with us on a scavenging run on bicycles. That bit of optimism ended with me being bitten and all of us believing I would soon be dead. Now we have a world where the infected are faster, are coordinated, and are almost as dangerous as the remaining criminal element of society.

The night is falling fast, and I'm terrified while driving down the road. I keep looking at Simone in the passenger seat and wonder what we will encounter on our drive, and if we will even make it back.

"We can't go into Grants Pass, Simone. Not even for Hannah."

"I know, Eddie," she says quietly. "What are we going to do? Where are all of the runners coming from?"

"I don't know. Even Erde doesn't have a clue about it, no one does. None of it makes sense. A week ago we never saw them before, and now hundreds are running around, maybe more. Erde says the parasite has obviously evolved, but it is statistically impossible for it to be evolving the same way in all of the walkers."

"You don't think all of the runners were survivors that just got caught, do you?" she asks concerned.

"No. At least I don't think so. I would hate for that to be the case. Can you imagine surviving for this long just to be infected by a runner?" The discomforting question hangs in the silence for a while. "It would make the most sense if that was the case, but it doesn't explain what we've been running into."

"I know. Do you remember that man that attacked us two days ago, the one pulling the barbed wire and post? He had to have been infected a long time ago."

"Yeah, he looked like he spent a month outside stuck on a fence and only recently broke free. If he was out in a field somewhere stuck on a barbed wire fence, there's no way the Zeus parasite in him could have changed identically to an infected in town. But he was definitely a runner now. So something happened to him."

*

"I see one there, by that building. Do you see it?" Simone asks as we drive through Rogue River.

We are in late dusk, and in another five minutes I know we wouldn't see the infected unless they run out in front of our headlights. As we climb the *on* ramp to the interstate and begin heading toward Grants Pass, I realize I have been giving the steering wheel a death grip, and my shoulders are raised up and tense as well. I ease back and roll my head around a bit to loosen the muscles, knowing the first gauntlet of Rogue River is behind us.

When we drove into Grants Pass the morning after Jeremiah's men went missing, we took three trucks and twelve people—just to be safe. Even then we noticed a runner looking out from behind a building or darting around a car in the distance, trying to figure out a safe way to approach us and attack. We had to shoot six of them before they seemed to get the message that our group was too dangerous to approach. As scary as it was to know these things can think and reason so well, it was good to learn that we could send in smaller groups than twelve to do scouting and scavenging. All we have to do is make sure the group going has good visibility during the daytime and one or two decent shooters set up to kill any advancing infected.

Two days ago we managed to send in a team of six, and they searched a block or two for supplies, clearing buildings of any infected that they came across. The supplies they loaded into one building and a pick up team arrived later in the day to bring the gathered supplies back to the ranch. The same system worked yesterday as well on a team I joined.

We knew we would have to send in larger groups as we ventured deeper into Grants Pass but figured the six man teams would work fine on the outskirts of the city. Hopefully this wasn't a stupidly optimistic outlook, because if it was, it just cost me my oldest daughter.

I glance over to Simone, and ask, "I shouldn't have let her go should I?"

"Eddie, look out!" Simone screams at me reaching for the wheel.

I look back to the road and catch a glimpse of something huge flash out of the headlights. There are more giant bulks moving just off the road in the blackness. I can't tell what they are, but they are they are headed toward the truck. My overstressed condition from worrying about Hannah and the few milliseconds of seeing what these creatures are is enough to convince my brain that we are about to encounter the latest mutated example of something out to destroy the human race. I swerve the truck left, away from the oncoming horde, and nearly crash into an abandoned vehicle in the median. I slow the truck down so none of them can jump in front of us, destroying our chance to escape.

"Eddie, stop the truck," Simone says in a peculiar tone.

"Stop the truck? Are you out of your mind? Whatever those things are, they're huge!"

Simone switches on the cab's overhead light. "Oh Eddie, you should see your face..."

I can tell she wants to say more but can't, because she is in hysterical laughter. I finally see what's so funny when one of the huge creatures lumbers onto the road ahead of us, and I am face to face with the ultimate scourge of humanity. The grotesque creature that will finally erase the last remnants of the human race, a cow.

I stop the truck and look at Simone, who is in full stress induced laughter. She is hunched over in obvious pain at having to laugh so hard, and tears are streaming down her face. She looks at me and is able to regain control for only a fraction of a second before my sad look of embarrassment sends her right back over the edge.

I would love to be able to join her in this laugh-fest, but my time to laugh at this episode will probably occur at a later retelling of events rather than right now. I grab my flashlight off the seat next to me, un-holster my pistol, and step out of the cab into the dark night to see these bovine terrors up close and discuss things with Timothy and his group in the SUV. I walk straight back to them, and Timothy leans out of his window at my approach.

"Eddie, what are you doing out of your truck? Is everything okay? You didn't hit one, did you?"

"No, I didn't hit one. I think it's probably safe to be out here. I doubt these cows would let the infected run up to them and take a bite. As long as they aren't spooked we should be fine."

Dianne opens her door on the passenger side and steps out. Her attention seems focused on the shrieking laughter still bellowing from my own vehicle.

"Is Simone all right, Eddie?"

"She's fine. Just a well-deserved tension release at my expense." Her curious expression as she looks at me in her flashlight's beam coaxes me to explain. "I didn't exactly react stoically when I first saw the cows. I mean, I didn't realize they were cows and didn't know what they were."

She graciously turns away to smile out of the light as she realizes that I was just terrified by this group of walking steaks and burgers. I hear a horse give a sputtering breath in the darkness and begin to wonder the same thing that Timothy asks next:

"Where do you think they came from?"

"They could be from anywhere, I guess, but that gives me an idea."

I stand in the headlights of Timothy's vehicle so the animals can see me and let out a whistle and a couple of clicking sounds, calling the names of horses we had at the ranch before our large attack. About thirty seconds later, our horse, Buster, walks up to me. He is a good sized tan colored horse that wasn't one of my favorites. He is sixteen hands tall and had a *no nonsense* attitude, all work and no fun. He liked working and getting a job done, but when it came to brushing or pampering, it seemed he just wanted to be left alone. With his attitude, I know how he survived after we set him free and even how these other animals are alive if they follow him or are anything like him.

"Some of these are animals we set free before the ranch was overrun during the winter," I mention to Tim and Dianne.

I pat Buster lightly on his muzzle, give him one of the sugar and dough survival bars from my pocket, and head back to my truck.

"I wish we could take them back to the ranch," Timothy calls out.

"They've survived this long on their own in this area, so I'm sure we'll eventually figure out a way to get them back home," I call back to him. "Let's get moving. We only have two or three miles left before we hit the edge of the city."

The horses and cattle continued their journey south of the interstate, heading toward the river. They probably learned to hide out in the wooded hills. We'll have to keep that in mind when we do a search to pick them up in the future.

Leaving the animals to go their own way gives me a little hope. If they can survive in this world as large and dumb as they are, maybe we have a chance as well. Hannah's chances aren't so good, however. We only have a small bit of road to go, and I haven't seen any sign that they attempted to come back to the ranch. I haven't seen their vehicle broken down anywhere.

CHAPTER 13
INTO THE OCEAN

Coast of Mexico.

Thomas steps down the loading plank into the sailboat, followed by the others. This section of dock was designed for larger military ships, so the forty foot sailboat looks tiny moored to the concrete wall.

Jack is a bit unsteady so the others have to help him walk aboard.

"Hello, I'm Keith. This is George, Frank, Jack, and Thomas," he says while lowering Jack to the deck where he can sit and relax.

The man and woman nervously look at each other.

"You do speak English, right? We were told you were Americans."

"What do you plan on doing with us?" the man asks, and the woman grabs his arm and shakes her head at him like he said the wrong thing.

"We don't plan on *doing* anything to you, unless there is a reason the military was holding you. You aren't criminals, are you?" Keith asks

"We haven't done anything," the man says in his defense. "You are the people that drove onto a military base loaded with weapons and confiscated our boat. Are you drug runners? Arms dealers? How do we know you won't kill us once we're past the blockade?"

Jack laughs first, and the other men laugh and chuckle.

"It looks like there is plenty of distrust to go around," Keith says. "Please get us underway before the military changes its mind about letting us leave. We aren't criminals, and you don't have to worry about us unless you try dumping us overboard."

The sailboat motors its way through the blockade line and into the Pacific. Once in the open ocean, the man and woman, who still haven't given their names, cut the engine, raise the sails, and cruise their boat into open water. After the flurry of activity the couple performs to get them underway is completed, Keith figures it's the right time to attempt introductions again.

"We aren't criminals, although the man we arrived with might have been a gun runner, we aren't sure. He helped guide us across Mexico from the Gulf in exchange for some of our supplies. Other than Thomas, who we met in Coatzacoalcos, we all made it here from New Orleans."

Keith spends ten minutes briefly explaining to the couple how they made their way from an oil rig to Mexico, across the land bridge to the docks of Salina Cruz, and that they plan on reaching Oregon. He finishes by apologizing for the quantities of supplies they have brought, which nearly fill the interior of the boat.

The two start to relax after hearing the men's stories but are still on edge, probably over their captivity in Salina Cruz.

"I'm Carl, and this is Ellen. I'm sorry for how we reacted. We haven't had much information since we got stuck in Salina Cruz. All we know is we stopped in there to do some shopping and get more fresh water. We stayed the night, and the next morning, the city was locked down. The military told us about a blockade and we couldn't leave. Then they told us someone was coming to take our boat, and they would let us go if the people taking our boat allowed us to come along.

"They haven't really told us any more than that. We don't know why the city was closed, why they were willing to give our boat to you, or what all the construction and military activity is about. Was there a terror attack or something? And why didn't you people take a plane if you wanted to go to Oregon? Is this some strange race around the world you're involved in?"

Carl shoots off his questions in rapid succession as he vents his frustration at being kept in the dark over what is going on. With each question the expressions on the men's faces diminish from excitement to be underway to depression at remembering why they are out here.

Carl and Ellen seem nice. About the same age as Keith and George, in their mid-sixties, probably enjoying retirement and sailing wherever they want. No one wants to explain to them the world is coming to an end, but of the group, Keith has the kindest touch when dealing with people. So they look at him to explain the world events.

"Where do you and Ellen live?" Keith asks, wanting to know what their situation is before he gives the bad news.

"We live in Monterey," Ellen says with excitement. You can see the way she lights up that she loves her home. "It's a beautiful community along the coast in California. We've been there for ten years. After Carl retired we moved there and go sailing all the time..." her voice fades and she stops speaking when the looks of the five men don't reflect joy at her words but increased sadness.

"Salina Cruz is locked down because a plague is spreading. The plague already reached Tehuantepec, which is only six miles away. They are trying to build a wall around the city to keep the infected out, but I've seen how the infection spreads. They have little chance of keeping it out."

"The infected? Do you mean infected people?"

"Yes."

"Aren't they trying to treat them?"

Keith chooses to be blunt at this point. "They are trying to kill them."

Ellen puts her hand to her mouth in shock. Carl scoots back, repelled at the words he is hearing.

"The plague makes people attack each other. When an infected person bites someone else, the plague gets spread. It transmits rapidly and every place it arrives shortly gets overrun. Coatzalcoalcos fell in four days from one person bringing the disease. Three hundred thousand people gone from a few bites."

"We have to get back to the U.S." Carl says with optimistic pride. "The U.S. military will be able to keep this thing out. Now I know why you want to get back so badly."

Keith shakes his head. "The U.S. military is gone."

He gives a second for Carl and Ellen to absorb what he said.

"The military, the police, the entire country has collapsed or is collapsing. This thing is all over the world right now. It doesn't start with a bite. It begins with an injection of a drug called *Zeus*."

*

Carl is at the bow of the ship holding on to Ellen, who is sobbing into her hands. Keith laid bare every detail of the disease that he knows.

George is at the wheel and the others are sitting around him.

"Ellen is devastated. You better be right about this," Carl demands, walking back to them but he can see in their eyes this isn't some cruel joke. "What are we going to do?"

"The five of us are heading to Oregon to meet up with Keith's son. We didn't have a way of making it to the rest of our families. No survivable way, that is."

"Our children are in Washington. I'm sure Ellen would want to see if they are all right. I just don't know if we can make that trip."

"It's right next to Oregon," George offers. "We have plenty of supplies, and it shouldn't take more than a few days to make it there after you drop us off."

"The supplies aren't the problem, the weather is. We were heading south because of winter storms. The waters outside of Washington and Oregon, heck even northern California, can be deadly going into the winter. We could try, but you should know we might have to stop somewhere over the winter. And if things are as bad as you say, we can't go to the mainland."

"I didn't think about the weather," George says. "As for stopping somewhere, I don't know where we could spend the whole winter. Even islands might not be safe. Lots of people in boats took off from New Orleans when it fell, and infected people can land anywhere a boat crashes."

"What about Hawaii?" Ellen asks, walking up while wiping tears from her face to join the conversation.

"Could we make it there in this?" Jack asks.

"In this?" she asks in an admonishing tone. "Don't say it like this is a little rowboat. This is a forty foot sailboat, young man, and we have been to Hawaii in it before."

"We could make it there a lot easier than we could get to Oregon or Washington," Carl says. "It would take a month, maybe two. It would depend on how long it takes to get to L.A. with the winds. It took us nineteen days the last time we left from L.A."

"It sounds nice," George begins. "But it won't work. Pearl Harbor is on Oahu, and there are military installations on some of the other islands as well. It would be a two month trip to an infected wasteland."

Ellen walks back to the bow in tears.

"Great job, George," Frank says. "Maybe you should filter things through Keith before you share them.

"Since I'm already being a downer, there is another problem we have to worry about out here: Pirates. Senior Maldonado gave us the guns and ammo for a reason, and we should have them ready for any other boats we encounter."

"I don't think people would come after a sailboat," Carl rebuts. "Criminals would want speed boats or to raid luxury yachts."

"And anyone with brains that wants to survive on the ocean will want a sailboat. That's why I didn't want a cruiser like the one we escaped from New Orleans in. We won't be able to refuel often with the land covered by infected people. The wind is free, as long as it's blowing."

"You could have made it all the way to Oregon without refueling in the right motorized ship."

"And the General wouldn't have let us take it. He is only letting sailing vessels leave because his navy can't use them. They have a refinery in Salina Cruz so I understand his thinking, but he may want the sailboats in another couple days when the city falls."

"You seem certain it will happen. How can you be so sure?"

"Acapulco, it isn't too far, is it?" George asks in a seemingly unrelated way.

"Just a few days up the coast. We were there for a week before we went to Salina Cruz."

"Good. Let's head there, and you can see for yourself what's happening in the world."

George is taking a chance with Acapulco. They haven't heard anything about the infection arriving in that city, but there is a very good chance that it is there. Two or three days of sailing should present Acapulco and give all the evidence Carl needs with what this sickness can do.

*

Carl and Ellen began teaching everyone how to sail and operate their boat, everyone but Jack, who has gotten too sick to be active. They chose to sail away from land to avoid any encounters with other vessels on their way to Acapulco, and aside from Jack's worsening condition, it has been a peaceful two days.

They are headed back toward land now and can already see a dark smudge of cloud on the horizon, which seems like smog, but shouldn't be visible this far out. George knows it is smoke, and Acapulco is probably in flames the way New Orleans and Coatzacoalcos looked after the infected destroyed those places. He doesn't want to be the one that makes Ellen cry again, so he keeps his opinion to himself.

"That isn't smog, is it?" Ellen quietly asks her husband, knowing the answer for herself with the view of smoke becoming clearer on the horizon.

*

"I don't think we should get any closer," George tells Carl as they approach the Mexican coast.

Through their binoculars they can see Acapulco is in flames. There are ships of various sizes scattered over the water, drifting without owners to steer them, some are in flames like the city behind them. Even in a fishing or speed boat it would be difficult to maneuver through the mess of broken, abandoned, and burning boats that are floating along the approach to the coast. It would be a slow motoring task without their sails if they wanted to get a better view.

"It looks like people are standing all along the shore," Carl says before handing the glasses to George.

"They're infected."

"That's thousands of people. They might be trying to get away from the fires!"

"Carl, I saw the same thing in Louisiana, and then in Coatzacoalcos. The infected spread out and head to sources of sound. They crowd along coastlines because of the noise crashing waves make."

"There's a boat heading toward us," Frank says looking south of the city.

It's a speedboat and is approaching them from the side.

"It's coming up fast. Get your guns ready."

122

"You people are paranoid," Carl says trying to diffuse the tension and keep Ellen calm.

Ignoring him, the four of them lay along the deck from bow to stern. Rounds are chambered into their guns and the safeties are switched off.

Jack is lying down below deck.

Ellen ducks into the cabin as the boat approaches just in case Keith and the others are right about the situation and her husband is wrong.

"There's another boat coming up behind the first one," Carl calls out. "They can probably tell us what is happening on shore."

"I can't get a good look at the people in that boat with the front end of it bouncing up and down. Can either of you see anything?" Frank asks knowing they can see as little as he does.

They know it isn't an infected crew, because the boat starts to slow as it gets closer, which is fortunate for them. That boat would have crashed right into the middle of the sailboat if it continued, since Carl is making no effort to get them out of the way.

Carl just stands there with his hand in the air, waving as the speedboat turns to ride adjacent to them. No words are exchanged, only gunfire.

The tunnel vision of criminal activity has the three speedboat thieves focusing all their attention on the compliant target Carl is turning out to be. When they open fire on him with their handguns, a return volley of bullets fly back at them. One falls facedown into the water, and the other two slump into the boat, obviously dead from their wounds.

Carl falls back onto the deck grasping his arm, with blood running out between his fingers.

The second larger boat begins turning away before it is close enough to be a danger of crashing into them, but it is still close enough to be a threat if anyone on that boat chooses to shoot. Keith and the others begin firing at it before it is able to come about. More armed men are on board, and they shoot back at the sailboat as they attempt to make their escape. Like the men in the first vessel, they are all firing handguns and don't have the aim or distance accuracy that rifles do. Of the seven men that were on the second boat, only one is still standing as it speeds away, but he too leans over and then falls before he is out of shooting distance.

Carl is sitting at the doorway to the cabin still holding his bleeding arm, and Ellen is sitting next to him in tears.

"George, can you fix him up?" Keith asks. "Ellen, you need to get us underway. Ellen!" he yells. "There might be more of those men out here. All of those abandoned and burning ships are probably caused by thieves. We need to get underway."

Ellen walks to the wheel and starts calling out orders to Keith. Frank and Thomas reload while scanning the coast for more approaching threats.

"You're lucky they only hit your arm," George tells Carl as he opens the first aid kit to treat the superficial wound.

"I didn't think it would be so bad. How can people do that to each other? How could you shoot those men and be so calm?"

With those words reminding him of what he just did, George's hands begin to shake. He has trouble putting the bandage on Carl's arm, and his face blanches white. None of the men had to fire on another person before today. They had their guns and watched a lot of horrible things happen, but throughout their escape from New Orleans and the trip across Mexico, it was always someone else that pulled the trigger. Usually Senior Maldonado's men.

Frank and Keith are having the same reaction to the encounter. Keith is kneeling with his head against the mast and looks as pale as George. Frank is vomiting over the side.

Thomas seems to be doing a little better, but his face is etched with fear and he looks like he is trying to fold his rifle in half the way his white knuckled hands are gripping it.

"That's the first time I shot anyone," George is finally able to mutter quietly to Carl.

CHAPTER 14
STRANDED

Grants Pass, Oregon.
Present Day.

The roads are still such a depressing reminder of how fast this disease hit. Almost every disaster movie I remember had images of roads and freeways jammed with cars from people trying to escape whatever calamity was being portrayed. None of our roads are packed with abandoned vehicles. There *are* accidents here and there, and the occasional one car wreck caused by recently infected drivers, all while trying to make a hasty escape to nowhere. But there are no telltale signs that a mass exodus occurred or was ever attempted.

"There's a runner," Simone calls out, probably pointing out the direction in the dark cab.

I keep the truck at a steady speed of thirty miles per hour hoping that I will be able to stop or maneuver enough to avoid getting in a wreck by hitting one of the infected.

"There's another on this side," I say. "A half mile more and we'll be at the ramp to Redwood Highway."

"There's two more!" Simone says a bit too loudly, expressing her building fear.

"I see them too. It looks like they are starting to close in on us."

"Eddie!" Simone screams as a softball sized rock appears in the light of the headlights before it smashes the windshield right in front of her. I hit the brakes and bring us to a stop, not reversing the truck right away, because I don't want to hit Timothy's truck coming up behind us.

"Tim, back up. Get out of here!" I yell into our radio when a branch hits our trucks windshield this time. I start spinning the truck around in reverse and hit one of the infected that was coming up behind us. Tim's truck is disappearing down I-5, backing up the way I should have done. Spinning our truck around lost us the few seconds I didn't know we still had. At least seven infected run past our headlights between Tim's retreating truck and our own, more of them are staying in between our trucks.

"Simone, hang on. I have to try and ram our way through!" I yell and stomp down on the pedal wishing my pressure on it could make us fly.

I don't have enough distance to get a decent speed up to plow through and make it to safety. Our first two impacts are enough to destroy the trucks front end, so I have to turn the wheel hard left to head off of I-5 before the engine dies. I keep my foot on the gas and bounce us down the hill in the direction of a former UPS package delivery center that is somewhere ahead of us in the dark.

"Eddie, I can't see a thing!" Simone yells right before we plow over another small grassy median and mostly miss the back end of a semi-truck trailer. The trailer's edge caves in the corner of the cab over my head and knocks the previously shattered windshield into our laps. We finally come to a rough stop when the truck rolls into the side of the UPS building.

Simone is able to jump right out with her flashlight and gun and starts shooting at the approaching runners. After vainly trying to open my jammed door, I turn to head out the passenger side.

While she is climbing into the truck bed in an attempt to reach safety, I struggle over the seat cutting my hands and arms on the glass fragments. I take one step out of the door just in time to be slammed back into the truck by a runner. The wind is knocked out of me, and I struggle to regain the ability to breathe while looking up to see Simone standing on top the truck's cab. I still can't breathe normally and feel a familiar sensation on my right shoulder as the runner that hit me takes a bite. I fumble in my attempt to get my gun free of its holster since this asshole or bitch is holding on to my gun hand. Simone shoots another runner as it approaches me and while dead, its continued momentum causes it to hit me and the leach trying to eat me, pushing me back into the cab. I almost drop my gun.

I finally switch the gun to my left hand and bring it up to the zombie's head, blowing it open, and freeing me to try and climb to where Simone is. I have no luck even getting into the truck bed. Every time I grab onto the side of the truck to boost myself in, a new body appears from out of the darkness. Lucky for us there are no vision enhancements for these things. They are as blind as I am right now and are simply following the direction the truck took off the interstate and the noise it made when it crashed several times. The bodies of the infected keep bouncing off the truck and running into the building, unable to stop when they finally see an object in their way.

"Eddie, you need to grab the shotguns. I can't reach the roof without your help."

I shoot three more infected that make it to my side of the truck from the freeway and another that nearly grabs me, but its full run velocity takes it right past me and it smacks into the corner of the truck's open door, either killing it, or knocking it out. I don't bother to ask if it's okay. I just shoot it in the head before reaching in and grabbing our two shotguns off the truck's back window. Simone shoots another runner that is close to getting me and several more rounds at an unknown number of infected trying to climb onto the truck to get at her.

"Here! Grab it!" I yell, reaching up with my aching right arm to hand her one of the weapons that will hopefully save our lives tonight. If there was a God, there would certainly be a place in Heaven for the Creator of these beautiful pieces of machinery we are holding in our hands. Kel-Tec's KSG's are wondrous short bodied beast shotguns. Each holds fourteen rounds of 12 gauge ammo, and they are a definite comfort to be using at a time like this.

I pump a round into the chamber, pull the trigger, and watch an approaching infected get picked up and knocked back about three feet. After two more thunderous roars from my shotgun I am able to climb into the bed of the truck.

Simone is able to light a flare and throw it out into the parking lot away from us.

The light will allow the infected to see us, but they will hopefully be attracted to the flare long enough for us to climb onto the roof of this building. She is just a few inches too short to make the jump and reach the roof's edge on her own. After she tosses her gun up there, I boost her up so she can begin her climb. Turning around, I see one infected that didn't get attracted to the flare that is climbing into the truck bed. I don't want to shoot it and redirect the attention of all the others back to me, so I let it scramble up, and then I kick it in the chest, knocking it back out of the bed.

Simone is hanging back over the side to grab for me, but I hand her my gun instead and tell her to back away. I jump up and have my arms up to my elbows over the edge. I try to pull myself up when I feel something hitting my right leg and am sure I'm about to be pulled back down. Managing to scramble my way onto the roof, I see the thing hitting my leg was my thigh holster that came loose.

"I've been bitten again, Simone. My right shoulder. I need you to look at it," I say while stripping off my shirt.

"I didn't grab the first-aid bag out of the truck!" she says frustrated and out of breath while looking over the side of the building at the congregating infected below.

"And I didn't grab the radio. So we don't know if Timothy made it out of here, and they won't know we're alive."

"Wait, look out there," she says pointing up the interstate from where we came.

Out in the distance someone is blinking their flashlight in a Morse code signal saying *RESPOND*. Our flashlight is down in the truck as well, but I do have a lighter in one of my pants pockets. I grab my bloody shirt, light it on fire and wave it over my head hoping they will see it. After a few waves the flashlight blinking stops, and we wait for the next message. About a minute later we decipher *SEE YOU ALIVE. HOME NOW. BACK MORNING*. And so starts our impromptu vacation under a beautiful starry sky.

"We shouldn't have both come," I tell Simone. "I should have driven slower. I knew it was going to be bad here."

"But we didn't know how bad it would be, and you couldn't have stopped me from coming to get my daughter if you tried," she says forcefully. "Donald and Karen always take great care of them when we are away, not to mention how good Samantha and Conner are. Everyone wants to be around Gabriel. Sometimes I have to literally peel him out of people's arms because they want to keep holding him. It isn't easy for me to think about it or say this as their mother, but I know they will be taken care of by everyone in our group if something happens to us."

I remain silent, and she asks the exact thing I am thinking about, "Do you think Hannah is okay?"

"I hope so," is all I reply quietly before a crash below us reminds me that our immediate situation isn't over or necessarily safe.

"Check your pockets for anything we can use," I say while starting to dig through my own. I usually wear cargo pants since I'm paranoid, and the extra pockets let me carry items that only a paranoid person would bother weighing themselves down with. In these pants I happen to have a small shotgun shell shaped flashlight, and the battery is still good.

"I wish I knew about this earlier." I have an unnecessary compass, a pen, a highlighter, a few loose bandages, a handful of nails, and a box cutter along with a few gun magazines and some loose 12 gauge ammo. Simone only has empty gun magazines.

"I'll walk around the edge of the roof and see if there is any other place these things can get up here besides the truck's cab."

It just so happens that the spot where our truck crashed has a higher roof level than the rest of the building. If there were any vehicles parked close by, it would have made an easy access for the infected to get to us. There is nothing around us, however, and our truck provides the only access to the roof. Getting up here was difficult enough for us to accomplish that we have little to fear from the infected being able to make it up.

"We should be safe, but obviously, I don't think both of us should sleep at the same—"

My sentence is cut off by two echoing gunshots coming from deeper in Grants Pass. I shine the light at Simone and see her face register the possibility as well.

"It could just be some random stranger trying to survive," I say, playing Devil's advocate.

Simone gives me a look and shakes her head. "And how many people that have lived this long would be attracting the attention of the infected back to them after we probably pulled half of the city toward us with our shooting?"

"Good point, I agree."

I point my shotgun in the air and shoot, pump, shoot, two shots just like we heard. Two more distant shots reach our ears, and we know the shots were meant for us. Most likely one or more of our people alive in the city that heard our little gun battle and decided to let us know they were all right once the noise died down.

Simone throws her arms up around me for a hug and manages to scrape the bite on my shoulder, reminding me that it is there.

"We need to get your wound cleaned up, Eddie. Get on your hands and knees."

"Getting kind of kinky on me?" I say with a chuckle. "Can't I just sit down?"

"You can sit upright or bent over, but I don't have any water or peroxide with me."

Not knowing where she is going with her directions, I can only shake my head in the darkness and wonder if men will ever understand what women are thinking or talking about.

"Clue me in, Simone. What's the point then?"

"I have to pee on it," she says flatly, but I can tell she is holding back a giggle. She waits just a moment, probably to contain the laughter that is ready to erupt, and continues, "I'll have to pee on it and rub it while I'm peeing to clean it out. You can sit instead of getting on all fours, but I doubt you want that running down your back."

"Wow, we haven't done anything like this since we were younger," I say while kneeling down and bending over. Simone kisses me on the cheek, and then proceeds to clean my wound.

CHAPTER 15
FEEDING THE SHARKS

Pacific Ocean.

The boat is skimming over the water with speed, and land is somewhere behind them. The coast disappeared beyond the horizon a while ago. After the attack at Acapulco the group looked at Carl and Ellen's nautical map of Mexico's west coast to discover what other hazards might lay ahead. The map is a portrait of a thieves' and pirates' paradise. Puerto Vallarta, Mazatlán, and Cabo San Lucas, all of those cities lie along the route back to the U.S. The fact that they were major tourist destinations and had homes of the wealthy means, like Acapulco, they will attract large criminal populations that would likely be stealing and killing as much as possible until they too are dead.

The destination they chose to try avoiding more criminal encounters is Isla Socorro, an island far to the west of the mainland, with a small Mexican naval station. It will take two days to zigzag their way across the ocean to reach the island. They hope to get any information they can about the situation around the world and in the U.S.

When they pick up someone that is still broadcasting on Carl's world band radio, it sounds like panicked gibberish to them since they don't understand Russian, German, or French. The little news they hear in English or Spanish is always bad and usually vague, speaking only about rioting and violence, but never with city names or locations.

*

"Should I bring us in?" Carl asks from the wheel.

"I wouldn't recommend doing that, they're all infected."

The infection has reach Socorro Island. Several people are standing at the end of the concrete dock built into the small harbor next to the naval base. They are staring at the sailboat with anticipation as it sits in the mouth of the bay.

"We can't land here, and there is no other port on the island according to the map."

"We're going to have to do something. Jack is getting worse, and we're almost out of anti-diarrheal medicine."

"What do you expect me to do about it?" George yells at Frank. "I'm sicker than you are and almost as sick as Jack. I know better than you what he is going through, but we can't go on that island with the infected here."

"But the base might not be infected yet, and they will have medicine."

"Right," he says with slow sarcasm. "And if the people on that base are alive, do you think they'll let you walk through the gate and say hello, or shoot you on sight thinking you have the disease?"

Defeated, Frank sits back down.

"I don't think we should land either," Ellen says. "I've been trying to contact them on the radio ever since the island crested the horizon. If anyone was free of infection at the base, they would have responded either to ask our condition or warn us to stay away."

"You've sailed this area. What's our next option?" Keith asks Carl, who is looking at the map.

"Cedros or Guadalupe Islands. Guadalupe is farther away and has only a small population. If the infection is there it would be easier to make it onto the island and survive, but they may not have what we need."

"Cedros Island is close to the Baja peninsula, maybe only sixty miles from it. It's a nice place and has about a thousand people that live in the main town, so they will have some medicine. There is also a company town on the south end. It's smaller, and I think they do salt mining or something. It will take another two or three days if we go straight there, or we could try going along the Baja coast and see if there is an unaffected town along the way."

"But that will expose us to any pirates."

"And it will add to the time, making the trip take a week to get to Cedros."

"Have you been to the smaller town on the south of the island?"

"No."

"What do you guys think?" Keith asks the others.

"Let's go to Cedros. They respond."

*

The sails are full and the mast is creaking as the ship cruises over the glass topped ocean. It is a carefree and beautiful day by anyone's standards, so they insisted Jack should be brought outside so he can enjoy it as well. The five men, and Ellen, are sitting at the bow, letting the cool wind caress their faces and the sun tan their skin. Carl is at the wheel.

"You better not take any chances at Cedros on my account," Jack tells the others. "You know it's meaningless at this point."

"You shouldn't be saying that about yourself," Ellen offers trying to end his self-defeating attitude. "Getting you better is worth any risk we can go through."

"Thank you, Ellen. I appreciate that. It's just that I won't be getting better, I'm dying."

She wants to protest but knows enough from his serious tone and the looks on his friends faces that Jack isn't embellishing.

"Is it your cancer?" she asks. "We know four of you are sick, but you haven't mentioned it so Carl and I didn't want to pry. Jack, you're starting to lose your hair, so I figured you were going through chemotherapy when you had to escape."

"It wasn't chemotherapy, Ellen. We were all exposed to radioactive fallout," Keith explains. "The oil rig I told you about, we left it because the nuclear plant in New Orleans melted down. Strong winds blew the radiation to the rig and set off the alarm. Jack and George were outside before Frank, Maggie, and me and were probably exposed to more of it than we were."

"Who is Maggie?"

"She is my wife...She was my wife. She was dying of cancer and didn't survive the escape from the oil rig."

"I'm so sorry Keith," She offers.

"We scrubbed ourselves trying to decontaminate, but George and Jack were wearing necklaces and I had on a ring. The metal absorbed the radiation by the rig and kept exposing us while we wore it. We didn't know to take them off until the military scanned is at Juchitán de Zaragoza and told us it was still radioactive. Even with the initial exposure there were significant health issues we would face, but we made it to the coast with the jewelry and continued exposing ourselves the whole time."

"It might not be so bad for Keith, who only had a ring on," Jack adds plainly. "But George and I were wearing death around our necks the whole time."

Ellen looks at the men.

"So, it is with all of you?"

"Not Thomas," George says. "We met him in Mexico. But Jack and I are dying. I have a few weeks or months at best, and Jack, he has..."

"Days," Jack finishes.

"I'm sorry, I was sure you had gone through chemotherapy."

"I wish it were something that was controlled."

"Even with the hair loss and your exposure, what you're feeling could just be a bug or seasickness," she says in a motherly tone full of confidence but tinged with worry. "You know you shouldn't drink the water when you travel. You could be all right, Jack! He could be all right."

"I started bleeding today, Ellen. You were worried earlier that Carl's wound opened up and he was losing more blood, it wasn't him, it was me. Dr. Morales gave me some medicine that is helping with the pain. I hardly feel a thing and don't get too loopy or confused, so it's great. George has been injecting it in my back. That's why I needed help getting out here. It isn't only because I'm weak. I can barely feel anything."

Ellen puts a comforting hand on Jack's shoulder and sits there in silence. The sail is still full, the sun still warm, and the water as smooth as it ever was, but the day is no longer a carefree beautiful, now it is a beautiful sorrow.

*

"How could the reactor melt down?" Carl asks the group after dinner. "They have too many safety protocols for that to happen. I should know, one of our son-in-laws works at the Columbia Generating Station in Washington."

"All of our children live in Washington, although most of them are around Seattle," Ellen says with a smile. "That's where we were from too until Carl retired, and we moved south for the warmth and sailing."

"All I'm saying is," Carl continues, "you might have been exposed to radiation, but I doubt it was from a reactor melting down. No one would let that happen."

George looks at the couple and smiles. "You're probably right Carl. New Orleans is a big city. It could have been something else."

A short time later the men leave the cabin to sleep under the stars on deck.

"Are you turning into a softy?" Keith asks George.

"I'm just tired of making Ellen cry. If they have family that worked at the Washington station then they have good reasons for not wanting to accept the truth."

*

The south end of Cedros Island looks abandoned. Carl sailed the boat back and forth twice to make sure. Right now he is motoring up to a large dock at the north end of the company town. They originally planned on heading to the town proper a few miles up the coast, but once they saw no one on the streets or along the shore, it was a quick and easy

133

decision to stop here. This facility will have its own medical office, and they won't have to risk running into thieves or the infected.

The pier extends several hundred yards into the ocean to make docking possible for the enormous salt tankers that this facility filled with salt. Carl brings the boat in and ties it as close to the island as possible, so Keith, Frank, and Thomas don't have as far to walk.

George's radiation sickness has returned, so he is staying on the boat. He is lying on the deck and trying to rest between bouts of nausea. Jack is below deck barely able to move. He is beginning to get disoriented, which is another sign of the worsening effects of his exposure. Carl and Ellen are staying on board as well and are prepared to get the boat moving as soon as their three scavengers return.

"The medical office should be in the largest building to the north of the salt fields," Keith says. "Most accidents are going to occur during processing or getting the salt out to the ships on this dock, so the company that ran the place would have it easily accessible."

"I would put it by the houses," Ellen offers.

"I worked at shipping docks on the Mississippi. Trust me, it makes more sense to have it in that larger building. You keep these guns ready in case anyone approaches. We left guns by Jack and George as well, but they won't be much help to you if you get in trouble. The safety is off on both guns, so don't hit the switch again, or you'll stop the gun from firing or make it go automatic, both of which would be bad."

Carl was a city boy all his life, and he never liked guns. He places his down by the wheel carefully. The training he received out on the water was exhilarating and frightening. He knows he can make the gun work if he is asked to, he just isn't sure if he can make himself function in a situation of desperation.

Ellen knows how to use a gun but has been fortunate that she's never had to. While she was raised in cities all her life like Carl, she knew about the extra dangers being a woman in a city posed and learned to protect herself. Out of all the odd places to learn about guns, it was with her college theatre group that she had become exposed. They were performing a particularly devastating play about an abused woman, and the director of the play, Jennifer Lawton, took them all out to a shooting club throughout the rehearsal process. *You should never let yourself be overpowered by someone larger than you,* Jennifer had always told them.

*

The walk to the main building is dirt and salt, with the smell of rust and ocean in the air. There is no real point to paving the roadways because the salt or heavy equipment would break it down too quickly.

The salt is thick and on everything. The first few unsteady steps the men took on the dust covered ground had it coating their lips.

"I can barely walk straight," Thomas says. "I don't think I've ever been on the water for that long."

"Neither have I, if you don't count the rig. It didn't rock like the boat does. You worked at docks, Keith. How much salt do you think is here?"

He looks at the towering salt piles trying to calculate what he sees.

"Over a million tons, I would think. Enough to make anyone rich in future spice trading."

The door to the large structure is standing open, and like Keith expected, the main room is an equipment repair facility. At the back wall there is a door with a large red cross over it and the word *clínica* written underneath.

"Simple enough," Frank says and walks in.

"You don't watch many horror movies, do you?" Thomas says filing in behind him.

"What don't you like?" Frank says turning to walk backward and embellish his next words. "The ghostly abandoned town or the dark interior of the rusted and creepy warehouse?"

"All of the above, actually. Oh, and walking into this place like an idiot without looking to see if any infected people are inside."

Reaching the clinic door, Frank opens it quickly and walks right in. This room doesn't have the skylights that the main warehouse did, so it is dark until Keith hits the light switch on the wall just inside the door.

Keith opens a cabinet to look inside and turns to Thomas.

"I can't read any of this. You'll have to find what we need. Anything for diarrhea and maybe something for seasickness as well. It might help with the nausea they are having. Frank, I want to talk to you," he says and pushes him out into the workshop, closing the door behind them. "What the hell was that all about?"

"I guess I just don't care anymore. You see what's happening to Jack and George. We're going to be that way too. Maybe in a few months, maybe a year."

"If you don't give a shit. Next time tell me before I take you on land with me. I'm relying on you to survive this trip."

"Against what? There's nothing in here."

"But you didn't know that. The whole damn town could have been packed behind that door when you opened it up. If you want to die, you have a gun in your hands to make it happen. Don't try getting the rest of us killed in your bid to be free of worry."

"Hey Keith?" Thomas calls from the door. "I need your backpack. I'm loading us up on bandages and pain meds just in case."

"Did you find the other stuff yet?" he asks walking back in.

"No, but I did find something to take your minds off that little lover's quarrel you just had."

"Screw you, Thomas."

"Keith's right, Frank. You're putting us all in danger if you act like that. Anyway, close the door and listen to this while I find the other meds. You grandpas were probably in college when this came out."

"Oh, that's good stuff. *Peter Frampton*, "Show me the way." A little off on your timeframe for me," Keith says. "1975. I was living the life and just got out of the Army. Good times."

"I don't know how old you think I am, but I was in high school when this came out. It's a great song, though. I went to a lot of parties that year."

"Jackpot. I found the medicine, but they only have six bottles."

"Let's just grab it. I'm taking this player and the discs with us too. I could probably check every digital player between here and Oregon and not find these songs again."

Frank slowly opens the door and looks out.

"See, I can learn."

"Great. Let's get back," Thomas says. "Being on solid ground is messing with me. Everything feels like it's rocking."

The bright sun makes them squint slightly but only for a second. The salt processing facility is still deserted. Keith, Frank, and Thomas hum and mumble different parts of the song they just heard as they walk back to the dock.

The men are three steps from walking around the building closest to the dock when they hear a gunshot. Keith ducks, but Thomas takes two quick strides around the side while raising his gun to see what's happening at the boat. Bullets rip through him and bounce off of the wall he stepped around.

If Thomas didn't die from the initial hits, the subsequent bullets do the job. Whoever is firing by the boat keeps shooting at Thomas and the wall, making Frank and Keith stay where they are. When the shooting stops they hear someone yelling in Spanish, and then another gunshot followed by Ellen screaming.

"They must have shot Carl. What do we do?"

"Let me take another look"

Keith crawls back to the edge getting ready to take a quick look and pull his head back.

*

From inside the cabin, Jack hears new voices speaking in Spanish. *I'm still dreaming*, he thinks to himself and drifts back out. His last two days have been filled with vague dreams. The headaches from the radiation sickness are gone now or the medicine is keeping them away, but he has been getting disoriented. That damn book of George's said it was a possible side effect. Too bad it didn't say anything about staying away from metal.

Jack's eyes flash open. *What was that? I know I heard something this time.* He slowly rolls onto the floor. When more gunshots ring just outside of the cabin, he grabs the rifle from the table. He is able to take one step without holding on, but then falls flat on his face. The shooting outside continues.

Jack struggles to get back up and hears more yelling. He pulls on the knob to get out but the nausea returns causing him to vomit. He spits on the floor, takes three deep breaths and slaps himself hard in the face to reorient where he is. *Take the gun off safe*, he thinks.

Another shot rings out, and Ellen begins screaming. Grasping the door handle, Jack opens the door to the blinding light, raises his gun, and shoots a figure standing in front of him. The strange man's face opens up, and the body starts falling back. Jack steps out of the cabin holding on to the trigger and turning the barrel to face each new attacker he sees until his gun is empty five seconds later. He doesn't have the strength to move farther and falls to the deck.

*

"That's full auto!" Keith says and looks around the building's edge.

Keith watches Jack turning with his gun. One man next to him is already falling and another gets shot as his rotation continues.

Ellen has a gun and kills two men at the bow of the boat in front of her.

Jack finishes his turn, and his remaining bullets empty into the last two bodies standing on the deck. They fly into Ellen's back and a man that is wrestling with her for the gun. Both people fall and Keith turns his gaze to the ground wishing to erase the image of what just happened.

Frank steps around the corner and quickly scans the surrounding area before stepping over to check on Thomas.

"Thomas is dead. Let's get up to the boat."

Frank runs up behind Keith, scanning the area around and behind them as they go.

The body of one attacker is hanging over the railing at a contorted angle with his foot stuck somewhere on the deck. The rest of the boat looks like a slaughterhouse floor.

Keith checks Ellen first. She is face down next to her husband, with six entry wounds across her back. Her body is still. Carl has a bullet wound to his head.

George is lying face down between the two men Ellen shot. He has blood on him but it must be theirs, there are no entry wounds that Keith can see. He turns him over and sees a large welt on George's forehead. His chest is still heaving.

"Jack is alive but too weak to move. How are the others?" Frank yells.

"Carl and Ellen are dead. George is just knocked out."

Keith looks back to Thomas' body and beyond him to the road that leads to the other town.

"Frank, make sure these bastards are all dead. I'll be right back."

"Where are you..." Frank looks at the road. The infected are starting to appear and walk to the dock. "You can't make it in time!" Frank yells after Keith as he runs.

Keith reaches Thomas' body and starts dragging him away from the approaching group of infected. He is pulling with all his strength but is still moving slower than the crowd seeking his flesh. He rolls Thomas onto his stomach, pulls off the backpack, and continues dragging the body to the boat.

Frank walks past Keith and starts shooting into the crowd. Heads, necks, and torsos pop open with red. The bodies in the front of the pack fall, allowing Frank to grab the backpack before turning to help Keith get Thomas' body back to the dock. Together they load Thomas' body and jump back to the dock to untie the boat and make their escape.

Frank starts the engine and steers them slowly away from the island. Keith walks over to the edge to free the leg of the dangling body, while Franks slows the boat and shuts off the engine. The body splashes into the water, and the anchor follows a second later.

Frank pulls the body Jack killed at the door to the side and raises him over the lifeline to drop him into the water as well.

"Not a good time to go swimming," Frank tells Keith and points into the water.

Several sharks are swimming around the craft.

"The dock is filling up as well," he replies, and they watch the growing crowd of infected walking toward the buildings at the end of the structure.

"They aren't watching us. Do you think someone is down there?"

"That's where these men were probably hiding. If someone is in there they'll get what they deserve," Keith says using an evil tone of revenge before dropping another body over the side to feed the sharks.

Frank grabs the body of the man that was shot next to Ellen and lifts him over the side, slightly sickened at the sight of more fins appearing from the depths.

The next body Keith grabs lets out a moan, so he steps back.

"Frank, this one is alive."

Frank walks over and raises his gun at the man, but Keith pushes it away.

"Wait. Help me turn him over."

They turn him on his back, and the pain from the movement makes him open his eyes wide. This one has been shot in the stomach. He says something in Spanish in a pleading tone.

"*No hablo español,*" they both reply.

"Bring the last body here, Frank."

Keith stands the man up and makes him look at the sharks consuming his friends in the water below. Frank drops the last man into the ocean, and a shark promptly grabs one of the legs and drags it under the water while shaking its head from side to side.

The man starts speaking rapidly, and then screams when Keith pushes him over the side. He isn't able to scream for long. There are too many sharks, and they've worked themselves into quite a frenzy with all the blood and free meat being thrown to them.

"We'll bury the others when we make it deeper into the ocean. They deserve better than what these scum received."

The wind feels good, so Frank gets the sails ready while Keith brings up the anchor.

Once the wind begins carrying them away a woman's scream carries over the waters, and they look back to the dock. The infected finally flushed the remaining bandits from their hideout. The two people run to the end of the structure and jump into the water. They try swimming toward the retreating sailboat.

"Should I turn around?" Frank asks.

"There's no point," is the answer followed by his finger tipped arm pointing to several fins converging on the fear-filled bathers.

CHAPTER 16
FREED FROM THE KEEPER

Oregon.
Present Day.

Timothy and the group in his SUV fared better in our reconnaissance to the edge of Grants Pass. One infected was able to jump on their hood, before they threw their vehicle in reverse, but it wasn't able to grab hold and just slid off when they moved. Two more that moved into the road behind them after they passed were plowed down by their SUV in its escape.

Timothy only reversed a short way down the road and killed his headlights to watch as the infected in the area all converged on my slower moving truck attempting to turn around. They lost sight of us as soon as the front end of our truck was damaged ramming into the infected, but they heard my truck moving until it crashed and then listened to our continued gunfire which only stopped when we were safely on the roof.

"Eddie, Simone, are you there? Eddie, Simone?" Dianne tries reaching us on the radio but we no longer have ours and can't respond.

"Try flashing the headlights," Jeremy calls from the back.

"If I do, too many infected will see us, and we'll have to leave right away. I'll try my flashlight first. Two of you get out with me and cover my side and rear so I can flash in the direction they crashed."

"No way are we getting out! You can use your light from inside the cab," Diane yells at Tim while slapping his arm. "We can't see a thing out there, so if you put one foot out that door we'll all probably be dead."

"You're right. I'm not thinking straight," he says and starts flashing the light in Morse code in the general direction we should be.

The inside of the SUV shines like an intermittent lighthouse each time the beam is lit and it works to safely guide the infected to the vehicle Tim and the others are in. Two infected hit their truck shortly after the light message begins. Those two are shot and killed, but everyone knows there will be others.

"How long are we going to stay here Timothy?" Jeremy asks. "We could get surrounded just like—"

"There!" Dianne yells and points out of habit in the dark interior.

"I see it," says Tim. "They're burning something and waving it. Let me just send another quick message and we'll get out of here."

Three more infected hit the truck while Tim is sending the final message. The group inside can barely hear and are seeing spots from the reports and flashes of the gunfire in the cab. Tim is especially night blinded from the reflection of the flashlight off the windshield in front of him and has to turn on the headlights in order to drive them out of danger and back home.

Once the headlights come on, the same scene of horror from earlier reaches them. Infected are all over the road, and some are already approaching the SUV in response to the gunshots and lights. If Tim and the others were able to stay a minute longer they would have heard the two shots reaching out from the city and the impromptu gunshot conversation that occurs, but the spread out group of infected on the road all run at the truck when the lights come on. They have to leave quickly if they want to escape.

*

Everyone is silent on the drive down the interstate. Successfully making it away from Grants Pass put them all on heightened alert. Knowing that they still have to drive through Rogue River is a threat that increases everyone's tension as each mile disappears behind the vehicle. There is no sign of the horses or cattle that had been on the road when they passed earlier. They slow down and several flashlight beams shoot out from each side of the SUV's windows as they drive through the spot, but nothing is seen.

"We're almost at the turnoff," Timothy says. "Make sure your guns are ready and roll your windows down."

There is a comfort in having the windows up in a vehicle. As fragile as they are, it is still a welcome barrier to the world outside. That feeling of safety is just an illusion that can lead to deadly consequences, if trying to take aim at an attacker with a face full of glass fragments. That point is made perfectly clear as they drive back into Rogue River and a runner hits the right side of the vehicle while carrying a rock. Its hand with the rock bounces off the window frame by Megan's face, saving her a glass shower that evening. Tim is able to keep the vehicle at a speed that prevents any of the runners in the area from making a significant obstacle or grabbing on to the SUV somewhere.

Rogue River doesn't have the numbers of the infected that Grants Pass does. The town wouldn't have any if Eddie's group decided to clear the place out. It is a small enough town that they could have killed all of those that aren't stuck in buildings in a day or two. It was decided not to kill them off because anyone wanting to get to the ranch by road has to go through Rogue River, and the infected are considered an initial line of defense. No one can set up shop in the town to shoot at or otherwise harass the regular traffic from the ranch that comes through here.

The rest of the drive home is quiet, and the release of tension can be observed in the slumping shoulders and rolling heads of relaxing muscles. Tim calls ahead to the ranch from a mile out, and the gate opens for them as they drive up. Behind the guards at the gate's entrance is what seems like every other survivor living on the land; Isaac's people, the Stick People, and the original ranch members as well. There is some well-deserved confusion when only one vehicle returns and Simone and Eddie aren't with Tim as his group gets out of the SUV.

The people of the ranch had started to think that they were invincible or at least Eddie and his wife were. Nothing bad ever seemed to happen to them that they couldn't overcome, and most of the people gathered were expecting to welcome back not only the search team but the members of the missing crew that everyone went out for.

"Where are Eddie and Simone?" Arthur asks as the murmurs of speculation in the crowd start to grow.

"They are alive but trapped on a rooftop by the on-ramp into Grants Pass," Dianne tells Arthur loudly enough for the assembled crowd to hear.

The floodgate of questions is opened up, and everyone asks at once:

"Are they okay?"

"Where's the missing team?"

"What happened?"

Tim puts his hands up in a pushing motion to stop the crowd from talking. "I'll give you the basics of what we know right now and fill in the details to whoever wants them at the fire pit."

A fire pit was set up for people to gather around when important community messages were shared. There weren't any buildings that had the space for everyone to gather. Even the riding stable was filled up with partitioned living spaces instead of being an open area until enough camping trailers and RVs can be brought up for people to live in.

"We almost made it to the on-ramp into Grants Pass when we were surrounded by runners. I'm guessing the sound of our approaching vehicles drew them to us. I was able to back out quickly, but there were already about a dozen runners between our SUV and Eddie's truck. They tried to turn around and ram their way through to us, but they hit too many runners."

"After that, we heard more then saw them crash into something and then shoot their way to safety on top of a building. I don't know if one or both of them made it or if they are injured. They must have lost their radio, because we couldn't contact them on ours. We only know someone is alive because they lit something on fire and waved it to us after we shined a message with our flashlight."

"What about the missing group?" Isaac asks.

"We didn't pick up any radio messages, and we were calling regularly right up until we were surrounded."

The larger group starts to disperse. Most of the Stick People and Isaac's people leave but all of the ranch people stay. Along with Isaac, Jeremiah and their sister Mariah, Gayle stays to find out about her missing husband and son. A man named Jordan, whose brother, Aaron, is also with the missing crew, stays as well.

From the Stick People, Dave Cromwell and Sheila Jackson stay. These two spend most of their time around Jeremiah and Isaac or their people. Dave particularly understands how precarious his position is and only credits his survival to the arrival of Isaac's group. He isn't aware that Eddie had initially planned on killing him and the other's that weren't welcome, but understood that he wouldn't have survived anyway if they had been left behind.

"So what's the plan?" Arthur asks.

"We put a huge group together and go after them in the morning," Donald says.

"We shouldn't go after them," Jeremiah says to everyone's not so astonished looks.

Jeremiah is still bruised by the fact that he lost a group of men when he didn't take Eddie's advice. In fact, he is upset over every experience he has had with Eddie and his family, from needing to live at the ranch, to being insulted by the Atheist regularly whenever he expresses gratitude to the Lord. The worst part of the Keeper family is that they have everyone fooled as to the true evil they represent.

Jeremiah knows this isn't a disease but the devil's work and Eddie is evil to the bone. He is using food and shelter to buy people's loyalty. Eddie is evil and his helpful attitude and smiling demeanor are only there to pull people away from God and into the arms of Satan himself. That part he is sure of, but he can't get all of the others to accept it, not even his own brother Isaac. He has had some success with the people that survived the winter with him and some of the Stick People understand as well.

Mike is the one that Jeremiah appreciates the most. Eddie killed Mike's father, so Mike knows exactly what Eddie is capable of and what is truly in his heart. According to Jeremiah, that is why Mike asked Isaac to be able to stay with their group. Mike needed to be away from Eddie or he thought he would be killed next.

Jeremiah continues talking in the face of the surprised and angry looks that they shouldn't return to Grants Pass for a rescue.

"Eddie told me how dangerous it was going out there. I didn't listen and it cost my men their lives. Even tonight Eddie said no one should go but went along because he knew no one would listen, and what happened to him? Maybe they were alive when you left, or maybe they weren't. If Simone or Eddie did signal by burning something, how do you know they weren't warning you to stay away and not return?"

Isaac grabs Jeremiah's arm and shakes his head *no*. Even Isaac can see Jeremiah is more interested in Eddie not returning than in protecting anyone at the ranch from possible danger.

Jordan steps out away from Jeremiah and stands by Donald.

"I don't care if it costs me my life. My brother is out there, and I'm going to find out what happened to him."

Then Gayle, who was too frightened to go earlier, says she will head out with them as well. In fact, aside from Jeremiah and a few of the older survivors that wouldn't be able to help, all of the remaining people expressed a desire to go on the rescue.

For many of them, Eddie and Simone have become the glue that keeps the place held together. The Keepers have become a landmark that reminds people that they are home and safe. Even though it is an illusion, in a world where everyone has lost something or someone, there is a strange comfort in being associated with someone that has lost nothing. The Keepers are survivors and everyone wants that luck to rub off on them.

"Spread the word to everyone else that if they want to go on the rescue in the morning, they should be ready to go at first light," Donald says and the group begins to break up.

"I think we'll have to turn a lot of people away in the morning," Arthur says.

Donald smiles while they walk, and responds, "That's your job, Arthur."

Arthur stops in his tracks. "And who put you in charge?" Arthur calls out in a mock annoyance.

"I'm not in charge, Arthur, you are. That's why you have to decide who gets to go. I just feel bad for the poor slobs you tell aren't going."

Moving again to catch up with Donald, Arthur figures he should start his work now.

"If you want to feel bad for someone, feel bad for yourself. You aren't going either."

"Hey, wait a minute. I wasn't trying to be mean, so you shouldn't take it out on me."

"I'm not. You and your wife are taking care of Eddie's children while they're gone. That's what you have always done when they've gone away together, and I know they trust you to care for their kids if something happened to them. There are people here like Jeremiah that want to see Eddie and Simone fail, even if it brings the rest of us down as well. You have to watch their kids and make some plans in case they don't return."

This time Donald stops walking and gets lost in thought as Arthur heads back into the house.

*

"What the hell are you thinking?" Isaac asks Jeremiah. "Eddie and his people have taken us in."

"Damn it, Isaac. Eddie is evil. Why can't you see that? He's pulling people in with kindness and spreading his sickness of doubt and disbelief in God. He is evil! And it looks like he's pulled you in as well."

"I haven't lost my faith in God. I just don't believe this sickness is caused by demons. It is evil but it is the evil of man that made this sickness. If it were demons then Mariah would have been lost as well, but some people are immune, just like Eddie and his group have explained."

Jeremiah gives one last look filled with anger and frustration, and then all expression fades as his face goes blank. He turns and walks off angry that his brother can't see the truth of what is happening. His sister Mariah died at the store the day she was bitten, and whatever is in her body now, isn't the soul she was born with. No one is immune, bitten people are either possessed by lower demons and attack, or are possessed by higher demons to confuse the survivors and draw them away from the Lord. If this wasn't the case then he wouldn't have killed his wife and daughter. If there were really immune people then he could have let them live, but there is no immunity, only possession. He knew the moment after they were all attacked, killing them was exactly what he had to do.

I need to talk to my people about this, Jeremiah thinks to himself, and walks around the ranch gathering those that believe in things the way he does, to have his own meeting about the morning rescue operation.

CHAPTER 17
STANDING ROOM ONLY

Pacific Ocean.

Keith and Frank take the sailboat out, away from land. Each man is silent and in his own tortured world. Light clouds drift by high up in the soft blue sky. The hull running against the water sounds like the hushed roar of a waterfall, randomly interrupted by the slapping of a wave.

"George is still unconscious," Keith says from the bow.

"I don't know what's going on with Jack. Come here and take a look at his eyes. He's just staring out, and they look strange, all glossed over. Do you think he's in shock? You said he shot Ellen. Maybe doing that put him over the edge."

"I don't think it's shock, Frank. I think he's dying. His eyes look like death."

*

The sails are lowered and the boat is drifting. Keith and Frank say their respects to Carl and Ellen before lowering them over the side. The remaining few hours of daylight are spent hauling buckets of water out of the ocean and scrubbing the blood from the deck.

That night they have a fitful sleep complete with twisted versions of the gun battle and the infected arriving, this time without anyone escaping alive.

George woke up in the middle of the night long enough to scream and vomit. They aren't sure if his regurgitation was caused by radiation sickness or the concussion he received from the blow to his head. Whatever the cause, he has a rough couple of days ahead of him.

Frank wakes up and opens his eyes to the brightening morning sky. He looks over and then back to see Keith standing at the wheel and looking at the instruments.

"You don't look so good. Did you get any sleep?"

"No not much," he says in a distant voice still staring at the instrument panel.

"What's wrong?"

"The GPS is out. It might be because of where we are, but more likely, the satellites are starting to drop out of their orbits without ground based corrections. We still have the compass, but without the coordinates and our drifting through the night I can't tell exactly where we are."

"Let's head east, back to the mainland. Either we'll get a signal or we can figure out where we are based on what we see on land."

"Yeah, that's fine. It's just bothering me."

"What, the GPS?"

"No. Well, yes. That and everything else. I've been up for the last hour thinking about where we were and what we've lost. I don't mean us specifically, I mean the human race. We had seven billion people on the planet a month ago. How many do you think are left?"

Frank doesn't answer, and Keith didn't expect him to. He just frowns a bit and shakes his head.

"Have you checked on George and Jack yet?"

"No. I didn't want to go in there until you were awake. I don't expect Jack to still be alive, and I don't want to be the one to find him otherwise."

*

"George is awake," Frank calls out.

Keith lowers the sails and heads below.

"I feel like a mule kicked me in the face. Can you get me some aspirin?"

Frank hands him a bottle of pills and a cup of water.

"Don't drink too fast. You don't want that coming back up on you. Or on us, for that matter."

George swallows the pills and holds his hands to his head before asking, "What happened with those guys that tried to rob us?"

Keith and Frank exchanged glances. Frank shakes his head and points at Keith.

"They're all gone. The thieves and the others."

Frank brings his hands down and slowly looks around the cabin before returning his gaze to Keith.

"They shot Thomas and Carl first. Ellen died during the shootout while killing the attackers. Jack died last night from the radiation poisoning. We buried him at sea an hour ago."

"Just the three of us then?"

The two nod in reply, and the group shares a moment of thoughtful silence.

"We were moving when I woke up. Is there a destination we're headed now?"

"The GPS is out so we're heading back to the coast to get our bearings. After that we will head north and travel as far as possible before the ocean is too rough for us to continue. Then we either go to the mainland to be killed, stay in the Pacific where we can sink and drown, or find a small unpopulated island to spend the rest of the winter. My vote is go to the mainland and hang out with the locals."

"I'll vote against that choice, if you don't mind. I'd like to stay down here and think about what you just said. Let me know when you see land."

*

"George, the GPS popped back on for a while. We're right here on the map and heading toward San Diego."

"What do you think we should do?"

"I want to stop there and visit the zoo, of course. What do you mean what should we do? Head north, avoid any large islands, boats on the water, or shorelines."

"I know there is a certain danger involved, but I would like to get closer to the coast. I want to see if it is as bad as we imagine, but also think it will be safer for us. We should stay along the coast in case the GPS goes out completely."

"We still have the compass, but I get what you're saying. It's always safer if we know where we are."

*

Over the next eight days the trio sailed north. From San Diego to Santa Barbara all along the coast there is nothing but people visible on the shore. Two hundred miles of shoreline filled shoulder to shoulder and as far back as the eye could see, nothing but infected bodies standing and crying out to the ocean.

"We were approached three times by other boats and what did we do? We shot at them as soon as they headed in our direction," Keith says to the others.

"You shot at them too. Are you saying we should have done something differently, maybe let them get closer and ask if they were friends?" George snaps back.

"No, that's not what I mean. The people on board those boats could have been friendly but this isn't the kind of world where we can take those chances anymore. We did the right thing. Friendly or not, there are only so many supplies on board. We don't have a set destination to wait out the winter or a certain time frame where we think we can get to Oregon. We need to figure out what we're going to do."

"I agree," Frank says looking at George. "Going along the coast to see what was happening was a good idea, but we can't keep doing that.

148

Eventually a boat that we shoot at to scare away will keep coming. And no matter how much you want it to happen, no section of coast is going to open up for us to park the sailboat and go out for a stroll. Those infected people are everywhere."

"I guess I was hoping to make it onto the mainland somewhere."

"It isn't going to happen. The entire coast is a death sentence and the more time that passes the fewer resources other survivors on ships will have. People will get desperate and not care if we shoot at them, like Frank said. They might even try to ram us and sink us both in desperation. We still have bullets so they'll figure we still have food as well."

"I'm hoping you two have an idea where to go then, because I have no clue."

Frank just shakes his head, and says, "I was going along with Keith but don't have any ideas. Staying on the water by the coast will get us killed sooner than later."

"I think we have two options. The first one I don't like and give my *no* vote to right now. Oil rigs. We passed seven outside of Santa Barbara already, and I bet there's more along the coast. We could try for them, but I bet anyone on the water has tried them or is already there. They could also be filled with infected people like the islands."

"My second idea is outside of San Francisco. There is this little spot of an island on the nautical map. I checked in Carl and Ellen's maps for San Francisco, and it's called the *Farallon Islands*. It's closer to the mainland than all of the other places, twenty miles, but it's small and listed as a wildlife refuge. No one lives there."

"How are we going to survive the winter on an empty island?"

"It isn't empty. It has two houses or buildings. No one lives there permanently, look at this brochure I found. They must have gone there at some point or wanted to. I'm thinking the water up there has been rough for the last month, so many people might not have thought to head there."

"Or it could be covered with infected as well."

"That's fine too, because it's a small island where we can probably see from side to side. If the infected are there, we can kill them all and still go ashore. Once we're on the island, we can defend it from any boats that crash there with infected on board."

"And if there are people on the island already?"

They all look at each other entertaining the possibility of someone rejecting their ability to land.

"We deal with that when we have to and based on how they react to us."

"You seem pretty enthusiastic about this, Keith. I'll agree with you on the oil rigs. I don't want to try sailing up to one. It would be too easy to be shot from up above. What about you, Frank?"

"I say we go for the island. I want to get off the boat and sort through things on dry land."

"Okay. I'll go along as well. Let's head to the Farallon Islands."

*

"Maybe we should try for Hawaii after all," Keith says mockingly after their arrival to Farallon.

They circled the main island with tremendous effort due to the large ocean swells and found no dock or berthing point. The island's shore is a rocky mess that will tear apart the sailboat if they try getting close. It is covered with birds, seals, and many infected people who are scattered around attempting to catch and eat anything that moves.

"I think this will work," Frank says with mock confidence.

"I know you were joking, Frank, but I do think we can make it here. The land isn't packed with the infected, and they are too distracted to bunch up at one point or on the shore. They haven't even noticed us with all of the other boats anchored around the island, so we could go ashore in the dinghy and start killing them one by one."

"It looked to me that all the anchored boats have been here a while and no one seems to be on them, so no prior claims to the land. And the biggest positive is the boats themselves. If something happens to the sailboat over the winter there will be at least one or two other boats out there to choose from come spring. If they all wash away then the island with probably wash away with them."

*

Three days, one hundred and eighty six rounds, and fifteen dinghy rides later, the men are satisfied the island is clear of the infected. It will take several more days to transport all of the supplies onto the island and up to the researchers' buildings.

George is feeling nauseous again so they are leaving him on shore to guard the supplies. It seems seals are curious creatures and will gladly climb on top of any boxes people leave on the shore. Luckily it isn't December yet. Elephant seals are supposed to arrive then and there is no way to make an elephant seal move off of a spot it chooses to lie on.

*

Scavenging trips were made to each of the boats anchored off the island over the following two weeks. Various supplies were found, from guns, to food, to medicine. Nothing which they didn't already have but they appreciated finding it anyway. The real boon came from two different sailboats. They were both older craft, one was larger than Carl's boat and the second about the same size, but both were definitely older and had seen a lot of sailing. There were Ham radios in each of them. Those would come in handy in the spring when they were able to get off the island.

A treasure trove of board games, cards, and music was found the first night in one of the buildings. The three of them spent each night playing chess, checkers, and poker while turning through the channels of the Ham radio trying to find someone to listen to.

Turns were taken for cooking meals, they did laundry and dishes together, and they each had a generally good time. It was like being on an extended vacation in a cabin by the ocean.

Every morning the trio would walk around the island and check for newly arrived boats, parked or crashed, and any infected they may have brought with them. They never found a new arrival. If anyone made it out of San Francisco, they made it out early and went south if they were on the water. The waves really do get bad out here during storms.

The three managed quite well together until this morning. George died in his sleep.

He hid his increasing pain and sickness from them well. They had no clue he was dealing with anything other than occasional bouts of cabin fever. Frank and Keith were waiting for him to come down for breakfast and discovered his stash of empty pain medicine bottles. Things they collected at Cedros Island. He wasn't the type to abuse them and they didn't suspect an overdose, but with so many bottles, they couldn't be certain of anything.

The truth arrived when they moved his body and discovered his notebook. He must have found it among one of the scientist's things because there were notes about the wildlife on half of the pages. If the name *George* wasn't scribbled on the front, they would have stopped looking at it after the third page describing the actions of the Tufted Puffin.

The island is too rocky to dig a grave, so they brought his body to the shore and took him out on the sailboat to give him a burial at sea like all of the other friends they lost.

They spent the next few days taking turns reading the notebook to each other. He wrote about their whole adventure, the highs and the lows. The last ten pages he filled with descriptions of the pain he was going through and his sorrow at first discovering blood in his stool. On that entry, he wrote that he probably had a week left to live, and he died on the sixth day after the note.

In his final entry he wrote that he was happy with his decision not to tell them what he was going through. He didn't want to burden them with the constant thought of him dying. He knew they would miss him when he was gone and wanted to continue enjoying their final days together instead of becoming a poster boy of pity and pain.

George was a good man and a good friend. It was another week before Frank and Keith pulled out the card table the three of them had spent so much time at together. That night was spent with anecdotes about George and life. Only two hands of cards were played.

*

Time continued to stretch and the fun repetition of their activities turned into monotony and boredom. Cabin fever was setting in just in time for spring to arrive. The calming waters allowed them to once again head out on the sailboat and see the world. The coast was still full of the infected. Keith and Frank both thought they should have died out by now.

One bright note was discovering someone alive in Oregon that has become their regular radio pal. Frank made contact with a woman named Katherine on the Ham radio, and she knows who Eddie is. The bad news is she hasn't seen him since the first day of the collapse. It was still nice being able to speak with someone and get a perspective of what is happening on land. Not much of it is good, although Katherine says her group stays mainly on lockdown on a secluded property. She is always vague about her location, as if Keith and Frank could run to her house and knock on the door. The caution does make sense, though. Anyone could be hearing the conversation they are having if they tune in to the right frequency.

CHAPTER 18
THE RESCUE?

Grants Pass, Oregon.
Present Day.

It is approaching dawn and nearly a hundred of the ranches' current occupants are gathered outside the main house to find out if they can participate in the rescue. There are a mixture of reasons the people in this group have for wanting to go. Some are wanting to rescue their friends. Some are afraid things will fall apart if Eddie and Simone don't return. Others are just bored out of their minds at the ranch after living almost a year with the adrenaline of always being in danger. There is also a group wanting to make sure Eddie and his wife don't return.

"Not everyone will be able to go today, but we will still take a sizeable force to deal with however many infected we run into," Arthur calls out to the crowd. "We will be taking ten trucks and forty people.

"You could fit a lot more of us than forty in ten trucks," someone calls out.

"Yes, *we can*, but we won't. If the numbers of running infected in Grants Pass were the same as they were a few days ago, then we could get by during the day with a much smaller group. However, things are worse. Our problem is that we don't know how much worse. It could be so bad that even the forty people that go might be in danger of not returning." Arthur pauses to look around before going on. "You have to understand that if you are chosen to go, even though you will be with a large group of shooters, you might be riding to your death."

"That's an even better reason to take more people," another person calls.

"We did think of that. However, if the situation is so bad that forty people can't make it out of the city, then an extra ten or twenty people probably won't make much difference either. It is either safe enough for forty or it isn't safe enough for anyone."

"This isn't just a rescue mission either," Donald says. "If we are able to clear areas safely then we are going to take this opportunity to pick up as many camper trailers as we have running vehicles, so ten campers.

Those of you that aren't leaving in thirty minutes should prepare your gear as if you were going, because if everything works out, we may send a second group out to get more campers after the first group returns."

"I'll be calling out the names that I decided can go," Arthur states and starts calling names.

Jeremiah isn't very happy to see Arthur deciding who will and won't be going. He thought everyone that wanted to go would be able to. He had arranged with several of his men that they would go out and try to kill Eddie instead of allow him to come back to the ranch. Fortunately, his brother brings up the point of freedom to travel quite forcefully with Arthur.

"I thought we were free to do what we think is right on this ranch? Why are you telling us who can and can't go? We have eight working vehicles just among my group, and I think I will go whether you say I can or not," he says fiercely to Arthur and the crowd. "Don't think you can exclude us just because we aren't from your original ranch group."

"Please calm down, Isaac," Arthur says in a placating manner. "Anyone that wants to go is free to do so, of course, but I spent a few hours last night splitting people up based on their skills to make sure we didn't send all of our bakers or mechanics or nurses into danger at the same time. For instance, Isaac, you are on the *don't send* list not because you aren't an original ranch member, but because you are your group's leader and we can't have our group and your group both potentially lose their leader. You can go if you want, but I would hope that you don't put your people, and frankly the rest of us, in that position. If I don't call on someone and you are dead set on going, please check with me first and I can ask one of the people with your particular skill set to stay behind on your behalf."

"You could have mentioned that first," Isaac says a bit embarrassed and receives some good natured chuckles that break in the tension.

"I'm good at getting things done on the ranch, tools and equipment. I never said I was good at dealing with people," he offers, causing more chuckles and a few outright laughs, and then he continues with the list.

Jeremiah is surprised when his name gets called and is pleased when two men of his trusted group also make the cut. This could be the opportunity he needs to take out Eddie Keeper and his wife. Unfortunately, the seating arrangements for each vehicle have also been decided. Jeremiah has been separated from his men because, like himself, each of them have experience with hooking up and towing camper trailers. He doesn't have time to make new plans before they leave, but each of his men nod at him and at each other to signify they know what to do if given the opportunity.

The trucks leave the ranch and drive into an uncertain fate as the morning grows brighter, and the sun is fifteen minutes from rising.

*

"Simone, wake up. It's getting light enough to kill some of them," I say looking out at mob of infected that are circling or just hanging out near the building we are on.

"How many are there?" she says with her eyes closed and refusing to move.

"Take a look. It's about fifty, I think. If the damn things would stay still I could get an accurate count."

"I guess we're not waiting for a rescue party then?" she asks still not wanting to get up.

"The more we kill the safer it will be for anyone that comes for us or the missing scavenger team. I don't want anyone driving in here to have fifty of these bastards jump on their trucks like they did to us last night."

"Okay fine, I'll get up, but let me pee first."

"I think my shoulder will be fine now, so you can keep that stuff away from me," I say jokingly.

"You're in a good mood this morning. Why is it you are so cheerful? I feel like crap."

"I think it's the bite. I got a fresh batch of Zeus into my system, so I'm feeling kind of numb and invincible."

"All right, Hercules. I'm all done, so you can start your rampage," she says smiling at me while pulling up her pants.

I walk up to Simone and kiss her. "I think Hannah is alive. I think that was her shooting last night."

Simone smiles back at me, and I step away to begin shooting at the people waiting for breakfast to fall off the roof.

"We only have twenty three rounds to shoot, so I need to clear the area around the truck to get more ammo. Let me do all the shooting. I plan on taking slow shots and let these sickos know that if they hang around they will all be eating pavement."

My first shot kills a man by the truck that was trying to climb up to us. The shot gets all of the others attention and about ten of them move closer to the truck to attempt their own climb.

"Is that how you cleared the infected out of the area when your group went in?" Simone asks.

"Yeah, pretty much. Our shots were slow and deliberate, and after a while, you could see the infected moving off to try and find easier prey. These things don't like dying any more than we do apparently." I shoot one that managed to climb into the truck bed and it falls into the small crowd of them below causing that section of bodies to stumble backward.

"Oh my God! They are looking at the one that fell?" Simone says while pointing.

The infected are working through the problem before them. They see that one of their own has been killed, and they are hesitating to continue their assault on the truck.

"Now watch this, Simone. I'll try to get them to back up."

I take careful aim and kill three more infected that are six feet away from the truck. The remaining infected look at the fallen zombies and back away. All of them are now at least six feet away.

"See, they still understand distance and are trying to get outside of the kill zone. You know what this means, don't you?"

"Yes, but what do you think it means?" she asks not completely aware of what could be going through his head at the moment and braces for him to tell some sick or corny joke.

"It means these faster infected have either retained more of their humanity than the slower ones did or the parasite is able to control them to a much finer degree using the former cognitive functions of the host. I have to assume for the sake of my own sanity that the human side of them is gone forever, and they are just brain dead eating machines."

"Okay, that's what I was thinking too, and if they're not?"

"If they're not then I'll feel worse about killing them at the end of the day, but they are still just people trying to eat us if that's the case. Unless one of these things starts speaking or holds up a white flag one day, I'm going to assume that they aren't running up to me to give me a hug."

With a shake of my head and a shrug, I start shooting at the crowd again, which is starting to edge back in closer to the truck. Four rounds later my pistol slide locks back. It's empty, so I switch to my shotgun. The blasts from it are louder and more devastating to look at for everyone involved. The infected are retreating back to the road, and while a few are still just backing away, most of the others are already running away in the opposite direction trying to find easier food or trying to get to safety.

I feel pain with each shot now, like I did several days ago in the city, when we first saw the infected behaving in such a careful way. As dangerous as these things still are to everyone, I feel like I'm a poaching hunter that isn't just killing one or two lions, but I'm killing the whole pride just for fun. Of course it isn't a fair analogy, because I wouldn't feel the same remorse if a whole pride of lions was a threat to my family. The difficulty is that these were once regular people, and by their new behavior, maybe they still are.

There are seven shotgun shells remaining, and I load four into Simone's gun and three into mine.

"I'll jump down to the truck and lift the ammo bag back up to you," I say right before I jump down.

Only one of the infected at the road makes a run for me. The rest seem content to wait and watch to see what will happen, and not so surprisingly, when Simone kills the runner as it approaches, the rest of the infected at the road turn away and run back toward the city.

*

When the group of trucks reach the edge of Rogue River they are greeted with a small crowd of the infected that were drawn to the road by the vehicles passing through last night. The people in the first four trucks are only able to stop and wait while fifteen infected surround them in an attempt to get at the tasty people inside. Everyone except the drivers from the last trucks step out and start shooting the infected as they walk up to the front of the line. In less than four minutes all of the infected that surrounded the first trucks are dead, and several more that were attracted by the shooting also lay dead in the road or off to the side.

Arthur even organized the placement of the trucks for their drive into Grants Pass based on people's abilities, and this first encounter proved how vital his planning is to the group. The best shooters were made to ride in the rear vehicles for encounters like the one they just had. As a result, even with the infected pressing against and trying to climb onto the first four vehicles, there were no close calls or errant shots going through a window.

The shooters of Eddie's ranch have spent the last eight months practicing. Every day there was practice, even during the winter months, and often indoors. They would usually use the airsoft guns in one of the houses, but it wasn't odd to find them shooting a pellet rifle for practice in the bunkhouse. In the riding stable, a pulley system was set up for targets to give them motion. Someone would run the lines making the targets move erratically and the others would practice.

The only time shooting dropped off was in the month after the huge attack. People weren't sure then if it was worth fighting for their existence anymore. Slowly, people started to practice again, and as soon as each person took their place behind a gun, they remembered the comfort and security it can provide when pulling the trigger. Eddie mentioned to Simone after that experience that he will make daily target practice a requirement immediately following any tragic event at the ranch to help rebuild people's confidence. The constant practice and reliance on guns as therapy has turned his group into exceptional shooters.

The convey makes its way through the rest of Rogue River and experiences no other crowding incidents. Several more individual infected are shot at or shot and killed as they attempt to approach the passing vehicles, but none pose a risk to stopping or slowing the group's progress.

There are no infected to be found, at least no runners now that the trucks have made it onto the highway. There are two slow moving infected walking along the road away from Rogue River that don't even seem interested in the passing trucks. The policy of avoiding gunfire to prevent detection has been decidedly changed with the behavior of the new runners. Now, any infected person that someone see's should be shot immediately if there are enough people to deal with any extra infected that may be attracted by the noise. Now more than ever it is a numbers game that the remaining humans have to overcome. They can no longer wait for the infected to starve to death. The arrival of the runners has turned the disaster survival clock back to day one. Kill them now or they kill you later.

"What do you think of it so far, Erde?" Samantha asks their resident scientist and ender of humanity. "How are the runners getting here if they are staying in the towns?"

Erde was chosen to go on this trip because he should have firsthand knowledge on how the infected are behaving. Before now he was discouraged from accompanying any groups because his particular skill set has the potential to help create a cure or at least inoculate everyone to help them become immune to the disease like Eddie and a few others are. If at all possible on the return trip, they are going to try and capture a runner and a walker, if any walkers can be found. A holding cell has been created just outside the walls of the ranch to contain the infected. It's a place where experiments can be safely done.

"It is strange that the infected don't appear to be leaving the towns and cities. At least none of them appear to be following us. What is more likely, though, is that they are keeping to the forests for concealment as they travel so that they are able to surprise any prey they come across. That is a guess. My specialty is not in animal behavior."

"Still, you haven't been out here very often, so what do you think about what you've seen so far? I mean, them seeking cover and leaving an area if too many of the infected are getting killed. They don't seem to be mindless creatures that have forever lost their humanity any more. That part is bothering me. It's bothering a lot of us that these are really just sick people that might be able to be cured one day and we are just killing them."

Erde sits quietly thinking for a while. He isn't thinking about the questions Samantha asked him because he has gone over those same things on his own over the last few days trying to figure it out. He has tried to understand what people have told him they've been seeing in the new behavior of the infected. What Erde is trying to figure out now is how to respond in a compassionate way.

Two days ago, when he had this discussion with Eddie, he came right out and told Eddie that more testing is needed to find out what is going on. He would have to have infected test subjects and possibly some regular people to infect as well to find out what the relationship is between what a person once was and what they become. Eddie let him know that he appreciated his frankness but Erde should be careful around the others on speaking so coldly and scientifically. Especially about infecting regular people just to try and find out what is going on. He said what happened at Wal-Mart with Stockton's people was a one time deal and not to expect coming across any more murderous or rapist gangs they could capture to do testing on.

So Erde is trying to come up with a way to tell Samantha what he truly believes must be done in order for him to understand and conquer this disease without her thinking him a monster.

"I am a chemist by training and expertise. All of my skills are in laboratory work, in research, so it is most natural for me to want to get into testing right away. If I could get hold of a good supply of chemical testing supplies and laboratory equipment I could start testing blood samples of the infected by introducing it to blood samples from uninfected individuals. Eventually though, without the ability to conduct tests on apes or other primates, I would need to progress to human transmission studies. I would need to study an individual that I knew a good deal about before the infection to properly determine what if any of that individual remains after infection."

Samantha looks at Erde with a slight expression of distaste at the subject but understands where he is going with his thoughts.

"So would that tell you how to beat this thing, or if it is curable, by testing people?"

"Unfortunately, no. For a real study of what this does to a human, we would need a functional Magnetic Resonance Imaging machine. We would scan the brain before and throughout the infection process to be able to determine to what extent the parasite kills off the human side of the infected brain and replaces it with its own programming or needs. Without an active MRI during the change, all of the things I am able to determine through laboratory testing will just be speculative. So, unfortunately, I fear we will never know for sure."

"Thank you," Samantha says and turns to look out at the passing tree line to ponder about the lives that once belonged to the occasional wrecked or abandoned vehicle they pass.

*

"Are you up for a stroll?" I ask Simone.

Looking down at me from the roof, she smiles and nods. "I want to find my daughter." she says and lowers herself over the edge, and then drops down to the truck's hood.

"Do we have enough ammo?" she asks jokingly knowing there is an extra backpack full of ammo and other supplies that I keep in our truck.

"I'll split the ammo between our two packs if you write a note to our potential rescuers where we've gone."

"They're going to think we're crazy heading into the city on our own after what we went through last night."

"They think we're crazy anyway, Simone. At least they think that about me. You're just guilty by association."

We start walking into Grants Pass to find Hannah and the rest of the missing scavengers after duct taping a note to the back window of the truck's cab and loading all available magazines.

*

Timothy Weyland is the in the lead truck for this trip back into Grants Pass. His and Dianne's experience with what happened last night are essential for the trip's success. A mile out from the city he calls out over the radios to remind people of what they will be heading into.

"Last night the road up ahead was overrun with the infected. There were too many for us to even consider attempting a rescue in the dark, and the noise of Eddie and Simone crashing and shooting undoubtedly brought more. Even with our numbers it could be an overwhelming situation. If it looks to be that way, we'll need to turn around and head back or at a minimum stay at a distance to try and clear some of the numbers. Let's play this smart and not lose anyone else. Hopefully we can save everyone and still pick up some campers as well."

Jeremiah is hopeful that the situation is desperate and horrific. The more chaotic it is during the rescue attempt the easier it will be for him or one of his men to shoot Eddie and Simone. Any friendly fire *accidents* will be blamed on the inexperience he and his men have with shooting at the possessed people. Jeremiah and his two men are each in one of the first three vehicles, so whatever they run into on the road ahead, they will be able to make some of the first shots.

"I can see some bodies on the road in the distance but don't see any runners yet. Everyone slow your vehicles down and watch to the sides to make sure the runners haven't spread out to form an ambush. The bodies you see are most likely the ones that attacked our vehicle right before we left last night. We should start seeing the crowd of runners soon."

The vehicles drive in at a crawling pace. They are keeping things slow, expecting a wave of the infected to wash over them like the quick onslaught of an avalanche, but no such danger presents itself. Only two runners are seen up ahead in the distance, and they appear to be running away instead of getting closer.

Everyone's morale is on a roller coaster ride this morning while they approach what was obviously Eddie's and Simone's last stand. There is a turmoil of anguish and excitement in some at seeing so many of the infected lying dead in the area around Eddie's crashed truck, but the turmoil is from not seeing them on the roof of the building against which their crashed truck rests.

Jeremiah feels only elation that the devils are dead. With Eddie and Simone out of the picture he is confident that his brother Isaac will take charge of the entire group and his leadership will keep all of their combined people safe. Not just from the demons in this world, but Isaac will keep their spirits strong and rejoicing in God's love so they can be taken into his loving arms when they die. Jeremiah knows there isn't a place for him in Heaven and only feels contentment that he will soon be able to have someone remove himself from this world the way he did for his loved ones after they were bitten.

All of the vehicles pull to a stop at safe distances from each other so some form of maneuver and escape is possible if they need to retreat again. The passengers exit the trucks somewhat clumsily while holding on to their assorted rifles, handguns, and shotguns. Still, no infected descend upon them.

"Set up a perimeter and check the bodies for Eddie and Simone," Timothy calls out. "They have to be out here somewhere." *They must be here. They wouldn't have gone off on their own,* he thinks to himself.

After a cursory look, no one finds their bodies.

Jeremiah smiles at the idea that Eddie and Simone are now walking around and possessed somewhere. His smile ends quickly though when he remembers that Eddie has been bitten before. *Is this what Eddie wanted?* Jeremiah thinks to himself building a horrible realization in his mind. *He wanted me and my men to come out here so he could lead hordes of the possessed against us and wipe us out. Or worse, right now he is leading an army against the ranch.* He is about to yell out his fear that the ranch is under attack and they should head back when one of the men finds something at the truck, and calls out:

"There's a note here!"

After Eddie and Simone left earlier, a runner came up to the truck and pulled off the note that they had stuck to the back window. It remembered that things people leave on paper can be important and wanted to get rid of it but didn't have the cognitive capabilities remaining to destroy or carry the note away from the area. The note was dropped on the ground by the truck, where it was only noticed among the refuse of this littered and destroyed world because it is paper and couldn't have survived the elements in its clean condition.

Before the note is read, gunfire is heard not too far in the distance from where this rescue group is set up. That sound can only mean survivors, and there is a collective intake of breaths as heads rise and turn in the direction of the noise which gives them new hope.

"Read the note," Timothy yells at the man.

"It says, *We heard a gunfire signal last night after you left. Our missing group is still alive and we are going out to find them. The infected fear us, but use caution. Stay in the open away from blind corners where they can approach. Simone and Eddie.*"

"Should we walk or drive?" Timothy asks Dianne.

"Both. If we take all the trucks with us the entire way, we'll get jammed up if we have to make an escape. We can drive in and leave a truck turned back this way every few blocks. That way if we need to fall back with injured people we can truck hop all the way down the line until everyone is able to get in. It will allow us to have a walking line of shooters until that point also."

"Did I tell you I wanted to marry you before the world fell apart?"

"You might have mentioned it," she says and smiles.

"Well, I still want to."

Most of the group has moved back to the vehicles expecting to load up, but a few are standing by Timothy and Dianne and hear their exchange. They are all fighters. Not by trade before the collapse, of course, but have grown into the hard, watchful men that we all used to watch in movies. When they are on the job they are always looking for danger.

Nine months ago every one of them would have given Timothy a hard time about his open tender moment with Dianne and included her in a bit of good humored ribbing about holding on to his balls. Now with more bad than good occurring, none of them say a word, and a few of them even smile at the interaction. They hope that they too can find a woman that can not only be deadly accurate with a gun but lay out a sensible ambush and escape plan the way Dianne does.

More shots ring out in the distance ending the few seconds spent in a better place.

"Everyone get in the trucks. We're going to slowly drive into the city to the area the scavenger group was supposed to be set up. Dianne suggested that we drop off a truck every few blocks so we have vehicles along an escape route out of here if we need them, so that's what we're going to do, any questions?"

Jeremiah wants to ask why they can't just leave the Keepers here but knows not enough of these people view them as a threat yet.

"What should we do?" whispers one of Jeremiahs men to him before they split up to get in their respective vehicles.

"If you get a clean shot without being obvious, then take it. But make sure it doesn't look like you are targeting them. We need to get rid of them, but I don't want people to start distrusting Isaac. He is the only one that can lead our people once the Keepers are gone."

"What about you, Jeremiah? I thought we were doing this to get you in charge?" the man asks clearly confused.

"I'm lost already. I can't guide you any more than Eddie can, and I'm no leader like Isaac either."

For the briefest moment the two men see pain flash across Jeremiah's face and seem to understand how he wouldn't want to be in charge of leading the group after losing his wife and daughter the way he did.

"Let's get going," he says to his men and they get in the trucks.

"Some rescue, huh?" the driver asks Timothy and Dianne when they get in. "We should have known. Eddie seems to have spent so much time around cats that some of their nine-lives rubbed off on him."

CHAPTER 19
CHANGES, DECEPTION, HEARTACHE, DEATH

Grants Pass, Oregon.
Present Day.

Mike feels the slow pull of waking hit him as his body is being rocked back and forth. He can faintly hear his name being called, and it feels like he is waking up in his bed back home in a time before the world fell apart. His mind puts together the pieces of where he is and what happened last night, and wakes up seeing Hannah leaning over him and shaking his shoulder.

After hearing the returned gunfire message last night, Mike and Hannah knew they were going to survive. Until that message came though they had spent the better part of the day trapped and believing they would never escape their rooftop prison. The infected were behaving differently, more aggressive, and didn't give them the opportunity to make it back to their vehicles to escape. At least being trapped enabled them to find out where all the runners are coming from.

"Mike, wake up. They're shooting again. I think my parents are starting to make their way to us."

As comforting as the news of rescue is, facing Hannah's parents after everything they have been through together puts a bit of fear in him, especially the prospect of seeing her father. Eddie seems to be a fair man and being trapped in Grants Pass isn't Mike's fault, but blame for Mike and Hannah's current situation lies squarely on his shoulders.

"Your father is going to kill me."

"It's not your fault we got stuck up here together."

"Being stuck here isn't what I was thinking about."

"Nothing that happened is your fault or something you should feel guilty about. You may be two years older than me, but it was my decision to be here and to do the things that I have done. If my dad didn't want me going off with the scavenger groups then he shouldn't have trained me to be such a good sniper," she says and then smiles. "Besides, I was the designated sniper yesterday, so if anyone is responsible for us being here, it's me."

"The shooting stopped. Is that bad?" he asks.

"No, the shots were all in one place so they haven't moved anywhere yet. They're probably just driving the infected away from them. I'll know when their gun shots are moving closer to us."

"You won't really be able to tell the difference, will you?"

"A few years ago we were visiting my mom's grandparents in France. The first big Muslim uprising happened while we were there. It wasn't just in Paris like, they said on the news. They were driving around everywhere in the backs of pickup trucks. There were huge groups of them driving from town to town—killing anyone they found along the way."

"We heard the sounds of gunfire approaching the village we were in, and were lucky to be far enough away from the city that the French military forces drove past us, to stop the terrorists advance before we were reached. You'll be able to tell when gunshots are approaching us, trust me."

*

The morning walk is anything but relaxing and fun. Simone and I are circling each other as we continue moving west down NE E Street. With just two of us, we can't simply walk back to back because our sides would be left open to attack. Staying in constant motion and letting the infected know that any approach means death is how we are staying alive. Most of the area we are walking through is still open space, no buildings or trees, but we are reaching the problem area now. The greatest causes of danger are the spaces between buildings. Any infected person can make it to the center of the street to attack us quite easily at a full run, and they can build that speed up in alleys, roads, or open property between the buildings we have to pass.

At the first intersection one infected does make a run for us as we move through and become visible. Two more make the attempted run after we pass a few more buildings. When we cross into the fourth intersection we see four infected just standing there to the south of us, not moving, just watching as we cross.

"Don't shoot them," I say. "Just keep walking through and see what they do."

Once we are out of their line of sight, we move out of the street and over to the door of an abandoned Domino's Pizza. I raise my shotgun to the ready and motion for Simone to follow me to the edge of the building. I creep to the corner and expect to have the runners bolt around in pursuit at any moment, but I don't hear footfalls to indicate movement, fast or slow. I peek quickly and pull my head back, but don't see anything. I look again, and then step out away from the building.

"They aren't there anymore."

"I see one," Simone says and points to the other side of Domino's.

At the opposite end of the store, one of the infected has its head popped around the corner, just the way I did.

"They knew the direction we were headed and were going to get us on the other side," Simone whispers.

With the apparent element of surprise gone, the four infected bound out from the side of the building and charge at us as we fire and back away at the same time. My first shot hits the lead runner square in the chest, the blow knocks him back into the second runner and they both fall. Simone shoots with her pistol. Three quick shots and a third runner falls. She starts to spin around to make sure we aren't getting attacked from behind, and I shoot at the fourth runner that is attempting to weave in avoidance of being shot, but disturbingly, is still running at us.

My first shot hits his shoulder and makes him spin around. I pump my gun to load the next round, and when he is facing me again, he just stops. It is probably his spin that caused him to stop, but for a split second before I pull my trigger it seems like he has given up. Not just given up his pursuit of us, but given up his will to live. Before now they would always run away when injured, or at least try, and he just stands there looking right at me as I pull my trigger.

Simone shoots several times behind us at a threat I don't yet see. I'm focused on the second runner that seems to be trapped under the first one I shot. It is smaller than the one on top of it and looks like it broke one of its legs in the awkward impact and fall, but that doesn't explain why it isn't struggling out from under the dead infected to come and get us.

"Eddie, there are several more behind us, but they're too far off to hit with my pistol. Use your rifle and let them know we have a long reach."

"Okay. Just watch that the one that's stuck over there. I don't know if this is another trick, but it isn't coming after us."

I let my shotgun hang by its sling and pull my rifle off my back. Raising it to my shoulder, I look three blocks down the road through my scope at the infected hoping to sneak up on us at some point. I pull the trigger, and the body falls showing me my hit is good. I scan again and spot one trying unsuccessfully to stand behind a tree. I pull the trigger again and that one falls as well. Three others that must have been hiding behind other objects run in scattered directions away from us. I watch for a few seconds to make sure no others try to approach.

"Is everything good?" I ask

"No Eddie, something is wrong."

"I mean are we clear?"

"Yes. No infected on the sides or where we are headed, but there's something wrong with the infected that's trapped."

We both walk up to it, and it doesn't give the gurgling moan that we have grown accustom to. It almost hisses at us, but the sound is still too deep and throaty to be called a *hiss*. It looks at us and snaps its teeth a few times in our direction, or rather I should say, *she* snaps her teeth at us, because this infected is a woman. Her right arm is stuck under the body that has her trapped, but her left arm reaches up to us a few times and grabs at the road in a vain attempt to grasp our shoes.

"Maybe the fall hurt her back," Simone offers as an explanation, but the woman's legs are still moving around a little, so she isn't paralyzed.

"I don't like it. Whatever is going on with this one, she is too human for my liking, but we can't leave her here." And I point my gun at her head.

Simone turns away. I'm not sure if she is checking behind to make sure we are still clear or if the scene playing out in front of us is just too disturbing to witness, but she misses what I have to watch. This woman, the infected I am about to shoot, drapes her arm over the body she is lying under and lowers her head to the pavement looking straight up at the sky. Her jaws continue to snap at a meal she is no longer interested in, and she lets out a moan I am familiar with. There is still the gurgle that comes from the infected when they are trying to get us and can't reach, but the tone is all wrong. It sounds like she's in pain. It is the sound of sorrow.

I pull my trigger, and the sound of mourning stops. Looking at the woman and the man again, I understand why she didn't struggle to get away. Her sound of defeat and sorrow all make sense, and I grab Simone and pull her around to show her what I see.

"That's the reason she didn't struggle to get away," I say while pointing at the woman's hand.

They had matching wedding rings.

*

"You do know where the scavenger group is, right" one of the men asks.

"I know where they should be," Timothy replies. "They were supposed to check out what was left in the Safeway Grocery store on G Street. There is also a food supply warehouse right next door. Between the two places there would have been plenty of items to stockpile for pick up, so they should be near one of those buildings."

"It feels good being out like this. I mean, it gives me a strange hollow feeling seeing everything empty and quiet, but being able to be out here, just walking along the road feels good."

Timothy just nods. He understands what the man means but isn't able to share in the feeling. All he feels as he walks down the road is dread and apprehension. He is bothered by the fact that he doesn't see any infected running around or any bodies lying in the road. The city looks like all the people just disappeared. The fact there are no bodies is also bothering him, because if Eddie and Simone came this way they should have been attacked at some point, and there aren't any freshly dead infected anywhere.

"Has anyone seen anything?" Timothy calls out. "Any infected or any bodies?"

He watches as one man runs up from the rear. It's Jordan, a man from Isaac's group. Jordan's brother was with the scavenging group that went missing.

"I saw a body on the road to the north. We're on F Street now. If they took E Street they could have pulled a lot of the infected that way," he says.

"Hey Timothy, I think we have something that needs checking out up here," a man calls from the front of the group.

The group is all coalescing at the front, and Timothy runs up to see what is so distracting. A small gun shop named *Fox Firearms* is set back off of the road.

"You know Eddie's rule," Dianne tells Timothy.

He nods. The ranch has more than enough firearms and ammo for people to use, but Eddie made a rule for when stockpiles or gun shops are found. Firearms and ammunition are a priority when out scavenging. The goal is to keep large amounts of guns out of the hands of people like Stockton. So even on a rescue mission like this, unless someone is known to be injured, collecting the guns takes precedent over everything else.

This store has a closed door and barred windows with no broken glass. It looks completely untouched, and the business sign is the only thing that has been damaged. It is laying on the ground. If the group had been driving by they probably would have missed the small sign on the door saying what the place was.

"Are we stopping here?" Jordan asks, clearly irritated.

"If the group is stopping for now, why not let me and a few men scout ahead to see if we can find them?" Jeremiah asks before Timothy can reply to Jordan.

"You want to take a small group ahead to look for Eddie and Simone?"

"I want to look for our missing people. I do know some of them, like Jordan's brother, Aaron."

Timothy is unconvinced by Jeremiah's good intentions but doubts the man would be dumb enough to try attacking Eddie when so many people are out here looking for him and his wife.

"How many people and whom would you take you?" Timothy asks.

"I have two men with me that I know and trust. No offense, Jordan, but I think you might be too wrapped up in seeing your brother and might compromise a smaller group if we had to run and you didn't want to."

"You feel confident you and two other men can safely move around out there?"

"Yes, I do."

"Just as confident as you were when you sent those men here that died?"

The statement was a slap. It was intended as one and that is how it was received.

"I know I underestimated the possessed people before, but this isn't the same situation. It's daytime now. We haven't seen or heard a thing since we got here, and I am offering to go as well." It takes everything he has to keep the answer on a level tone and not draw his gun and blow Timothy's brains out. *Your time will come, Timothy, but right now I need to get Eddie.*

"Good, grab your two men and follow me," Timothy says walking in the direction they just came.

The four of them stop at the back edge of the group, and Jeremiah looks at Timothy like he has lost his mind.

"I think we're facing the wrong way," Jeremiah says.

"No, this is the right way. I'm not going to send three men with minimal experience into the heart of unexplored territory in a city that could have thousands of infected individuals running around. Not even men that are loyal to you, Jeremiah," he says hinting at his distrust. "I am willing to send you three to the last truck we left and for you to bring it back here to the gun store.

"We will need a truck to load up whatever we find inside. If you want to be helpful, go get that truck." Timothy then steps up to Jeremiah to tell him directly, "I don't believe for a minute that you are so desperate to see Eddie, his wife, or any of the other missing people return that you are willing to go out ahead of our group alone to do it. Come back with the truck or don't come back." And he walks back to the front.

"Jordan, pick nine other people to go with you and check ahead for your brother," Timothy says when he returns.

*

"Do you hear that?" Simone asks while gripping my arm tightly.

"My ears are still ringing. What am I listening for?"

"Someone is banging something, down that way, I think," she says while pointing south.

"Let's check it out."

We start walking south on 9th street and ahead on the right side of the road I see the food distribution center that was one of the scavenging targets.

"Damn. I had us walking too far north. That's one of the buildings they were supposed to check."

"I told you to ask someone for directions," Simone says in a smart aleck tone.

I want to respond in kind but my thoughts are pulled back to the infected couple we just had to deal with. *I wonder if Simone and I would stay together if we were both infected.*

"Mom! Dad!"

Hannah and Mike are waving to us from the roof of the Safeway sitting at the other end of the parking lot we are next to. Simone grabs my hand, gives it a squeeze, and starts running across the parking lot. I do a fast walk toward them but keep scanning the area for any infected surprises. There are bodies scattered everywhere, and I don't want to have any of us jumped by an infected that is playing dead.

At the ground below Hannah and Mike is a pile of bodies, many of which are lying on top of the ladder that should be on the roof.

"Eddie, help me move these bodies so we can get the ladder out."

"You stand guard while I move the bodies. We don't know if you're immune yet, and I don't want you getting cut or getting their blood on you."

She smiles, nods, and starts talking to Hannah while I begin getting my hands dirty.

"Hannah, did anyone else make it?"

"I don't know. Tyler is on the roof of that building over there," she says pointing east. "We can see him, but he hasn't moved since yesterday. I think I see him breathing when I look through my scope, but I'm just not sure. Mr. Bradley is dead. I saw him get killed when the infected swarmed out of that building next door. I don't know what happened to Aaron or Ashley. They were on the north side of the building where Mr. Bradley was attacked."

"I've got the ladder free. Help me get it up."

"You did not just say that Mr. Keeper," Simone says while shaking her head at me.

I shrug and give a small smile. Normally I would be laughing along with her about my unintentional sexual reference, but the things we've been dealing with are hitting me harder than I thought they would. I don't like ambiguity surrounding my actions. Either I do something good or I do something bad. If it's bad, I hope I have a good reason to do it.

Simone pulls me into a hug, but our assorted hanging firearms clang into each other and prevent a true embrace making the comforting gesture somewhat awkward.

"Are you all right, Eddie?" she asks quietly.

"I don't know what's going on. I can kill people if I think they are a threat to us, and I haven't lost sleep at night when I've done it. I can kill the infected when I know they are mindless eating machines, but I'm having a serious problem killing the infected if they are just extremely ill people, no matter how dangerous they are. That couple back there, it's really getting to me. And not just that, another one earlier just seemed to stop and wait for me to kill it. It seemed like it just gave up."

"Eddie, you're so sweet," she says in a loving and non-sarcastic way, but it still makes me feel like a heel. "I remember just over a week ago you were going *on and on* about how unfair it was that Jim Margrove and his wife were killed."

"Yeah, but he was killed by a drugger."

"Yes, a person with an illness that makes them violent and dangerous to be around."

"Okay, I see your point, but I still feel horrible about that couple."

"I'm not going anywhere, Eddie. I love your tender side, and I wish you knew how great it makes me feel when you say things like that. I think you're projecting."

"I am worried about losing you, Simone. I don't know what's going to happen with Jeremiah."

"Mom, Dad, Hello! Do you think you could put the ladder up?"

"Thank you, Hannah," I say sarcastically. "I appreciate your timing as always. I see your ammo bag is down here with the ladder, should I bring it up to you or was it an offering to the infected?"

"Dad!" she says in a frustrated tone. Her demeanor has changed in the last few days since other kids and teenagers arrived. She is reminding me more of the carefree young girl that she used to be than the cold, monotone girl she became after Steven died in our attack.

"Let's get up there so we can find out what happened," I say finally smiling.

I sit on the edge of the roof and enjoy the sun hitting my back. The early morning air is still cold. Hannah and Mike are sitting too close together for my liking. This is a huge empty roof, and they are side by side.

"How about we get some space between you two?" I suggest bluntly.

"Oh my God, Dad," Hannah mumbles.

Mike, however, gets a look of sheer terror on his face, and all color drains from his features as he moves away from her.

"Why don't you let us know what happened yesterday?" Simone offers trying to get us all back on course.

"Well, we have some great news," Hannah offers looking at Mike and smiling, and then back to us.

"Hannah, if you think Mike is your boyfriend or that you are even old enough to have a boyfriend, it isn't great news," I say more angrily than I should.

I get a chorus of *no's* in return. Hannah says *no* in a hopeful questioning way. Mike thrusts both of his hands up fearfully and says *no* with his eyes wide and a shaking head. Simone looks at me and tells me *no* like I just farted loudly in an elevator.

"No?" I question.

And again I get three *no's* in return.

"Dad, you are so embarrassing. The good news is that we know where the runners are coming from."

Finally some information I can wrap my head around.

"Hello up there? Anyone send for a rescue party?"

Everyone gets up and looks down to the group below.

"Hello, back. We didn't hear about a need for a rescue party, but if you're in need of one we'll gladly help out," I say back to some smiles but one very concerned face.

"Mr. Keeper, is my brother Aaron up there with you?"

"Hannah was just starting to fill us in on what happened yesterday. She says Aaron and Ashley were on the other side of that building when a horde of runners came out of it. You have a good sized group with you, so we can come down now and help you check it out."

"Hannah, Mike, I'd rather have you stay up here than down checking the building."

"Dad, I'm fine. We got rest and had food to eat. The only thing we dropped yesterday was the bag of ammo. I want to help."

"I didn't mean stay out of the way. I meant stay up here. Load your gun and watch for trouble."

Hannah gives me a smile before I head over the side on the ladder.

"Aaron was at that building?" Jordan asks while pointing.

"On the other side, she said. Wait, Jordan. Don't just run over, listen. Most of the bodies lying here came from inside that building. We need to be careful when we go over to check it out. Let's spread out and go slow. Two of you should head over to that other building and check on Gayle's son, Tyler. Hannah said he's on the roof but hasn't seen him move since yesterday. Be careful in case he's infected."

The group slowly spreads out in the parking lot and heads for the last known whereabouts of our missing persons. The east end of the building is an unusual design, like two Quonset hut buildings squished together, and they are connected to two large warehouse sized squares. The piecemeal structure is large and stretches almost the entire two blocks in length.

Semi-trailers are parked along the side of it, and as we move past the third trailer, we see a large hole, ten feet tall and six feet wide, in the side of the building. It looks like a truck trailer backed into the building at some point and made the hole.

"Jordan, do any of you have radios?"

"Shoot, I forgot to tell you. We have another thirty people just down the next street at a gun shop we ran across. They're only two blocks away. I didn't grab a radio when we left, but we'll be able to see them if we go to the intersection."

"Okay, two more of you split off and go down the street to let everyone know where we are. Ask them to send us another ten people. We might have a big building to search. Who's in charge of the group?"

"Timothy. And he's not real happy with Jeremiah right now."

"That's Jeremiah's problem, not mine."

"It's about you."

"Jeremiah's just jealous that I'm so good looking," I offer as a joke to take away from what I am sure is a serious situation. Timothy is an easy going guy and wouldn't get upset unless it was justified.

"Jordan, it's your call on how we proceed."

"You trust me even though Jeremiah's causing problems?"

"I trust Isaac and Isaac's people. If you were one of Jeremiah's men, Timothy wouldn't have sent you out here to find us. You also seem military, so you should be able to get us through the searching we need to do in and around this building without major issue."

The two that went to check on Tyler return and don't have positive expressions.

"Tyler is alive, but not doing too good."

"Was he hurt or bitten?"

"No, we couldn't find anything. There were no bites or blood. He just lays there or sits there. However we moved him, that's the way he stayed."

"Catatonic?"

"That's the word. Yeah, I think he just checked out. We tried to give him water but it just poured out of his mouth. So we laid him down and came back."

"Thanks," I say. "We'll grab him when we leave. Jordan, what are we doing?"

"You six stay here and guard the hole. All of those infected his girl Hannah killed came through here, and there could still be more inside. Eddie, Simone, Charlie, you come with me and we'll check along the north side of the building for any other entry points or signs of where Aaron went."

"What makes you think Hannah killed all of those infected?" I ask as we walk around the side of the building and into the street.

"I came on the first scavenging run, and she was the lookout for us as well. Your girl can shoot, but Mike, not so much." Pointing to three bodies up the street next to the building, Jordon asks, "Did you and Simone shoot them earlier?"

"No, we came down from E Street, straight to the Safeway. Let's go see."

"Simone, Eddie, I'm so glad to see you're all right." Melissa and Brian carpenter walk up with a group of eight other people from Timothy's group. "Is Hannah here?"

"She's up on the Safeway roof. Do either of you have a radio?"

"Yes, take mine," she offers.

"Thank you." I grab it wanting to get re-established with the world. "Hannah, we have a radio now, can you hear me?"

"I hear you dad."

"Timothy, do you hear me."

"Good on this end, Eddie."

"There are some bodies outside of a second entrance into this building. We think Aaron and Ashley might have been forced inside by runners and might still be trapped by them. We're going to clear the building—"

I stop talking when I hear the report of distant gunfire. Coming from the east, the direction we all came. It isn't just a few shots either, someone or rather several someone's are shooting a lot of rounds.

"Hannah, Timothy, do either of you have eyes on that?"

"It's too far away, Dad, and there are buildings in the way."

"That's the direction I sent Jeremiah to get a truck," Tim says.

The shooting stops, and we all start jogging east to meet up with Timothy and the rest of the group.

*

"Hi Timothy, Dianne." I nod at them. "Erde, I'm surprised to see you here," I say with a stern look at Timothy.

"He needed to see how the infected behave in person."

"I'm also hoping we can capture one or two for blood tests," Erde says in his own defense.

"You know what happens to us all if you die, Erde. Don't kill the human race twice in your lifetime."

It is a horrible thing to say, but it's the truth. So far no one else we know is alive that has any grasp of working with or identifying toxoplasmosis in order to culture an immunity drug for the remaining uninfected. He created this illness and released it on the world, and right now, only he has the ability to protect us from it.

A truck is speeding up the road at us so we all step off to the side. Jeremiah is driving and starts to slow down, but when he is right next to the group, he slams on the brakes and slides another twenty yards past us. He struggles to get out of the cab, and I see a body in the back.

"Phillip's been shot. He needs help!" he yells while grabbing the man in the back of the truck and trying to pull him out. "They're coming. We have to get out of here!"

"Mom, Dad, you need to run!" Hannah yells over the radio. "Look east! Look east!"

The group as a collective turns around and looks down F Street from where Jeremiah just arrived. A swarm of infected are running right at us from half a mile away.

"It takes two minutes to run half a mile. Samantha, get Erde on the Safeway roof now. GO!" I yell. "Everyone else follow Jordan to the building we were going to clear. There may be infected inside but that is your best bet to survive. There aren't many entry points and we can kill a lot of them as they try to squeeze in to get us. Run now!"

"It looks like hundreds of them," Erde says from behind me.

I turn and grab his arm trying to get him to leave.

He pulls his arm away, and tells me sternly, "If you want me to save the rest of us, I need to see them." And he puts binoculars back up to his eyes.

I kneel down and get my FAL aimed at the oncoming crowd. Several other shooters line up next to me, standing or kneeling, depending on their preference.

A minute and a half.

"This is interesting."

"Erde go!" I yell and start shooting at the rampaging death ahead of us.

The bodies start falling in the distance, but the swarm doesn't stop. I have to change my magazine and look quickly to make sure Erde is gone.

One minute.

I stand to resume shooting and slowly start walking backward. One step, two shots. One step, two shots. The bodies keep falling. The runners keep running.

Thirty Seconds, time to run.

I turn to run and only Simone is still with me. My FAL is empty so get ready to toss it in the back of the truck as I run by. I don't have any more 7.62 ammo on me right now so I won't be needing it. I didn't calculate the time right. We have our guns and packs on and won't be able to outrun this group. If we drop our packs we lose all of our ammo.

"We have to drop everything and run or we won't make it," I yell.

She waves at me and climbs into the driver's seat of the truck, which is still running. I jump in, and she takes off just as the leading edge of the runners are about to hit the tailgate.

"Tunnel vision," I yell to explain myself.

"That's why you have me," she says as she speeds toward the building everyone else is trying to climb into. "Once we're in the yard, I'm going to jump out and run to Hannah. You take the truck and block that hole in the wall."

I don't have a chance to respond before she takes the corner, hops the curb, and knocks down one the few remaining portions of fence still enclosing the semi-trailer parking area. She mostly stops the truck but leaves it in gear, and does exactly what she said she would. She jumps out and makes a beeline to the Safeway building. There aren't any runners here yet, and she has Hannah on the roof to cover her progress so I know she will make it. I do an awkward jump-slide across the bench seat and twist the wheel to get the truck turned around.

The last few people jump into the hole in the side of the building, and I drive the truck up against it to help block the hole. I open the driver's door and lean to get out but remember in time to lock the passenger door. Unlocked car doors don't stop the runners.

I hear shooting farther inside the building so there are still infected inside the place. I take four gulping deep breaths of air to calm my nerves and clear my head before I turn back to the entrance with my KSG raised.

Bullets are flying through the opening as the runners pile up outside and start climbing over each other to get in. It is a sickening feeling to watch them continue to advance on us when there are at least twenty guns pouring lead at the bodies coming through the hole.

My shotgun is out, so I switch to my pistol. The shotgun is more devastating, but I don't have the time to reload. A runner makes it in and jumps from the truck onto one of our shooters, someone I don't know. The infected are starting to pile up in the hole, but it is too large to get plugged up and the bodies of the dead keep shifting and rolling over each other onto the floor. Another one makes it in and bites into a second shooter. He looks familiar but I can't remember his name. We have to start backing up as more runners are making it into the building.

They aren't making much progress once inside, but it takes our aim away from the opening helping the infected increase their foothold in the building. I switch to the next magazine and keep shooting. Jeremy is a few feet off to my right, trying to pick up a magazine for his gun that he dropped. I shoot a runner that is headed for him and turn to shoot another just before it makes it to me.

There are too many of them, but I keep shooting. We all keep shooting. What else can we do? I watch Jason Anderson get killed, a runner bites into his neck before any of us can adjust our aim to save him. Jason's eight year old son Christopher died in our attack over the winter. I hope for a second that his wife Rebecca isn't here but that second passes, and I see her run to his fallen body.

The slide on my gun locks back again, so I load my last magazine. I put the gun in my left hand and I draw my machete with my right. My left hand isn't as steady as my right but accurate aiming isn't required at a distance of two or three feet. I step forward into the infected onslaught, shooting and slashing until I am between Rebecca and the oncoming horde. There are still too many making it in. I shoot, they fall, more advance. One grabs me and is shot by someone else. Another grabs me and I shoot it away. Shoot, slash, shoot, shoot, slash.

My gun is empty. I drop it and continue swinging wildly with my blade at anything that tries to get to Jason's body or Rebecca. Four more shooters appear to my right moving forward and are able to start pushing the runners back. They are finally killing the runners faster than they can come in. I turn to grab Rebecca wanting to get her farther into the building, get her to safety, but it's too late. She is lying on the floor next to Jason with her gun still resting in her mouth.

I turn back to the fight with my machete raised and see that we are winning for now. The infected have been pushed all the way back to the truck again. Then everything goes black, and I feel like I am falling.

CHAPTER 20

RECOVERY, DISINTEGRATION

Oregon.
Present Day.

It must be late. It so dark I can't see a thing. Reaching up to my face I feel bandages covering my face. I try and lift my head to sit up but feel the room start to swirl and it falls back down.

*

I can hear a mumbled conversation somewhere nearby.

"Who's there? I hear you. Why can't I see, what's going on?"

"Your vision is fine, Eddie. I'll get Simone so she can tell you what's going on. Stop trying to sit up."

"Don't push me back down, tell me who you…."

I feel the room spinning.

*

"I'm sorry, he hasn't woken up……I think we just need……Maybe tom..."

*

"Is someone there?"

"Eddie, it's Simone, I'm here. Don't try to move or get up. You'll just pass out again if you do."

"Is that what's been happening? Why can't I see?"

"There are bandages covering your eyes," she says, and I feel her grab my hands. "Eddie, you were shot. Don't tense up, just relax. You were shot in the head, but it mostly grazed you."

"What is mostly?"

"The bullet chipped the back of your skull on your left side, took off most of your ear and scraped along your cheek. You were shot from behind. Do you remember anything that happened?"

I think about the question for a while and remember where I was before things first went black. The scenes all flood back and the fear of battle makes me try to jump up and continue fighting.

Everything spins.

*

"Are you sure you don't want to get some rest? It could be a while before he comes back around."

"I'm awake," I say to whoever is there.

"Eddie, it's *Michael Palmer*."

"I'm here too, sweetie," Simone says.

"Eddie, I'm going to change your dressing. If you can stay still and remain calm, we can make sure your vision is okay as well."

"I thought you said I could see?

"You didn't take any direct impact to your eyes," Michael continues talking while un-wrapping my head. "But any time there is major trauma to the head certain processes can get damaged or affected in minor ways. You'll know when we take off the bandages if there is any change to your vision."

I grunt my understanding, and then ask the next thing I need to know, "How many were lost, Simone?"

"Maybe now isn't the best time."

"How many?"

A few seconds pass before she quietly says, "Sixteen."

I purse my lips, take a deep breath, then rub my eyes and open them to a dimly lit room. One lantern is on in the corner and is burning on a low setting.

"Erde?"

"He's alive, and so is Hannah."

"How is Rachel doing?"

Rachel Anderson is the sixteen-year-old newly orphaned daughter of Jason and Rebecca, the two people that died next to me before I was shot.

"I wasn't sure if you knew what happened to her parents."

"I was six feet away from Jason when he got bitten, and I saw her run to him. I moved out to stop the infected from getting to her as well, but she killed herself while I had my back to her. That was right before I blacked out."

"Rachel isn't doing very well, a little better today, but yesterday was extremely bad for her. It was pretty bad for all of us."

"Have I been here for two days?"

"Just for a day and a half," Michael responds. "Do you remember everything that happened around that time?"

"I can still see it all pretty clearly. We were finally starting to push the infected back to the opening, or at least other people were. I was out of ammo. I turned to get Rebecca away from the front but saw that she was already dead. Then I turned back around to see the infected being killed at the truck before I went black…Where was Jeremiah?"

"He didn't shoot you, Eddie," Michael offers. "He was shot before he drove up to your group in Grants Pass. Timothy stayed by him in the warehouse during the fight to make sure he wouldn't try anything."

"Then one of his men did it."

"The two men that he took with him, Phillip and Greg, were killed when they were first attacked by the infected. Greg was attacked by an infected and shot wildly hitting both Phillip and Jeremiah. Phillip was dead in the back of the truck when he pulled up to your group, according to several people there, including Timothy."

"Someone shot me intentionally!"

"Someone did shoot you, but from what I heard it was crazy in that building and not everyone is a good shot. We have three other people that were shot. One of them shot himself by mistake."

"We were winning, Michael. The infected were fifteen feet in front of me and our people were between me and the infected. There was nothing left in the warehouse to shoot at where I was standing."

"I don't know what to tell you or what you should do about it. Get better and then you can start talking to people yourself to find out what happened."

I nod slightly in agreement, knowing there isn't much I can do right now.

"I have to see some other people, I'm sure your lovely nurse will be able to take care of anything you need."

Simone smiles, and waves. "Bye, Michael. Thanks."

He walks out the door, and Simone sits on the bed next to me.

"How are the kids?" I ask.

"They're fine, when they aren't being terrible. They're calling you *Zombie Dad* now," she says while holding her hands up and making claws. "Because you can't die. I think Olivia came up with the name. I was crying, of course, and she said *Don't worry mom, dad is better than a zombie cause he can get shot in the head and live. He's super zombie dad.*"

"I would prefer *Super Dad* over *Zombie Dad* but I guess it'll do. Tell me though," I say grabbing her hand, "who did we lose?"

"I need to get Erde and Hannah in here first. They both have information that you need to hear that is connected to who we lost. I think they're both in the house. Just give me a minute."

"Could you bring Arthur in, as well. I need to know what he knows."

She gives me a strange smile and nods before heading out.

*

I'm sitting up against the bed's headboard as they walk back in. I need to see people's faces when I speak with them to gauge how serious things really are. While I feel a bit nauseous, the throbbing sound on the side of my head goes away.

Simone walks in, followed by Arthur, Erde, Hannah, and Mike. I don't want Mike here, but I'm glad he is here just the same. He has been living on the farm with Isaac's people, and I can get an idea of how things are going there by his reactions and answers when I speak to him.

Hannah leans over and gives me a hug, and then sits in one of the chairs. Mike stands next to her, and Erde stands at the foot of the bed.

"Eddie wants me to tell him who we lost. So I think your information on *why* is important to give him now as well." Simone sits down by me again and begins the new list of losses. "You already know we lost Rebecca and Jason. We also lost Joshua Langford, Randy's son, and Jessica Palmer, Daniel's wife"

"Jessica was out there?"

"She went to rescue her sister, Ashley," she says with sadness. "We also lost Brian and Melissa Carpenter, and Randy, Arthur's brother."

I look at Arthur and understand why he has been leaning in the corner with his head down. The people we lost were close to us all, but Arthur lost his brother and nephew.

"I'm sorry, Arthur. I can't believe anyone let Randy go to Grants Pass. I don't even remember seeing him there."

"He didn't go with the group. He had a heart attack yesterday," Arthur explains. "The losses of the winter attack destroyed him. He couldn't take the stress of losing his son as well."

"How is Patricia doing?"

"She is taking it better than I am," he says. "They both knew his health wasn't the greatest anymore, and I think she was preparing herself for him to be gone these last few months."

We exchange nods and commiserating looks the way men do in silence and give one last nod as a signal to move on.

"What about Brian and Melissa? Where were they?"

"They were in the building with you. I was told they were killed at the other end while they were clearing the infected from the back, they were attacked from the side by some infected that were in a small office. They were bitten and weren't immune," Erde explains.

I count them off on my fingers, seven so far.

"And the rest?"

"The rest weren't from the ranch. Phillip and Dale Gregory, they were brothers from Isaac's group. Greg and Anthony Whitlock, they were a father and son from Isaac's group. Luke Simpson, the man from Isaac's group whom we met on the drive back to the ranch the day they arrived. Peter Gregory, a cousin of Phillip and Dale. Stephanie Clayborn and Joanna Sutton, who both came in with the Stick People. And of course, Gordon Bradley, Gayle's husband.

"Who the hell let any of the Stick People go into Grants Pass? They aren't ready for that."

"None of us were ready for what happened in Grants Pass, but they weren't there. They died here at the ranch due to complications...they starved to death. They were weak when we rescued them and they were too sick to hold any food down. We had simple saline bags set up, but it wasn't enough. We couldn't save them. There are another four, possibly five from that group that won't make it another two days for the same reason. Another three possibly from infections, but we have them on heavy doses of antibiotics so they have a chance. A small chance."

Mentioning Gayle's husband, Gordon, reminds me of the catatonic boy that was stuck alone on a roof for a night. "Is Tyler okay?"

"He is doing better. He's eating and looking around now. His mother is taking care of him. He shouldn't have gone with the scavenging group into Grants Pass. He wasn't ready, but his father insisted that he go. Then he had to watch what happened." She turns her attention to our daughter. "Hannah, you should tell your father this part."

"They ripped him apart," Hannah says bluntly and shakes her head in anger. "We were still setting things up when the runners broke out of that warehouse. Tyler had his ladder up for the escape route onto the building he ended up stuck on. Mike and I didn't have time to set up our sniper position, though. We were still carrying our ladder and supplies to Safeway when it happened. The hole in the side of the building was blocked when we walked by it, but the runners were obviously able to pull whatever was blocking it away and stream out at us.

"I heard something crash and turned to look. Runners were pouring out of the building right at Mr. Bradley. I watched Ashley and Aaron disappear around the side of the building, and Mr. Bradley ran toward Tyler who was already climbing the ladder. Mike and I had to run the rest of the way and put the ladder up quickly. Thankfully I made him go up first. He grabbed me and pulled me up when the infected hit the ladder—knocking it down. I dropped the bag with most of our ammo, and our radio and would have fallen down as well if he wasn't there." She puts her hand on his shoulder, and says, *thank you,* to him. "Once Mike pulled me up we looked back to Tyler. He was lying on the roof, and the infected below were tearing at what was left of Mr. Bradley. That's when we found out where the runners are coming from."

I look at Erde, expecting him to take over, but he points me back to Hannah.

"The runners are infecting the walkers!"

She smiles knowing this is a good piece of information and continues.

"All the noise the runners were making attracted few walkers. When the runners saw them, they ran to attack. The walkers even tried to turn to get away but they were bitten anyway. They didn't get torn to pieces, like Mr. Walker, each one was bitten a few times and then they were left alone."

"I'm not following you," I say.

"And I'm not finished," she retorts giving me a stare. "So I start shooting them. I keep shooting expecting that they will take off like they always have when they start losing too many in a group, but they hang around and give me more target practice. I keep shooting, but I leave the walkers alone. I like seeing them moving around slowly like they used to. Then, about six hours after the walkers were bitten, they start to run."

She ends her speech in a *ta-da* kind of gesture, like she just pulled a rabbit out of a hat.

"So the runners are infecting the walkers? But we tested a walker biting Stockton's men and it made them run. I thought they already had the running variant in them."

"The walker we used for testing had been bitten by a runner recently," Erde explains. "I noted some fresh bite marks on that walker, but it seemed irrelevant at the time. Now we know where all of the runners are coming from. Any remaining walker will be attacked by the runners to increase their numbers. And with each walker they infect, their swarm grows. But that is not even the interesting part. I think I know the answers to *why*. *Why* there are runners, *why* they are attacking walkers, and *why* they are swarming."

"Enough with the dramatic pauses. Could you just tell me, please?"

"They are starving to death," he says with a shrug implying simplicity. "If you remember, the infected were finally starting to starve to death. That is why everyone felt it was safe to start travelling. But the Toxoplasmosis gondii parasite is a living creature and requires a living host. The late stage of starvation the infected are in is essentially causing the body to eat itself. The breakdown of the body systems caused a mutation, or rather a change, in how the parasite manipulates its host. It needed the infected host to become faster and more dexterous in order to catch diminishing prey.

"The runners are attacking walkers to increase their numbers just as they did during the initial outbreak. But walkers would most likely turn into runners eventually anyway, once their bodies reach a critical starvation point. The runners attacking the walkers is just speeding up the process.

"They are swarming together in an effort to cover a greater area and find more food. They are no longer interested in infecting the remaining human population. They will do to us what they did to poor Mr. Bradley. They will consume us entirely if we are caught."

"So making people immune is irrelevant at this point?" I ask.

"Oh no, immunity will still help people survive if they are attacked and can get away. And it will be even more important two or three months from now."

"What happens then?"

"By then the infected should all be dead." He puts his hand up to stop me. "Yes, I know what you want to ask, why seek immunity if the infected are dead? The infected will be dead but not the parasite. The dead bodies of the infected are already in our lakes, rivers, and streams. They are rotting around the world and animals are consuming their corpses, allowing the parasite to continue existing. My engineered parasite could possibly never go away, but as long as the remaining human population is inoculated with the unaltered parasite, there will be no more outbreaks of this zombie disease."

Erde finishes his speech and everyone's expressions fall into concerned frowns, the exact opposite of the cheerful smiles I expected from this news.

"Let me guess, none of this matters because a giant meteor is about to strike the Earth and kill us all," I offer trying to lighten the mood.

No one is amused.

"The infected are swarming now," Erde continues. "They are desperate and virtually unstoppable, like locusts sweeping through a field. We are already unable to leave the ranch and go into the cities for supplies because they might follow us back when we return."

"So we wait them out. We have wells for water and enough food to last for another five months at least without rationing anything, more than enough time for them to starve."

"They will find us before they all die. Some already have," he says.

"We have been getting runners at the fences throughout the day," Simone tells me. "One or two at a time, but they are coming. And those are just the loners, eventually we could get hit with a swarm. There are runners swarming in Medford as well, which means we could see a larger group of them hit us than during our winter attack. And this time it won't be an army of frozen, barely moving people that are easy targets."

"How do we know they are swarming in Medford?"

"Greg called us," Arthur offers. "They got set up south of Medford and let us know what they were seeing in the city."

"Does he have enough food for him Lilly and Jessica to make it until the infected starve?"

He shakes his head. "They don't have enough food, and there are eight of them."

"Who went with them?"

"That new group of people you ran into on the way back to the ranch. The ones forced to trade sex for supplies."

"They all left?"

He nods.

"That woman named *Heather* took her baby out there?"

"Yes, she did," Simone says cutting in. "They all spoke to me the night they got here and I explained how things used to be."

"How they used to be? But you weren't sure what the future at the ranch would be like," I ask.

"Basically, yes. With all of these new people I don't know what's going on now or what will happen. And with you letting that psychopath Jeremiah live next door, I don't know how long any of us have left, with or without the infected."

I flush a bit red at being chastised by Simone in front of everyone.

"I thought we agreed that there wasn't much of a choice in letting Isaac's group come here."

"I don't mean letting them come here, I mean letting Jeremiah live. Apparently Jeremiah wasn't very supportive of the efforts to send a rescue party out, and Timothy personally thought Jeremiah was going to try and kill you when he offered to go ahead of the group to *look* for us. If he is sending people out to kill you or trying to do it himself, how safe do you think our kids are?"

The outburst has me and everyone else stunned to silence. I don't know what to say and not just because she has information that I don't. She has to be pretty pissed for it to come to the surface like this right now.

"I didn't know what Timothy thought or that Jeremiah was causing problems for a rescue mission. I assume he didn't like us being on the rescue list. If you think he is posing a threat I'll look into it, but don't know exactly how to take care of him," I say all of this while looking back and forth between her and Mike.

Mike, of course, has been living with Isaac's group, and from what I understand, has been spending most of his time around Jeremiah and not Isaac, so the issue is particularly sensitive in this setting.

"That's what I don't get, Eddie!" she is fully yelling at me now. "I've had to deal with you nearly dying, *how many times in the past week*? I'm getting sick of it. I don't know if it was that damn bite you got, but you've changed. Jeremiah is a threat to you, he is a threat to me and the kids, and when there is a threat to our family, you deal with it. You always have, but not now, and I want to know why?"

"Mike, would you mind leaving Hannah here for a little while? Go on downstairs but don't leave. I'll need to speak with you before you head back to the farm."

Simone puts her hand to her face in an obvious sign of frustration. Whether she is frustrated more with me and my inaction or her own betrayal of confidence in front of Mike I'm not sure. Once Mike is gone, Simone shakes her head at me.

"I am so sorry, Eddie," she says. "I completely forgot he was living at the farm. He is with Hannah so often now I just forgot."

"But you aren't sorry for yelling at me I take it?" I ask and smile.

"No, I'm not. Now what's going on?"

"I am trying to keep track of what's going on but my main reason for not acting on anything is *Isaac*. I'm not doing anything because I think he's a good man, and he has a lot of good people in his group as well. As much as I like Arthur, and Timothy, or the others that have been here since the collapse, they aren't going to be running things if something happens to us, Isaac is. And if Isaac has any kind of bitterness to our family and friends because I execute his brother with no just cause—"

"No just cause?" she says interrupting me. "Everyone knows he wants you dead and us gone. Even you think one of his people tried to kill you when you were shot. I know you have your own way of doing things, but I'm afraid for our kids on this and I'm used to you keeping me informed."

"Eddie, I have to side with Simone on this one," Arthur says. "Jeremiah is a danger to us all, and it was his own brother that brought that to your attention in the first place. How can you give him the benefit of the doubt when you weren't willing to do it for those others at the store?"

"I know what most of our people think I am capable of, and yes, I guess most of your opinions are right. That doesn't mean I will continue killing potential threats if the group thinks I shouldn't. I've been trying to deal with this in a more reasonable and civilized manner since you intervened with how I planned on dealing with Dave Cromwell and the other people we weren't going to bring with us."

"They aren't exactly the same type of threat that Jeremiah is," Arthur offers.

"What were you planning on doing with them? You weren't planning on just leaving them behind?" Erde asks.

"No. I was planning on killing them when we left. I thought they posed the same type of threat that a reporter named *Chad Hansen* did. He wanted help, and I refused him. That refusal ended with him amassing the army of infected that attacked us last winter. Leaving Dave and the others behind would have been no different. They knew they would die without us and would have every reason to join up with the next bunch of criminals that came through to try and kill everyone here at the ranch and steal the supplies."

"So you knew them for a few hours, thought they might be a threat, and decided the best thing to do would be to kill them?" he asks.

"Yes."

"And you planned on doing this on your own?"

"Yes, of course, but I was talked out of going through with it by Arthur and several of our other ranch leaders. I am often brutally vindictive to those that could harm people I love or care about. By any measure of rules, it is wrong, but I stopped living by the rules when your Zeus creation erased everything else. Playing by the rules and being civilized puts me and my loved ones at a disadvantage against every hateful criminal that is still alive out there. So *no*, I'm not ignorant of the severity of my decisions, and I do understand it is an extreme and morally wrong thing to do. However repugnant someone may consider my actions to be, my family is alive and well because of them."

"Mr. Keeper, I think you are misunderstanding what I mean when I question how quickly you decided those people should die. Out of everyone left alive, I have done considerably more evil, albeit unintentional, with Zeus. I also did not make it from Portland to Grants Pass with Emily without having to do some very questionable things to survive. I'm just surprised that you came to the conclusion that they should die so quickly, but then determined you were wrong and let them live."

I pause for a moment, curious that his words weren't an outright denunciation of me.

"I don't think I was wrong about them. I didn't go through with it because I value the opinions of my group. That's also one of the reasons why I haven't done anything about Jeremiah. I don't want to run this place on the fear that anyone I dislike will get killed. I respect the opinions of the people here and don't want to alienate them."

"I think Arthur and Simone should have let you do exactly what you planned to keep everyone safe," Erde says firmly. "I was speaking with Mike earlier. He mentioned how frustrated Isaac has been since the day at they arrived here because Jeremiah is spending most of his time with Dave Cromwell and Sheila Jackson. Mike said Jeremiah spends more time with those two and himself than he does with his own people now. They seem to have a fair amount of interest and input into Jeremiah's actions. You should speak with Mike about it. He was very candid with me. For the amount of time he said he spends with Jeremiah, I wasn't convinced that he really liked the man."

"I am aware of Dave's and Sheila's influence on Jeremiah. I've been keeping track of what he has been doing, or had been until a few days ago. Now before Mike runs and tells Jeremiah that I am being encouraged to kill him, would you all mind leaving for a while and sending Mike up here so he and I can have a chat?"

Simone gives my hand one more squeeze, and before she heads out I say, "I will still do what I need in order to keep our family safe. With so many more people involved, I'm just trying to be smarter in how I do everything."

Erde nods and leaves as well.

"Arthur, I'm sorry about Randy. My life wasn't worth the trade for any of the people we lost, but especially not your brother. He was a good man."

"Thank you," Arthur says and walks out.

CHAPTER 21

SETTING SELF-DESTRUCT

"Eddie, you need to do something," Simone says desperately. "Jeremiah is in the riding stable again preaching about demons."

"I know."

"Don't tell me *I know* all calm like that," she yells. "He has most of the Stick People on his side now, along with Isaac's people as well."

I stand up and pull Simone into an embrace she tries to struggle away from at first.

"There's nothing I can do to stop him now, except walk in there, and kill him. You know what would happen to us and the kids if I did that. Those people aren't just his friends. They are obsessed followers."

"Go out there and talk to them," she says forcefully while pulling away. "Tell them—"

"Tell them what, Simone? Tell them what they already know but don't want to accept?" I say back in frustration over the whole situation. "Every one of those people knows what Erde did in creating this mess. They all know where this thing came from and have the same information we do, but they are scared about something we can't change. Jeremiah has them fearing for their imaginary souls and craving an un-provable happy afterlife. Facts and evidence can't compete against that kind of storytelling when people are waiting for thousands of infected to climb over the walls."

"What are we going to do? He isn't attacking us yet in his sermons, but it can't be far off."

"I'm going to take care of this, but I have to send the kids away first."

"That's why you're so calm. You have a plan, don't you?"

"Yes."

*

"Greg is that you," I ask over the Ham Radio.

"I'm here, Eddie."

"How is your set-up there? Michael tells me you have a secure location where you don't have to worry about the swarms."

"We have to worry about them, but we set up some remote control sound towers to pull them back to Medford if they start heading out our way."

"I have been working on something like that myself today." I lower my head unable to keep the happy banter going. "Greg, I want to send you my children."

There is a pause before we hear back from him. "Eddie, I have to warn you, we didn't take much in the way of supplies with us. Only what we could carry in one truck. We are lucky to have made it where we are with what we have."

"Supplies aren't a problem, Greg, but a safe place is. I want to send my kids along with Erde and anyone from the original ranch group that wants to go to your location. Simone and I will be staying here, but I want a place at least for all the younger people like Donald's son and daughter, and Ashley Dixon. I was hoping to send the people out to you with two semi-trucks full of food, guns, and ammunition. I even want to send Michael Palmer and his family out there so you'll have an EMT on hand."

"Eddie, is it that serious?" A woman's voice asks over the radio.

"Who is this?"

"It's Katherine Montgomery, from your store."

"Katherine, you made it! I can't believe it. How did you end up with Greg?"

"One of our spotters saw a truck trying to outrun a small swarm the other day, so we set off one of our sound towers to draw them away. Some of them turned away, but we still had a good fight on our hands to kill the rest that were after them. We brought Greg and his group to my place after they told us their story. He didn't tell me who the crazy guy is that keeps letting people onto his ranch, and I didn't think it would be you. What happened to building an Ark and not letting strangers on after the rain started?"

"You remember that huh? I was never good at taking my own advice."

"Or you are too big a softy to turn people away."

"Katherine, I bit off more than I can chew on this one. I tried keeping my enemy closer, but the guy that is the lead troublemaker seems to be insane and now there are a bunch of good people here that are in danger. I need a place to send them before a swarm shows up or Jeremiah blows his top. I think I can send you the two semi-trucks full of supplies like I mentioned if you can take these people in."

"So it is that bad, isn't it."

"At the rate Jeremiah is building people into a religious fervor, I'm not sure if I have two days before he comes after us."

"You are all welcome to come here even without the supplies, Eddie."

"I appreciate the offer, but I'll have to stay here to finish this. He might let my children out of here, but he would come after me anywhere I go. If I came to your place, I would just be putting your people in danger without helping mine in the process."

"I'll let you know where to come. You have a paper, right?"

"You can tell Michael the directions after I'm gone. It's better if none of us that are staying behind know where you are."

"I'm sorry to hear that. It's a shame people can't come together in days like these. Good luck, Eddie."

"Thank you, Katherine. Good luck to us all."

*

"Dad, what did you say to Mike? I tried talking to him earlier, and he told me to leave him alone and that I should talk to you if I want to know why."

"Mike is one of Jeremiah's people now, Hannah. He heard us talking about the threat Jeremiah poses to us the other night, and I told him he has to stay away from you."

"He wouldn't avoid me like he has been if you just told him to stay away. He cares about me."

"Hannah, you are twelve years old, and he is fourteen. What do you think I'm going to say? Do you think I'll invite him in to the house so he can live with us?"

"So what if I'm twelve! I've done more things at twelve than you probably did in your first thirty years. I'm the team sniper, and you treat me like a child."

"Being good with a gun doesn't make you mature enough to be in a relationship."

"Great! Well let me ask you two things. How old do I have to be before you think I'm old enough to start dating, and do you really think I can survive long enough to reach that age?"

"I don't know, Hannah. I don't have an answer for you that I can honestly give."

"I only have a few months before I turn thirteen, and you know what, I'm counting every day because I don't think I'll live that long."

I take a step back at the brutal truth of her words and they keep coming with increasing volume and emotion.

"Each and every day since we came to this ranch, I have wondered if tomorrow will be my last day. Am I going to die right away or will I get infected and have you or mom kill me? I have struggled with that constantly after the infection showed up in the world, and now I have to deal with you bringing psychopathic murderers onto the ranch that take my boyfriend away. He cares about me. I know he does, so you had to say something to him to make him to stay away. What did you say to him?"

It hurts to see Hannah so upset with me, but I am doing what every father is supposed to do for their children. I am keeping my child safe.

"I told Mike I may not be able to do anything about Jeremiah, but I could kill him at any time and no one would bat an eye. I told him he is a threat to our family and to stay away from you or I would kill him."

Calmly and sincerely, she says, *I hate you*, and walks off.

*

"How are the defenses against the infected coming?" I ask Arthur.

"Good, so far. You can see we removed the dirt mounds circling the storage towers and placed all that dirt and some more inside them to fill them up. That gives us two towers of steel reinforced hills to fight from. It doesn't matter how many infected press against the sides now, they won't collapse."

There are two towers on the property made of old shipping containers that were used for survival training on the ranch before the disease arrived. Each tower is a set of four containers stacked two high.

"Those towers helped us survive the last attack. Let's hope they will do the same during the next one," Arthur says.

"What's with the ditch?" I ask pointing beyond the towers.

There is a groove carved in the earth about twenty yards east of the towers where I assume they got the remaining dirt to fill the bottom containers.

"It's a moat," he says smiling broadly. "At least it's a good beginning to one. We needed the extra dirt and started digging and it just took shape. If you walk past the tower you'll see the moat stretches from the north fence line to the south fence. If we continue to work on it, we could surround the whole property and dump our fuel or oil into it to burn if we get attacked. The slow infected would have walked right through it, but I bet the fast ones will avoid the fire."

"That would have been great to see, Arthur. Unfortunately I don't think we'll have the time to finish it. About the towers, I need you to make one change if you could."

"What is it?"

"I would like one more storage container placed on top of each tower right in the center. Use the ones that we are emptying of stored goods. Then in the tops of those cut large holes in the top and weld steel bars across the opening so any infected that manage to climb up there aren't able to get inside."

"I could do that."

"Good. How about the sirens? How many do we have?"

"Four of them, we just have to hook each one to a battery, and then run."

On the scavenging trip before Hannah and her group got trapped, sirens were picked up to draw the infected to specific areas. We couldn't decide what would be the best siren to look for but my daughter Olivia solved that problem for us. She recommended the civil defense sirens. *They are big, loud, and if you can get them to work, will be heard for miles*, she had said

"I'll need one of them placed in each of those storage containers you cut the holes in and some type of pull line set up to activate them from the ground."

"You can't set them off in the containers. The sound will get amplified and pull every infected from Medford and Grants Pass to the ranch!"

"And the poor goats and chickens we're going to leave in the containers are going to keep the infected here until they starve."

Arthur looks at me like I've lost my mind.

"The ranch is lost, Arthur. Either it will be Jeremiah and his delusions or the infected and their disease. We can't stay here, none of us."

"I thought we were going to stay and fight?"

"Fight for what, this ranch? It's a small piece of land in a world without people. We can take any property we find that isn't occupied and build a new ranch. The supplies are replaceable as well. Not as easily right now, but in three months the world will belong to us again. I want to make sure there is someone around to enjoy it. Tomorrow, after the trucks leave with the kids, I want you to take everyone else from our group north on Wards Creek Road. Follow it around until you make it to The Oregon Vortex. I had Donald drop off a few truckloads of supplies there over the last month."

"I was wondering why he was coming back occasionally with an empty truck."

"Yeah, that was my doing."

"You don't sound like you're coming with."

"The goats and chickens are the bait to keep the infected here, and I'll be the bait to keep Jeremiah and his group in place."

*

"Isaac, I need to speak with you."

"The towers at the end of the property look great, but how are we going to get so many people on those single storage containers at the top."

"Those containers are only for the animals, not us. That's not what I want to talk about."

I guide him by the arm into the house and sit him down with Simone and me.

"I need to know your final assessment of Jeremiah. Is there any hope of reasoning with him?"

Isaac looks between us and shakes his head. "I don't know him anymore. Ever since we met your group he has been obsessing over immunity and demons. He was never this bad before about the infected, or at least, I didn't notice it before he was around other people."

"You do know what is going to happen then? He is fixated on me and my family. I don't think he will stop until I am dead, maybe all of us. I will do everything I can to prevent that from happening. That means I have to kill him. You understand that, right?"

"I thought if we came here, if we joined with your group and Jeremiah saw that our people don't have to worry about starving or freezing this winter, that he would turn back from the path he was on. He has gotten worse, though. I haven't been able to speak with him at all lately. I know you have to keep your family safe, but he is my brother, and I can't condone your killing him. Can't you just send him away?"

"Do you think I can just send him away?" I ask in return.

"No, you can't. Give me one more chance to try and reach him. Mariah has said she wants to speak with him about her immunity, and she is convinced he will understand once they talk."

"I hope for her sake—"

"Dad, Mike is coming to the house. I saw him through the window."

"Hannah, I'm speaking with Isaac."

"I don't care. Sorry, Mr. Johnson. I'm not leaving. I'm going to hear what Mike has to say."

"I should let you go, Eddie."

"Actually Isaac, I think you should stay for this. It might be in both of our interest to hear what he has to say."

There is a knock on the front door before Mike lets himself in and looks around the first floor for somebody.

"If you're looking for one of us Mike, we're in here," I call

"Mr. Keeper," he starts speaking, but sees Hannah and Isaac and pauses.

"It's okay, Mike. Tell me what's going on."

"It's starting. Jeremiah is going to challenge you. He's with Dave and Sheila right now, and he's getting ready. He wants to confront you today. Dave said they should wait until tomorrow, but Jeremiah said *no*. He's going to find you in two hours."

"Is he getting ready to fight?"

"Yes. He says he will challenge you in a way that will make everyone see you for the demon you are, and you will have no one to back you up when he's done."

"Do you know why is he taking two hours to do it?"

"It's a ritual," Isaac offers. "He will pray for guidance first, and then dress himself in all white to signify purity for the confrontation. It is what we would do when confronting alcoholics or drug users in our parish."

"Isaac, I suggest you get everyone you care about and trust off the ranch right now. If you think they have any loyalty to your brother, then leave them behind."

"You're kicking me out?"

"I'm sending you next door to the farm. I'm trying to save your life. My people will not know which of your people can be trusted, only you know that."

"You can't kill them all, Eddie! There are good people that he is just controlling. They're my people and some of them are just kids."

"Good people don't threaten to kill my family over imaginary *sky friends*, Isaac. And I would think twice about informing everyone in your group. Jeremiah has a strong hold over his followers and you would be considered the worst type of traitor there is to fanatics like them. You are working with me and will be a blood traitor to most of them. It isn't just my life on the line now that this has escalated."

Isaac looks at me with turmoil on his face.

"Why did you warn me about your brother that first day?"

He pauses before replying, not wanting to face the truth of his own words. "Because I knew he was a danger to others, and your group specifically. I will have Mariah speak with him quickly while I prepare my people to leave."

"You should try arranging a prayer group before you go," I say flatly.

"Why would you make jokes about my religion when people are going to die?"

I look back at him a bit confused, and say, "I'm not trying to ridicule you, although Jeremiah wouldn't have convinced a bunch of Atheists that I am a demon. What I meant was, throw together a quick prayer group for the children in your group and get them out of here as well. Take all of the kids to the farm with you and make sure they survive. I bet most of their parents would be happy to get them out of danger. They probably think I'll sprout wings and spit fire at them all when I'm confronted."

Isaac nods, and then walks slowly out of the room with his head slightly down. We hear the door close as he leaves the house.

"What should I do, Mr. Keeper?" Mike asks.

"You should probably stay here now. Hannah, I'm sorry I lied to you about Mike being on Jeremiah's side, but it was for his protection. His loyalty could have been questioned if he kept spending so much time over here with you. I sent him to live with Isaac's group the first day they arrived. It wasn't Mike's choice or idea."

"What?" Hannah says in a confused tone.

"I sent Mike to keep tabs on Jeremiah for me, so I would know when something like this happens or when he decides to attack. Because I am responsible for the death of Mike's father, the hatred that everyone expected him to have for me was a perfect cover for him to gain Jeremiah's trust. They didn't know about the issues Mike had with his father, mostly regarding Mike's mother's death, that helped him forgive me for what I did. Mike will have to explain the rest to you. Your mom and I have to get everyone ready."

"How did you know you could trust him? How do we know we can trust him now?" Simone asks in defiant concern.

"I've seen how he looks at Hannah. It's the same way I look at you and the kids. He's not going to let her get hurt. Hannah, get your brothers and sisters ready to leave. You're going to stay with Greg and Jessica for a while. Mike, you should go with her."

Simone looks at me and shakes her head before we both leave the house in search of Arthur.

*

. "Ashley, I need you to load all of the animals you can into that semi-trailer," I say pointing to an empty trailer next to the one Donald and his son are loading for tomorrow.

"I should wait until morning to load the animals. I don't want them locked up in there all night."

"The trucks will be leaving soon, possibly right after you finish loading the animals."

She looks at me with pain and anger in her eyes.

"My sister died trying to take care of this place and our group. I can't believe you're letting them make us run. What happened to you?"

"What happened to me?"

"Yes, what happened to you?" she says it slower in a derogatory way as if I was having trouble understanding her. "You killed the men that sent the infected after us and didn't blink with the things you did. After we were overrun, everyone was ready to give up and leave, but you kept pushing and kept working, so we did as well. Even with Stockton, you walked right up to the man knowing that he had fifty people behind him and made him give up without losing anyone on our side. But I look at you now and I see fear and uncertainty. You look weak."

"Weak?" I say in a frustrated tone.

She steps back knowing she is crossing a line with me she hasn't done before, but she is too upset to stop.

"Yes. You are being weak and a disappointment. The man I knew as *Eddie Keeper* didn't care about dying if what he did was right. He would have walked over to Jeremiah at the tents and killed him. He wouldn't have stopped until every asshole that is threatening our home was dead. Why are you letting them force us off the ranch?"

"I didn't change, Ashley, and they aren't chasing me away. I'm sending all of you away, but I am staying here to fight."

"Alone?"

"Yes, alone."

"Well, that's just stupid."

"I'm sure it is, but I haven't changed. Everything I have done so far has been to keep the people at the ranch safe. Do you know why I didn't go guns blazing against Stockton like you expect me to do with Jeremiah?"

She shakes her head no.

"Because there were innocent lives involved. If we charged the store, all of the Stick People would have died. Probably most of us as well. I am perfectly capable of killing people I think are bad if I think doing so will keep everyone safe, but I didn't have that guarantee with Jeremiah. I could have killed him and had five more unknowns just like him come after us from their group. There was only one way I could have dealt with them to ensure everybody's safety and that would have been to kill them all. I am not ready to do a wholesale slaughter of Isaac's entire group just because some of them are under the delusion I am a demon possessing this body."

"I doubt he really believes you are possessed. He wants to kill you because you're an Atheist."

"It doesn't matter."

"Doesn't it piss you off?"

I look at her for a moment wondering why she cares.

"I'm possessed or I'm an Atheist. Why he wants to kill me isn't important. Whatever his reason is, I can't kill that entire group just because some of them are zealots or insane. And as for what I've done before, up until now violence and brute force has worked to keep the threats away, but that won't work with Isaac's group or the Stick People. I've been trying to solve it diplomatically and with restraint, but now I know that they can't all continue to exist if I want our group to live."

"Then why send us away? If they are a threat that has to be dealt with, how can you stop them all? You'll be killed before you get them all, and our people will still be at risk. We should all stay and fight like we were prepared to do against Stockton's group."

"There is no way for our group to survive an attack on Jeremiah's followers. There are only twenty-five of us left, and that includes my children. Jeremiah has a hundred people that are listening to him now, and at least thirty of those are close followers, like *Jim Jones* kind of followers. He wants me and Simone dead more than any of you. That is why she and I have to stay. It will keep him here allowing all of you to escape."

She looks at me strangely, and Donald walks up interrupting the conversation that is eating into the loading time.

"The first truck is almost loaded, Eddie. If you two help out instead of talking, we could get the supplies started in the second truck," Donald says trying to chastise us.

"Finish with the first truck, and then help Ashley get the animals loaded in the other one. In fact, forget finishing with the supplies. Just load the animals and the ranch people in the other truck and leave. I want the trucks headed to Katherine's place in forty-five minutes."

"What changed?"

"Jeremiah is getting ready to confront me. Some sort of ultimatum that I supposedly won't be able to back out of. We have just over an hour left due to some ritual he goes through. Arthur said he has a way to clear the swarms in Medford from your path. I'll find him and send him over to see you."

As I begin walking away I hear Ashley ask Donald, *Who is Jim Jones?*

*

"Eddie, I was just going to look for you," Arthur says as I approach him by the storage towers near the back of the property. "I have the sirens hooked up in the top containers and there is a rope hanging over the side of each one that can be pulled to set them off."

"Thank you, Arthur. How long do you think they will run once I start them?"

"I don't know, but after our talk earlier I figured longer would work better, so I hooked up four car batteries to each siren. It will take a long time for those batteries to drain completely."

"Great, longer is better. Especially now that we're taking the animals instead of leaving them as bait. It's time for everyone to go. Jeremiah is making his move and you need to tell Donald how you plan on drawing the infected swarms away from the trucks."

"I was going to set up one of the sirens in Medford to draw the infected away from the area our group has to go. I will need to leave an hour before the trucks to be able to get the alarm positioned and have time to escape before a swarm gets to me."

"That's not enough time then. The trucks are leaving in just over thirty minutes, is there any way you can get it done in that time?"

"I guess I'll have too," he says and walks quickly back toward the trucks.

I look at the moat he built earlier and think it could come in handy once the sirens are blaring.

Several pickup trucks loaded with people drive out of the main gate while I am getting the tractor started. Either Isaac got word to the people that he trusts to leave or people are leaving of their own accord. I wish them the best of luck out on their own. The farm is no place to be if a swarm shows up, but the ranch is no place to hang out if you want to avoid a fight.

I use the tractor to drag some of our fuel tanks to the edge of the ditch and pierce the container walls with the tractor scoop. The smell of gas from the first tank hits me and makes my head swim. When I puncture the side of the oil tank, the smell is tolerable but still not pleasant. The job is done, and this moat will create a half circle of fire that should work as a barrier to let Simone and I escape from Jeremiah. We will have to go on foot to make it through the woods to our first fall back location with supplies, and the fire will let us do that.

I watch the two semi-trucks roll out of the gates. I hope Arthur was able to get a siren set up in time outside of Medford. Those trucks are just meals on wheels for the infected if they get caught by a large swarm. Jeremiah's people don't seem too concerned about the trucks leaving. I guess as long as they see I haven't gone anywhere they are content to let Jeremiah finish his full two hour prep time.

Timothy walks up to me at a brisk pace while I am removing the spark plugs from the tractor. "Eddie, you need to get back to the house. You're not going to believe who is on the Ham radio."

Ignoring his statement, I have to ask him, "Why didn't you leave with the others? You at least got Dianne to leave, didn't you?"

"Don't you want to know who it is?"

"I'll find out when we get there. Just tell me why you didn't leave."

"Are you kidding? This is the classic *good versus evil* fight. We wouldn't miss it for the world."

"So Dianne stayed as well?"

He nods *yes*.

"*Good versus evil*, huh? And who are you rooting for?"

"You and Simone, of course."

"You must know most of the people still at the ranch think I'm pure evil. Supporting me won't do you any favors in survivability once Jeremiah makes his show."

"Jeremiah is insane. He may hide his insanity well behind a front of Christianity, but what he is doing is anything but service to a higher power. We won't let him destroy what this place stands for without a fight. Now get in the house and take the call," he says as we arrive at the door and he opens it for me.

I walk into the room with the Ham radio and hear Simone and Dianne speaking excitedly to someone on the other end. I am also not too pleased to see my daughter Olivia sitting in a chair behind them. She was supposed to leave with everyone else in the trucks. Hopefully no one else in my family decided to take a losing gamble with their lives by staying here.

"Who is this person I need to speak to so badly?" I ask getting their attention.

A new level of tension hits when they turn their faces toward me, and I can see they have both been crying. Simone is not one for hysterics, so I doubt she had any kind of emotional breakdown over our current certain death scenario. They don't say anything, just look at each other, and smile.

"Eddie is here now. I'll let you speak with him for as long as we have," Simone says into the microphone before getting up.

A long dead voice from the past sounds out of the speaker, "Eddie, are you really there?"

Now I understand Simone's tears. My own eyes well up as I take my place in a chair facing the radio.

"Dad, is that you?"

"Yeah, Eddie, It's me!"

"How many people survived in New Orleans?"

"I'm not in New Orleans anymore. We left right after your call eight months ago and spent some time in Mexico, but that's not important right now. Simone told me what you're up against with the swarms and also with this *Jeremy* fellow."

I don't bother interrupting to correct him on Jeremiah's name. My mind reels a bit knowing that my father made it out of Louisiana and is still alive.

"We have seen the swarms of the infected as well. They have been running along the coast in California. Listen, if you can convince Jeremy to relax for a little while longer you won't have to worry about the infected."

"You've lost me, Dad. You said Mexico and California, where are you?"

"I'm off the coast of Oregon, right now. Me and a friend I've been surviving with are on a sailboat. I've given Simone the rough details of my location, but you need to know the infected are dying out right now. You won't have to wait more than a couple of weeks before they are all gone."

That has my attention. I sit there stupidly nodding at the radio expecting him to see my encouragement to continue.

"Are you sure?"

"Yes, I'm positive. We've been watching them from the boat for the last six to seven months. The coast is filled with them. It looked like millions of them were along the shore by San Diego and Los Angeles. I think everyone infected by the coastal cities went to the beach. I'm pretty sure they were attracted by the sound of the waves. We started seeing runners two months ago outside of San Francisco, it was a sickening sight. Instead of millions of bodies standing along the shore moaning at us, it was millions of them running. Just a huge mass of movement heading north along the coast.

"We tried sailing ahead of them and noticed them falling down by the masses along the way, and didn't know what was happening. After seven more days of watching, huge sections of them were falling over, thousands at a time it seemed. We kept seeing them die like that, and then two weeks after they started to run, we woke up one morning to a dead coast. They are all dead out here. They start running when they have two maybe three weeks left to live. The running infected are starving to death, just like you were told by your man. But they don't have months left to live, just weeks, by what we've seen."

The elation that this news should bring, as well as knowing my father is alive, is short lived. A loud knock on the door lets me know my time is up. I look over to Simone standing in the doorway to the entry hall, and she nods at me with a frown to confirm my suspicion that Jeremiah must be outside.

"Dad, I have to go. Jeremiah is outside. I'll see if we can use this new information to tide him over, but his main concern is an afterlife, not this one."

"I know it doesn't mean to you what it means to me, but I'll pray for all of you to make it out of there."

"I love you, Dad."

"I love you too."

CHAPTER 22
BROTHERLY LOVE

Isaac walks around the groups of praying followers spread throughout the riding stable. He is looking for Mariah, who should be speaking with Jeremiah, and wants to get her to leave the ranch. The faces looking up at him when he passes are a mixture of his own emotions and something more. He sees fear, anger, resentment, and a few truly evil looks of hatred shown his way. *Eddie was right. They think I'm a traitor. Maybe I am.*

The two men guarding the entrance to the partitioned room Jeremiah is in hesitate before letting him pass. They know what he will find inside and aren't sure if they should let Isaac in. If he is with the demon, Eddie, then he could be a threat to the man they've grown to trust.

"Wait here, Isaac. I'll check with your brother if he will allow you in."

"Charles, are you serious? It's me!"

"You've chosen your side, Isaac, and if you are with Eddie then you are against Jeremiah. You are against God!"

Charles opens the door and nods to Peter, the other man, then he walks in closing the door behind him.

"You've made a mistake Isaac," Peter says, stepping in front of the door to block the way should Isaac try to walk in after Charles. "Jeremiah told us everything. Even how he knows what Eddie is. You took the path of evil and—"

His words are cut off as the door opens behind him. Dave Cromwell, Sheila Jackson, and Charles all file out and stare at Isaac as they go by.

"He will see you now," Charles says while drawing his gun on Isaac. "You won't be needing any weapons. Take them all off."

Isaac removes his guns and blades and is thoroughly searched before the two men open the door to let him in. Dave and Sheila have begun leading the prayer groups in singing religious hymns, and the pit in Isaac's stomach grows as he suspects the start of singing is to cover other sounds that may arise in the room with his brother.

He doesn't get to go in alone. Isaac is followed into the room by Charles and Peter, and the door is closed and locked behind them all. The small room is brightly lit with two lanterns on wall pedestals across from each other. A large leather chair is on the right side and seems out of place in the world which they now live. Jeremiah is standing in front of a table in his pristine white suit. The clear plastic body suit he is wearing has protected his ritual outfit from the blood that is dripping down the front of his body and pooling by his feet on the floor.

Isaac sees Mariah lying on the table behind their brother.

Jeremiah steps to the side, giving access to the grotesque vision of Mariah's mutilated body, a large knife protruding vertically from her chest.

Before being able to take his first step, Isaac's head is knocked sideways from a blow and he blacks out.

*

Stinging pain. Isaac's cheek feels like it's on fire.

"Use the water. I want him awake."

A bucket of cold water is poured on Isaac's head and that revives him. He is now seated in the large leather chair with his hands duct taped together in front of him. He tries to stand but his legs are taped up as well, so he sits there and focuses all of the hate he can conjure in his gaze at Jeremiah.

"You murdered Mariah!"

"No, Isaac. I murdered the demon that was in Mariah's body." Isaac follows his brothers glance and sees he is also speaking to Charles and Peter. "That is the same thing I killed in my wife's and daughter's bodies as well."

"You're fucking insane, Jeremiah! There are no demons. This is a disease and you know it."

Jeremiah shakes his head and gets an expression of pity on his face as he looks at his brother and walks up to him in the chair.

"I know for a fact that any person who is bitten is controlled by demons. I've proven to many people how I know and that only those that are close to God like you and I can flush them out and eliminate them. Would you like me to show you the proof?"

Isaac looks at the other men, and then back to his brother.

"If you have proof the bitten people are demons, I will look at it."

Jeremiah takes off the transparent plastic jacket and then begins to remove his white suit top and shirt. He lifts his left arm and points to a scar on his armpit and chest. A mouth shaped scar.

Isaac's eyes grow wide as he looks at his brother.

"You see now, Isaac. I know the people bitten are possessed by demons because I have been one of them since our attack on Christmas day. I have fought the demonic urges but know that only my strong faith in the Lord have truly protected me from its total control up until this point. I had to kill our sister because she gave herself over completely to the demon and allowed herself to be swayed by the evil which Eddie Keeper spews. Because of my bite, I am not fit to lead these people, Isaac, but you are. Everything I am doing here, this is all to make sure you and those that worship God are the people that continue to rule this Earth."

Jeremiah motions for the other men to go, they nod and walk out.

"Why didn't you show me this earlier?"

"I wanted to, but I think it was the influence of the demon keeping me at bay," he says while pacing back and forth in a sincere and determined manner. "I was only able to regain control when I was challenged by Eddie that first day at Wal-Mart. I knew he was protecting the demon in Mariah, and it woke me up."

"And at Christmas when you told everyone to kill the people that were bitten?"

"That was me breaking through the demons grasp again. I was mixed up by the fever at first. But once my mind was clear I knew everyone had to kill the bitten, and I had to kill my wife."

"After the fever you got from being bitten?"

"Yes."

"The fever from bites doesn't happen for six hours, but you killed Angela and Rachel after thirty minutes."

Jeremiah stops his pacing and looks straight at his brother.

"You've always been too smart for your own good Isaac," he yells. "I was going to give you all of this. All of those people out there would have worshipped you, would have followed you anywhere even with your betrayal of me. All I had to do was go out there and tell them you were one of us and all you had to do was believe it too."

"But it's a lie!"

"Who gives a shit if it's a lie? You would have ruled the world."

"Why did you kill Mariah? Why did you kill your own wife and child?"

"Angela was leaving me. She filed for a divorce before the gathering at the camp. Rachel wanted to go with her and told me I treated her mother like dirt. They were disrespectful."

"And Mariah?"

"Mariah was for show. These people need to know what I'm willing to do to people that won't follow me. You should understand that since you like Eddie so much. He did the same thing to the men that attacked the ranch."

"He did it to protect the people at the ranch not to control them."

"You're a fool if you think that, Isaac. Everything he has done has been for power and control, just like me."

"You are insane," Isaac says with a sad tone of understanding.

Jeremiah puts his white jacket back on and replaces the plastic cover over it as well.

"This could have all been yours, Isaac. You could have rebuilt God's kingdom on Earth for his followers, but now I have to send you to him."

With those final words Jeremiah begins the process of beating his brother to death.

CHAPTER 23
THE FALSE PROPHET

Oregon.

I check that my guns and knives are all in their corresponding holsters and sheathes, and then open the front door. I am expecting to see Jeremiah and a throng of people wanting some kind of show, but only two people are there; Gayle Bradley, the cook, and her son, Tyler. Tyler is still a bit shell-shocked from witnessing his father's death and doesn't go more than five feet away from his mother at any time.

"Gayle? Where's Jeremiah?"

"You only have a few minutes, Eddie. They are all in the riding stable, and Joanne let me know I needed to hurry."

I don't know who *Joanne* is, but Gayle is motioning for us to follow her. So I grab Simone's hand and Simone grabs Olivia's, and we file out of the house together. Timothy and Dianne come out behind us.

"Where are we going, Gayle?"

"To the back of the property. I saw you fill the ditch with fuel, and I put a plywood ramp over it so you could leave."

She picks up the pace as we walk past the stable. Two men outside that were keeping an eye on me earlier disappear inside as we walk by.

"If you're with Isaac, why didn't you leave with him earlier? I saw the vehicles go out the gate before our trucks did."

"Isaac is dead, so is Mariah," she says in an upset manner, and Simone grips my hand. "Jeremiah is in that building right now bragging about how he killed one of the demons, his own sister. Mariah tried to talk with him about being immune but he just cut her down. Isaac found out when he went looking for her, and Jeremiah beat him to death."

"He beat him? Are you sure Isaac is dead?"

"There isn't much left of Isaac's face. Once Jeremiah knocked him down he kept punching him and calling him a traitor to God. If Isaac isn't dead now he will be soon."

I stop and look back to the stable where people are starting to walk out following Jeremiah in our direction.

"He's going to do the same thing to you and your family if you don't go. He wants to make an example of you. He thinks if he kills you all of the demons will go away."

The irony of the situation isn't lost on me. If I stay and Jeremiah kills me, in a week or two when the infected all drop dead from starvation, he can claim he was right. If I run then he can still claim running us off our farm is what sent the demons away. Either way he will have a win for his new cult ideology.

I start walking toward the back of the property again at a quick pace. When we reach the plywood plank, I have everyone walk across, and then I throw the plank into the ditch leaving me stuck on the this side with Jeremiah.

"Eddie, what are you doing?" Simone yells pleadingly pacing back and forth along the ditch looking for a way to get back over to me.

"I have a surprise set up for him. Just stay on that side. Everything will be okay," I say calmly. "It's not just you and me anymore. You have to get Olivia out of here now." Olivia and Simone both start crying and I prepare myself to face Jeremiah, who has almost arrived.

I turn to face him as he walks up. He is flanked on either side by two of the Wal-Mart trouble makers, Dave, and Sheila. I instinctively put my hand on the gun in the holster at my side. At least twenty assorted firearms rise up to point at me and everyone behind me, so I move my hand away and wait.

"Eddie, Simone, I'd like to talk to you," Jeremiah says like a politician looking for votes.

"You want to talk to me the way you spoke to Isaac?"

"He betrayed God! He knew what he was doing, and he got punished for it."

"You mean he betrayed you, right? Everyone here knows Isaac never stopped believing in God."

He turns his back on me to address the crowd.

"Those are the words of the demon. Everyone bitten becomes possessed. We all know this. Isaac knew this, yet he still sided with him?"

I have to admit Jeremiah has a flare for preaching with drama. He is good at it. The fiery speaking, the finger pointing, and accusatory inflections in his tone. He even turns on the spot to face me again when he points at me and says the word *him* in a long drawn out rumbling way.

"You are a demon, Eddie. Ever since you were first bitten you have been possessed."

"If I'm not immune then why don't I run around and try to bite people like everyone else you say is possessed?"

"You know why, beast! But I will entertain your dishonesty to prove to these people what you are, so they know without a doubt that we are doing the will of God."

I have to shake my head and roll my eyes at the ridiculous spectacle of it all. I can understand one madman like Jeremiah being in a group, but looking around at the faces in the crowd, I see fear and anger looking back at me. They are all looking at me as if I were about to burst into flames and consume them with fiery evil. It's the same look of fear I've seen on the faces of people fighting the infected.

When Jeremiah takes a dramatic pause for breath, Olivia matches my sentiment in thoughts when I hear her ask, "Is he serious? What's wrong with him?"

"The monsters that bite are all lower demons, the ones that run around spreading their satanic filth. You, Eddie, are a higher demon. That is why you can control your behavior and why you survive the attacks."

He spreads his hands out to the sides and nods his head as if he has explained some big truth to the world. If all of these nervous people didn't have guns pointed at me he would be dead ten times over.

I want to take him seriously, I know that is exactly what all of these people believe, but a smile starts creeping onto my face. Simone starts laughing behind me, followed by Olivia, and then I burst out laughing as well. Once again I am doubled over at the most inappropriate time trying to catch my breath and wiping tears from my eyes at how asinine the world and the situation I find myself in has become. It must be a full minute before I'm able to stop laughing enough to say anything. Each time I try, I look at him attempting to be serious and official, and it cracks me up even more.

"Oh, Jeremiah, thank you. I needed that. I'm sorry for laughing but look at you. That show might work on the regular faithful that attend your church, but I think you're going to end up in a home for the overacting. Cut the theatrics and tell me what you want."

"I want you to admit what you are. Tell them you are a demon."

"I am not a demon. Demons don't exist. I don't believe in gods or devils, angels or demons. Is this the work of a demon in your eyes?" I say pointing at the ranch and the people in the crowd. I am trying my hand at Jeremiah's game but with less gaudy embellishment. "I've been keeping all of you alive, fed and healthy. How is that the work of a demon, Jeremiah?"

"That is the work of a higher demon. You aren't just trying to kill us. That isn't your way or your purpose. You want to fill our stomachs with food, give us a safe place to live and steer our souls away from God. You want to take away our eternal life in Heaven and a comfortable life on Earth, is the way *you* are doing it."

I know I can't win against Jeremiah's fantasy with a logical argument and it pisses me off. No matter what I do or say, I can't win.

"That right there is why I don't believe in God. Look what happens to you if you believe in things without evidence. I mean, look at all of you, your belief in God has totally screwed up your perspective on reality! This is a fucking disease like the bird flu or Ebola. Some people survive it, and some people don't, but you start throwing your ideas about God bringing about the end times and suddenly all bets are off. Now anything is possible from pigs farting peanut butter to imaginary demons controlling human bodies. There's nothing I can say that you can't counter with some magical explanation Jeremiah, so why don't you just kill me and spare us all the torment of your proclamations."

"I don't want to kill you if you aren't a demon, Eddie, but I have a way for you to prove whether you are or aren't to these people. My group and I want you to accept Jesus Christ as your Lord and Savior," he stops speaking and is waiting for a reply.

At this point most of the people in the crowd nod their heads at his statement. People from his group and the Stick People.

I understand their sentiment, even though I can't agree with it. Religions have been calling for judgment day ever since man first created gods. Now that the world of man has truly gone belly up the people in front of me are turning to the easiest explanation they can wrap their heads around. They want there to be a better life after this one, something to look forward to after the suffering they experienced in this one. I just can't make myself believe in something in order to feel better. Either it is or it isn't, and if I don't know, then I don't say yes.

"Is there anything else, Jeremiah? Any specifics you want to add to your invitation to find Christ?"

"Yes, you need to accept that what we are dealing with are demons and possessions. If we keep trying to deal with these things as if it is a disease, we will lose sight of the lesson that the Lord is trying to teach us. We should be humble in his presence, and the demons will leave us alone."

"You think if we all pray real hard and accept that these things are demons they will just go away?" I say shaking my head, unable to grasp the convoluted reasoning behind such a thought.

"They are still here because you and many of those around you question the existence of the demons. You even question the existence of God!" he says with genuine anger.

I hold my hands up in a calming motion, and say, "Okay, okay Jeremiah. I'm not trying to be rude but you know I don't believe in God, and your theatrics are great. Let's try this then, you have a large crowd of believers here, why don't you and anyone here that wishes, try to convince me. Convince me that God exists. Tell me why I should believe and what evidence I am missing that should lead me to believe even half as strongly as you do?"

To this Jeremiah straightens up and smiles. "That I can do, Eddie. The proof that God exists is you," he says while pointing right at me.

I look down at myself and back up at him shrugging my shoulders. "Not enough, Jeremiah. Care to elaborate?"

"You, Eddie. Your life. Look at what you have and tell me that God wasn't guiding you. You knew before everyone else that you should prepare for disaster. That was God's hand guiding you. You prepared this ranch like your own Ark to weather the coming storm that we are in. You took in all the decent people that came your way and fought, risking your life to protect and save the innocent people that Stockton captured. That is God guiding you.

"You have survived this plague with God's blessing, and He has chosen you to guide and protect these people. That is why he has spared your family while most of us others have endured such terrible losses. God has blessed you, and it is time for you to accept him for the gifts he has given you."

"And if I don't accept that these are the gifts of a God?"

"Not *A* God Eddie, *The* God! And if you don't accept him then you must be against him."

"So if I accept your God then I am his blessed messenger, and if I don't I'm a higher demon?"

"Either you accept God has blessed you with all of your success and swear allegiance to Him or we will know you can't, because you are a demon!"

"Sorry, not convincing. Is there anything else?" I ask, and he just steps back as if my question might hit him in the face. "Does anyone else have evidence that should prove to me that God exists?"

"He has a point, Eddie," this time it is Dianne behind me that speaks up.

"You believe the infected are demons, Dianne?" Simone asks in shock.

"No, not demons or possessions, but look at your life, your family all surviving. Even Eddie's father survived. How do you explain it without God?" she says.

I turn back to see many heads behind Jeremiah unfortunately nodding.

"Fine, let's say I believe God has blessed my family. I don't believe we have been blessed by anything, but let us say God exists. Because my family all survived, I should show my appreciation to God and?" I ask leaving the rest to be filled in by the crowd.

"You should convert!" one person says.

"Become a Christian," says another as the crowd begins to murmur in excitement.

I stare at these people and wonder how humanity was able to survive for so long when people can so easily twist the things they witness to fit their own agendas.

"Don't you mean you should all become Atheists?" I ask back at them.

The faces filled with hope at my possible conversion turn to looks of surprise and fear at what I have suggested. I know Jeremiah won't let me live. It doesn't matter if I say I believe in God or not. You could tell by the growing anger and frustration etched on his features as it sounded like I might be finding a way out of his trap. I'm not going to pretend to believe in God to save my skin any more than a devout Christian would pray to Allah to keep their head from getting cut off. All I can do is speak the logic that I know and accept my fate for not having killed Jeremiah, Dave, and Sheila that first day at Wal-Mart.

"I'm serious, you should all become Atheists. I mean, look at you, look at your losses. Not just what you lost but how you lost them. Most of you had to watch as your loved ones got violently murdered. A third of you spent your time after that starving and afraid, moving from group to group, and watching countless others die. Then there are the rapes and abuse you endured."

Simone calls out trying to stop me, but I am too pissed off that we are being threatened by this crowd to let it go and I ignore her

"All of this suffering and abuse was while you prayed fearfully to your all loving, all knowing, and all seeing God, right? And then there is me and my family, the lowly Atheists, the evil nonbelievers. Here we are untouched. And you know what? I just found out my father is alive and well in a boat just off the coast of Oregon here. He made it from Louisiana to Oregon. How he did it I have no idea, but I spoke with him just a few minutes ago. Of course, in your minds we must be evil because what, because God hasn't chosen to touch us with the gracious love of his destruction that he has shown you people. Well I say *no thank you* to that. If God is real then he obviously show's favor to us Atheists above those that worship Jesus Christ."

"You are the Devil," Jeremiah shouts at me.

"Oh shut up!" I yell back. "I know why you want me to be a demon. You need me to be the Devil because your belief in God made you murder your wife and child."

Jeremiah lunges at me screaming, but I was expecting it the way he was leaning into my words, and I kicked him in the chest knocking him back and draw my gun on him and anyone else in the crowd that wants to have at me.

"Jeremiah needs every one of you to believe that I am a demon because I am immune," I yell. "He murdered his wife and daughter after they were bitten, but they weren't showing any signs of infection. His claiming that this illness is demons allowed him to get away with murdering his own flesh and blood without hesitation or remorse. He was getting away with it too until that day at Wal-Mart, when we explained there were immune people."

"Shut your mouth," Jeremiah yells and wants to come at me but is being held back by several people that were on his side. Whether they want to protect me from Jeremiah or him from my bullets I don't know yet.

"Why don't you finally tell the truth to all of your *followers* and under the watchful eyes of your Lord," I say with heavy sarcasm. "After all, I'm sure you believe He is here. If I am immune from exposure to cats and if others are immune also because of cats, then your wife and daughter that owned several cats were probably immune as well, and you just murdered them."

"Eddie, that's enough," Gayle says. "You made your point, but you weren't with us then. We all thought these were demons and didn't know about immunity then."

"Sure, I wasn't with you then, but you have learned what this outbreak really is since then and that didn't stop him from killing Mariah or beating Isaac to death, did it! I don't care what this disease or illness is. It doesn't matter what it could do to me if I wasn't immune and got bitten. I would never harm my wife or children if they were bitten and not showing symptoms. Jeremiah and several other people in this self-righteous group of yours killed innocent people and worse, you killed loved ones that showed no signs of turning.

"I was told some of the people your group killed were bitten early in the Christmas attack and had been fine for over twenty minutes before you put bullets in their brains. We have been living with Mariah for over a week with no issues, and he still killed her.

"Believing in God and demons is the reason people in your group willingly murdered trusted loved ones. So no, I will not join you in your delusional fantasies of demons and Heaven and Hell. I refuse to join you in hunting down and murdering immune people just because you think they are possessed by higher demons, and I will not allow anyone that thinks that way to stay on this ranch any longer."

Jeremiah is furious. He is being forcefully held back from getting to me and disarmed by the people he whipped into a frenzied mob of religious retribution. I have no intention of letting him off the hook for what he has done or them for following him.

"Everyone here knows if the world didn't come to an end Jeremiah would be sitting in prison for what he did to his wife and daughter. I admit I have killed my share of people and regret only Craig, Mike's father, but I would not change what I did if I had to do it again. But you, your own flesh and blood. You will have to deal with the guilt of that until the day you die.

"The rest of you can believe in whatever God you want or none at all, I don't care and never have, but I want everyone that believes that the infected are possessed by demons off of my property now. If that is all of you then you'll have to kill me to stay, but I'm guessing most of you see what Jeremiah was trying to do and why."

For a split second I regret what I have just said. I had everyone on my side and now realize with my proclamation of eviction I have turned many, if not all of the people in the crowd, back against me. The ranch is all they know of safety and survival, even with its limitations against a running horde.

The regret is short lived because the attention of the crowd turns from me to a rumbling in the woods to the north beyond the fence. The sound is coming from the front of the property, the way we assumed a swarm might arrive if following the roads to us. The people in the crowd begin to scatter in fear. Where they can run to in an enclosed fence, I'm not sure, but with the first appearance of an infected runner the panic will set in and everyone will scatter to their own little corner to face death. This group didn't train for attacks, and outside of our recent encounter in Grants Pass, they haven't survived a major attack the way my ranch members did either. Even with the training we had, I'm not sure most of my group would stand their ground this time.

What breaks through the tree line is the same terror I encountered on the road the other night. A herd of cows and horses is running along the fence. Everyone still in the group in front of me collectively sigh and release a small chuckle at the fear they were feeling, but my fear is increasing. The cattle aren't just running, they are panicked and frothing. They have been on the move for a while and have no intention of stopping.

Turning around, I yell, "Simone run, they're coming! I'm going to jump."

The six on the other side of the moat turn and start running to the back fence. Once they make it into the woods they can follow the animals that hopefully know the safest direction to head, and I will follow.

I get ready to run to make the jump and get hit from the side. When I land, Jeremiah is leaning over me trying to grab one of my guns. I kick him twice in the balls, and he doesn't flinch. I punch him square in the throat, and he still relentlessly tugs at the gun on my hip trying to get it free from the auto-lock holster that holds it in place.

"Jeremiah, turn around!" yells a bloody pulp of a face that I barely recognize.

Isaac is standing behind my attacker. When Jeremiah straightens up and turns to face his brother, I finally understand why my attacks were having no effect on him. There is a knife sticking out of Jeremiah's back and barely a trickle of blood appears staining his shirt. Far too little an amount of blood for the size of the knife or for the identical hole next to the protruding handle where the knife must have first been stuck.

Jeremiah is immune.

I stand and am about to pull my trigger and kill this lying sack when the back of Jeremiah's head opens up and its contents hit me in the face and chest. Isaac pulled the trigger that ended his brother's life. This scene of fratricide and me covered in brains and blood is horrific enough without the shouts of terror that rise from the now scattering crowd. The swarm that was chasing the cattle is here and has turned its attention to the screaming human delicacies that are enclosed within the property's fence like sheep locked up for a wolf's dinner.

"Isaac, get to the tower," I yell and point the direction for him go.

He moves off in a slow and pained way.

I pull the knife out of Jeremiah's back and use it to cut a large piece of his shirt free. I set it on fire with my lighter and toss it into the ditch causing a roaring flame to burst skyward and spread out along the length of the canal.

I run past Isaac, who is still trying to make it to the nearest tower, and pull the rope that Arthur attached to the siren turning it on. Any infected that had an idea of continuing their pursuit of the horses and cows should be pulled to the spot where I am standing. I lift the ladder that is laying next to the tower and begin my climb to hopeful safety.

The noise is deafening at the top, but at least here I have a slim chance of life. I also just have one ear to worry about losing my hearing in.

Isaac is climbing up the side followed by someone from Isaac's group that I don't know. Gun fire is erupting all over the ranch now and the infected have breached the fence in several locations. There are too many of them, in fact, it is probably all of the remaining infected in the area that are converging on the ranch. I cut some of my own shirt off, wad it up, and shove it in my good ear. It barely helps cutting down the noise.

I help Isaac up once he reaches the top and look over the side to see the next person's progress. I don't like the look on this guy's face, he isn't fearful enough about what is going on down there. I look at Isaac and hand signal him to look at the man that is near the top of the ladder. Isaac shakes his head *no* and rubs his finger across his throat—signaling death. I kick the ladder to the side and watch the man and ladder fall into the growing mass of infected below.

I gaze at the scene of horror for a few minutes, amazed that anyone is able to survive as long as they do with so many infected around. The crowd of over one hundred people is no match for the thousands that pour onto the property. Every person hiding is eventually found and ripped to pieces while they are consumed. Some people managed to hide in a few of the small sheds or in the rafters of the riding stable, but those buildings are either already crushed or are being pulled down while I watch.

No infected followed Simone and Olivia into the woods that I could tell. The swarm is staying on this side of the burning ditch and several feet away from it, none are attempting to cross it or find a way around.

Isaac is lying down. He is either sleeping, passed out, or dead. I'm not sure which. There isn't anything I can do, so I lie down as well and watch the clouds move across the sky as I listen to the continuous, headache inducing blare of the siren.

CHAPTER 24

OUR WORLD

Oregon.

Hannah and Mike are sitting in the cab of Donald's truck. Benjamin is sitting in Hannah's lap in the front passenger seat next to Donald, who is driving. Donald's wife, Karen, is in the back with their daughter Katy. Mike is entertaining William and Amelia. Donald's son, Joshua, is driving the other truck in front of them.

"Tell your son to drive north. I don't think we should go through Rogue River," Hannah tells Donald.

"So you're the navigator now?" he asks.

She nods confidently back at him.

Donald grabs the CB radio, and calls to his son, "Joshua, drive north on Wards Creek Road and follow the loop on Sardine Creek Road to Highway 99."

"Got it, Dad," they hear back.

"Now I want you to drive to the farm and pick up any of Isaac's people that we can."

Donald idles his truck at the intersection wanting to follow his son's truck north. "Your father wanted me to get you and everyone in the back to safety."

"If Isaac did what my father told him, most of the kids and teenagers from Isaacs's group are at the farm. We have to get them to safety. The farm will be more of a death trap than the ranch is right now. Once we pick up everyone we can head out the same way as Joshua."

"You're the boss," Donald says and calls his son on the CB to explain what is going on as he turns south.

When the truck pulls onto the farm, no real explanation is given to the people and children standing around, and in this world, details are often not needed if you know to say the right thing.

"If you want to live, get in the back of the truck, or follow us in your vehicles."

Nothing more has to be said. For almost nine months the remaining human population has had to follow one mantra and that is *listen* when someone offers you a way to survive or die. Fifteen children and teenagers are loaded into the back of the truck with the ranch survivors and their animals. Nine adults are going in their own trucks, and six people choose to stay at the farm and take their chances with Jeremiah's wrath once he is finished with Eddie and Simone Keeper.

Donald tells the other drivers which way they should head, and they drive off to catch up with the other semi. He double checks with those saying they are remaining and closes up the back of the truck after they repeat their refusal to go.

Donald drives the truck north to begin their trek that will take them past The Oregon Vortex and the supplies they dropped there. They can't see onto the ranch from the road as they drive past, so they don't know what state of trouble Eddie and the others are in.

"Would you look at that," Donald says while looking in his side view mirrors behind the truck.

Everyone peers into the mirrors to see a large herd of cows and horses run across the road behind them toward the property.

"Do you think they are finally returning to the ranch?" Donald's wife Karen asks.

"Donald, get us out of here," Hannah yells. "They must be running from a swarm."

Donald accelerates the truck and drives out of view around a corner before the tail end of the cattle herd goes by. There may not be anything chasing those animals, but this isn't the kind of world where you wait to see if you are right about nothing happening.

"We can't see them now. Stop the truck."

"What?"

"Stop the truck, Donald! I'm getting out," Hannah says handing Benjamin to Karen in the back.

While she is strapping on her backpack and grabbing her gun, Mike is doing the same.

Donald brings the truck to a stop but isn't about to let her go without an explanation. "If there's a swarm back there you can't help your parents now."

"Olivia stayed behind, and I'm going to get her. I know the woods better than they do. I'll run to the back fence and guide them to The Vortex if we can make it out. You get everyone else to Katherine's place."

Hannah jumps to the ground from the truck step, and Mike hops out of the cab following her. Donald watches as they take off running through the trees. Karen moves up front to sit next to Donald and puts her hand on his arm, giving him a squeeze as she moves by. Benjamin, in her arms, just looks between the two and seems content to be with these familiar faces that have cared for him so often before.

"We have to trust that they know how to survive," she says to her husband.

The truck moves on.

*

The beeline Hannah is making through the trees has her angled to intersect the path the cattle herd took just beyond the back of the fence.

"They lit the fire," Mike yells looking at the smoke rising through the blinking flashes of ranch they can see through the trees as they run. His inattention costs him with a sharp pain and a quick fall onto his back when he runs into a low branch. He's a bit dazed but gets up and continues running to catch up with Hannah, who didn't slow down or stop when he fell.

Hannah turns to run out of the tree line into the open land they made beyond the fence for security. She has to make a running loop like she is rounding bases on a baseball field to go around one of the piles of burnt bones and ashes from the bodies of the large winter attack.

"I see them," Hannah calls out finally turning back to see Mike running much farther back than she expected him to be. "Mom, over here!" she yells getting the escaping groups attention while slowing down for Mike to catch up.

Mike finally catches up, while Hannah waits at the fence for the others to reach them.

"What happened to your head? You're bleeding."

"I hit a branch when I wasn't looking."

Hannah looks at him like he managed to sink an unsinkable boat. "How did you hit a branch?"

"I'm taller than you, duh. I was looking at the—"

His words are cut off by the piercing yell of the siren. Simone, Olivia, Timothy, Dianne, Gayle, and her son Tyler, all climb the fence while Hannah and Mike look at the ranch. In the distance, they see sections of the fence near the front of the property collapse as the infected pile up against it. The infected burst onto the property through the openings to get at the wailing sirens sound.

"Where's Dad?"

"He isn't coming, Hannah."

A split second is all she has and is all she takes before moving the small group away from the open area by the fence.

"Follow me. I can get us through the woods to The Oregon Vortex. Dad made me hike the way there and back after he let those idiots move here."

They all take off running to the cover of the trees.

"Are you going to be okay?" Hannah asks running next to Mike.

"Yeah. It isn't bleeding bad, is it?"

"No, just a little." She smiles and gives him a playful shove toward another tree, and then her face turns serious and into a frown.

"You're worried about your dad?"

She nods and looks to the other side to see her mom returning her look of concern. Their worry is overshadowed by the fear they feel with the sounds of the occasional gunshot from the ranch that can be heard over the siren.

"Do you know what your father planned with the siren?"

"No, but that sound will echo through the hills and could bring every infected in Grants Pass and Medford to the ranch."

"Hannah, we got a call from Grandpa Keith before the fight started."

Hannah looks at her mom with surprise but doesn't say a word.

"He told us that the infected are dying off. He said once they start running, they die within two weeks. He saw it happen all along the coast."

"Are you serious?"

"Yes."

"So if we survive this we just have to wait a week or two and no more infection?"

"Hannah watch out!" Mike yells too late to stop her.

She runs right into a cow standing in the woods. Getting back up from her awkward fall she sees spread out in the forest before them all the horses and cattle that were running from the infected threat. They are all breathing heavily and most have white froth dripping from their mouths.

"Either they think it's safe or can't hear the infected anymore because of the siren. We should keep moving in any case," Hannah tells everyone.

"Keep going forward. I'm going to look for one of our horses," Simone tells the group. "If I can find him and bring him with us, this group might follow us as well."

Looking for Buster their lead horse turns out not to be necessary. The cattle start following Hannah, Olivia, and their mom through the woods as soon as they started walking again. It helped of course that they were offering carrot and cucumber slices from their packs.

"It's only three miles to the Vortex, but it will take us a few hours to walk there over the hills, longer if we run into any water before we get there and the herd stops to drink," Hannah explains and continues moving northeast after checking her compass.

*

"What do we do now?" Mike asks as the group arrives at some houses and buildings to the south of The Vortex.

"We wait," Hannah says preventing her mom Simone from giving a response.

"Hannah, there's a truck here that your dad brought. I think we should try to join the rest of the group with Greg and Katherine."

"You can't go, Mom," Hannah says and grabs her mom's arm preventing her from making it to the truck. "You're not in charge out here. This is our world."

"Hannah, you are twelve years old and won't speak to me like that," she says with a desperate anger while pulling her arm away from her daughter's grasp. "We are going to catch up to Donald in the trucks or meet them at Katherine's place. I am getting what's left of our family back together."

"Mom, I can't let you go. If you take that truck you will get us all killed."

"What are you talking about?"

"I have to show you on the map," she says and continues talking while taking it out of her backpack and placing it on the hood of the truck. "Mike and I have been going on the scavenging runs together and have a better idea what things sound like echoing through the hills than you do, Mom."

"We all heard the second siren when we were at the top of the first hill. Arthur sent someone ahead of the trucks with another siren to pull the infected swarms in Medford away from the route we had to take to Katherine's place. The reason the other siren we heard was changing pitch was because it was driving around and not in one place. It should have been heading north on Table Rock Road to Sams Valley.

"We didn't hear it anymore once we got to the top of the second hill, only the one from the ranch is still blaring, which means that truck must have been overrun. The Medford swarms were probably closer to the west side when the truck went by."

"Who took the siren ahead of the trucks?"

Hannah doesn't want to answer her mom. "Mrs. Langford."

"Patricia?" she says with shock. "Who went with her?"

"She went alone. I heard her and Arthur speak before she left. They said their goodbyes and said they would meet again, but they didn't mean in this life. She wouldn't have stopped the truck to turn off the siren. It would only stop if she was overrun."

Bringing her mom back to the present, Hannah continues talking and pointing to the map. "With the other siren off and a swarm so close to the hills, the entire population of Medford will be heading to the only sound left to hear, the siren at the ranch. They will be crossing Sardine Creek Road to the south of us. If you drive down there, you will either be killed by a swarm or you'll bring it back up the road to us if you can escape. Katherine's place is south of Medford, and we have no way of getting there while the siren is blaring and the infected are still alive."

Simone pulls Hannah and Olivia into a fierce motherly hug. "That isn't what I wanted to hear Hannah," she says.

"I know, Mom, but it's the truth. Dad wouldn't have let me go on the runs if he didn't think I was ready. I know what I'm doing out here."

"Okay, young lady. I guess that puts you in charge. What should we do?"

Hannah looks at the faces of the group all turned to her for direction. It is one thing to blindly say the truth in the heat of the moment and quite another to be expected to come up with a plan for survival for more lives than your own.

"The truck bed is already packed with supplies, and Dad had Donald fill these buildings with more. We can come back here for extra things if it is safe, but now we should take the truck and head north."

"Sams Valley is directly to our east on the map so if any infected are pulled to the siren from that area, they might cross where we are right now. If we head north a few miles, we should be out of any danger area. We can find a house and either wait for the siren to stop or the infected to die off."

"The horses and cattle have all gone down to the creek. Should we try to get them?" Mike asks.

"We can call for them when we get moving and see if they follow. It would be nice to have them around, but we don't have any feed for them, so they'll have to manage on their own the way they have been."

Everyone climbs in or on the truck and they begin driving slowly up the road calling out clicking and kissing noises to the herd at the creek. At first it seems the animals are too tired to follow anymore, but the horses at least decide they want to return to some type of non-dangerous human companionship and walk out of the tree line to follow the truck. Cows wander out of the trees behind the horses, and the unusual exodus parade makes its way north to find a home that will keep them safe for the next week or two while the remaining infected die out.

CHAPTER 25
PURGATORY

It has been three days since I set off the sirens. Isaac is alive but won't ever look like his former self again. The swelling on his face from the beating Jeremiah gave him has subsided somewhat, but there are two open cuts that will heal badly. He has a cut on his forehead and one on his cheek just below his left eye, and I don't have anything to stitch them closed. Luckily I had a tube of triple antibiotic ointment in my pocket and lubed up his wounds. Hopefully that prevents him from getting an infection.

Arthur left the usual setup of firearms and ammunition on the tower for a normal defense but no medical supplies. I'm happy he thought to put a week's supply of food up here this time. Isaac and I can stretch the food to last a long time with just the two of us. When our big attack happened last winter we weren't prepared to be stuck on top of the tower over night, and as terrified as we were with the surrounding horde, we were still hungry and thirsty.

I think I am deaf now. I no longer hear the tone of the siren, all I hear is a constant ringing. Or maybe the constant ringing is the siren, I'm not really sure. Isaac and I will both have permanent hearing loss to some degree, if not complete, once we make it off the tower. I would like to speak with him but hearing each other's voices right now would be like doing sign language to each other in the dark. Neither of us had a pen when we made it up here and none were in the supplies, so we aren't able to write messages either. All we can do is sit and wait.

It started raining yesterday, and what I was thankful for then I am irritated at now. I doubt there is anything a human could experience that they aren't able to complain about in one form or another. This beautiful rain allowed us to refill our water bottles and is dropping through the barred hole in the storage containers top to accumulating inside on the floor ensuring that we won't die of thirst. But I am not thirsty now and have little fear of dehydration at the moment, so the continued downpour is only acting as an irritant to me.

The infected are dying off in mass like my father said they would, but that is creating another problem for us. The bodies that fall dead are piling on top of each other. We are twenty-three feet in the air on top of the third storage container on this stack, but the infected are almost able to climb onto the lip of the second stacked container. The dead must be piled eight or nine feet deep now for the running and stumbling swarm to reach that high.

The burning moat is extinguished and lost below the infected, and I no longer see a standing structure on the ranch besides the one we are on. The main house partially collapsed yesterday, and I can see the tilted roof being occasionally scrambled on by an infected. I don't know if the infected tore at the house to knock it down because someone was hiding in it or if it was just the relentless pressure of all the bodies crushing against it that made it cave in. I was sorry to see it go. All of the kid's toys were in the attic playroom.

I am sure my family is alive and well out there somewhere. With nothing to do but think these last three days, I have entertained every possible horrific outcome that could have befallen them. The uncertainty and helplessness of my current situation nearly drove me mad the first two days, but now I am feeling better. I have hope on my side that they are still alive. They were headed to a safe location before the swarms entered this area, so I have that small comfort.

Isaac has no optimistic thoughts to keep him from devolving in to sadness and depression. His people left the ranch for safety but only went to the farm next door. We were never able to fortify that property as well as this one, so everyone that went there to escape Jeremiah's wrath is dead. Isaac has lost everything. Every remaining member of his family has been killed, either by the infected, or by his own brother. I still can't believe Jeremiah was immune to this disease like I am. I wonder how long he knew?

Jeremiah must have gone completely insane at some point. In this twisted world none of us were able to see it. I thought it was just religious extremism driving his motivations. I wonder if we'll ever know for sure what happened to him.

*

It has been five days now. Isaac just woke me up to point out the infected are finally able to climb onto the wide ledge of the second storage container below the one we are on. The containers are each eight feet wide and ours is placed in the center of the two below us, so there is a four foot ledge on each side for the infected to climb on.

The height that the infected are at now means the ones that are still running are doing so on probably fifty thousand bodies or more. The swirling mass of stumbling infected never seems to decrease in size. As far as I can see, from tree line to tree line, there are runners doing their best to maneuver over the bodies of their fallen brethren. For two hundred yards to our front and sides the bodies of the dead must now be twelve feet deep based on the level the runners are standing compared to us. Behind us it is the same thing out to seventy-five yards. Any future archeologist that digs at this site will have a hell of a time figuring out why so many people came here to die.

Another two days of bodies dropping in these numbers and the infected will be level with the top of the second storage containers. At that point the pressure of all their bodies against this empty container will crush it. We will be ripped apart if we stay on the outside, but we will have some hope for survival on the inside if we can stay in a pocket that isn't completely crushed.

*

It's the evening of the sixth day. The flow of infected onto the property has increased. They are arriving faster and dying faster than they were before. Now it seems once the masses reach us, they run around for only an hour or two and then collapse into the heap below them. Before morning, the dead will most likely be piled to sixteen and a half feet enabling the infected to exert all of their pressure on the sides of our metal island of solitude.

Isaac used a chocolate chunk from the food supplies to write the first words from him since our exile up here. *Should we shut off the siren?* he asked.

No, the infected should all come here to die. Save any survivors left out there, was my reply and our only conversation ended.

We transferred our remaining supplies into the container along with our firearms and ammunition. We haven't fired many shots in the last few days, only here and there when a particularly enterprising infected person would make an extra effort to get up here by climbing. We don't want the crafty ones showing the others how to get to us. I think the siren is disorienting the infected when they arrive, either that, or their advanced stages of starvation are preventing them from targeting me and Isaac directly. We know they see us up here, but once they arrive they get caught up in a circular death march around the tower. The slow rotation of bodies reminds me of an insane prison scene I remember from a movie. I think it was called *The Four Feathers.* I'm happy to be up here away from the crowd below.

*

I had to tie up Isaac. He turned off the siren in the middle of the night. There wasn't much change in my ringing ears to notice anything, but there was a definite pressure change in the container and it caused me to wake up. I think he is claustrophobic and being trapped in here finally

225

made him snap. Or maybe he still has some hearing left and is just tired of the constant headache the sound must be giving him the way it's giving me. Whatever the reason, he disconnected the siren, and it has to stay on.

I've come to peace with the fact I won't be seeing my family again. I will die here with my last friend surrounded by the bodies of the diseased and those that betrayed us.

*

I was wrong about the ability of the infected to crush the shipping container we are in. There isn't a way for the feet of the infected to make purchase on the bodies below them in equal measure, so there will never be enough constant pressure on all sides. At least they won't be able to crush the container.

I woke up to the ground rumbling like an earthquake but it was just our personal sarcophagus being shifted by the horde outside. Every so often, the infected on one side has a better footing than the other, and the container moves. I lifted the barred door at the top and climbed out to see how the landscape looked.

It is the same field of moving bodies, all pressed together, running around and around the tower with the song of the siren. The tops of some of their heads are just at the edge I am standing on, so I'll have to start locking the door when we're inside. I don't want it pulled open once the infected are finally able to climb on top.

I untied Isaac today to make sure he could move around. He hasn't made an attempt to turn off the siren but looks at it constantly as he moves past it. His pacing exercise takes him the length of this place. I wish we could speak to each other. I can only imagine the suffering he has been feeling with all of his losses.

*

I'm not sure how many days it has been, nine, maybe ten. I haven't been tying up Isaac anymore. I had to let him free to keep him from getting hurt. The container started rotating and shifting a few days ago, making it feel like we are in a ship's cargo hold. Apparently the rotating mass of infected finally moved us off the tower, and we are sliding around on top of the bodies. Rotating and bouncing all day and night, stopping only when we dip into a soft spot making the container stick for a moment before it lurches violently forward again.

We'll be out of water soon. We collected as much as we could, but once the container started shifting, the remaining water on the floor got contaminated with our waste when our ammo can toilets tipped over. I should have seen that coming and secured them or locked them closed.

I don't know which is more oppressive, the heat or the stench. The temperature must be a hundred-ten degrees in this thing. Isaac and I are just in t-shirts and underwear now and are either covered in flies or mosquitoes, depending on the time of day. The smell of the rotting bodies outside helps to hide the stench of our own waste and our own motion sickness induced vomit.

Neither of us can sleep, even though we both desperately need it. There isn't a way to rest. The movement of the container has us roll against the walls anytime we try.

*

We unlocked the door and are climbing to the roof now. The container stopped moving for longer intervals, so I wanted to see why. I also need to know why we haven't been covered and buried by the infected yet. They should have been on top of us several days ago.

I'm not sure what I see when I first make it outside. Even with the heavy cloud cover the day is too bright for my eyes to adjust and focus properly. Spending days inside our dark, spinning room has also disoriented me, and I can't determine which direction I am facing.

Once my eyes adjust I see the horrifying landscape. There are still thousands of infected surrounding us, but they don't stretch off into the distance the way they once did. Beyond our container, out to twenty or thirty yards, are the infected that are still circling and trying to move it. Beyond that initial perimeter is just a scattering of single infected people hunched over or crawling in the process of dying. There are still enough infected around us to keep us spinning but the container must have wedged itself against something below their feet. It is probably the broken hulk of one of the buildings preventing them from getting it in motion again.

Isaac waves to me and climbs back below to get something, and I continue looking around trying to figure out exactly where on the property we are. The tree line is buried as deeply as everything else has been, so nothing looks familiar. Finally I see a dip, a curve, and a space between the trees that I recognize, and while I can hardly believe it, we are most likely stuck against the remains of the main ranch house.

Isaac starts throwing guns and boxes of ammo up to the roof. I lay down and lean into the hole to have him hand them up to me.

*

We take our time loading the magazines and getting our guns ready. There isn't a need to rush. With the siren still hooked up and probably blaring the infected aren't going anywhere, and there are not enough of them anymore to pile up to where they could climb and get us unless we started shooting at only one spot.

227

When we are both ready I nod to him and let him take the first shot. My hands are shaking badly from the effects of our ordeal, so I don't even try aiming for my shot. There are so many of them out there I can't miss. I can't hear the report, but the recoil feels good. No, I take that back, it doesn't feel good, it feels great. It feels incredible, amazing and fantastic all rolled into one. I look over at Isaac, and he is smiling. I am too.

I motion for him to watch and I quickly pull the trigger, unloading my magazine and sending the bullets in random directions into the crowd. I feel like a kid playing a video game. I watch Isaac give a wolf howl or a yell to express his joy and he unloads his gun quickly in the same manner.

I reload and continue shooting. It feels good finally having some success after our time in purgatory. Even the stench of bloated and rotting bodies is welcome in the free flowing air out here. Hope and joy have returned to our world, and then I feel something on my skin that nearly brings me to my knees. I rub my hands against my face to help the falling rain wash the grime away. It is a light but steady rain that probably won't last long, but its effects are instant. I feel alive again, reborn. Instead of simply surviving, I feel like I can live.

*

The infected are all dead. After the needed shower in the rain we continued to vent our mixed emotions with volleys of bullets at the runners who wanted us dead. We each laughed, yelled, and cried as we removed what we hope are the last vestiges of the terror we have faced these last nine months. Isaac and I decide to stay another night on the storage container and let the siren ring. With no place to go and no way to get there it seems too risky to walk across the piles of human remains on the blind hope that no other runners are out there.

*

The stars are out, and the earlier storm brought cooler air along with the rain. It's pleasant to lie here and contemplate my smallness in the scheme of things again. That is something I have been missing and I'm only realizing it now. The ability to feel insignificant and not have it terrify me because of the dangers that are out there.

I hope everyone made it, but more than that, I hope the human race makes it. These last few weeks have been brutal for my group of survivors. I can only imagine how many of the few humans remaining lost their lives once the infected started to run. Even if there are only small pockets left in the world, I know the human race will rebound.

*

The morning light wakes me, and I turn to see Isaac is already awake. He is sitting and watching the sun rise.

No infected arrived at the container last night, and I can still feel the vibration of the siren so I know it is working. I eat a brief breakfast from an MRE, but the building anticipation of leaving this metal prison keeps me from finishing it.

We have two duffle bags that we can load the remaining supplies in. They won't be easy to carry, but I'm hoping we can find some backpacks soon. Anything we leave behind will likely rot along with the mountain of flesh it is standing on, and I don't want to lose any more weapons than the ones that are buried below us.

I motion to Isaac to follow me and mouth the words as well. I am still dead set on getting a pen and paper, and the best place for that is the farm next door. We awkwardly maneuver ourselves over the bloated bodies around us until we reach the downward slope of death in the woods between the ranch and the farm.

The farmhouse is still there, but it is ruined. All of the windows are broken, the doors are missing, and it looks like the infected decided to peel the siding off. The fields are also destroyed. We would be lucky to find one potato in all the acres that were planted. I'm glad a potato isn't what I came here for.

I walk through the ripped open entry and only have to search for a few seconds in the kitchen before I triumphantly walk back out with the holy grail of communication raised above my head.

The two of us sit down on the front steps and begin to write our thoughts and questions to each other in a black and white composition notebook.

Eddie - *I'm glad we made it but I'm sorry about your losses.*

Isaac - *I am too. On both counts. Do you think everyone else made it?*

Eddie - *I hope so. I'm mostly concerned about Simone and Olivia going into the woods.*

Isaac - *I thought they left with the others.*

Eddie - *No. They were still here when Jeremiah confronted us. Did you know he was immune?*

Isaac - *I didn't know until he beat me up. He told me he was first bitten the night of our Christmas attack. He killed his wife and daughter and he knew he was bitten himself. I heard what you said when I walked up to him that night. You are right, he was just a murderer. I'm sorry.*

Eddie - *He was your brother, that makes it more difficult to see or accept. He must have been bitten again in Grants Pass because he wasn't reacting to pain when he attacked me.*

Isaac - *He tried to kill you in Grants Pass. It was one of his men that shot you.*

Eddie - *I figured as much. Can you hear anything or have any ringing?*

Isaac - *No. It's all gone.*

Eddie - *Mine too. At least you still have both ears so you look somewhat normal, except for those scars on your face.*

Isaac - *Is it bad?*

Eddie - *It would look bad on my pretty face but it doesn't change much for your looks.*

Isaac - *Ha ha. So what do we do now?*

Eddie - *Let's check the house for backpacks. I want to hike over to The Oregon Vortex today. Lots more supplies and a working truck if Simone didn't take it.*

*

The walk to the Vortex is taking longer than it should, but we don't have any appointments so I probably shouldn't be worried about it. We have at least eight hours before the sun goes down and will be at the supplies in forty-five minutes. There is no sign of any living infected in the woods even though their bodies are scattered everywhere. They fell in the spots where starvation finally led them to death, and I think they truly are all gone. At least in our little part of the world.

*

We have finished checking the buildings. The truck is gone, and while that makes our situation worse, I know at least someone made it here to take it. It gives me hope that Simone and Olivia are alive.

Isaac hands me the notebook.

Isaac - *We should eat. I'm going into that house. I want to sit at a table for this meal.*

I nod at him and follow.

We walk into the house and Isaac looks back at me waving his finger in my face. He steps past me and closes the front door. I can imagine his words *were you born in a barn?* but in truth, there is the possibility more infected may be out there. I shouldn't get lazy so quickly.

While we are getting our food ready a truck pulls into the driveway outside. Hannah, Mike, Gayle, and Taylor hop out.

"I told you the roads would be clear now," Hannah says to Mike punching him on the shoulder.

"I know, I know. It just seems too good to be true."

Taylor is happily banging on a pot with a large metal spoon. They have been driving up and down Sardine Creek Road making as much noise as possible trying to flush out any infected in the area.

"I think I remember that song," Hannah says to Taylor at the tunes random beats he is making with his drumming.

Hannah begins an impromptu victory dance making them all smile and bringing tears to Gayle's eyes. She wasn't sure if Taylor would ever be the same again after what happened with his father in Grants Pass. Seeing them smile, dance, and being able to make so much noise again is a luxury she didn't think she would live to see.

"We should probably get going, Hannah. Your mom will be getting worried," Mike tells her.

She sticks her tongue out at him but happily bounces back to the truck smiling the whole way.

Back in the house I hand the notebook to Isaac and walk to the door.

Eddie - *It's too hot. I have to open the door. We'll have to keep watching it after it's open.*

I open the door as the truck pulls out of the driveway. I don't see it and Isaac and I are unable to hear the horn blowing several times as it pulls away.

*

The day has been nice. Out of cautious habit, Isaac and I are on the roof of the house getting ready for nightfall. He hands me the notebook.

Isaac - *Head into Medford tomorrow?*

Eddie - *Yes. I still think that's our best bet. Just have to watch for more Stocktons or remaining infected.*

CHAPTER 26

REUNIONS

"Mom, wake up."

"Hannah, what? Is it time for my watch?"

"No, the siren stopped. Not even a minute ago. We need to get ready to go."

"Hannah, the battery probably died. It's been twelve days."

"Fifteen. We've been here for fifteen days. Mom, just get up so we can start getting ready."

"Hannah, it's still dark out. What time is it?"

"Just after five. It's going to start getting light soon."

Hannah runs off to the next room to wake up some of the other people. Simone isn't in such a rush to get up. For the last three days they have been scouting as a group farther down the road attempting to find any living infected. Hannah hasn't wanted to leave the area, because she is certain her father is still alive and he will turn off the siren when things are all clear. The first thing Hannah will want to do is drive back to the ranch to pick up her dad, who will no longer be there. It isn't something Simone wants to face or deal with.

"Mom, are you up yet?" Olivia asks walking into the room. "Hannah told me the siren stopped."

"There is no stopping you girls, is there?"

*

Down the road from Eddie's ranch, two men walk along the pavement at dusk.

"We're close, aren't we?" Frank asks.

"His place is supposed to be just up the road according to the map," Keith replies.

"Do you think the siren is coming from there?"

"Yes, it seems like something he would do."

"But that would bring all of the infected in from miles around."

"I know. That's probably what we smell."

It hasn't been an easy journey for the two men. They have lost a lot on the way here and feel like they only gained a little. What Keith expects to find is *closure*. His son survived the war but lost the final battle. No one could live through the tidal wave of bodies that the blaring siren would attract.

Once Katherine told them Eddie was alive they sailed to the coast of Oregon. Keith was avoiding making that final step of their journey, because he didn't want to know the truth which he expected to be bad. When he was finally able to speak with Eddie he heard the defeat in Eddie's voice and understood the hopeless position Jeremy had put them in from Simone's explanation. He is filled with sadness knowing he travelled across the globe only to say goodbye when they were still miles apart.

"We probably only have half a mile more to go up the road, but it's getting too dark. There are too many trees for an infected to hide in. We should stop."

"We haven't seen one for days, Keith."

"And I don't want to see another one for as long as I live. That doesn't mean they aren't out there. We'll stay on the roof of that house tonight and head out in the morning. I want to see if my son is alive, Frank. It is difficult being so close the ranch and not finding out, but you and I both know with the siren and the smell there is no way he can be alive. Eddie knew the infected were attracted to noise and probably thought setting up a siren would clear out the countryside to make things safe for any other survivors out there. I just hope he was able to get Simone and the kids out of harm's way before he activated it."

*

Back at Katherine's retreat, she is getting an update on the situation in Medford.

Katherine sits down and wishes the words she is hearing are true but isn't able to accept them. "Are you sure?"

"No. I thought I would lie to you so everyone can run into the city and get killed by the infected!" Greg replies sarcastically. "Of course I'm sure. The infected are gone from Medford. Four patrols drove all over the place honking their horns and nothing came out. We even had a spotter spend the day on the hospital roof, and they saw nothing but us."

"That *is* good news. Have you told the others?"

"No, not yet. I wanted to tell you first, but a few of them were on the patrols so I'm sure everyone else already knows."

"Well, go call them in here so we can plan what to do next."

Arthur, Donald, Samantha, and Timothy walk into Katherine's dining room, which has become her makeshift office since receiving so many survivors from Eddie's ranch.

"Greg tells me the infected are gone," she says and sports a big grin while looking at the group. "I know you have wanted to head back to the ranch to see what happened, and I will let you go tomorrow, if you want."

Because the runners posed a greater risk to Katherine's retreat than the walkers did, she had to lay down the law and take away everyone's ability to travel. The trusted leaders of Eddie's group were newcomers here, and she didn't need any of them running to the ranch and bringing back a horde with them. They were only allowed to go outside the retreat with Katherine's patrol's one at a time.

"How many of us can go?" Timothy asks.

"You can all go if you want. I will be sending one of my patrols along with a siren remote just in case we are wrong about the infected being gone. You know the routes you should take if you run into trouble, and if it is an overwhelming horde, my patrols will make sure you don't make it back here to threaten the lives of the others."

Outside of their tents, the larger group of Eddie's ranch refugees discuss who should go.

"I can't go," says Donald. "I promised Eddie and Simone that we would take care of their children. I already broke that promise when I let Hannah get out of the truck that night. I can't do anything that will take me away from Benjamin, Amelia, and William."

"I have to go," Arthur states firmly. "The ranch was my home. I have to see what has happened to it."

The group debates but mostly discusses for the next several hours what the possibilities are if the infected are really gone. After night falls, most of the people have uneasy sleep, if they are able to find rest at all, with the excitement of being free to travel again and see the world.

*

Back by the Oregon Vortex, Eddie and Isaac climb down from the roof as the morning light begins creeping into the night sky. The sun will rise in about thirty-five minutes, and they will be on the road heading south in ten.

Before getting on his bike Isaac hands Eddie the notebook.

Isaac - *You know we might not find anyone right?*

Eddie - *I know. The infected were everywhere and still might be.*

They nod to each other, get on their bikes, and start pedaling toward Medford.

*

At the Carpenter farm next to Eddie's ranch.

"I'm glad the siren stopped," Frank says. "It was giving me a headache. Did you get any sleep?"

"Not much. It's light enough now. Let's head up the road."

234

When they arrive, the view before them is pure horror. Grotesque and disgusting fit to describe it as well, but it is mainly horror. At road level Keith and Frank don't even have the whole picture of what is on the ranch.

"How many bodies does it take to make a wall this big?" Frank asks shaking his head at the impossibility of it all.

"I can't imagine," Keith replies. "We need to get over this wall to see where the siren was coming from. Maybe there is a house or building on the other side."

"Can you climb this with your leg?"

Keith has been having severe pain in his right knee making him limp. He didn't twist it or hurt it anywhere, so he is at a loss for what might be going wrong.

"I'll manage. Just help me stay balanced. I'm sure these bodies will shift occasionally."

Frank rubs two rags full of Vicks VapoRub ointment to combat the smell of the bodies and hands one to Keith to wrap around his face.

The light of morning is increasing, but the sun is still fifteen minutes from rising when the two finish climbing to the top. They each take a few steps and freeze, their minds unwilling to absorb the vision before them. Frank doubles over and vomits, while Keith drops to his knees and cries.

From tree line to tree line and as far back as they can see, the land is a level field of human bodies. The only blight on this wasteland of human suffering is a large metal storage container sitting a hundred yards away.

Keith struggles to his feet and begins limping his way toward the structure. Frank follows at a distance, unable to travel far over the bloody and bloated mess before dry heaving over the corpses again.

"Frank, come here!" Keith yells with excitement.

"Is someone there?"

"No, but someone was here."

The bodies immediately around the storage container show signs of life. Not that they are moving but that they were killed. Most of the field they walked over were runners that had fallen over and died.

"None of the bodies out there had bullet wounds that I could see," Keith says excitedly about the macabre details.

"They looked covered in blood to me," Frank replies with disgust.

"They were bleeding from their mouths and ears, probably due to the normal breakdown process after death. Look at the bodies next to the container here, they are riddled with bullet holes, and there are bullet shells scattered around as well.

"Boost me up. I want to see what's on top," Keith says walking over to the container's side, and Frank offers his hands with intertwined fingers as a step.

"Whoo hoo!" Keith yells

"What? What?" Frank asks frantically wanting to see as well.

"No bodies, but lots of shells," he replies. "Someone was up here till the end, but there are no fresh bodies around this thing or inside. I see the siren as well. It was inside this shipping container."

"What do we do now?"

"First, give me your backpack. There are some guns and ammo still up here. I want to take it all."

"Keith, I think I hear something."

"It's probably just the ringing from this damn siren. My ears are still messed up. Just give me your backpack, and we can look around for any survivors once we get back to the road."

Backpacks loaded, the pair walk back to the edge of the bodies where they first climbed up. There is a truck parked in the road and six people with guns standing in front of it staring up at them.

"I told you I heard something," Frank says.

The rising sun is behind the men standing on the wall of bodies preventing Simone and the others from seeing who they are.

"That's not Dad or Isaac," Hannah says

Keith recognizes three of the faces below.

He takes off his mask, and calls out, "Simone, It's Keith. We're coming down, okay?"

The scene by the truck is heartfelt and powerful. Fierce hugs are had by all as well as free flowing tears as a result of the reunion.

"I'm sorry, Keith," Simone tells him. "Eddie is dead. He stayed here at the ranch when the runners arrived and set off the siren."

"I don't think he's dead," he says in rebuttal. "There's a storage container on top of all the bodies up there and no one is inside."

She begins to protest at the obvious, but he waves off her attempts.

"Someone was alive and on top of that container shooting at the infected. The bodies close to it were shot, so I think he waited until there were only a few runners still alive. He killed them and then left."

"Were there any guns still up there?" Simone asks.

"Just a few and some ammo. We have them in our bags."

"Let me see," she says with a glimmer of hope.

She knows if Eddie was alive he would take anything he could and also which guns he would leave behind if he could only carry so much.

Simone jumps up from the bags and grabs Hannah and Olivia in a fierce hug, and then steps back and leaves a hand on each daughters shoulder.

"Your father is alive," she says and bursts into tears again. "It's all 9mm." she says through the sobbing. "The guns and the ammo. That's what he would have left behind."

"Eddie!" Simone yells out, stepping away from the others. "Eddie, can you hear me?" Turning back to Keith, she asks, "Did you call for him when you got here."

Keith frowns like he knows something she doesn't.

"What?"

"He won't be able to hear you, Simone. Frank and I stayed at the farm down the road last night, and my ears are still ringing. If Eddie was next to that siren for the last two weeks, he may never hear again."

"How do we find him if we can't call?" Olivia asks.

"Which way did you come?" Simone asks Keith.

"We came up the road from Rogue River."

"And you stayed at the next farm over?"

"Yes. But there was no sign of them there. We searched through the house before we climbed up to the roof."

"So he left yesterday or earlier. He would head to The Vortex, that's the only place nearby with supplies. You were there yesterday, Hannah, did you see anything?"

"No, but we didn't go in any of the buildings. We were making a lot of noise, but if he can't hear he might have been there."

The group climbs into the truck and drives up the road, heading to The Oregon Vortex. At the same time a group of four SUVs from Katherine's ranch approaches the Rogue River turnoff from Interstate 5 on their way to the ranch.

*

When the ranch refugees arrive at the entrance of their former home they are all in various stages of shock. They knew the siren would pull all of the infected to this spot, but there is a vast gulf between the scales of devastation which people are able to imagine as opposed to that which can actually occur. As with Keith and Frank earlier, Arthur and the other climbers of this human plateau are physically drained and mentally shattered by the tremendous scope of it all.

"It looks like someone was still here shooting at the end," Timothy says to Arthur

Leaning into the opening, Arthur says, "The siren is still hooked up, and there aren't any bodies or supplies inside. Whoever was up here might have survived."

*

"He was here," Hannah says excitedly walking around the houses by The Vortex. "That ladder wasn't against the house yesterday."

"The houses are all empty," Mike calls out. "But there are some fresh open food containers inside."

"There are two bicycles missing as well, so someone else survived," Simone says. "We know we didn't pass them. Let's drive down the road and find your father, girls."

They hop back in the truck to begin what they hope will be the final leg of this emotionally turbulent game of Hide-N-Seek.

*

Timothy and Arthur are walking slowly across the human cobblestone pavement to tell the others what they found.

"Do you hear that?" Timothy asks?

"It's an engine," Arthur says looking north in the direction of the sound. "Eddie had Donald stash a bunch of supplies at The Oregon Vortex. He said they also left a truck there!"

"There aren't any abandoned vehicles left in the world that are running. It has to be some of our survivors."

"We hear a vehicle," Samantha yells to the men as they climb down from the bodies.

"We do too. Arthur thinks it will be at the Vortex where Eddie stashed some supplies."

"What's the quickest way there?"

"It depends on the direction they are travelling. We should send one vehicle north in case they are coming back here and the others south to find them if they are going to Medford."

The group splits up and speed off to find out who survived the last battle in the end of the world.

"I hope it isn't Jeremiah," Samantha says to her husband Conner. "I don't care how much death we just saw out there. If Jeremiah survived, I am killing him."

*

Eddie and Isaac have reached the end of Sardine Creek Road and have parked their bikes on Highway 99. The Rogue River is flowing twenty yards in front of them and down a bank. The rain that fell on them was a relief while they were still on the storage container, but they still had a night of sleep and a walk across the valley of the dead to regain their filth when they escaped their potential metal tomb.

Eddie hands Isaac the notebook.

Eddie - *I need a bath.*

Isaac - *We do have fresh clothes in the packs.*

Eddie - *And shaving gear!*

The men leave the bikes and carry their gear to the river. They will have a bitter cold yet refreshing bath over two weeks in the making.

*

Simone parks the truck next to the bicycles in the road and steps out, Olivia climbs over the seat to exit as well, unwilling to wait for Grandpa Keith to leave the truck. Hannah and the others climb or jump out of the truck bed, and Simone looks in every direction trying to see her husband.

"Where are they, Mom?" Olivia asks with frustration.

"I don't know, girls. Maybe you should check by the river."

A few quick thoughts flash through her mind, and she screams at the girls, "STOP!" It suddenly dawned on her that the survivors of the attack could have been anyone, including Jeremiah. That man would not hesitate to kill her and Eddie's children if he had the chance.

Simone raises her rifle and begins to walk toward the river but stops with the sound of a new approaching danger.

"I hear a car up the road behind us," Olivia calls.

"It sounds like it's going fast. Everyone get ready to fight!" Simone yells.

"There's another one coming from the west. We're boxed in," Keith says. "I can see it."

Like the boats that approached them in the Ocean, Keith doesn't wait to find out if the occupants are friend or foe. He starts shooting at the approaching truck, hitting it in the grill and tires before Simone can knock the gun out of his hands.

The reunion almost turned into a blood bath when the new arrivals to the scene drove up and were either shot at or witnessed the shooting. The people that fill the three vehicles pour onto the road and aim their guns at Keith, the man they don't know who tried to kill them.

Simone stands in front of him with her arms out to the people she knows and yells at them not to shoot.

"This is Eddie's father! He thought you were attacking us."

"Keith, these are survivors from the ranch. They were sent to Katherine's place."

Several apologies later, the group finally turns their collective attentions back to the bicycles on the road.

Samantha slowly walks to the top edge of the river bank, still unsure of what or who she will see. The rest of the group follow in similar fashion, ready to face the worst.

Down at the river's edge are two men sitting across from each other, with traces of white foam on their faces. Isaac has just finished the last swipe of shaving Eddie's beard and spots the group standing on the ridge. He waves up at them and motions to Eddie, urging him to turn and see who it is, with a huge grin on his face.

Simone puts her hand to her mouth and starts crying. Hannah and Olivia run down the bank to grab their father, and Keith stands next to Simone, unable to keep his tears from flowing over his cheeks.

Eddie just stands there smiling up at Simone as his girls try tackling him with their hugs.

*

The day ends with a celebration at Katherine's retreat. Isaac was elated to find out most of the people he sent to the farm survived due to Hannah's urging. All of the young people and children from his group survived.

The following week was filled with storytelling or story writing for the benefit of Eddie and Isaac. Mixed into the discussions of world adventures and calamities were ideas of rebuilding and exploration. Several of the people spoke about trying to preserve some of the former technologies and modern conveniences that would disappear without regular upkeep, and they all expressed a desire to prevent mankind from falling into a base Stone Age form of existence.

One evening, after a very good meal, Donald gets out his guitar and strums away. Eddie and Isaac enjoy the heartwarming show of the kids smiling and dancing to what must be a lively song. Isaac passes the black and white notebook over to Eddie.

Isaac - *More than one blade of grass I think.*
Eddie - *It's a whole field.*

CHAPTER 27
OREGON COAST
THE LAST BLADE OF GRASS

It has been seventeen years since the Zeus Plague, as it is now called, brought the human race to near extinction. Lines of communication have been established with various parts of the world. Originally relying on Ham radios, now they are using some other form of radio transmission that people have attempted to explain to me and I still can't understand.

Erde Fleischer's name is used as a warning for when people want to do something good but it ends horribly wrong. Just saying his name has replaced the phrase *"The road to Hell is paved with good intentions."* He did manage to develop an injection to protect people from his Zeus parasite. The risk of infection is still out there since Zeus can still be found and contracted along with normal toxoplasmosis.

Dogs are beginning to make a comeback as pets popular for people to own. Cats have dominated that sphere ever since we were able to start rebuilding the world. If an alien race came to the planet today they would rightfully conclude the dominant species is the cat with their numbers and elevated level of pampered comfort.

Only one major outbreak of the Zeus Plague occurred after the large event we all survived, and that was in a town of anti-cat fanatics living in Asia somewhere. They refused to keep them as pets and also rejected Erde's toxoplasmosis injection. It cost over three thousand lives before that second outbreak was wiped out.

My family has been living on the Oregon coast in the hills above a town once called Gold Beach, now we call it Christine. We renamed it after my mom when we moved down here. The population is close to four thousand people now, and it's a beautiful place to live. It sits on the ocean with the mouth of the Rogue River just to our north emptying into the Pacific.

Little Benjamin isn't so little anymore. He's eighteen years old, six feet one inches and was the last of our children to get married. He married a wonderful girl named Julia, who reminds me of Simone at her age.

Hannah married Mike three years after they met. They have their own twelve year old daughter now, and they named her Evangeline. That girl is the spitting image of her mother, attitude and all.

Olivia started her own trade company and is usually travelling the coast between towns with her family.

All of my kids are grown, and the pride I feel having them around me right now is immeasurable. They didn't just survive the end of the world, they thrived in it. Simone and I were able to be there with them every step of the way.

I wish Keith was able to live longer and watch them grow up, but I'm happy that we were at least able to see him again and spend a few more years in each other's company. Keith died a month after Hannah was married. It was cancer, probably a result of his exposure at the oil rig outside of New Orleans. Frank died a year after him.

Arthur seems determined to outlive us all. He is here with the rest of the survivors from the ranch. Samantha, Conner, Timothy, Dianne, Daniel and all of the others came to send us off.

Of all my friends that came today, I appreciate Isaac showing up above all others. He stayed with our family for ten years following our reunion at the river bank. He only left after he found a woman that he couldn't live without. She was driving through with a travelling trade caravan, and it was love at first sight.

Neither Isaac nor I regained our hearing, and over the last two years, my eyesight has largely gone as well. Too many nights of writing notes and papers by lamplight.

Isaac hands me a familiar tattered black and white notebook.

Isaac - *Are you sure you have to go?*

I look down at Simone. She is lying on my lap and the small waves are making the little boat we are in rock slightly. Years before the collapse Simone had her Thyroid taken out due to cancer. She had to take thyroid replacement hormones for the rest of her life after that. We had stockpiles of the medicine, but after seventeen years, everything ran out or lost its potency. We knew without the medicine she would eventually fall into a coma. She passed out of consciousness a few days ago.

The world of medical care is returning to some level that it was at before the collapse, but it will be years or decades before medicines are available beyond simple aspirins and creams. Even in the past, with full medical care, her current condition would be difficult to reverse.

I write a short while in the notebook and hand it back to my old friend before mouthing the words *goodbye* and picking up the oars to row out into the Pacific.

Eddie - *I have lived my life and it was a good one. I couldn't ask for a better family or better friends. My children are grown and I have nothing left to teach them. My eyesight is fading, my hearing is gone. All I have left is the opportunity to be a burden to the people that have earned the right to live their lives for themselves and survive the best way they know how.*

I know most of you would be willing to take me in and care for me until my dying day but what none of you can know is I am already dead. I used to say that all I needed in life was for one blade of grass to exist somewhere in the world. That was enough to sustain me. What I never told any of you was Simone was my one blade of grass. Without her the world is nothing but barren fields.

I love you all. Celebrate the experiences we had together and cherish your one blade of grass.

THE END

 SEVERED**PRESS**

CHECK OUT OTHER GREAT APOCALYPSE BOOKS

XY
by D.S. Lillico

An iron fortress protected by automated gun turrets is the only world Elsie has ever known.

When tragedy strikes, Elsie is forced to leave the sanctuary of her home and out into a brutal new world. A post-apocalyptic wasteland filled with savage mutants.

Hunted and alone Elsie stumbles into the care of a giant named Punch, but the world is now full of worse things than giants. Cannibals are starving, bandits are roaming and war is coming.

Elsie's arrival plunges the new-world further into darkness... and is there really something hidden inside of her?

SANCTUARY
by Ian Page

Deeta Nakshband, a Connecticut physician is attacked by a local surgeon while on duty in the hospital. Her friend, Janelle Jefferson, has similar experiences in Miami. Both of them become aware of an increasingly violent world as acts of isolated brutality escalate into civil unrest. They grapple with their paranoia as family members and coworkers become dangerously unpredictable. Worldwide, military units go rogue, war begins in Korea and cities implode as people slaughter each other in the streets. Martial law is declared in an attempt to maintain order. People are arrested, detainment camps are set up and interrogations end with tragic consequences as modern civilization crumbles. Deeta and Janelle band together with family friends and coworkers to save each other and find sanctuary.

www.ingramcontent.com/pod-product-compliance
Lightning Source LLC
Chambersburg PA
CBHW020100180626
46812CB00006B/2415